The Macken Wives

by the same author

Trespasses
Too Much Too Young

THE MACKEN WIVES
Caroline Bridgwood

SINCLAIR-STEVENSON

First published in Great Britain
by Sinclair-Stevenson
an imprint of Reed Consumer Books Ltd
Michelin House
81 Fulham Road
London SW3 6RB

Copyright © 1993 by Caroline Bridgwood

All rights reserved. Without limiting the rights under copyright reserved, no part of this publication may be reproduced, stored in or introduced into a retrieval system or transmitted, in any form or by any means (electronic, mechanical, photocopying, recording or otherwise), without the prior written permission of both the copyright owner and the above publisher of this book.

The right of Caroline Bridgwood to be identified as author of this work has been asserted by her in accordance with Copyright, Designs and Patents Act 1988.

A CIP catalogue record for this book is available from the British Library

ISBN: 1 85619 215 6

Phototypeset by Intype, London

Printed and bound in England
by Clays Ltd, St Ives plc

PROLOGUE – ONE

Savannah, Georgia 1980

AL MACKEN IS DEAD.

He stared down at the words he had just written, finding it oddly comforting to see them there, on the desk blotter. He imagined the headlines in the late edition of the *Savannah Morning News*, the photographs of the grieving family at the funeral, the obituaries in the *New York Times* and *Washington Post*. The inevitable media speculation and fantasy about the future of the Macken dynasty. It was a privilege, in a way, to be able to foresee your own death, to know exactly how it would be.

Al thrust his hands into his pockets and strolled over to the picture window that gave a panoramic view of the Savannah River. His suite of offices was on the penthouse floor of the MackenCorp building, a square tower of plate glass that dominated the skyline of the city. Al smiled as he remembered the outcry there had been when he built the damn thing. Until then, the headquarters of the Savannah Bank and Trust Company, a graceful neoclassical stone construction, had been the city's tallest building at a modest fifteen storeys. The municipal planners didn't want elegant Savannah to become a city of skyscrapers. Al had promised them that his new head office would also be fifteen storeys high, not a storey more, not a storey less. But at the last minute he hadn't been able to resist sticking another storey on top, just so that he could be king of the castle, top of the heap. The trustees of the Savannah Bank, whose boardroom he was looking down on now, had started a petition, and there had been a string of angry letters in the *Morning News*. But, hell, Al Macken was the city's wealthiest businessman, head of the biggest corporation in the state and one of the top fifty in the

USA. No one was going to tell *him* to tear his building down and start again. They only had to look at what he'd done for this town, the money he'd poured into it. He was as much a part of the place as the Cotton Exchange, or the golden dome of City Hall. Or the river itself, winding its lazy way round the islands to the ocean. In front of him on the wall was a framed plaque that bore testimony to this fact. The words printed on it were from the old Johnny Mercer song:

> *Pardon my Southern accent*
> *Pardon my Southern drawl*
> *It may sound funny*
> *Ah, but honey I love y'all*

The plaque had been given to him as a well-meaning joke by business associates in New York, and Al had laughed with the rest of them when it was presented, but he still hung it in pride of place because it summed up how he saw himself: Southerner first, American second.

Al opened his desk drawer and took out the bottle that his doctor had brought round in person that morning. His hand shook with a tell-tale tremor as he read the label. Just one word, scrawled in the handwriting of his personal physician and old friend, John Morrow: 'Amytal'. A barbiturate which, combined with a generous dose of alcohol, would slip him nice and gently over the edge into irretrievable unconsciousness. Much less unpleasant than strychnine or cyanide, John had assured him.

Of course it was illegal for John to conspire in his death in this way, but arrangements had been made. In return for her silence, Winona, his loyal secretary, had been given a handsome financial settlement that would keep her in comfort for the rest of her life. Al knew that she would not let him down, she was far too devoted to him. At the appointed hour she would come into his office on the pretext of returning for some papers. She would remove the Amytal bottle from his body and call John Morrow, who would register the cause of death as a heart attack and sign the death certificate. Once all the medical formalities had been observed and the body removed, Winona would break the news to the family.

Al liked the neatness of it, the dignity. Better to go quietly than to surrender to the ravages of the disease that was set to destroy his pride as well as his life. He was determined that no one was going to see Al Macken looking and acting like a goddam cripple and least of all his two sons.

He looked over the document on his desk one final time. He'd wrestled with the wording of it for some days, but it still sounded strange when he read it back to himself, probably because it referred to an unseen future where he would not be around to control things. And that was pretty hard to imagine. He tried to picture the reactions of his family at the formal reading. It started off with all the stock phrases, but there was plenty of surprises in there, to make them all sit up.

'I, Alexander Wilson Macken, being of sound mind . . . declare this to be my last will . . . that all net assets and corporations leased and owned by the parent company, MackenCorp, shall be gifted to the federal purse of the State of Georgia unless the following terms and conditions are met . . .'

Which was a fancy way of saying that unless everyone did what they were damn well told the whole show was going to be given away.

'. . . the holdings listed above and hereafter referred to as "the Corporation" shall be held in joint trusteeship by my two sons, TRAVIS PEABODY MACKEN and MICHAEL PEABODY MACKEN, each holding the position of executive vice-chairman, with a voting share of forty per cent. The said trusteeship to be enforced for two years from the date of my death, at the end of which period, overall control and the appointment of chief executive of the corporation shall be decided by the board of directors. In the event of the corporation's gross annual sales having increased by a margin of less than ten per cent of their value on the first anniversary of the date of my death, the above condition shall be null and void and the corporations and all holdings shall be bequeathed to the state of Georgia as detailed above . . .'

A scam, his attorney had called it, with clear disapproval. A power struggle, and one that could only be bad for MackenCorp. Al preferred to think of it as a division of talents. The image fitted perfectly with his own Southern, Bible-belt roots. Besides, it allowed him to be as fair as a father of two sons could be. True, he kind of expected Travis to come out as top dog, but that was because he had more experience. On the other hand, Michael probably had more brains. . . .

Anyway, this way they would be forced to work together, however fierce their natural competitiveness. They would *have* to pull together and make MackenCorp grow, or that last proviso about profitability would mean they lost the lot anyhow, just as surely as if they refused to accept the terms of the will.

Al checked his watch: it was 6.30. Winona would be here in an hour and a half. He turned back to the window for one last look at the river. The sun was setting, a real Georgia sunset with cobalt blue sky merging through shades of smoke and gold to a brilliance that was not quite orange, not quite scarlet. To his left, the dun brick towers of the Savannah Electric Company had become a solid silhouette of black, fading into darkness, while the coloured lights on the tugboats glittered like gaudy decorations on a Christmas tree. The deep boom of a ship's horn brought him up with a start, made him jump. No matter how many times he heard that sound, he always jumped.

His hand shook slightly as he opened the bottle and swallowed all the tablets, washing them down with a slug of decent malt whisky. Within seconds he was unconscious. Within an hour he was dead.

Winona arrived at eight o'clock, exactly as planned. Fighting back her tears, she removed the scribbled words on the blotter, and the empty bottle of Amytal. She checked Al's wallet and removed two photographs, one of a pretty blonde woman, the other of an elegant redhead. The former she replaced, the latter she destroyed.

She left a message with John Morrow's answering service, then began the round of calls to inform the family. Travis was unavailable, travelling on the company jet to a shareholders meeting in Chicago. Michael's whereabouts were initially unknown, but she managed to track him down at an exclusive ski lodge in Vail, Colorado. It was part of her duties to inform Al's sons, in very general terms, of the contents of the will, just in case any information leaked to the press before the reading.

The line to Colorado was a poor one.

'Michael, are you there – did you hear what I said?'

There was a silence, then Michael's voice came crackling down the line. 'The son of a bitch!' was all he could say. 'The manipulating son of a bitch!'

PROLOGUE – TWO

Liverpool, England 1961

John Anderson was strolling along the marina at New Brighton, screwing up his eyes in the fierce August sunshine.

'Hang about, kids. . . . just a tick. . . .' He eased his hand from the sticky grasp of small fingers, pulled out a handkerchief from his pocket and knotted it in all four corners. Then he pulled it down firmly over his head and continued walking. All right, so it didn't shade his eyes, but at least it made him feel as though he had some protection from the sun's rays. And OK, so he probably looked a bit daft, a bit of a soft lad, but he didn't care. Strolling along on a summer's day with his son and daughter, a humble ship's welder could feel as much of a man as any titled gent, Prince Philip Mountbatten even. His two happy, healthy kids were more precious than rubies. He was lucky, and he knew it.

The children were silent, taking in everything around them. There was a lot to see today, on top of the peeling paint and salt-bleached canvas deckchairs that you could see on any old day of the week. Busloads of trippers from outlying parts of Cheshire and Lancashire. Gangs of beatniks posing behind their dark glasses. Teenage girls huddled round a transistor radio. A Punch and Judy booth that had seen better days in his opinion, but which entranced the kids all the same. Everywhere was strewn with the flotsam of chip papers and sticky puddles of dropped icecream melted underfoot.

'Here, our Peg, give us one of those!'

John had given them each money to buy sweets. Jimmy had finished all his first, as usual, and was pestering Peg for one of hers.

Eight-year-old Peg gave her older brother a calculating glance from under her fringe. 'Tell you what, you can have all the liquorice I've got left for a penny.'

'But they only cost a ha'penny, the whole lot.'

'There'll be a ha'penny left over for me then, won't there?' Peg gave him a guileless smile. 'Tell you what, since it's you, I'll throw in the sherbert dib dab too.'

John laughed at his daughter and ruffled her hair. 'You little scally, you! You'll be selling icecreams to the Eskimos next!'

'But it's fair, Dad.' Peg was sweet reason itself. 'These are the only sweets we have left between us, so they're worth more now than when we started. Also, it's saved him the trouble of having to go back to the shop.'

'And greed has its price, eh? . . . Come on, we'd best be getting back. Your mam'll have the tea spoiling.'

He swung the girl up onto his shoulders, knocking the knotted handkerchief askew. 'Look how tall you are now . . . if you look hard enough you'll be able to see America!'

Peg squinted hard into the distance, beyond the mouth of the Mersey to the Atlantic, invitingly blue today. 'I can! I can see it, Dad!' She grasped the sides of his neck as he quickened his stride and declared solemnly: 'I'm going to go to America when I grow up, to make my fortune.'

Jimmy sneered. 'Girls don't make their fortune, do they, Dad? Girls get married and have loads of babies!'

'Not me,' said Peg, defiant. 'I'm going to be too busy getting rich, aren't I, Dad?'

'If you say so, Peggy.' He squeezed her fingertips. 'Now, wave goodbye to America and let's get back for that tea of ours.'

He turned through a half circle, so that the ocean was behind them. Peg went on looking back over her shoulder, narrowing her eyes at the horizon until it was just a faint grey blur and she couldn't see America any more.

PART ONE

ONE

Georgia 1939–1945

The sun was low in the sky by the time Al Macken woke.

He stretched his stiff limbs, taking a few seconds to remember where he was, and why. The quiet lapping of water brought it back to him. He was stretched out on the River Street jetty in the city of Savannah. And there it was, the magnificent Savannah River; much wider than he had imagined and somehow mysterious, leading to the invisible ocean. The sky had warmed to a rich flamingo pink, against which the passing boats were black silhouettes, studded with lights like jewels against ebony.

He shouldered his bag and began to walk, heading downtown. The esplanade was deserted now, but the rest of Savannah was coming to life. Al stared in frank amazement at what he saw. A country boy like himself could never have imagined that a city could be so beautiful. The original grid of squares and tree-lined avenues still survived, but its Georgian houses now vied with neoclassical and colonial mansions, and Victorian extravagances built by the merchants who had made their fortunes since the Civil War. The eighteenth-century streets and squares were filling up now with promenaders, who strolled beneath tendrils of Spanish moss and branches heavy with azaleas; elegant, worldly people who seemed at one with the laughter and music drifting out from open windows. These sights and sounds were so unfamiliar to Al that for a long time he wandered about in a daze, just looking and listening. His daddy would have called it Babylon. But he had already decided that if this was Babylon, then Babylon was where he wanted to be, and where he wanted to stay.

He was hungry; very hungry. Over the past forty-eight hours he had walked forty miles or more, with little more to eat than some bread and cheese. On the corner of one of the streets on the western edge of town he was seduced by a cheerful neon sign: RUDY'S DINER – GEORGIA'S FINEST SINCE 1910.

The interior was warm, despite the expanses of shining metal and tiles, and filled with the comforting hiss of steam from the coffee machine and the sizzle of pancakes from the griddle. Al studied the menu intently. He only had two dollars to his name, and everything seemed very expensive.

'Kin I help you, boy?' asked the pot-bellied proprietor with a hint of impatience.

'Just a black coffee and a jelly doughnut, please.'

The man narrowed his eyes. 'You ain't from around here, are you?'

'No. My folks come from Walthourville.'

'You run away from home?'

'No . . . well, not exactly.' Al sipped his coffee slowly. 'My daddy used to whip me something mean. And one day he figured that I'd grown bigger than him, and I could whip him back if I wanted. But I just walked out instead.'

'That so? And what d'your daddy do for a living?'

'He's the town preacher.'

'Uh huh. . . . And you've come here looking for work?'

'I'm seventeen, almost eighteen.' Al was suddenly defensive. He gestured down at a broad, sun-tanned forearm, sinewy with muscle. 'Reckon I could pass as older if I had to.'

The proprietor refilled his coffee cup. 'What kind of work you after?'

'Anything really.' Al grinned. 'Just until I get me a business of my own and make my fortune.'

'You and all the others!'

'That's the New South, that's what it's all about. My daddy always told us making money was sinful. So I thought I'd give it a try. . . .' He set down his cup and wiped his mouth on the back of his hand. 'Know anywhere I could stay?'

'You could try Miz Bailey's boarding house, a few blocks along here.'

Al had little trouble finding the place. The queue for the dining room stretched out half way along West Jones Street. The others were working men, dressed in rough denims and plaid shirts, weary from their day's labour. He fell into place at the back of the line, savouring the most delicious smell that had ever tormented his nostrils. Suddenly the coffee and doughnut seemed like bread and water.

The man in front of him saw Al's trance-like stare and laughed. 'The best cook in town, is Euphemia Bailey. And she has rooms to let, too. If she likes you.'

Al followed the other men into the basement dining room and took his place at one of the tables where the diners were served family-style by Miz Bailey herself, along with her sisters and aunts, who bustled to and fro from the kitchen. Every inch of space on the three tables seemed to be taken up with a steaming dish of food; there was beef stew and fried chicken, red rice and creamed squash, sweet potato pie and corn bread and plenty of piping hot gravy, all washed down with jugs of iced tea.

Euphemia Bailey was a small, sprightly woman of about forty, with neat auburn curls and a sharp eye which was kept on proceedings at all times. She said grace before the meal started, and when it was over she stood at the door and collected a dollar from everyone who had eaten.

'See you again, Miz Bailey,' they said as they filed out, or 'See you at breakfast.' She seemed to know all of them by name, and there was a quizzical look on her face as she held out her hand to Al.

'You're new in town,' she said, with a smile.

'Al Macken, ma'am.' He hesitated, feeling ashamed. 'Ma'am. I only have seventy-five cents. But I could help you with the clearing up. Sweep the floor, or something.'

'We got all the help we need, Mr Macken.' She looked at him gravely, but her eyes were warm, and there was a smile hovering at the corners of her mouth.

'Well, I'm fixin' to get myself a job in the morning, I'll pay you back just as soon as I'm paid.'

'Really? And where you goin' to find this job of yours? Don't you know how many men walk into this town looking for work?'

'I don't know, ma'am. I'll find something.'

'And where you going to stay while you're finding your job?'

'I don't rightly know, ma'am.' He looked her straight in the eye.

Euphemia considered his face; she saw plenty of strangers, maybe a hundred each month, and she had learned to judge a man correctly on first acquaintance. The face she saw looking back at hers was handsome, but most of all it was proud. There was pride in the uplifted angle of the jaw, and in the unwavering gaze from the bright blue eyes. But they were eyes of astonishing clarity; there was no shiftiness or guile there, no hidden depths. She could believe in this face.

'Reckon we might have a room for you upstairs,' she said. 'And as for a job, I recommend you start with the rail depot. They always need strong young men for the railroad. Ask for Mr Wilkes, the foreman. He knows me.'

She led Al upstairs to a small room at the front of the house. It had a polished wooden floor, a rocking chair and a narrow bed with a patchwork coverlet. The curtains were open, and Al went to look out at the gardens on the other side of the street and the row of houses beyond them.

'Oh, Miz Bailey, will you look at that! I'n't that house something!'

He pointed to a redbrick Queen-Anne-style villa, with a circular turret and stained glass windows. The massive brick porch was covered with ivy and had ornamental arches and fancy cast-iron trellises sheltering massive steps which led down to an immaculate manicured lawn. Brilliantly coloured shrubs were illuminated with whimsical outdoor lights, and at the end of the garden Al could make out the silhouette of a summerhouse, which was like a miniature version of the main house, built from wood.

'That's the Peabody place,' said Euphemia, plumping up the pillows on his bed. 'His daddy made a fortune from lumber and built the house about fifty years ago. Reckon it's pretty ugly myself, but then folks have different tastes, I guess. . . .'

Al stared at the house again. On the first floor there was a light shining through flimsy curtains, and he could make out a slender figure against the tall window.

'And that's the Peabody girl,' said Euphemia, with a tightening of the lips. 'I advise you to stay away from *her*.'

★ ★ ★

Everyone in Savannah knew Euphemia Bailey, and with her personal recommendation, Al had no trouble getting a job at the railroad depot loading up the freight cars that took imported goods to Atlanta – rubber tyres from the Far East, fruit, coffee and timber from South America. It was hard, physical work and Al was exhausted by the end of each day, having no more energy than was required to walk back from the railway terminal to Euphemia's boarding house, shovel back his evening meal and fall asleep on his narrow bed, usually without getting undressed. His tall frame filled out with muscle and sinew, and the skin on his hands coarsened; he looked like any other railwayman, most of whom were many years older. Two of the younger ones had become his particular friends: a slow, sweet-natured boy called Bluey, and Wyatt Neely from Minnesota, who stood six feet five inches tall and had a broad grin and tow-coloured hair so pale it shone white in the sun. Bluey had never known any other life than the railroad. His father was a 'red-cap', an attendant who served the passenger cars on the steam train to Atlanta, and Bluey wanted to be a red-cap too. Wyatt was more ambitious. He was studying accountancy at night school and aimed to apply for a white collar job on the railway board as soon as he had graduated.

Al worked hard, volunteering for overtime and nightshift as often as he could to boost the steadily growing pile of dollar bills under his mattress. Euphemia took a motherly interest in his progress and let him do odd jobs around the boarding house in lieu of rent.

'But don't you go working too hard now,' she would say, when he went to fetch the small bag of tools he had brought with him from Walthourville. 'A young man like you, you should be out socialisin', meeting some nice young ladies.'

In what spare time he had, Al liked to go down to the river and watch the boats coming and going; he would have sat on the wharf all day if he could. Best of all was when a really big ship came in. He liked to look out for the ship's mark and try and figure out where it came from, and what it was carrying. And the ships came from all over: Panama, Greece, Norway. As likely as not, he would be loading some of their cargo on to the freight cars the next day, his arms and back straining with its weight.

This was as close to happiness as Al could recall. There hadn't been a great deal of it around when he was growing up. Home in the tiny Georgia town of Walthourville had been a faded weatherboard shack with a crooked stoop and peeling paint. It was a mean sort of house and James Macken, the town preacher, was a mean man, waging a one-man battle against sin that had dried up any human kindness and left uncontrollable anger in its place. Al still had the scars on his back to prove it. His younger sister Martha was living alone with their widowed father now that Al was gone. He just hoped that she could keep on the right side of James Macken long enough for him to earn the money for a decent place for them both to live. Then he would send for her.

One afternoon he came back from the river and went straight into the parlour to ask Euphemia if she needed any jobs doing.

'Oh, I'm sorry, Miz Bailey. I didn't realise you had company.'

Sitting opposite Euphemia in her best velvet armchair was a man of about fifty, tall and handsome, with thinning hair which was still a bright enough shade of red to make an odd contrast with his dark eyebrows. Even in his ignorance about clothes, Al could tell that the fine wool suit had been custom made and the green tie was pure silk.

'Al, I'd like you to meet Mr Clermont Peabody. Mr Peabody, this is the young man I was telling you about.'

Peabody stood up but did not offer his hand. 'I was asking Mrs Bailey if any of her boarders were interested in doing some work for me. I understand you do some odd jobs about the place.'

'Yes, sir.'

'Ever do any house-painting?'

'Yes, sir. Painted the whole of our house back in Walthourville. Every two years starting when I was twelve. That was if my daddy could afford the paint.'

'Al's a very good worker, and he's awful strong, Mr Peabody.'

Peabody looked Al up and down, like a plantation owner judging a male slave. The gaze made Al feel uncomfortable.

'My wife wants the gazebo painted.'

'The gazebo, sir?'

'You know, the summerhouse. At the end of our garden. Has

a mind to change the colour to match the blossoms on some shrubs she's planting. There's $50 in it if you finish the job and my wife is satisfied.'

'I'd be happy to, sir.' Boldly, Al extended his hand and waited for Peabody to shake it. Peabody smiled, for the first time.

'I can only work evenings, but I can start as soon as you like. Tonight, even.'

'I'd be obliged.'

'What's Mrs Peabody like?' Al asked Euphemia after supper as he packed his tools and brushes into his bag.

Euphemia sniffed. 'Very proper. How do you say? . . . Refined. In fact, she's what you'd call a real Southern belle. Her daddy owned a plantation, out Bethesda way. And she likes you to know it, if you know what I mean.'

'And the daughter?' Al fastened his overalls and slung his bag over his shoulder. 'Is *she* a real Southern belle too?'

'No, she ain't.' Euphemia swept up a pile of plates and carried them through into the kitchen. 'She's no better than she should be, that Miss Peabody. Like I said before, you stay away from her.'

Al realised when he called at the Peabody house that Euphemia must have been teasing. The heavy oak front door was pulled open by a coloured maid.

'I'm Al Macken. Is Mrs Peabody at home?'

'No, she ain't.'

'Who is it, Clara?' A young girl of around Al's age appeared in the hall. She had fair hair scraped back into a pony tail, and though her face was pretty, her expression was timid, nervous even. She wore a plain blue cotton dress with a square neck that accentuated the fact she had no breasts to speak of, and not much in the way of hips, either. On her feet she wore white bobby socks and plain Oxford loafers.

'It's the young man come to do the summerhouse, Miz Cordella.'

The girl extended a hand; her grip was cool and limp. 'I'm Miss Peabody. I can take you out to the back if you like, I know where Daddy told our boy to put the paint.'

Al followed the girl out into the garden, where it was still

17

light, and there was a pleasant breeze. She shivered and pulled her thin arms around herself. 'I swear these evenings are getting too cold for me. . . . Well, here we are. There's the paint that Mama picked out, and I see you have your own brushes with you. I guess I'll just leave you to it.'

She gave Al a brief, nervous smile then turned and ran back to the house, her arms still clenched tightly across her chest as if she was afraid he was trying to see through her dress.

Al started painting the wooden slats of the summerhouse in the pale blush pink that Mrs Peabody had selected, but the light faded before he had completed two walls. He would have to return the following afternoon, and possibly the one after that too if he was going to do the window frames and door. He started to wipe down his brushes with methylated spirit and pack them away in his bag. Without looking up, he became aware of someone watching him. In the half light he could make out the figure of the Peabody girl crossing the lawn.

No, it was not the Peabody girl, he could see that now. She had come to stand in the arc of one of the fancy garden lamps, and the light on her hair gleamed a rich red, somewhere between copper and gold. Her skin was pale and creamy, her full curving mouth outlined with dark lipstick. She wore a flimsy voile dress, cut low to expose a generous cleavage, and her shapely legs were encased in silk stockings that shimmered in the lamp light.

Al, kneeling over his brushes, realised that he was staring at her ankles. Even worse, he was trying to imagine what was above them.

'I . . . I'm sorry,' he stammered. 'I thought you were Miss Peabody.'

'Why, I *am* Miss Peabody, silly!'

'But the young lady I spoke to earlier said – '

'That was my sister, Cordella. I'm Beulah.'

She did not offer her hand, merely smiled and put her head on one side, as if inviting him to admire her curvaceous form. Al suddenly remembered Euphemia's words and realised she had been quite serious after all, and this must be the Miss Peabody she wanted him to avoid.

'What are you grinning at?' she asked sharply.

'Tell me, there aren't any more Miss Peabodys back there in the house, are there? You don't have any more sisters?'

'No, it's just me and Cordella. And Mama says Cordella's no trouble. . . .'

'Well, I'd best be gettin' along now. . . .' Tearing his gaze away from the silk-clad ankles, Al started to pack away his brushes.

'They said on the radio just now that the war in Europe's started. Just a few hours ago, they reckon. I'n't that just awful?'

'Yup. . . .'

Beulah swung her skirt from side to side, an action that was guaranteed to make Al look up, since the voile made a distracting rustling sound as it moved against her silk stockings. Once she knew he was looking, she smoothed the front of her skirt, pressing it back to reveal the outline of her slim thighs.

'They say that if it goes on a long time, our troops might have to go and fight too.'

'Nah!' said Al. 'It'll be over before then, you'll see.'

'Well, what a shame.' Beulah smoothed her thick curls. 'I was just thinking how cute you'd look in a soldier boy's uniform. . . .'

'Well, I guess I'd better be on my way now.' Al picked up his bag of tools and waited respectfully for her to step aside. 'I'll be finishing up tomorrow,' he added, but by then Beulah was already out of earshot, and all he could see was her slender shadow floating across the lawn.

On his return to the Peabody house the following afternoon, Al could not help but be disappointed when the maid let him in and there was no sign of Beulah. A figure hovering in the kitchen doorway turned out to be Cordella, even more nondescript with her thin, dirty blonde hair hanging down straight.

As he went into the garden he saw that Beulah was sitting on a swing seat on the porch. She wore a white cotton dress, crisp and starchy, and a wide-brimmed straw hat. She was swinging her legs to and fro to keep up the momentum of the seat, and there were no silk stockings this time, just bare feet with red-varnished toenails.

She waved when she saw Al. 'Hey there! Like a mint julep?'

'No thank you, ma'am. I'd better get right on with the summerhouse.'

She shrugged and poured herself another glass from the jug on the table. Then she kicked out her legs again, rucking up her skirt to reveal a glimpse of her firm thighs. The gesture had such nonchalance, Al simply could not make up his mind whether it was deliberate or not.

'I am *so* bored!' she lamented. 'I declare I have *never* been so bored in my entire life!'

Beulah scowled at Al's retreating back as if she held him partly responsible for this state of affairs. And while he worked he was aware of her watching him from her vantage point on the porch, not watching in the idle way of someone sitting and watching the world pass by but with a provocative air, as though she were intent on distracting him from his chore by her presence alone. And though he moved the brush steadily up and down the wall, covering the white clapboard with fresh paint, Al was distracted. He found himself looking back frequently at Beulah. She managed always to have her face turned away, yet it was as if she had just invited his glance.

Al started to sweat, although he was in the shade and there was a pleasant breeze. He pushed down his overall braces and stripped off his shirt. When he raised his eyes to take in the porch, he saw Beulah stand up and pull off her hat in a gesture that mirrored his own. Her hair drooped and swung against her shoulders, the same brilliant gold-red as her father's.

'You still painting?' she called.

'Looks like.'

'Can't you finish up now, and come and talk to me? I swear I am so bored I am goin' to *die!*'

Cordella came out of the house, carrying a glass of lemonade on a tray. 'Mr Macken doesn't want a drink!' her sister shouted at her. 'Least, he didn't want any of mine!'

Cordella handed the lemonade to Al with a shy smile and scurried away across the lawn. Al drained the glass in a few seconds, pausing to wipe his hand across his brow.

'Well, I declare. . . .' Beulah was coming across the lawn towards him. She swung her hips as she walked with the measured grace of a panther. 'So you *do* have a thirst after all.'

Her eye lighted on the wet paintbrush that Al had laid on one side. Quick as a flash she grabbed it, flipping the bristles to and fro so that tiny droplets of pink paint sprayed out into the air. Some of them splashed across Al's forearms. 'Well, look what we have here, this ole paintbrush that you think so much of. . . .'

Al tried to grab her wrist and take the brush from her, but she was too quick for him, darting away and skipping across the lawn. 'You'll have to catch me first. . . .' She ran up to the main house and stared at it quizzically with her head on one side. 'I think maybe this place would look better with a bit of pink paint on it. Starting with the bricks outside Daddy's library, maybe. . . .'

'No, stop. . .! Miss Peabody. . .!' Al ran after her and tried to grab the brush, but once again she slipped away from him. She ran round the side of the house to where the gardener had left a ladder, and started to climb up it to the first-floor windows. The wet bristles smeared the wall as she climbed, leaving snails' tracks of pink against the red bricks.

She turned round to grin at Al, who was gripping the foot of the ladder.

'Hey – give me that thing!' Al tried hard to concentrate on the dripping brush, but his vantage point below Beulah's ankles gave him a disturbing view of her legs, all the way up to the top of her thighs. He could even see the delicate lace that edged her panties. A strange wave of heat passed up his backbone, making his pulse race.

'If you want the brush, I guess you'll just have to come up here and get it!'

Al's legs trembled as he climbed the ladder. He stopped two rungs below where Beulah stood, but she waved the brush high above his head, taunting him. He moved up another rung, and because he was some inches taller than she, their faces were now on a level. He saw for the first time that her eyes, slanted like a cat's, were bright green. He grabbed her wrist and tugged, and suddenly her lips were on his and he was kissing her, fiercely, desperately.

After what seemed a long time, Beulah pulled away, her eyes wide with a mixture of surprise and amusement. Al recognised the expression on her face; he could tell that she was searching for the most flippant or sardonic riposte in her repertoire. The fact he could see inside her mind, that he felt he already knew her so well after such scant acquaintance took his breath away. Before she could speak he grabbed her with his free hand and kissed her again, allowing his fingers to travel down from her neck to her large breasts and the curve of her hips.

'Now that's something like. . . .' She breathed in his ear, pressing herself against him with enthusiasm. 'C'mon, let's do it! I mean, let's *really* do it! There's an old blanket in the gazebo . . . no one would see us. . . .'

Al struggled to control the desire snaking its way through his body, and to ignore Beulah's fingers, gently manipulating his erection. He wanted to, God he wanted to. He'd never done it before, not properly, but he could tell it would be wonderful. He didn't even care about Euphemia Bailey's warning, or the fact Beulah might have used the blanket in the gazebo on other occasions just like this.

It was the thought of Clermont Peabody that stopped him. Not because he was Beulah's father, but because he was going to give Al $50 if he did the job properly, and Al did not want to put the money at risk, not for all the hot little rich girls in the world. He needed that money if he was going to get on in this town, and become as rich as the Vanderbilts, and if he played his cards right with Peabody there might be more of it coming his way.

'No,' he said to Beulah firmly, unpeeling her fingers from the paintbrush. 'Not right now. I've got to work. I know it, and you know it.'

And he climbed down the ladder and walked back to the summerhouse.

Al did not see Beulah Peabody again for almost a year, but he thought about her. He dreamed about her too, her green cat-like eyes and the sun glancing off her red-gold hair. He would dream he was on the ladder again, with the hem of her flimsy dress just brushing against the tip of his nose. The tantalizing glimpse of lace-edged panties disappeared from view as she moved further up the ladder, but in his dreams he pursued her and grabbed her, pinning her down hard so she couldn't move. He could hear her laughter, her gasps and finally her moans of pleasurable surrender, but he could never see her face. The dream culminated with Al yanking her panties away angrily and pressing himself against her, but always at the moment he was about to enter her he woke up, panting and sweating and with an angry erection.

He woke like this one morning in the summer of 1940 but the erection quickly wilted as he put all thought of Beulah from his mind. Today he had more important things to think about. He leapt from his bed early and went about washing and dressing in a purposeful way, with a broad smile on his face. Today he, Al Macken, was going to change his life for ever.

'What you grinning at, boy?' Euphemia demanded as she served him with a bowl of grits and a plate of hot biscuits. 'You look pleased with yourself, I must say.'

'Today's goin' to be a great day for me, Miz Bailey.' He put his arm around her waist and gave her an affectionate squeeze. 'Just you wait and see.'

'Great day or no, you'd better hurry up and eat those grits while I put your eggs on. You're surely going to be awful late getting down to that railroad depot. Mr Wilkes in't going to like you any today.'

'I ain't goin' down to no railroad. I quit.'

'You quit? How in thunder do you intend on paying your board then?'

'You'll see.' Al wiped his mouth with his napkin and slid out of his seat. 'And hold the eggs. I ain't got time this morning.'

His first call was at the Savannah Bank and Trust Company on East Bay Street, where he withdrew all the money he had saved from his wages since he started work; nearly $1000. He rolled the billfold carefully and carried it like that, all the way down Bay Street. He didn't dare let go of it, put it away in a pocket where someone might steal it, for that money represented his whole future.

He headed west down the waterfront to the loading bays where cargo ships docked and stood on the dockside, studying all the vessels that were tied up.

'Kin I help you, boy?' someone shouted.

'I'm looking for Brad Gilbert.'

'That's me.' The man hauled himself up so that he was standing on the deck of his boat. He was short and squat with a thick neck and massive forearms baked brick red by the sun. 'What kin I do for you?'

'Hear you've got a boat you're wanting to sell.' Al climbed down the stone steps onto the jetty. 'This her?'

'Yup, this is her.' Gilbert gestured proudly from one end of the deck to the other. His pride and joy was a tugboat, squat and low in the water, with peeling black paint and the evidence of much patching and repairing on her sides.

'It ain't just *Rose Marie* I'm selling. It's the whole business. You get the office over there as well.' Gilbert pointed to a crumbling shack a few yards back from the jetty. 'With a telephone.'

'And how *is* business?' Al asked, squatting down on his haunches to inspect the sides of the boat. He rubbed his hand along her side and the crumbling paint came away.

'Well, you know . . . kind of quiet since the war broke out. And with the federal government takin' over so much land in these parts for them military camps . . . a lot of people's seen their businesses go under, you know.'

'I guess so.' Al was thinking about what he had read in the *Savannah Morning News* that week, about the anti-aircraft training facility they were going to build up at Fort Stewart. And they were talking about a submarine base on this stretch of coast too. All of which was bad news for residents whose land was being repossessed, but good for the state's long-term economy. And building those installations was going to take a lot of raw material, which would mean a lot of ships coming in and out of these waters. . . .

'Tell you what,' he said, straightening up. 'Since times are hard, with the war an' all, I'll give you $600. For the *Rose Marie*, the office, and any goodwill that goes along with it.'

Gilbert scratched the fleshy folds on the back of his neck, frowning. 'Well now, I don't know. The *Rose Marie*, she ain't in what you would call the first flush of youth, but we've been in this business a long while now, me and my daddy before me, and I reckon it must be worth a bit more than that, even in these times.'

'Eight-fifty,' said Al quickly. 'Cash. That's my best offer.' He unrolled the billfold and started counting out hundred-dollar bills.

'Well, all right,' said Gilbert grudgingly. 'I guess you'd better come on up to the office and I'll git you the keys, and *Rose Marie*'s papers and all the other damn fool bits of paperwork you're goin' to have to deal with from now on.'

There was a great number of Gilbert's damn fool bits of paper in the office, most of them piled in grimy heaps, others trampled underfoot on the bare floorboards. The place looked as though it hadn't been tidied or cleaned for years; there were broken panes of glass in the windows and a smell of bad drains. Later, thought Al; I'll worry about all this mess later. For the time being he had other more important things to take care of.

As soon as he had dealt with Gilbert and taken the keys, he headed back down West Broad Street to the railway depot. The Atlanta train was in the yard, being loaded up with bales of cloth from the mills out near Monroe. Al recognised the cartons they were packed in. He also recognised the tall, stooping figure moving amongst the bales, his hair glinting white in the sun.

'Hey, Wyatt!' He put his fingers in his mouth and cat-called. 'What y'all doing?'

Wyatt Neely straightened up and grinned at his friend. 'What am *I* doing? It should be me that's asking you that question. I thought we'd seen the last of you round these parts.'

'Hey, you having a good time, Wyatt?' Al stood with his head on one side, his expression mocking. 'Y'all *enjoying* yourself down here?'

Wyatt shrugged. 'You know . . . it's Monday. And we've got to get the Atlanta wagons on the road before noon. I don't have time to stand and talk to idle types like you. You know that.' He sighed and ran his hand over his forehead, beaded with sweat.

'Do what I did then. Go and tell Wilkes that you quit.'

'Yeah, and do what?'

'Come and work for me.'

Wyatt wrinkled his nose suspiciously. 'Do what?'

'I just bought myself a business. And I need a Yankee college type like you to come and do the books for me. Keep the money straight.'

Wyatt laughed. 'Get out of here! I'm aiming to be one of the big boys too, you know. I'm going after real qualifications though, not just . . . well, messing about with boats. Little boy's games.'

Al's eyes narrowed. 'This ain't no game, Wyatt. I'll even make you a partner if you like.'

Wyatt rubbed his forehead again and looked around him at the hot, dusty railyard, at the bales of cloth heaped up around his ankles. 'Well, I don't know. . . .'

'Tell you what, I've got me some things to do, so why don't y'all think about it? And if the answer's yes, I'll meet you on the waterfront tomorrow morning, eight sharp. Brad Gilbert's place. Except that it's not any more. It's Al Macken's place.'

Al went straight back to Miz Bailey's house, took a shower and changed into a fresh shirt. He dabbed a bit of lime cologne on his wrists and his chin and ran a comb through his hair, singing cheerfully as he teased the ducktail on the back of his neck. Things were going well for him, he could just feel it. He was really on a roll. What better time could there be to pay a visit to the Peabody house?

Al had never come across Clermont Peabody's wife during his previous visits to the house, and he was somewhat shocked when she answered the door. Shocked because he had expected the coloured maidservant, and shocked because he had never met anyone quite like Mrs Juliette Peabody before. The only two women he had ever known intimately (unless you counted Beulah) were his mother and Euphemia Bailey. His mother he only remembered slightly but she, like Euphemia, had been small and rounded, giving off an aura of softness that would yield to the touch. Mrs Peabody, on the other hand, was immensely tall and thin to the point of gauntness, though this was disguised by the excellent cut of her cashmere costume. The colour of her pale hair had faded, as Cordella's would one day, but it had been expertly tinted gold and elaborately dressed into a rigid mass of pleats and curls. Her expression was rigid too, rigid and cold.

'Yes?'

'I'm here to call on Miss Peabody, ma'am. Miss Beulah, that is.'

'Oh. *Beulah.*'

The emphasis which she placed on her daughter's name spoke

volumes. It said, '*Yes, you are the unsavoury type of young man I would expect Beulah to keep company with.*'

'Is she at home?' Al asked boldly. 'Only I do have one or two business appointments to keep.'

Without another word she led Al up to the first-floor parlour which had a harp and a piano and a large chandelier that tinkled slightly in the breeze from the verandah. Over the mantelpiece was a portrait, in the style of Singer Sargent, of a woman Al guessed was Mrs Peabody's mother. She stared back at him with the same haughty and indifferent gaze as she twirled a long string of pearls between her fingers.

The door opened abruptly and Beulah entered. Al started slightly, so great was the contrast between her sensuous warmth and the chill of her grandmother's image. She exuded colour too, in that pale room whose silk drapes had been faded by years of afternoon sun. Her brilliant red curls and primrose yellow dress were startlingly bright, making Al want to blink and rub his eyes. She stood a few inches away from him and he caught a gust of her perfume, tainted slightly with the warm odour of perspiration.

'Well, lookee here. . . .' Beulah put her hand on her hip, smiling broadly. 'I thought I'd scared you off.'

For a few seconds Al was unable to speak. He was staring fixedly at Beulah's breasts, at the curve of her waist and her hips; the stuff of his fantasies made glorious flesh.

'I've been working,' he said finally, dragging his gaze upwards to her face. Her sparkling green eyes were laughing, challenging him. 'That's what I came to tell you. I've been busy getting the money together to start my own business . . . and I've done it. Started my own business, I mean. I've bought a tugboat company.'

'Uh huh.' Beulah nodded slowly.

''Course, I'm fixin' to expand just as soon as I can. Pretty soon I'll be a real big name around here, just like your daddy.'

'So?'

'So I came to ask if y'all would walk out with me. We could maybe go to the movies, or to the fun-fair. . . .'

Beulah's smile disappeared as if she had just tripped a switch. Her eyes narrowed. 'Listen to me, *boy*. . . .' She thrust her face so close to his that he could feel tiny beads of spittle on his cheek. 'No man runs out on me and then gets to take me out after! And just because you bought yourself some dirty old boat doesn't make you nothing special. For pity's sake, why don't you just think about who I *am*! Those are the sorts of boys I date, over there!'

She waved her hand impatiently in the direction of the mantelpiece, where engraved white cards demanded the pleasure of the company of Miss Beulah and Miss Cordella Peabody at this levee, and that hunt ball and the other debutante's coming-out dance. Beulah's eyes shone with anger. 'I'm a somebody in this town and you're a nobody and that's why you don't mess around with me and then just walk away! So the answer's "no" – I don't want to go with you to a movie, or to a fun-fair, or even down the street!'

'Why, you arrogant little bitch!'

But Beulah didn't even hear him; she had turned on her heel and walked out of the parlour. He ran after her.

'You're wrong!' he shouted down the curving stairwell. 'I *am* somebody, you just haven't realised it yet!'

Rather than feeling dispirited when he left the Peabody house, Al felt exhilarated. Coming into contact with Beulah was like having a bucket of icy water thrown over him; after the initial unpleasantness he was left with a bracing glow. The skirmish had given him the extra fortitude he needed for his next task, which he wasn't looking forward to. He walked to the western edge of the city, to Highway 95, and took the bus out to Walthourville.

He checked his watch when he climbed down from the bus and started to walk to the house, passing the white clapboard church. It was 3.30. His father might be home at the moment, there was certainly a chance. But the later he left it, the greater that risk would be. He hung back at the top of the dirt track, watching. After a few minutes, he could make out his father's tall silhouette on the stoop. He looked gaunt, thinner than he had been a year ago when Al left. His father walked to the bottom of the scrubby patch of garden and started hoeing a bare patch of dirt, pausing occasionally to pull out a weed and toss it aside. Al hurried down the track and into the house. Martha was in the kitchen peeling potatoes at the sink, just as she had been on the day he left.

'Al!' She looked startled, then delighted, and then her eyes began to fill with tears. 'Oh, Al!' She hugged him fiercely. 'I di'n't know if I was ever goin' to see y'all again!'

'I told you I'd come back for you, didn't I? Quick now, go and get your things packed.'

'But what about Daddy? . . . I ain't finished makin' his supper.'

'You ain't goin' to make him supper tonight nor any other night. You've finished with all that. You're coming on back to Savannah with me.'

'You know, it wasn't so bad living with Daddy after you'd gone,' Martha confided to Al a few days later. They were in the shack that Brad Gilbert had described as his office, and Martha was hanging some curtains in the windows. 'He went kinda quiet after you left, never said nothin' very much. Just let me get on with keepin' house an' all. And he never laid a finger on me, as long as I got his dinner cooked on time. . . .'

Martha stood back to admire her handiwork, her head on one side. She was a sturdily built girl, pleasant-looking rather than pretty, with curling sandy hair and bright blue eyes, just like Al's. They got the blue eyes from their mother. James Macken had dark, dark brown eyes, the kind that glittered when they showed anger. Al had hated looking into those eyes. . . .

'Anyways, we've got the future to think about now,' he said gruffly. 'And I've got to either learn to dock and undock ships or find me a pilot to hire. They say gettin' those big boats around the riverfront is like threadin' a needle up a dark alley in a rainstorm.'

'Well at least you're not doing it alone,' said Martha, picking up a duster and polishing the telephone. 'You've got me and Wyatt to help you out all we can.'

Martha Macken threw herself into her new life as if she was entering a wonderful game. After settling her into a room at Euphemia's boarding house, Al took her straight down to the new premises on the waterfront, where she exclaimed with horror at the filthy state of the office and set about cleaning it up. She scrubbed down the walls inside and out with ammonia, removing layers of grime and mould. Then with Euphemia's help she found a glazier to repair the broken windows and polished them until they shone. She found a desk, cabinet and chair being sold cheaply in an office clearance on Factor's Walk and carried them down to the wharf herself. Wyatt put up shelves and between the two of them they devised a system for filing the hoped-for contracts. Then while Wyatt and Al repaired and renovated the *Rose Marie*, Martha pored over books on shorthand and typing, practising on the sturdy black typewriter Euphemia had brought down from her attic. The final chore was the nailing of a hand-painted sign over the door of the office, in swirling gold letters on a black background: 'Macken Tugboat Co'. The phone started to ring with enquiries as soon as it was in place.

Al had often stood on the walkway on River Street and watched the tugboats guiding huge ships nimbly in and out of the docking terminals. So many times, in fact, that he was sure he could start off by manning the *Rose Marie* himself. He had worked out what all the whistle signals meant, and he knew the precise moment when he was to transfer in mid-stream from the tug to the visiting vessel and twist and turn her alongside a pier.

Wyatt, however, was quick to talk him out of the idea. In his quiet, ponderous way he explained that the insurance to cover an untrained and inexperienced pilot would be prohibitively high. Patiently, he went through the projected figures with Al, talked about cash flow and overheads and liabilities. Some of the ships they might handle would be over 500 feet long; the channel they had to turn in was 600 feet wide. The narrow margin made for a high degree of risk, and it was human lives and valuable cargo at risk.

Al agreed reluctantly and they set about hiring a pilot, Captain Joe Costello, who was already well past sixty and so passionate about the river that he was willing to work for very little. Even so, his wages stretched their cash resources, so Al bought another tug, renovated it himself and hired another pilot, then a deepwater barge to ferry cargo around between the wharves. By the beginning of 1941, the construction of the military base at Fort Stewart had begun, bringing shipload after shipload of raw materials, and more and more business for the Macken Tugboat

Company. Within a year Al had acquired a fleet of half a dozen tugs and enough commissions as they could comfortably handle. With some reluctance, Al agreed with Martha that it was time for them to leave Euphemia Bailey's boarding house and put some of their mounting reserve of cash into a home of their own.

They found a two-storey Queen-Anne-style house on Whittaker Street, facing east towards the elegant fountains and tree-lined walks of Forsyth Park.

'It's too big,' said Martha as soon as Al showed it to her. 'It's just too big.'

'Pretty, though, ain't it?'

'Oh, it sure is. . . .' Martha sighed, looking at the delicate stained glass transoms over the window, and the twin turrets at either end of the generous verandah. She continued to sigh with pleasure once they were inside; at the ornate fireplaces and the handsome carved wooden balustrades. 'But we can't live in a place like this. There are seven . . . no, eight bedrooms. Who on earth is going to keep the place clean and decent? I won't have time to keep house if I'm at the office full time. We don't usually get finished up there until seven or eight.'

'We'll hire a maid, numbskull!'

'We can't do that!'

'Why not? Other business people do.'

'Yes, but we're . . . I mean, we're just folks! And you're barely twenty, I'm seventeen . . . everyone from round here will just laugh at us, say we're just bits of kids, playing.'

Al put his hands on Martha's shoulders and turned her to look at him. 'Martha, we *are* folks from round here, just you remember that. We're not a couple of hick kids from Walthourville no more, we're citizens of Savannah and we run a business here, a booming business. We can have half a dozen maids if we like. Now . . . do y'all like the house?'

'Yes. I like it fine.'

'Do you think Wyatt would like it.'

Martha blushed crimson. 'Wyatt? Why do you ask?'

'Because we could let one of the rooms to him. That way there would be three of us living here, and you wouldn't need to feel so bad about hiring a maid if we had a paying guest.'

'Well, I guess so. . . .'

'Good. That's settled. We're buying it.'

The house belonged to a widow whose sons had both joined up since mobilisation began. She was anxious for a quick sale, and Al managed to secure the property for only a fraction of its true worth by paying cash.

'It seems a bit mean . . .' said Martha, 'a poor widow lady being driven out of her home like that. She's lived here for ever. . . .'

'That's what happens in war-time; families get split up. Anyway, you heard what she said. She wants to go and live with her sister in St Petersburg. Can't wait to get away from here. And if we didn't take advantage of the situation, you can bet your sweet bippy that someone else would!'

Martha soon forgot all her doubts when their little household settled down in Whittaker Street, Wyatt occupying three rooms on the top floor. With the same energy and diligence that she applied to setting up the office, Martha set about finding furnishings and rugs and sewing drapes. She knew nothing about antiques or interior decoration, but in this as in all things she educated herself, spending her lunch hours poring over books and magazines at her desk, and in the evening continuing her studies on the swing seat on the verandah.

'She's playing house,' Al said to Wyatt, then added in a teasing tone, 'she'll make someone a damn fine wife some day.'

Wyatt's fair skin turned a vivid shade of pink. 'Aw, leave her alone, Al, she's just a kid!'

Nevertheless, Wyatt was in turns protective and chivalrous towards Martha, and it was a growing attachment Al was only too glad to foster. He had far to go himself, way beyond Savannah and even Georgia, and Martha was going to need someone to take care of her eventually. He fell into the habit of leaving them alone on the verandah in the evenings, talking quietly on the swing seat and sipping pink lemonade made by their newly acquired maid, Gracie. Sometimes they would look at Martha's books together, sometimes they would talk over the day's business and any new ideas they had, sometimes they would just sit in companionable silence, watching couples take twilight strolls in the park.

Like an old married couple already, thought Al with

satisfaction. He would keep a discreet distance, sitting on the front steps to go through the company books or repair some small piece of equipment from one of the tugs. He was sitting like this one evening, taking apart and cleaning a sextant, when a car drew up on the kerb.

Al noticed at once that it was very fine; a white Mercury convertible. The driver was a woman. She checked her appearance in the driving mirror and then swung a very slender pair of ankles onto the sidewalk. Al didn't recognise her at first; she was wearing a large picture hat and it completely covered the gleaming red-gold hair that Al had come to think of as her trademark.

'So, country boy. . . .' Beulah spoke softly, but there was a challenge in her stance, hands on hips with sunglasses tapped impatiently against her thigh. 'I come calling and I find you playing in the dirt.'

Al ignored her and continued to rub away furiously at the sextant with his oiled cloth.

'This your new house?'

'Uh-huh.'

'Hmmm. . . .' Beulah put her hands on her hips and scanned the roof line. 'Quite pretty, if you like the Queen Anne style . . . but then I can't abide the Queen Anne style.'

Al laid down his rag, but his eyes still did not quite meet hers. 'The Peabody house is Queen Anne, ain't it?'

'Well now, that's quite correct, it is. But then Grandaddy never did have any taste. Me, I prefer colonial-style architecture . . . or maybe federal. . . . Now, tell me, y'all didn't go and buy yourself a Queen Anne house just because you thought *I* might like it?'

Her tone was wheedling. Al looked up and allowed his eyes to meet hers for the first time. The look that smouldered in them sent little stabs of heat directly to his groin, but he managed to keep his own gaze steady.

'How d'you find me?' he asked.

'Daddy told me you'd bought yourself a new place.'

'Your *father* did? What's it to him?'

Beulah waved her sunglasses airily. 'Oh, you know . . . he just likes to take an interest. He says your business is going places, too.'

'He does, huh?' Al picked up his oily rag again and returned to his chore. Out of the corner of his eye he could see that Beulah was positively bristling with impatience. She came and stood a few inches away from him, so that if he were to raise his head his eyes would be level with her silk-swathed hips. 'Who's that girl over there?' she demanded.

'My sister, Martha.'

'That her beau?'

'That's my partner, Wyatt Neely.'

'So . . . aren't y'all going to introduce me?'

'No, I'm not going to do that. . . .' Very slowly and deliberately Al laid down the sextant and stood up, wiping his fingers on the rag. With Beulah in high heels, their eyes were exactly on a level. 'You and me are going to go for a ride in that fancy automobile of yours.'

'Aren't you going to clean up some?'

Al shook his head. 'No. You have to take us country boys just as you find us.'

Beulah ran her eyes up and down his torso and a smile curled at the corners of her mouth. 'I might just do that.'

They climbed into the car and Beulah threw it into gear, screeching away from the kerb and picking up speed rapidly as they headed down Whittaker Street. Al could feel warmth from the leather seat where the sun had been on it; there was warmth too, more imagined than real, from Beulah's right thigh as she pressed the brake pedal. There was a lipstick balanced precariously on the dashboard and a scent spray without its cap, tossed impatiently aside. The car smelt of scent, and Al imagined her spraying a cloud of it onto her neck as she made her way to the house on Whittaker Street.

Beulah continued to look at the road ahead, her concentration seemingly completely taken up with driving. They were heading out of the city now, still travelling very fast.

'Where are we going?' Al asked.

She shrugged her shoulders. 'I don't know. Nowhere really. I thought it would be kind of fun just to drive around some.' She increased the pressure on the accelerator slightly and Al realised with a blinding flash what she was doing. She was playing another of her games and this one was all about having power and taking control. As long as he was the passenger and she was driving she could do what she liked with him, he had made himself her prisoner. He shot a sideways glance at her, but she did not react, focussing her eyes on the horizon. He found he was more excited than angry; it was like being in close proximity to a rare wild animal, one that was both beautiful and dangerous.

He waited until they were on a straight stretch of road, driving through an avenue of dogwood trees. 'Stop the car!' he ordered.

'What?'

'I said, stop the car!'

He reached for the wheel and yanked it hard to the right, pulling on the handbrake at the same time so that the car squealed to a halt with a cloud of dust and a burning smell.

'You crazy, goddamn – '

Al stoppered her mouth by placing his firmly over hers. His hands moved up quickly and gripped her shoulders, pinning her back against the leather seat. Beulah tried to arch her body against him but he persisted and after a few seconds she relaxed, moving her lips against his and sliding her tongue teasingly between them.

A few cars passed them on the road, but it was almost dark now and most people were at home, cooking their evening meal, listening to news of the war round the radio set, arguing with their families. They were alone in the dark. The thought excited Al. This time it was not going to be like his dream. This time there was going to be no stopping, no holding back.

His fingers sought the buttons on the front of her silk dress and suddenly hers were there too, fluttering against his, helping him. He had thought that underneath she would be wearing a corset like the one in his childhood memories of his mother. That was the only experience of women's undergarments he had ever had, a grey bony thing that creaked slightly at the touch. But Beulah wore only a satin chemise supported by thin ribbon straps which she slid down from her shoulders. Her breasts swung free and for a few seconds he could only marvel at their full, slightly pendulous shape, the creamy colour of the flesh and the strawberry pink of the nipples. He buried himself in them like a hungry child, wanting not only to nuzzle and to suck but to feed. The novelty of this emotion overwhelmed him. The sweetness of her smell and her softness incited not only desire but the need to seek comfort, the only feminine succour he had known for years.

Beulah was making little wiggling motions with her hips, struggling into an upright position and pushing him back into the passenger seat.

'Hey, c'mon, I don't want to play momma. *This* is what I'm after. . . .' She unbuttoned his flies and wrestled his penis free from his undershorts. Then, with little grunting sounds she pushed her panties halfway down her thighs and somehow managed to lift her left thigh over his so that she was straddling him. Her successful manoeuvring seemed to please her, and a broad smile swept over her face as she lowered herself onto him, the first ingenuous smile Al had ever seen her give.

Then she began to move slowly to and fro, building up the hot wetness running down him, making him reach out for something to grab on to before he passed out with sheer pleasure. The leather car seat gave off gentle squeaking sounds and the car's chassis rose and fell slightly in tandem with her rocking motions.

'Oh Beulah . . .! Beulah. . . .'

And then it turned into his dream again. Suddenly she wasn't there and his rigid penis was twitching in empty space. Drops of semen shot onto the leather seat, and the dashboard, and the windscreen.

He opened his eyes and groaned. 'Oh, Jesus, what the . . .?'

'This is your first time, isn't it?' Beulah's voice seemed to come from far away. She was sitting behind the wheel again with her skirt pulled down and seeming remarkably composed. Only the swell of her naked breasts in the front of her shirtwaist gave away their recent coupling.

'I had to do that,' she said firmly. 'Because there's no way in the world I want to go and get myself pregnant. As it is, that was pretty risky. I just might not have been able to stop in time.' She smiled broadly again. 'Fact is, it felt so good I almost *didn't* jump off in time!'

She noticed Al's crestfallen expression and reached over to squeeze his hand. 'Don't worry, next time y'all can get some French letters. And there will be a next time, I know it. That was only a taster.' She giggled.

Al's tongue had cleaved to the roof of his mouth and he could only mumble, 'Oh.' He reached for his handkerchief and started to dab at the mess on the windscreen with shaking hands.

'Don't worry about that none, I'll clear it up later.'

Al tried to picture this: the car parked on the drive of the Peabody mansion and Beulah sneaking downstairs at midnight with a bucket in one hand and a cloth in the other. He didn't care to wonder how many times she had cleared up such sticky stains before. In fact the idea caused him pain; he could no longer bear the idea of her being with anyone else.

'Y'all want a cigarette?'

Al, who rarely smoked, accepted one, and gradually the nicotine calmed him. He put his feet up on the dashboard, leaned back in his seat and blew the smoke up at the night sky, now darkening to blue streaked with silver.

'You know,' he said, puffing contentedly, 'all of a sudden I feel like I know nothing about you. Nothing at all.'

'You know enough.' Beulah ran her scarlet-painted fingertips along the edge of the car door, then examined her nails minutely.

'Oh sure, I could work out what you're thinking for *now*, but what I'm saying is . . . I mean, I don't know what you think about things in general.'

'What things?'

'Like, are you happy with your life?'

Beulah gave a little laugh, exhaling smoke. 'Well . . .' she drawled. 'I guess I'm lucky. Other people would say I'm lucky. I come from a good family, with a decent home and plenty of money. Daddy gave us a decent education, I have a brain in here – if I care to use it. And I guess I don't look so bad.'

'But?'

She laughed. 'You could tell there was a "but"? The but is that I get so sick of my family, you know, feeling like I'm stuck with them for ever if I don't do something about it. They're just so dull, so small town. Daddy talks about his business all the time when he's home, but he spends most of his time at the Oglethorpe Club anyway, just to get away from Mama, who can think about nothing but the Social Register and the Junior League and the Savannah Historical Foundation, and how well connected other people are.'

'What about your sister?'

'Cordella?' Beulah snorted. 'She doesn't think about anything at all. She just does whatever Mama and Daddy tell her.'

Al screwed his cigarette butt hard against the window rim to extinguish it, then tossed it out on to the grass. 'So what do you think about, Beulah?'

'Oh. . .' Beulah leaned back and sighed. 'Adventure. Money. Men. Passion. . . . How about you?'

Al held his hand flat and levelled it at the horizon. 'I want to just keep right on moving forward. I ain't going to let nothing hold me back.'

'Wouldn't it be great if there was like this one long, straight road and it went on for ever and ever and you could just drive and drive down it, real fast . . .?'

'Hey, come on.' Al reached over and turned the key in the ignition. 'Let's get you back to that ugly, dull old home of yours.'

In the months that followed, the house on Whittaker Street became a place of escape for Beulah.

She and Al went out too, taking Beulah's car. They would drink in bars, dance into the small hours at Savannah's exclusive supper clubs or sometimes just drive down the new coast road, stopping to eat at a roadhouse, or to make love in the car when darkness fell. When fall drew in, then winter, and it became too cold to drive around at night, they spent more and more time in Al's room in Whittaker Street. Al worked as hard as ever to build up the business, but all the time he wasn't working he spent with Beulah. He waited for some signs of disapproval from Clermont Peabody and his wife, but none came.

'Don't worry,' said Beulah. 'He's not going to stop us now you're the up-and-coming young businessman in this town. He approves.'

Martha, however, did not approve. She was in awe of Beulah, especially her dress sense, which she made frequent attempts to imitate. 'I do believe that was a Norman Norell she was wearing,' she would say in hushed tones after one of Beulah's visits, 'I saw one just like it in *Queen* magazine.'

It was the sounds that Martha objected to, the sounds of sighing and gasping, sometimes even screaming, that emanated from Al's room when the two of them were in there. Sometimes they went on most of the night and then she would see Beulah calmly walking downstairs at six in the morning, smoothing her hair as if nothing were wrong. Martha and Wyatt were walking out together now, but they observed all the proprieties. They had barely started to kiss one another, and most of their conversations were concerned with where they would live when they married one day, and how many children they would have, and what they would call them. The animal passion, the openness of Al and Beulah's affair made them uncomfortable.

'I think Martha was going to say something to me this morning,' said Beulah, lounging on Al's bed one Saturday morning. They had just made love, and she lay in a whirlpool of damp, wrinkled sheets. 'I only asked her if she had a clean petticoat she could lend me because mine had got a little bitty stain on it.' Beulah's mouth curled at the corners. 'She went all red in the face and looked like she wanted to scold me.'

'You mustn't be too hard on Martha. She's still just a kid. And a preacher's daughter.'

'Well, the preacher's son sure seems to be at home with the pleasures of the flesh.' She reached her hand out to his crotch as he passed the bed, scratching her long fingernails lightly against his testicles. His penis stirred in response, but Al walked over to the bureau and turned on the radio.

'Aw, Al! Come on, turn that thing off now. You've done nothing but listen to that borin' old stuff about Pearl Harbor. You already heard what happened a thousand times. It got bombed.'

'That "stuff" is important. Things are goin' to change now, that's for sure. We're on borrowed time. The War Department's really goin' to come after us now.'

'But I thought you were planning on expanding. The new warehouse you're after buying – '.

'Oh, I am. There's never been a better time for those that are able to take advantage. With the draft taking most of the men away, businesses are feeling the pressure, especially family businesses. They're like ripe fruit, just there to be taken.'

Al pulled his shirt over his head and started to button it. He had not mentioned to Beulah that his call-up papers were already in his jacket pocket, had been for some days now. This really was borrowed time, but he might just make it, if he was smart. . . .

'Come on.' He slapped Beulah's bare calf. 'Get your dress on. I'm taking you to see my latest acquisition, remember?'

Martha stopped them at the bottom of the stairs. 'Al . . . Beulah . . . y'all going out?'

Beulah gave Martha her sweetest, most innocent smile. 'Why yes, Al promised me we could go and visit the new place you've just bought.'

'Only Wyatt and I have got something to tell you both. Wyatt!'

Wyatt came through from the parlour with a sheepish smile on his face. Martha took his hand.

'Wyatt and I are now officially engaged! On account of him just being drafted.'

Al narrowed his eyes. 'You going then, Wyatt? To Europe?'

'Well, yes, I guess I am,' said Wyatt in his slow, ponderous way. 'I want to defend my country. I guess we all do. It'll be your turn soon, Al.'

'I'm going to do Wyatt's work while he's away,' Martha cut in eagerly. 'We've been through the books together so many times I know exactly what to do.'

'Sure you do,' said Al. 'Hey, this is great news! We're delighted for the both of you, aren't we, Beulah?'

He took Wyatt's hand and wrung it firmly. 'We'll celebrate later, OK?'

'I think it's real sweet,' said Beulah later, as Al drove her car along Lathrop Avenue, heading west. 'Wyatt and your sister getting married.'

'Uh huh.'

'I mean, it must be nice having someone think so much of you they actually want to marry you.' She gave Al a sidelong smile.

'I thought you was hot for adventure and passion and such.'

'Well I *am* . . . for now. But it might be nice to marry and have a family some day, if I could find me the right man.' She put her head on one side and smiled coquettishly at Al. 'He'd have to be some kind of a man though.'

Al took his eyes off the road for a moment to grin back at her. 'I'll have to see what I can do.'

They pulled up outside a large, shabby warehouse, with

'Southern Cargo Company' painted on the side in letters so faded they were scarcely legibile. Outside on the wharfside there was a ramshackle congregation of cranes, pulleys and rolling ramps.

'So you just bought *this*?' said Beulah, wrinkling her nose. 'What are you going to do with it?'

'It's a stevedoring company. Contracted to load and unload cargo ships. There's an office on West Bay Street, too, that goes with it. I know it don't look like much, but when we get this place straightened up it's going to make us a whole load of money. After the war's over there's going to be a boom in the number of ships sailing in and out of here. I'm just trying to get the Macken company ready ahead of time.'

Beulah drew in her breath admiringly. 'A whole load of money! So we're going to be rich. What shall we spend it on?'

'The first thing I'm going to do is buy me a car. A car that's at least as smart and at least as pretty as yours. No offence, but a man should have a car of his own to drive.'

'Why of course he should!' Beulah linked her arm through his. 'As long as you let me pick it out . . . and think of the house we can buy. Wyatt and Martha can stay in Whittaker Street and you and I can build ourselves something real fancy. Out on the Back River, or Vernonberg maybe. . . . And I want to travel – '

'To New York!'

'We'd have an apartment there, of course, but I mean to Europe. To Paris and London and Rome! And think of the parties we'd give.'

'The best in Savannah, naturally.'

'The best in the whole South! Oh . . .!' Beulah hugged herself with pleasure. 'As soon as this damn war's over the future's just going to be so great!'

Al's hand dropped instinctively to his jacket pocket, where he fingered his draft papers. 'Listen, honey, I have a little bit of business to complete. Didn't you say you was fixin' to go to the beauty parlour or some such? How about letting me set you down on Drayton Street?'

Al was glad when Beulah concurred with this suggestion. After setting her down he drove to the Peabody house.

'Mr Clermont Peabody,' he told the maid firmly. 'No, he's not expectin' me, but I know he'll be willing to see me.'

Peabody was in his library, a polygonal room with a large stained glass window depicting a ship in full sail. He motioned Al to a chair on the other side of his desk, and proffered a box of cigars. 'I've been expectin' you to call.'

'It's not concerning what you think.'

'Isn't it?'

'I haven't come to talk to you about Beulah. Though I assure you, I hold your daughter in the highest regard, and I'm taking care of her just as well as I can.'

Peabody gave a gruff laugh. 'Beulah doesn't need a man to take care of her, Mr Macken, as I'm sure you must be aware. She goes her own way, always has and always will. So, shall we talk about what you're really here for? Which I'm assuming must be money.'

'Money?'

'I hear you put in a bid for Southern Cargo. You're going to need some money to get the business operational, and to finance it when it is. Stevedoring takes a lot more manpower than tugging, Mr Macken. You're going to be paying a lot of wage packets.'

'The Savannah Bank and Trust are going to back me. They know it's a good risk.'

'So. . . .' Peabody waved his cigar. 'Just why are you here?'

'I've been called up. I thought you might be able to tell me how I can get exemption from the draft. I'm single, I've got no dependents, my health is excellent; they're goin' to send me straight off to boot camp. But the business really needs me just now. This is the time I need to be here, when there are opportunities for expanding and diversifying – '

'And profiteering?' cut in Peabody. 'Don't worry. I think you're absolutely right to try and take these opportunities as they come. You obviously have vision, and great business sense. And that's why I'm going to help you.'

'You are?'

'I have many contacts on the local draft board. I'll make sure you get an exemption.' He smiled. 'I think the United States of America will benefit more in the long term if you stay right here in Savannah. And I want you to cancel that loan from the Bank and Trust too. I'll put up the money at a quarter of their interest rate.'

Al stared at him. 'Why? What do you want in return.'

'Nothing. Absolutely nothing.'

'Aw c'mon, Mr Peabody, you're a businessman too! You don't do something like this just for the hell of it. You must have a reason.'

Peabody pretended to be engrossed in examining the end of his cigar. 'Just let's say I'm doing you a favour.'

'And you might want that favour returned?'

'I might. I'll let you know.'

Al Macken was refused for active service by the United States War Department. The doctors who carried out his medical reported that he had a weakness of the chest that had hitherto failed to come to light. So while Wyatt Neely was with the Third Army in Sicily, Al and Martha and their new secretary, Winona, ran the ever-expanding Macken Company. Al continued to enjoy Beulah's sexual largesse whenever he had the time, which was less and less often. And he waited for Clermont Peabody to call in the favour.

The call came over a year later. It arrived in the form of an invitation to dine at the Peabody mansion. Black tie.

'Well, I don't know anything about it,' said Beulah petulantly, leaning over Al's shoulder to read. The invitation had been mailed to the office on West Bay Street, which had now been renovated and acted as the headquarters for Al's growing number of business interests. 'He hasn't invited me, I know that for sure. That's the night I'm expected at Shirley Anne Bligh's coming out dance at the Country Club. Daddy knows it is.'

'Maybe he wants to talk about you.'

Beulah picked up a magazine and pretended to read it, but a little smile curled around the edges of her mouth. 'D'you really think so? No . . . it'll be about business. That's all he thinks about, especially now he's not making so much money as he used to.'

Al was still wondering what Clermont Peabody's purpose was when he went there to dine. There were no other guests, and with both girls absent at the dance, Al was forced to spend the entire four courses making stiff small talk to Clermont and his wife over a candlelit table laden with exquisite silver and crystal. Mrs Peabody had stopped short of wearing a tiara in her heavily lacquered hair, but there was a diamond necklace sparkling in the crepey hollows above her low-cut satin gown.

They talked about their social circle and the activities of its members, explaining patiently to Al the particular status and significance of each one as though this information were somehow important to him. There was none of the hostility or disdain that Mrs Peabody had displayed when he came to visit Beulah two years earlier. By the time she excused herself from the table to leave the men to smoke, Al was on his guard.

'I'm supposed to offer you port,' said Clermont gruffly. 'But my guess is you'd prefer some of this.' He held up a bottle of Wild Turkey bourbon, and half filled two crystal tumblers.

'Rumour has it that company of yours is going to turn over a million dollars in this coming year. That true?'

Al smiled politely, but refused to be drawn. 'Like you say, it's a rumour.'

'No need to be so scratchy with me, boy. I'm just trying to show that getting you off the draft was a good move. A damn good move. And putting up that loan. You've turned that ramshackle place into pure gold.'

'And now you want to call in the loan?'

Clermont puffed his cigar smoke at an eighteenth-century portrait of an English ancestor. 'Not the loan, no. The favour.'

Al took a gulp of the bourbon. 'Shoot.'

'I want you to marry my daughter.'

Al stared at him for a second, then laughed out loud with relief. 'So *that's* what this is about! Well, that's OK, seeing as we're half-engaged already.'

'Not Beulah. Cordella.'

There was a chill silence.

'*Cordella*? What a damn fool . . . I've barely even spoken six words to the girl. What would she want to marry me for, anyway?'

Clermont made a gesture in Al's direction to indicate that his physical charms were obvious enough.

'If you want me for a son-in-law, why in hell's name don't

you want me to marry Beulah? She's the one I've been walking out with for nearly two years. Goddamnit, she's the one I'm in love with!'

Al's voice rose steadily as he sensed a trap tightening around him. Clermont stood up and started to pace around the room. He came to rest in front of the dining table, a few feet from Al. Leaning back on the edge of the table, he crossed his arms and closed his eyes briefly before continuing. 'Look, Al – you don't mind me calling you Al, do you? – the first thing I want you to get clear is that I love both of my daughters equally, and I care what becomes of them. I know that what I'm saying sounds strange, but let's just talk it out rationally. You are going to need a wife if you are going to be a force in this city. Business in the South revolves around hospitality, and socialising. Not what, but whom you know. You need a wife at your side. What you do in your private life is your own concern, but you need a wife to smooth the way.'

'But – '

'Please – just hear me out. Now Cordella also needs a husband. She's not like her sister, with a line of young men waiting to partner her at dances.'

The thought of Beulah's eager suitors pressing against her on the dance floor sent a shiver of jealous rage through Al.

'Cordella's quiet, and womanly and dutiful. She'd make an excellent wife. She needs the security of a home and family. Beulah, now, she's always been wild and uncontrollable. She's not the kind of woman to make you a good wife.'

'She wants to get married. She's told me so.'

'She might want that now, but that girl changes her mind as often as she changes her clothes. And if you did marry her, what kind of a wife would she be? Standing loyally by your side? Always there when you needed her? Come on, Al, you're a bright guy, you know what I'm saying is true. But if you married Cordella, well, you could be sure that she would be exactly the sort of wife you need to get on. Mrs Peabody and I would make sure that Savannah society was right behind you both.'

'Savannah society? Jesus . . .!' Al stood up. 'I'm sorry, but I just can't listen to this any more.' He walked out into the hall, wrenched open the front door and ran down the steps, still shaking his head in disbelief.

The problem was that everything Clermont Peabody had said was both rational and true. Al twisted and turned in his bed that night, unable to banish Clermont's voice, calm and measured, from his mind. Yes, he did need a wife eventually. Preferably one who was well bred, with the right connections. And Cordella fitted that description. But, damn it, it was *Beulah* he wanted, he needed. Beulah, with her voluptuously pale breasts, and slanting eyes. He pictured her now, lying in that same bed, naked. The neat concave dip of her stomach, the red-gold triangle between her thighs. He clutched his pillow against him, and when he slept it was in a state of fevered arousal, just as in the old days when he first met her.

It was different when he woke. His erection had wilted. And the first thing he saw when he opened his eyes was his favourite suit, tossed casually over a chair. He had asked Beulah to take it to the cleaners for him last time she was here, but she had ignored or forgotten the request, relying as ever on Martha to take care of his domestic needs. If he were to ask her about it she would just laugh, or brush him aside with her customary impatience. Clermont was right about her being unreliable. She came and went as she pleased, answering to no one, and that was fine for now . . . but if she was his wife? Beulah was born to be a mistress. She was perfect in the role.

He considered his reflection soberly as he shaved. He was thinking about fidelity now. Was that what her father had been implying, when he talked about her dancing partners? That she would not remain faithful? Had she been faithful so far, even? Or did she allow those eager young Southern beaux, many of them dashing in their officers' uniforms, to let their fingers wander to the cleft between her large, creamy breasts. . . .

Hell, this was getting him nowhere, just reviving the erection. The point was surely that he wasn't going to let Clermont Peabody tell him whom to marry, like he was James Macken himself! He really wanted to just go round there and tell the man to go to the devil. But there was the loan. Borrowing to pay it back would be disastrous for cash flow just when they were on a roll, about to make it big. More important, there was the draft board. If Peabody used his influence against him, he could end up shipping out to Europe. Or worse still, being sent to jail. Martha would never be able to manage the company on her own.

Al wiped the soap from his jaw with a towel and sat down on the edge of the bed. He was in the grip of a sensation that suffocated him yet at the same time made him feel powerfully sure and certain. Strong, even. He had felt it before when he'd turned down Beulah's invitation to make love in the gazebo. He'd needed to toe the line then, to keep his head above water and make the $50 Peabody was offering. To grab the break. He had been right to do so, but this was an even more important crossroads. If he accepted and married Cordella then that would be the pattern of his life for evermore. Business first, last and always, everything and everyone subjugated to the good of his company's name.

Al smiled. He could live like that, if it meant that he was going to get as rich as the Vanderbilts and the Morgans and the Goulds, who used the coast of Georgia as their playground. One thing was for sure, though, he was going to make enough to buy and sell Clermont Peabody ten times over. This was very definitely the last time he was going to dance to anyone else's tune.

TWO

Savannah, Georgia 1946–1952

Beulah Peabody tapped on the door of her sister's bedroom.

'Come in.'

Beulah stood leaning against the door jamb, one hand on her hip, holding a lit cigarette between crimson-tipped fingers. 'So. The bride prepares.'

Cordella, sitting at the dressing table to brush out her hair, looked up nervously.

'Lover boy stopped by, did he?' Beulah's eyes were narrow as she puffed on her cigarette.

'You know fine well that it's bad luck for the groom to see the bride on the night before the wedding.'

'"*You know fine well. . . .*"' Beulah mimicked her sister's high-pitched, girlish voice. 'How would I know that? I've never gotten married, see. I've never taken somebody else's beau for my husband.'

Cordella's face flushed as she turned back to the mirror and dragged the brush through her pale hair. 'I didn't steal anyone. Al asked me to become his wife, and I accepted.'

Beulah's lip curled slightly. 'You could have refused.'

'I didn't want to. I love him.'

'You love him, huh?' Beulah walked slowly into the room, pulling a package out from behind her back. 'Look, I bought you a gift. A wedding gift.'

Cordella unwrapped the package. Inside the paper was a silk teddy, soft and sensuous, gleaming in the light of the lamp on the dressing table. Cordella looked at it uncertainly, fingering the supple fabric.

'Reckon you're gonna need some sexy underthings to turn him on.'

Cordella turned her gaze up to her sister's face.

'You don't have a *clue* what I'm talking about, do you? You say you love Al, but you have no idea what loving a man is all about.'

Beulah turned on her heel and walked out. Back in her own room, she shut the door fast behind her and leaned on it. Her heart was pounding, her breath coming in great gasps.

Downstairs, the household was still humming. Her mother was discussing the last-minute arrangements with the cook and the maids, fussing over the floral decorations that draped the porch and the hall and the staircase, checking the crates of French champagne, making alterations to the guest list. Beulah walked slowly to the window and twitched the curtain aside. She saw a car making a right onto Tattnall Street and her heart lurched; she thought it was him.

It wasn't, but still she kept looking, waiting for him to draw up outside and come running into the house telling her it was all a mistake, that it was her he wanted, and not that damn fool Cordella. She was still there long after the bustle had ceased downstairs, the household had gone to bed, and Al Macken's future bride slept peacefully, unknowingly in her bed.

None of what had happened was Cordella's fault, Al reflected on the night of their wedding. Yet if that was so, why did he feel so angry with her?

He sat on the chaise longue in the dressing room of their suite in the Royal Poinciana Hotel in Palm Beach, listening to the steady rise and fall of Cordella's breathing. She was asleep, thank God, and tomorrow night they would be back in Savannah. Just one weekend away for the honeymoon, that was all he had offered her. The business needed him. 'Do you understand?' he had asked, testing her. 'Of course,' she had replied, but her eyes hid something.

That look in her eyes was there when she stood at the altar beside him. She had accepted her father's plans for her without question, smiled and said she was pleased even, but her eyes said she was not happy. It was as if she resented him. Hell, why should she resent him? He was everything a young bride could want, all the wedding guests said so. Tall, handsome, rich . . . soon to be very rich. Al had gone out of his way to be kind to Cordella, to be considerate, even to pay court to her a little during the eighteen months of their engagement. He sent her flowers and gifts, bought her some exquisite pieces of jewellery, picked them out himself. And the smile with which he had greeted her when she walked down the aisle had been genuine enough too. She had had her mousy hair tinted gold, and curled, and with a little powder and paint she had turned out to be surprisingly pretty. The simple cut of her ivory satin gown suited her slim figure, the haze of silk tulle over her face showed off her delicate complexion. She had even blushed, as brides were supposed to. You would think she had her heart's content. Unless you looked into her eyes.

The rest of the wedding had passed in a blur. Al had never been to a society wedding before his own, and had no idea what to expect. He had never seen so many people all in one place as were crammed first into the Christ Episcopal Church on Johnson Square, and then into the reception at the Jekyll Island Club. He had never even tasted French champagne, and didn't have the nerve to tell the passing waiters that he didn't much care for the way it tasted. No one would have thought the country had just survived a war, but then that was what good old Southern hospitality was all about. The guests all enjoyed the extravagance to the full and no one seemed much concerned by the absence of the bride's sister, who was 'unavoidably detained' on the West Coast.

Al managed not to think about her until he and Cordella were alone in their hotel bedroom, and then she was all he could think about. Cordella went into the bathroom to change, and emerged wearing a flowing silk nightgown and negligee. They were exactly the sort of thing that Beulah would have worn, but instead of magnificently full breasts the plunging neckline revealed only Cordella's scrawny, bony chest.

For a few moments Al was at a loss and just stared at his bride.

'What is it?' she asked quietly.

'It was just, I don't know . . . that's an awful pretty gown.' He put his arms around her and kissed the nape of her neck, running his lips down over her collar bone and sternum to the place where her breasts made two tiny protrusions under the silk. Her skin felt dry and smelled of soap.

A warm, familiar sensation started in his loins and spread with urgency through his entire body. He pressed himself against Cordella but instead of the heat and the yielding he had known with Beulah, the eager hands reaching down to touch him, there was only stiff resistance. He laid Cordella on the bed and raised the silk nightdress to position himself between her thin, girlish thighs. She braced, terrified, and it was only then that he remembered that his wife was a virgin. He had no idea what to do with a virgin, but he had heard that it hurt a girl terribly, and there would be bleeding, tears.

He rolled away from her and patted her hand. 'Hey, listen, there's all the time in the world. Let's wait a while until we're a bit less tired.'

'I guess it's not what you're used to,' Cordella said, in a small, tight voice.

He had gone out of the bedroom and left her then, and she had eventually fallen asleep, leaving Al sitting alone in the dark thinking of Beulah.

He had seen her only once after agreeing to marry Cordella. He went to the Peabody house that same evening, to try and talk to her about it face to face, though he was not sure what he would say. She refused to see him, which at least meant that he avoided having to think up a speech, but he had also fantasised that she might forgive all and they would make love one last time as a way of saying farewell. Now he would never be able to look at her or touch her.

It was raining when he left the house, a real Georgia downpour, cascading down rooves and gutters and dripping from the heavy tangles of Spanish moss. So he was surprised when he turned to look back at the house and saw Beulah standing on the verandah in a pool of lamplight. The rain darkened her hair, and it clung against her cheeks and neck like streamers of seaweed. She was looking right down at him, but she said nothing.

For the first time Al felt sure that he loved her. Or rather, he *had* loved her, because it was already in the past. Standing there, with her pale skin gleaming, the rain sticking her cotton dress to the luscious curves of her body, she seemed remote, a fantasy woman.

He moved under the street light to get one last look before he walked away, and it was then that he noticed she was smiling right at him. The smile was triumphant. I know you, it said, and I know my sister. I know what your marriage will be like.

She waited until he turned to walk down West Jones Street and then she shouted after him.

'It's not over yet, Al Macken!'

If Al's marriage to Cordella turned out rather better than he had hoped on their wedding day in 1946, it was largely because of the changes in Cordella herself.

As the years passed, the pale, plain girl receded and was replaced by a neat and elegant young woman who was a superb housewife and an exemplary hostess. Al gave her a generous personal allowance and she used it to good effect where her appearance was concerned, employing Savannah's best hairdressers and beauticians and, now that the war was over, travelled to New York to replenish her wardrobe. Thanks to her mother's example, she knew how to manage servants and devoted much of her time to the decoration and refinement of their new home. Al had given the house on Whittaker Street to Wyatt and Martha as their wedding present, and bought a gracious white mansion on the banks of Turner's Creek, facing east. The house occupied a beautiful moss-draped tract of land, with 800 feet of water frontage, a boat house surrounded by palm trees, and a landing jetty. Al thanked God that Beulah was not there to see it, for wasn't this exactly the sort of house that she had wanted; white colonial elegance on the banks of the river? She had described it, and he had bought it for her sister, and that made Al feel guilty as hell, about both of them.

Still, it was Beulah's absence that was helping Cordella to flourish. She had left for California when the engagement had been announced and had stayed there for a few years, playing bit parts at one of the movie studios and enjoying the fast social life. Then she had moved on to Paris and Rome, just like she said she would.

Cordella never spoke about her sister, so Al picked up these pieces of information from overhearing their friends gossip. He and Cordella gave a lot of parties and made friends together, which Al enjoyed. And everyone in Savannah wanted to be friends with Al and Cordella now that MackenCorp was the city's fastest growing corporation. Al had the golden touch, everyone said so. He always managed to be in the right place at the right time, and every concern he bought was turned around on itself and started to make money. It couldn't even be put down to the luck of being in Savannah in the post-war years when the fortunes of the port took a massive upturn, because Al had foreseen the new prosperity and invested heavily in shipping and cargo long before then. He bought a shipyard and started to buy transatlantic liners, refurbish them and sell them for a vast profit to the Norwegians or the Argentinians. He diversified his interests too, expanding into industries in the surrounding counties, buying sawmills and lumberyards, cotton mills and a chemical plant. His interests inevitably moved beyond the state of Georgia, and before long he was dealing with financiers in New York, and then Chicago, travelling away from Savannah with increasing frequency. . . .

He did not think about Cordella much when he was away. But he did notice that there would be a period of tension when he returned from a trip and that look would be there in her eyes again. It was there in the spring of 1948 when he came back from the successful financing of a New York subsidiary which would handle import and export.

'You know, honey, a guy I met up there was suggesting we go into marine re-insurance. There's a hell of a lot of money to be made, and we have all the right contacts.'

Cordella waited for Bonnie, their coloured maid, to set the food down on the table; as usual there were bowls of steaming squash and black-eye beans, beef stew with red rice and cornbread on the side. He insisted that they still eat Southern food at home.

She nodded. 'Sounds exciting . . . don't forget we have the Hackers, and your sister and Wyatt coming for dinner tomorrow night. And on Saturday there's a fund-raising garden party over at the Cavershams. Only I have to get to that early, since I'm on the committee. . . .'

She was avoiding his gaze.

'Honey, what's wrong?'

Cordella looked up. 'I want a baby,' she said fiercely. 'I'm your wife. I'm entitled to that at least.'

Al had never heard her so vehement, so impassioned about anything. 'Hey. . . .' He came over to where she was sitting, and took her hand. 'I want us to have a baby too, of course I do. And we will – '

'No, we won't! How can we? You know, Dr Morrow told me that you have to be sure to . . . be intimate . . . at the right time in the month, but how can we be if you're always going away on these business trips?'

She burst into tears.

'Cordella, honey . . . we'll try harder. And you can always come with me on the business trips, if that's what you want.'

She lowered her handkerchief. 'Do you mean it?'

'Sure. Now just stop worrying. It will happen.'

Cordella conceived two months later, during a trip to San Diego. Al's initial reaction was not joy at the thought of the coming child but relief. At least Cordella *could* conceive. If she had been barren then Beulah really would have had the last laugh.

In March, 1949, Cordella gave birth to a perfect boy, a son who was the image of his father, an heir to the kingdom. For the first time in his life, Al fell deeply in love. He broke the Macken tradition of giving the firstborn son his paternal grandfather's name and out of sheer gratitude allowed Cordella to name him. She called him Travis Peabody Macken.

It was a golden period in their marriage; they were equally delighted with their son, and now at last they really had something in common. They would sit by the crib watching him sleep and talking over their plans for the future.

'He's going to be the head of the most powerful corporation in America,' said Al. 'I'll see to that.'

'And he'll find himself a wonderful wife,' Cordella whispered. 'And give us a whole host of gorgeous grandchildren.'

Al reached for her hand. 'I love you.'

He had not meant to say it, did not even know for sure that it was true, but there it was. She gave his hand an answering squeeze, but in the half light he thought he caught a glimpse of that old look in her eyes again, the look that was half question, half accusation.

That conversation over their son's crib was their closest moment, and with the excitement of the birth dying away, marked the beginning of an inevitable drift apart. Travis's presence meant that Cordella was more tied to the home and it was not so easy for her to travel. She was a Mother now, with a capital 'M', the rite of passage had admitted her to the heavenly host of Savannah's society mothers, with all the attendant ritual activities: fundraisers, birthday parties, baby showers. And Al was working harder than ever, flying to a different destination every week, driven by the need to consolidate his empire for the next generation.

He was aware that on these trips he was starting to look at other women. Just to look, and take an interest, maybe flirt a little, nothing more. It didn't seem worth the risk of taking things further. Compared with Beulah, or at least his fading memory of her, they all seemed rather bland.

He was not tempted into infidelity, but his sexual thoughts about these women could be quite distracting. It became a game during dull board meetings to construct a complicated and torrid fantasy about himself and one of the secretaries or receptionists who was around that day. He supposed it was because his sex life with Cordella was humdrum in the extreme. It had never been great, not since the very beginning when he had made the mistake of comparing her with Beulah. Immediately after Travis's birth she had withdrawn from sexual activity for months, claiming that the demands of the baby made her too tired. When she did show an interest again, it was very sporadic. Most of the time she would be politely disinterested, then she would suddenly demand his attention voraciously, surprising him with her eagerness. Those were always the best times.

It happened one night when he had just returned from a visit to shipyards in Norfolk, Virginia. He arrived home late and very tired, but before he could retire to bed, he had to go through the papers relating to the day's meetings. He took a glass of bourbon through into the den and began to read through them.

Cordella came in behind him and put a hand on his shoulder.

'I hope you're coming up to bed soon.' The pressure of her fingers was intense.

'Soon. I need to spend a little time on this stuff first, hon.' He rubbed his forehead. 'Things didn't go too well today. I'm going to have to wrestle with these figures a little.'

'I could help you relax.' She tried to take the glass of bourbon from his hand but he raised it to his lips, so instead she let her hand run down the front of his body to his crotch in a gesture that was more desperate than sensual.

Al pushed her away. 'Don't, honey, not right now. Like I said, I'm tired, I want to get these – '

'And I want another baby! And I'd like to know how the hell I'm ever expected to have one!'

Al swivelled his chair round to face her. Her fair skin was flushed pink with anger.

'Cordella, we have a baby. A perfect child. Isn't that enough for you?'

'He's two now, he's not a baby any more! All my friends are having their second or third babies. Wyatt and Martha have got three! I want . . . I want you to make me pregnant.'

'Oh I get it. . . .' A grim smile crossed Al's face. 'Sex is just for having babies. You're only interested in me when you think you might wind up pregnant. Is that all you want me for?'

'It's better than not being wanted at all! It's better than having to marry your sister's lover, and knowing all the time that *she's* the one your husband wants!'

Cordella was shouting. But she never shouted, she was a nice, well-bred Southern girl who never raised her voice, especially not in front of a man. . . . And the look was there in her eyes again, burning with a fury he could feel. It was as if the pain in her had reached out and assaulted him too; he felt as though he had been struck.

They were both frozen for an instant, then Cordella grabbed the glass of bourbon and smashed it on the desk, sending a swirl of amber liquid over his papers.

'Jesus, no! That's the new petrochemical contract . . . you stupid goddam – '

He pushed Cordella hard and she stumbled backwards, losing her balance. It was all too simple then, to push her roughly to the floor and stand over her, relishing her vulnerability, aroused by it. Her negligee was rucked up, exposing her thighs. He hadn't meant to do it, but he found himself pushing it higher and entering her roughly. She wasn't ready, and he felt at once how much he must be hurting her.

'No, Al . . . I can't, please *no*. . . .'

She screamed and clawed at him with her nails, but it was too late. It was done.

Cordella suffered as much at her second son's birth as she had at his conception. The baby became stuck in an awkward position and needed forceps to free him, whereupon his mother haemorrhaged so profusely that without a swift blood transfusion she would have lost her life.

The guilt and remorse Al suffered that day as he paced to and fro in the hospital waiting room were an adequate punishment for the rape of his wife. Both he and Cordella were aware of this, though neither said anything.

'I thought I was going to lose you,' said Al when he was allowed in to see her. He clutched her hand and looked into her eyes, waiting to see it again . . . but no, the look said she forgave him.

'Here's your son, Mr Macken.' The nurse bustled in with the white, swaddled bundle. 'Your wife says she's going to call him Michael.'

The baby. In his fear for Cordella he had all but forgotten the baby. He looked down into the tiny face and almost gasped. His father's eyes were looking back at him accusingly.

'Most unusual, ain't it?' The nurse bent over to take the child back again. 'Almost all babies are born with blue eyes, then they change at a few weeks. But every so often you get one that's born with brown eyes. Very striking, don't you think? Makes him look real handsome. You're going to break some hearts, aren't you, my precious?'

When Al left the hospital his thoughts were with Cordella, rather than the child.

He asked the chauffeur to drive him down to River Street, said he needed to walk a while. The last few hours had drained him, terrified him. He pictured Cordella dead in childbirth, her thin girlish limbs stilled for ever, and the thought made his heart pound with dread. He hoped she would be happy, now she had her two children. If only she could understand that he *did* love her; he felt warm and grateful and caring towards her. The feelings did exist, but he found them so hard to get hold of. Like he reached out to touch something only to find it on the other side of a pane of glass.

The sound of a tugboat's horn made him jump. He turned to watch a majestic ship glide out of harbour and down the river to the Atlantic, headed for who knows where. England maybe. The ship's mark showed it was registered in London.

He would bring his sons down here to watch the ships when they were older. He had another son to look out for now. But would he be able to love the boy with James Macken's eyes?

THREE

Liverpool, England 1968–1970

Peg Anderson sat up and threw off the covers as soon as her eyes were open. She rarely lingered in bed, and especially not during the summer holidays. She could tell already by the pale glow of sunlight on the faded cotton curtains that today was going to be one of those great summer days, and she didn't want to miss a second of it.

She dressed quickly in shorts and a gingham blouse and tugged a hairbrush through her hair, barely pausing long enough to register her reflection in the small mirror on the bedroom wall. Even at the sensitive age of fifteen, Peg was not terribly concerned about her appearance, and that was the truth of the matter. The face looking back at her was pretty enough in an unremarkable sort of way. If she grinned, which she did now, her mouth looked too wide, and her grey eyes creased up at the corners and almost disappeared. A scallywag was what her father called her when she grinned like that. A little madam, was what Mam said.

Her nut-brown hair was thick and heavy and tended to flop into her face, so she tied it up into a ponytail. She didn't put on any make-up the way some of her class mates were starting to. Her skin was good, a healthy biscuit brown whatever time of year, and her eyelashes were thick and dark, her lips a pleasing red. With a touch of customary arrogance she told herself she didn't really need make-up, so it would just be a waste of time. And Peg couldn't bear to waste time.

She leaned out of her bedroom window, as far as she could go, and smiled. Summer days like this, with that sweet-salt smell in the air mingling sand and vanilla, were great for being a teenager in Liverpool and for living by the seaside. And she was lucky enough to be both.

She climbed up onto the windowsill and swung her legs through so they were dangling against the brickwork on the front of the house. It was a modest home, very much like all the others in Virginia Road, New Brighton; a shabby bay-fronted terrace with paint that peeled and flaked constantly with the wind from the sea. There was no proper garden, just a yard at the back and a small paved patch at the front. The red front door and the window boxes full of geraniums provided a splash of colour.

And at least they owned their own home, which was more than a lot of the people they knew could say. Dad had always been in regular work. He was a welder in the Mersey shipyards, and an experienced welder could earn a decent wage in these days of the post-war boom. The yard was receiving orders for enormous luxury liners, even with all the talk of too much competition from the Far East. And Mum worked too, as a part-time librarian, so the Andersons had more than a lot of their neighbours. In fact, some of the people round there thought they were getting a bit above themselves, especially when Mum, who was passionate about music, had started paying for Peg to have piano lessons.

Peg was wise enough to realise that their family's fortune lay not with their financial security but with their happiness. They were a close, loving family who teased and criticised one another but showed support and solidarity whenever they were needed. She had always idolised her father, a big, powerfully built man, quickly moved to anger but just as quick to laugh. She had loved the size of him when she was a little girl, the way he could toss her up in the air like a rag doll. John Anderson spoke his mind, he was known for it. So he made as many enemies as he did friends, but people always respected him and listened to what he had to say, electing him head of the local Labour club.

She respected him, too, for the way he worked so hard and so uncomplainingly. The shipyard was a place for real men, Peg had grown up understanding that. It was dirty and noisy and it was dangerous. Accidents killed men in the yards nearly every week. There was 'white finger', loss of feeling in the hands from continually clutching hammers, and there was welder's lung, which would usually kill a man in the end. The bosses would always say it was because a man smoked – they didn't like the idea of the fuss there would be if it was proved to be an industrial disease.

Life was harder for the welders than the boilermakers, outfitters and shipwrights. Peg could see that for herself when her father took her and Jimmy to visit the yard. The welders had to work directly under the keel with their necks cricked back in a biting wind from the river, welding seams above their heads. Their appearance had been quite terrifying to her when she was a small child. They wore leather aprons and hoods and leggings to keep off the fountains of molten metal, and under the masks their faces turned blue. The need to keep their eyes focussed on the blowtorch as they worked gave their faces a disturbing stare.

'Gives you a terrible stiff neck, that does, lad,' Dad had said to Jimmy. 'That's real man's work that is. Especially when it's your turn to go down the hatches and weld the ship's bottom.'

Jimmy had bitten his lower lip and stared. He didn't want to be a welder, or work in a shipyard at all. His ambitions were all to do with music. Nowadays that meant wanting to play in a skiffle group and be as famous as one of the Beatles.

On the same visit they went past the offices on their way home and caught sight of the chairman with his soft hands and white shirt and the gleaming signet ring on his finger.

'If you stick at your schoolwork and get yourself an education you could end up marrying a man like that. How about that, eh, girl?'

Peg had smiled uncertainly. The man in the tailored suit and silk tie looked like the inhabitant of another planet.

''Cos you're a right clever little miss, aren't you? Like your mum.' He squeezed her shoulder.

'Pah, anyone can be a soft jessie like that if they want to!' Jimmy wrinkled his nose in scorn. 'But I don't want to. I'm going to be in a rock and roll band!'

Peg craned her neck to the right, to see if there was any sign of Jimmy returning from his paper round. On the corner of Virginia Road was the Eat Inn, the fish and chip shop where they went on Friday and ate rock salmon or cod sitting at the high stools that flanked the shop's ugly tiled walls. If you turned left by the chip shop and followed the road down, you came to Marine Promenade, and beyond that, the beach. There were a few elderly ladies down there throwing bread crumbs to the gulls, but apart from them the place was still deserted. In an hour or so, the kiosks that sold chips and hot dogs and candy floss and Kiss-Me-Quick hats would raise their shutters and the people would begin to arrive, their numbers swelling until they turned into a crowd by the time the sun was high in the sky. And over to the left, where she could just glimpse the tussocky grass of Wallasey Golf Club, there would be golfers hunched over their clubs, their trousers flapping in the strong sea breeze.

At half-past seven, Jimmy's bike came tearing round the corner. Using his foot as a brake, he scraped to a halt outside the house and flung his bike against the railings.

'One of these days you're going to fall out of that flaming window!' he called as he marched up the steps and into the house.

Peg heard movement below; the shrill whine of the kettle and the clatter of plates as their mother made breakfast for Jimmy. The milk float slid into view round the corner of Virginia Road, and the milkman carried three pints to the front step, making the familiar clanking sound as he retreated with the empty bottles.

Peg swung her legs round and climbed back into the bedroom. Seeing the milk float had given her an idea. She sat down at her desk, a makeshift affair made by her father from two old tea chests. Notebooks, paper and pencils were neatly arranged on one side, and on the other there was a cash box. She opened the cash box and counted the money. Nine shillings and eight pence. So if a pint of milk cost. . . . Pausing occasionally to chew on the end of her pencil, Peg made some calculations and wrote out a list of figures.

When she had finished she went back to the window and stuck her head out as far as she was able without toppling into the street. Now all she had to do was catch the milkman.

There was a familiar figure on the other side of the street. Peg stuck two fingers in her mouth and whistled.

'Hey, Sand! Sandy!'

Sandra Wilson turned round. She was Peg's best friend, a plump, plain girl with a relentlessly cheerful nature.

'Sandra, you fancy making a bit of money?'

Sandra laughed. 'Oh yeah, what now, Peggy?'

'I've had this great idea. . . .'

'Not another one.'

'Yeah, another one. But listen, it's really good, we'll make loads of cash. Hang on there a second, I'm coming down.'

Peg slipped her feet into battered sneakers and thundered down the stairs. Her mother stuck her head out of the kitchen as the front door was wrenched open.

'Breakfast, our Peg?'

'Not now, Mam, I'm busy. . . .'

She sprinted to catch up with Sandy, linking arms and propelling her down the street.

'So what crazy scheme has old muggins here just let herself in for?'

'I'll explain later. Come on, walk a bit faster, will you? We need to catch up with the milkman.'

'What for?'

'Because we need a dozen pints of gold top, that's what for!'

After they had bought the milk and borrowed a crate from the milkman to lug it back to Virginia Road, Peg whisked a mildly protesting Sandra down to where the market stalls were just setting up.

'What are we doing?' complained Sandra. 'I haven't had my breakfast yet. I'm flipping starving.'

'Strawberries.'

'I can't have strawberries for breakfast – '

'No, we need to buy some, silly! And the cheaper the better.'

Peg roamed between the stalls, scrutinizing all the fruit and vegetables. 'Ah, here we are.'

She found a display of bruised and over-ripe strawberries, being sold off cheaply at nine pence a pound. After haggling with the stall holder she managed to come away with five pounds of fruit for three shillings.

Satisfied with the purchase, she slung the carrier bag of strawberries over her wrist and linked arms with Sandra again. 'Right, we can go back and have breakfast at my place now. Then we'll get to work.'

'Do you mind telling me what we'll be doing?'

'It's going to be a hot day, right? A real belter.'

'Right.'

'So what do people round here do on a hot day?'

'They go to the beach.'

'Correct. And what do they want to eat while they're down there?'

'Chips.'

'No, lame brain! Icecream! So that's what we're going to make. Lots and lots of lovely strawberry icecream. And we're going to sell it for a fat profit.'

After Mrs Anderson had served the girls boiled eggs and toast with a long-suffering air, they commandeered the Andersons' tiny kitchen. The milk was turned into a thick, creamy custard, and when it had cooled, the pulverised strawberries were stirred into it. Peg filled every available bowl with the stuff, slopping it all over the table and the formica work surfaces.

'Dear God, the state of the place!'

Her mother watched from the doorway, bristling with indignation. 'I hope you two are going to clear this lot up.'

Peg smiled sweetly. 'Of course we are!'

Mrs Anderson untied her apron and hung it up on the back of the kitchen door. 'Well, I'm off down to the library now. I want to see this place spotless when I get back.'

Sandy started running water into the sink, but Peg stopped her. 'Not yet, we haven't finished!'

'I thought we had. Look – icecream all over the flipping place.'

'But it's not icecream yet, is it, dummy? It's not cold. Icecream has to be frozen, and if we're going to make the lunchtime rush, we'd better get our skates on.'

'Where are we going?'

'To see Mike Finlay.'

Mike Finlay was the Irish owner of the Eat Inn. He had a soft spot for Peg, and she wheedled and cajoled until he had given her several plastic containers to put the icecream in, and sold them a catering pack of icecream cones on the cheap, because they had been sitting around the back of the shop a long time and were probably a little stale. Most important of all, he lent them space in his freezer for the morning to set the icecream. They scraped the sticky pink custard into the tubs and scuttled along the street with them, anxious not to waste any precious freezing time.

Sandy glanced up at the sky. 'There's a cloud up there. Looks like it might rain.'

'Think positive,' said Peg. 'It's only a small one.'

They set up their pitch soon after noon on a central stretch of beach, just opposite the crazy golf course and the Palace Ballroom. They charged nine pence for a cone, and sales were brisk.

'Oh, Peg, look at those little kids over there! They've been staring at the icecream like little puppies. Let's give them one each, eh?'

'No!'

'Oh, Peg! Just a little one!'

'Look, Sand, if you give a free icecream to one kid, you've got to give free icecream to them all, and that's hardly good for business, is it? Word'll get round and before we know it half of Liverpool will descend and eat up all our profits.'

'You're a hard case, Peg Anderson, you know that. . . .' Sandra squinted into the sun. 'Hey, isn't that Billy Walsh over there?'

She pointed to a handsome youth in a white T-shirt and jeans who was strolling towards them.

'Oh. . . .' Sandra exhaled with sheer pleasure. 'Everyone thinks he's exactly like James Dean.'

'And no one believes it more than Billy Walsh does.'

'Oh come on, girl, he's gorgeous!'

'And he knows it.'

'You know him, don't you?'

'He hangs out with Jimmy and the band sometimes.' Peg glanced in his direction, while pretending to brush sand off her hands. He was good-looking, she had to admit it, and he did have a certain style, sticking to denims and leather jackets while all the other boys were experimenting with pudding-basin haircuts, frilled shirts and cuban heels.

Sandra muttered between her teeth, 'Don't look now, but I think he's coming over.'

Billy tugged his cigarette from his mouth and exhaled. 'Hi.'

'Hi.'

'So what's all this?'

'You can read, can't you?' said Peg tartly. She pointed to the sign saying 'HOME-MADE STRAWBERRY ICECREAM'.

'Go on then, give us one.' He ground his cigarette butt into the sand with the toe of his boot.

'Please.'

'Please.'

He took the icecream from Sandra and put the other hand in his jeans pocket, shifting from foot to foot.

'It's melting,' Peg pointed out.

'Yeah.' He grinned at her. Licking an icecream while still managing to look as cool as James Dean posed a problem. He turned to go. 'Hey, if you two are interested, there's a party down here tonight. Nine-thirty. Bring some drink.'

'Peg, did you hear that? Billy Walsh asked us to a party!'

'And he got icecream all down the front of his jeans,' said Peg with satisfaction.

When John Anderson returned from the shipyard that evening, he found his wife on her hands and knees with a bucket of hot water.

'This is a funny time to be scrubbing the kitchen floor, love!'

'Well, it's not every day your kitchen gets turned into an icecream parlour.' She told her husband about the strawberry icecream. 'They did get as far as wiping down the surfaces, but they forgot all about the floor, didn't they? Great big sticky patches all over the tiles!'

'How much did you say they made?'

'About fifteen pounds profit each. Locked away in that little money box of hers, no doubt.'

John Anderson threw back his head and laughed. 'The crafty little. . . . I hope she's paying you to clean floors for her, because she can certainly afford it now!'

The look his wife gave him made it plain she was not amused by this idea.

'Oh, come on, Kath! Give the girl some credit. At least we can be sure she's never going to go hungry. She's got a bit of something about her. She's not a dreamer like our Jimmy. She's really going to get out into the world and achieve something.

As long as she doesn't forget how to enjoy herself along the way. . . .'

'Not much chance of that at the moment. She's upstairs getting ready to go to some beach party.'

John frowned. 'I hope it's not some rough biker crowd. The girl's only fifteen after all.'

Kath Anderson shrugged as she wrung out the dishcloth. 'Like you said, she's got to learn how to enjoy herself. I said no later than eleven o'clock. . . .' She gave her husband a wry smile. 'She's growing up, John. Before you know it this young entrepreneur thing will be forgotten and it will be nothing but boys, boys, boys.'

Peg was quite excited about the party, but she tried to quash the feeling. She didn't want to care about things like that too much; there were other things that were more important. She didn't ever want to become one of those girls who thought about nothing but boys, clothes and parties. It had occurred to her that her excitement had something to do with Billy Walsh's presence, but she disowned the thought at once.

She had only one party dress, and wearing it to the beach seemed daft somehow. So she changed into a clean white pair of shorts, and a short sleeved cotton blouse in a violet shade that was very flattering to her brown skin. She let her hair hang loose round her shoulders and dragged a brush through it until it gleamed. A slick of pale pink lipstick was her only concession to making up her face.

'It's not fair!' moaned Sandra when they met up at the end of the street. 'You always manage to look good without trying.'

Sandra had squeezed her plump body into a mini dress covered in acid green swirls, with complicated frills at the neck and wrists and a big brass zip down the front.

'You look fine,' said Peg, and added, 'It'll be dark on the beach, anyway.'

'You know, Peg, I really enjoyed myself today, selling the icecream. It was a good laugh.'

'Yes, it was.' Peg slipped her arm through Sandy's, as was their habit when they were walking along together.

'I was thinking, maybe when we've left school, we could go

into business together. Open a café or something. I know you're the one with all the ideas, but I can work hard.'

'Yeah, it would be great, wouldn't it? We might have to wait until I'd been to college though.'

Sandra pulled a face. 'Is that what you want to do, go to boring old college? . . . Oh, look, Peg!' They had arrived at the beach, and in the distance, the flames of a bonfire were just visible. People were arriving from all directions, clutching bottles. Someone was carrying a portable record player, which they set up on the sand.

'Look, Peg, isn't that Billy Walsh standing over there by the bonfire?'

Peg shrugged. 'Who cares?' She kicked off her shoes and relished the sensation of toes sinking into cold sand. 'Come on, they're playing The Equals. Let's go and dance!'

Billy Walsh had a bottle of Newcastle Brown ale in one hand and the other was thrust deep into the pocket of his leather jacket. He lifted the bottle to his lips from time to time in a measured, rhythmic way and in between swigs, he watched.

At the ripe old age of eighteen, he considered himself something of a connoisseur when it came to girls. Usually he wasn't interested in fifteen-year-olds, but Peg Anderson was different. She was a nice-looking kid, but that wasn't what made her stand out. After all, there were a lot of pretty girls at the party tonight. Plenty. They were all trying to look like Jean Shrimpton with their baby doll dresses and spidery false eyelashes.

There was nothing doll-like about Peg Anderson. She was incredible though. There was such an energy coming from her. You just had to look in her eyes, and you could see it shining out of her. And she was never still, always moving, laughing, talking. The other guys liked her too. Several of them had tried to chat her up, asked her to dance. They mistook that sparkle in her eye for flirting. They didn't understand that that was just Peg.

She looked across and smiled at him.

'Want a drink?'

She shrugged. 'OK. Fruit juice'll do.'

'Why not have something stronger? You'll have to get used to drinking some day.'

Her grey eyes widened slightly. 'Why's that?'

Billy hunched his jacket up around his shoulders. 'Well, everybody does, don't they?'

'I see. So I've got to be like everybody else, have I?'

A smile spread slowly across Billy's face. 'Little Miss Cool, aren't we? Don't you ever let go of that control just for a minute?'

Peg gave an impatient little shrug.

'How about a cigarette?'

'No, thank you.'

'What then?'

'Look, Billy, I'm just here to enjoy myself, have a good time. I just want to dance, OK?'

She turned and wove her way back through the crowd. He followed her retreating back, a flash of purple in the fading light.

'If it's dancing you want, I'll dance with you.' As if on cue, someone plonked a slow song onto the record player: *Hey Jude*. Billy wound his arms round Peg's waist and pulled her closer. Over his shoulder Peg could see Sandra, winking and gesticulating.

His lips nuzzled her neck. 'How about a kiss?'

She ducked. 'Don't, Billy!'

'Why . . . what's wrong?' He feigned innocence. 'I thought you liked me.'

'I *do* like you, Billy, I like you fine, it's just. . . .' She pulled free from his arms and started to walk away from the patch of flat sand that was acting as a dance floor.

He followed. 'Well, what then?' He caught hold of her wrist and pulled her back towards him. 'What's the matter?' He spoke more gently now. 'I thought that's what all you girls wanted, a fella to hang around with. A boyfriend. We could go out, if that's what you want.'

'No thanks.' She pulled free again and started walking up the beach towards the breakwater. 'I've got other things to think about right now.'

The other things on Peg's mind included returning to school for her final two years. She was taking 'A' levels in Maths, History and Economics, and desperately wanted to do well. The first year of the sixth form passed easily enough, but at the start of the second, with the exams looming, Peg's restless energy became directed towards her schoolwork.

'You're getting to be a bore, you know that,' Sandra moaned, as they trudged up to the playing field in what they termed their 'fag break'. 'It's just swot, swot, swot all the flipping time with you. They're only exams!'

'Yes, but doing well in them is important.' Peg accepted a cigarette from Sandra and puffed at it with a desultory air. She didn't really enjoy smoking, she just did it to keep Sandra company. 'Getting decent grades in my "A" levels is what's going to help me get away from here.'

'But I still don't see what you want to do that for,' Sandra complained. 'What's wrong with round here?' She gave an indignant little puff of smoke. 'Anyway, we're supposed to be opening our café together. Or have you forgotten?'

'I haven't forgotten. There are just other things I want to do first. Going to college, for starters.'

'Where are you going to go? Apply for Liverpool University, and then we can still open the caff.'

Peg shook her head. 'I want to go somewhere different. I thought I might apply to Durham, and to Bristol. They sound nice.' A gleam came into her eye. 'I might even have a crack at Oxford or Cambridge.'

'Christ, Peg Anderson, you're going to turn into a snob as well as a swot!'

Sandra ground her cigarette butt into the grass with her shoe. It was a raw autumn day, and she shivered, pulling her gaberdine coat around her and rubbing her cold hands together.

Peg was squinting at a gesticulating figure at the other end of the playing field. 'That looks like Lizzy Deacon down there at the other end. She's waving at us. Wonder what she wants.'

'She's probably trying to tell us that Bastock's on the warpath.' Miss Bastock was the games teacher, waging a constant war on smokers who defiled her territory.

They stood up and strolled towards Lizzy.

'Peg,' she called. 'The head wants to see you in her study. Now.'

'Shit!' Peg fanned her smoky breath away. 'Got a mint on you?'

Chewing frantically on a peppermint, she made her way to the headmistress's study, pausing to pull up her socks before she knocked on the door.

'Sit down, Margaret.'

Peg started at this unfamiliar use of her real name. No one apart from her teachers ever called her Margaret.

'It's all right; you haven't done anything wrong.'

The headmistress smiled warmly and Peg felt a pang of guilt about the sort of things that she and the other girls used to say about Miss Crosby behind her back. That she was a scrawny old spinster, that the tweed skirts and twin sets she wore were hideous and frumpy, that her backside was bony. In fact they all rather liked her, it was just that she was different from the other women they knew; their mothers and aunts and big sisters, who were all preoccupied with babies and laundry and cooking the tea.

'I had something in the post this morning that I thought you should see. It will be going up on the general noticeboard, of course, and I was going to mention it in Assembly tomorrow, but I thought it would be of particular interest to you.'

She reached into the capacious brown bag she used to carry her notes and books, and brought out a shiny blue leaflet with the words 'Morrison Trust' printed in gold letters.

'You may have heard of the Morrison Trust before. Charles Morrison was a Liverpudlian who emigrated to the United States and made his fortune, and when he died he left a trust to provide money to educate his fellow Liverpudlians. Some of the money for our new music block came from the trust.'

Peg nodded politely to show that she was following the thread.

'Anyway, the trust has endowed a Morrison Scholarship for the express purpose of financing a young Liverpudlian throughout their studies, as long as they choose an approved college or university in the United States. Secondary schools in this area are asked to put forward suitable candidates. And since your results during last year were so outstanding, I thought you should give some serious thought to applying.'

Peg, who had listened intently, gave her a little disbelieving smile. 'To go to *America*?' She breathed the word out. 'I could go?'

'Certainly, you could have a try. You stand a very good chance of success.'

'How long would I go for?'

'That would depend on all sorts of things. The scholarship is awarded for two years initially, but if the candidate makes a success of their studies, it can be extended to three or four years. The terms are quite generous. You wouldn't be living destitute in an attic, however you would be expected to find some of the money for the initial expenditure on books and clothes, et cetera. I don't know how your parents would feel about that.'

'Oh, we'd find it, Miss, even if I had to beg on the streets to pay my fare!'

Miss Crosby smiled at her enthusiasm.

'Well, you know what I mean. . . . What do I have to do?'

'You sit some examinations in the spring, and then if you do well, you go for an interview here in Liverpool. I myself would be responsible for any extra coaching you might need.'

She couldn't help but feel gratified by the girl's reaction. Margaret Anderson always had been a rewarding pupil to teach; she really tried hard. Telling her this piece of news had been like putting a flame to a touchpaper and watching the glow of enthusiasm start to burn in her eyes.

'. . . Anyway, perhaps it's best if you go off and have a little think about it.'

Peg stood up. 'Thank you, Miss, for considering me. I'd work really hard, you've no idea how hard!'

'What on earth d'you want to go to America for?' Sandra asked a few hours later as they walked home from school. 'You wouldn't catch me going to America. I think Liverpool's the best place in the world to be. It's got fab shops, fab clubs, fab guys. . . .'

'It wouldn't be for ever. It's just a chance to do something different, that's all.'

She could tell that Sandra didn't want her to go, and this made her feel guilty and defensive. 'What's wrong with wanting to be different?'

'You could try asking *him* that. He'd know the answer.' Sandra pointed to a large motorbike parked at the corner of the street. 'Your mate Billy Walsh.'

'Well, well, well. . .' said Peg strolling towards him and sounding more blasé than she felt in her scruffy school blazer and skirt, with her socks bagging round her ankles. 'If it isn't the elusive Mr Walsh!'

He had been away for a while and his absence had not gone un-noticed. Jimmy said he'd gone down south to earn some money working on a building site.

He grinned and shifted position on the seat of the bike. Sandra's presence seemed to inhibit him, and Peg had the impression that he had been lying in wait for her.

'I could give you a ride home.'

'What – both of us?' demanded Sandra. 'Give over!'

Billy looked at her, then at Peg, then back to Sandra.

'Oh I see. . . . Well, listen Peg, I'll see you in the morning.' Sandra shouldered her schoolbag and backed away, waving.

'That wasn't very kind.'

'Well. . .' Billy grinned. 'There's only room for one behind me.'

Peg folded her arms across her chest. 'So that's it, is it? You just expect me to hop on behind you and go?'

'Why not? Are you chicken?'

Peg laughed. 'Who, me? Never!'

She slung her satchel across her chest and climbed on the seat behind him, wrapping her arms decorously around his waist. The bike roared into life and took off, making her give a little shriek and clutch him more tightly. She hadn't expected it to go quite so fast, but she rather liked the exhilaration of it, and the way it felt as though the wind was pulling her hair out by the roots. And the truth was that she liked the feel of Billy's firm torso. She pressed her cheek against his back and inhaled leather and exhaust fumes.

'Like it?' he asked when they had come to a halt outside her house.

'It was OK.' Peg's eyes sparkled.

'You could ride it again sometime.'

'Are you asking me out, Billy Walsh?'

'Are you saying yes, Peggy Anderson?'
'Maybe.'
She smiled at him and skipped up the path to the front door. 'See you.'
Billy's eyes narrowed as he watched her go inside and slam the door. He looked at the house wistfully for a moment, then turned the bike around and roared off down the street.

'Mum!'
Peg flung open the kitchen door. Her mother had just returned from work at the library. Her coat, scarf and handbag were draped over the table and she was filling the kettle to make tea.
'Mum, guess what? I might be going to America!'
She told her mother about the Morrison Scholarship.
Kath Anderson pursed her lips. 'Your dad will be pleased. Really pleased.'
'And what about you, Mum? Aren't you pleased?'
'Well . . . America. It's an awfully long way away.'
'It wouldn't be for ever. I'd come back.'
Peg felt defensive, as she had with Sandra. 'The thing is, though, Mum, I'd need to get together some money of my own before I could go. . . .'
'Well, I don't know, Peggy. You know your dad and I would help all we could, but extras like that – '
'No, wait, I've had a great idea about how to make the money.'
Her mother sighed as she poured boiling water into the teapot.
'I could do a sandwich round at school. Loads of the girls hate school dinners, and want to buy something else to eat. I could make the sandwiches here in the morning, or the night before, and take them in and sell them. If I sold about half a dozen rounds a day at, say, three shillings a time. . . .' She chewed her lip as she did the mental arithmetic. 'Say I was turning over five pounds a week . . . I could come out with 150 quid profit at the end of the school year.'
'But, Peggy, be sensible!' Kath put down two cups of tea on the table. 'If you were studying hard for the scholarship exam, not to mention your "A" levels, where would you find the time to do all that? There's the time buying the stuff for the sandwiches as well as making them. It's crazy.'

'But Mum. . .' Peg grasped her mother's hand and squeezed it. 'I couldn't risk not being able to take the scholarship because we didn't have enough money. I really want to go, don't you understand? I really want to go to America!'

Sandra Wilson was in her bedroom, experimenting with her wardrobe. The transistor radio on the chest of drawers was turned up loud, and she jived and shimmied around the room, trying on first one outfit then another, before viewing herself from a variety of angles. Despite her size she was a good dancer, moving deftly, even gracefully between the wardrobe and the mirror. Occasionally she would grab a lipstick from her make-up bag and dab some onto her mouth to get an impression of which shade looked best with which outfit.

God, she was glad it was spring!

Sandra was in a better mood today than she had been of late. It was the first really warm day they had seen all year, and at last it felt as though summer was just around the corner. Spring also meant that final exams were looming, but Sandra wasn't really bothered about that. If she did well, she would go to catering college, if not she would find some sort of job. It was all the same to her.

She had spent quite a lot of time up here on her own over the past few months. It had been rather a dreary winter. A lot of that was down to Peg and the way she had been behaving. It was just work, work, work with her these days. She wasn't any fun any more. All right, so she had always been someone who liked to get on and get things done, but she used to laugh and kid around, too. Now all she thought about was her scholarship exams.

'*Sand*!'

Her mother's voice was just audible over The Small Faces.

Sandra turned the transistor down and flung open the bedroom door.

'Sandra, visitor for you!'

She peered over the banisters. Billy Walsh was standing in the hall. His face wasn't wholly visible from this oblique angle but she knew that it was him from the white T-shirt, faded denims and the shading of the stubble on his chin.

'Hullo, Billy.'

Sandra's tone was cool. Her heart turned over every time she set eyes on Billy Walsh, and yet she was a realist. She knew he wouldn't come here without a reason.

'Hullo.' He smiled. 'Just passing through, thought I'd drop by and see what you were up to.'

'Nothing much.'

He shrugged. 'Well. . .'

'Want a drink?'

Sandra went into the kitchen and fetched a beer for Billy and a glass of lemonade for herself. They took the drinks into the garden and squeezed on to the step next to her father's tubs of spring bulbs.

'Nice flowers,' observed Billy.

'Mmm.'

'There's a party on tonight at the Blue Lantern Club. Want to go?'

'Look, Billy. . .' Sandra shifted on the step so that she was facing him squarely. 'It's not me you want to see really, it's our Peg. And it's her you want to go to the party with, isn't it?'

'I could ask her if I wanted to.'

'Well, I wouldn't bother; she won't go.'

Billy fished in his jacket for his cigarettes, lit one and puffed on it thoughtfully, staring at the toes of his boots.

Sandra softened slightly. 'Peg's special, isn't she? Everyone else thinks so – there's no reason why you shouldn't. But you're not going to get anywhere with her. Not while this stupid scholarship business is going on, anyhow.'

Billy leaned forward and tapped his cigarette on the step, watching the ash fall into a glowing pile. 'I've already asked her to the party actually. She said "no".'

'Why not ask her again. You never know.'

He brightened visibly. 'You think so?'

Sandra sighed inwardly. 'Worth a try, I'd say.'

Billy Walsh's motorbike roared around the corner of Virginia Road. He braked slowly, then throttled back on the ignition until the engine phuttered and died. He leaned back on his heels for a moment, looking at the Andersons' house. It was going dark; upstairs someone switched on a light.

He swung his leg over the saddle and clattered up to the front door.

Mrs Anderson opened it. 'Hello, Billy.'

'Is Peggy in?'

She shook her head. 'I'm afraid she's at the library, studying. Sorry.'

'Oh.'

The door closed and Billy stood still for a few seconds, staring at it. Then he walked to the Eat Inn, bought a bag of chips and sat down on the kerb outside the Andersons' house, to wait.

Peg Anderson sat at the kitchen table, buttering bread. She buttered twenty slices, then slapped ham and tomato on half of them, cheese and pickle on the rest. Her movement slowed gradually. She was tired, very tired.

Her mother, at the stove, watched her anxiously but said nothing.

Peg cut the sandwiches, packed them in paper bags and stacked them up in the fridge. Then she took out a notebook, calculated that day's profits and wrote down the figures.

'There, all ready for tomorrow! I'm going to go up and do some history revision now.'

'Hang on a moment, love. . . .' Kath walked to the window and twitched back the curtain. 'He's still there.'

'I thought I asked you to say I was out.'

'I did, but he's obviously decided to wait for you. He's been there an hour.' She glanced at Peg. 'He's obviously very keen.'

'History revision!' said Peg briskly.

'Oughtn't you to have a word with him first, poor lad!'

'Poor lad nothing! If he's got all evening to waste sitting on the pavement, then let him!'

She carried her books upstairs and set them out on her desk. Every so often she would get up and look out of the window. At nine o'clock he was still there. And at 9.30. At ten o'clock she gave in.

'Haven't you got anything better to do, Billy Walsh?' she called from the top of the steps.

'I thought you were at the library!'

'I was studying here. Sorry.'

She came and sat beside him on the kerb. 'I'm surprised you waited so long.'

'Impressed?'

'Amazed, say.'

Billy sighed. 'I've never done this before . . . with a girl, I mean. There have always been loads of girls, some of them a fair bit older than you. It's never been difficult for me.'

Peg grinned. 'I know.'

'So why does it have to be different now? You're a great girl, Peggy, you and I could have some great times together.'

'Because. . . . Look, I can't answer that now, Billy. Just leave a few weeks until the exams are over. Then ask me.'

The summer of 1970 arrived, and long hot days were taken for granted. Jimmy Anderson joined a rhythm and blues band called the Neanderthals and spent all his waking hours practising in basement rehearsal rooms. Kath Anderson was promoted to senior librarian and started working longer hours.

John Anderson fretted over his daughter. Her exams were over, but she was like a cat on hot bricks. Her 'A' level results arrived in the second week of August, three A grades in History, Maths and Economics, but John knew it was the results of the Morrison Scholarship, due out two weeks later, that she was pinning her hopes on. For himself, he didn't quite know what to hope for. If Peggy failed she would be devastated, and all that hard work. . . . But if she passed she would be off to Harvard, and then who knew when they might see her again?

'It's not very fair, really, is it?' Kath Anderson complained on the morning that the results were due. She broke eggs into a frying pan and dropped slices of bread into the toaster. 'I mean, leaving it this long to tell you. You'll be off at the end of September; it only gives you a few weeks to prepare.'

'*If* I get in,' Peg reminded her, snatching a piece of toast and sitting down at the table to eat it.

'Even so, think of all the things – '

'Mum! I don't want to talk about it, all right?'

Jimmy thundered down the stairs and into the kitchen. 'Talk about what?' He glanced at Peg's face. 'Ooops, sorry!'

'Look, as far as I'm concerned, today is just a normal day, all right?' Peg finished her toast and licked her fingers. 'Let's just carry on as normal, please.'

'You could always come down to the club and listen to the Neanderthals rehearsing,' Jimmy offered. 'That will take your mind off it.'

'I should think it would, a racket like that!' John Anderson observed from behind his copy of the *Liverpool Echo*.

'Hey listen, I'll have you know that we're all set to become the new Rolling Stones!'

'In your dreams!'

Jimmy swatted at Peg with his fork. 'Cheeky mare!'

Kath frowned at them. 'Well if this is going to be just a normal day, Peggy, you can start it by sweeping the kitchen floor. It's covered from sand off your shoes. I don't know, the amount of sand off that beach that ends up in here, I could. . .'

'Build a sandcastle?' suggested Jimmy.

'Oh, Mum, do I have to? I was planning on going to see Sandra.'

'Oh . . . all right then. If it's going to stop you moping about here, go on then.'

'Anyway, it's off our Jimmy's shoes too!'

Peg walked slowly and purposefully down to the bus stop on the corner of Virginia Road. Today was going to be bad enough without rushing around like a headless chicken. She had planned plenty of things to do. She was going to take the bus over to Sandra's house and listen to records. Then they might catch a ferry across the Mersey to the city centre and do some shopping. Afterwards they would probably return to New Brighton and have lunch on the beach and fool around on the crazy golf course. Then, and only then, would she telephone Miss Crosby and ask her for the scholarship results.

'Hey, Peggy!'

Billy Walsh's motorbike was parked outside the Eat Inn and he was sitting astride it. He wore shorts and a white singlet that looked dazzling to the eyes against his dark tan.

'Have you heard then? Sandra Wilson told me you get your results today.'

'No, not yet. Later.'

Billy tried to look nonchalant. 'The thing is, there's a party on tonight down at the beach. I thought it would be a good opportunity for you to celebrate.'

'*If* there is anything to celebrate.'

'So you'll come?'

'If I fail, I won't much feel like a party, will I?'

'All right, I'll do you a deal, then. If you fail, I won't see you there, and I'll understand why. But if you get in, you've got to come.'

'Says who, Billy Walsh?'

'Oh go on, Peg, you'll enjoy it. You know how you like dancing. Say it's a deal.'

He stuck out his hand.

'Oh, all right, then.' Peg gave a little shrug. 'It's a deal.'

Sandra and Peg had a successful shopping trip. They found a wonderful new boutique in the city centre and Peg blew some of her sandwich money on a linen-look shift dress and a pair of matching shoes, little-girl shoes that fastened across the instep with a button, which the shop assistant assured her were exactly like the shoes from Biba in London.

Alone in her bedroom that evening, Peg tried the dress on again. It was in a shade of raspberry pink that flattered the brownish tones of her hair and skin. She put the shoes on too, and brushed out her hair, and applied some lipstick that Jimmy had given her for Christmas and she'd never used. Then she sat down on the edge of her bed and just sat there for a while, staring at the toes of her new shoes. All of a sudden she felt quite exhausted.

'So where is she then?' Billy Walsh muttered to Sandra. They were on the beach, shivering slightly in the cool wind that was blowing off the sea. Summer was on the turn; there was a touch of autumn around the edges.

Quite a gang had already arrived, maybe twenty or thirty. It was going to be a good party, when it got going. As usual there was a delay while someone tried to get some music set up. A bonfire had been lit, and most of the kids were standing near it, trying to warm the back of their legs.

'I don't know where Peggy is.' Sandra took the bottle of beer from Billy's hand and helped herself to a swig. 'I honestly don't know. I haven't seen her since three o'clock this afternoon, and I haven't a clue what happened after I left her. Not the foggiest.'

'So you don't know then?'

'If she's going to turn up? No I don't. . . . Hey, they've got the music going. It's *Get Back*, too. Come on!'

They started to dance, but all of a sudden there was Peggy, strolling towards them from Marine Promenade. She'd thrown a big baggy sweater of Jimmy's over her dress and it made her look small and vulnerable.

She smiled uncertainly when she saw Billy and Sandra.

'So?' Sandra was so excited the word was almost a squeak.

Peg's smile broadened. 'I've won the scholarship. To read Economics at Radcliffe College. That's Harvard, but for women.'

'Peg! That's just . . . I don't know what to say.' Sandra hugged her. 'Except that I don't want you to leave Liverpool, you cow. How long's it for?'

'Four years.'

'Oh, Peggy!'

'How did your parents take it?' Billy asked later, when the commotion had died down and Sandra had allowed them to go off and dance.

'Pleased, of course. Dead pleased. But sad too. A little bit upset, I suppose.'

'That their golden girl's going to disappear for four years.'

'Exactly.'

'And after the four years, then what? Will you come back?'

Peg nodded her head slowly. 'I suppose so, I don't know. I haven't thought that far ahead.'

Billy loosened his grasp on her waist and stepped back a pace. 'I don't believe that! I thought you planned your every move, had your whole life mapped out.'

'Don't you ever plan things, Billy Walsh?'

'I'd planned to kiss you tonight.'

And he did. His mouth tasted sweet, tobaccoey. It felt nice. It felt more than nice, it felt wonderful. Peg kissed him back.

'Anyone would think that you'd enjoyed that,' Billy lamented, as they walked away from the dance floor. They sat down on the sand and Billy lit a cigarette.

Peg put her hand on his arm. 'I did. You've no idea how much. Only don't tell anyone I said that.'

Billy's arm went around her and pulled her to him hard. She let him kiss her again, then extricated herself, but her eyes were still locked on his.

'You know,' she whispered sadly, 'I could really fall for you, Billy Walsh.'

'Fall away.'

She shook her head. 'I'm not going to do that.'

'Why the hell not?'

'Because I'm not going to let myself.'

'I don't understand, this is all too intellectual for me. . . .' He puffed savagely on his cigarette. 'I mean . . . feelings are just things that . . . you feel, right? You can't help it. You can't *control* them!'

'Oh, but you can . . .!' Peg jumped to her feet and pulled him up by the hand. 'Come on . . . I want to show you something.'

They left the beach and trudged up Albion Street to St George's Mount, right to the top so that you could only see the water of the estuary when the light reflected on it in the distance. St George's Mount was the nicest road in New Brighton, the one where the middle classes had kept their second homes in the days when the place was a new resort, an escape from the city of Liverpool. People lived in them all year round now, the pretty cottages and villas painted in faded icecream colours.

In daylight, the view was quite breathtaking from the top. You could see the tangle of cranes and warehouses along the docks, and beyond that the squat shoulders of the cathedral on the other side of the Mersey. You could watch the ferries go to and fro from up here, and the pleasure boats in the summer. And seagulls, always lots of seagulls.

'America's over there, somewhere,' said Peg, pointing. 'Dad used to bring us up here, when I was little, and then later I used to come up here by myself and just look that little bit harder, see if I could actually *see* America. I always wanted to go there, as long as I can remember.'

Billy put his arm around her shoulders. 'You mean that's why you're backing off? Because you're about to leave for America?'

'Partly. But it's not just that. . . .' She sighed. 'It's what it represents, and what you represent. I feel as if when I've over there, anything will be possible. . . . I could become a millionaire, head of some big corporation, anything. All right, so it might not happen like that, but the *possibility* is there.' She clutched Billy's hand. 'It's like this wonderful new world of opportunities opening up. Getting involved now, or in the future, might mess things up – '

'You've still got to *live*, Peggy!'

'I know, but it feels as though I'd have to give up something of myself, and that might make me unable to take the path ahead. . . .'

She looked out across the water and shivered. 'It's a big step. Leaving my family like this is going to hurt them. I need all my strength to make it.'

'So, there's no future?'

'I'm afraid not.' She kissed him again, lingeringly. 'Race you down the hill, Billy Walsh!'

'Peggy – !'

But she had already slipped from his grasp and disappeared into the night.

FOUR

Savannah, Georgia 1960–1969

People seemed to enjoy telling Michael Macken how rich his daddy was. Especially Al Macken himself. But then he would point to the plaque in his office, the words of a song by the famous singer, Johnny Mercer, himself a native of Savannah:

> *Pardon my Southern accent*
> *Pardon my Southern drawl*
> *It may sound funny*
> *Ah, but honey I love y'all.* . . .

'However rich you are, it's important you don't go forgettin' your roots. MackenCorp is a Southern company, and it's the South that's made us what we are. We may have offices in New York and Chicago but we belong here, we always will. . . .'

And it was very easy to belong in a town where your daddy owned or had an interest in every going concern. As Michael and Travis grew up, the Macken empire grew from the largest company in Savannah to the largest in Georgia and finally to one of the top five hundred in the country. Al Macken appeared on the front of *Newsweek* under a caption asking 'IS THIS THE FACE OF THE NEW SOUTH?' Inside, he told the interviewer that he was aiming to put MackenCorp in the top fifty companies, and described how his business interests, which had focussed initially on the river and the port, had expanded further and further into the hinterland, spreading from shipping into petro-chemical refineries, amusement arcades, lumber mills, textile mills, and latterly into communications; television networks and radio stations. 'And when I reached the state border I just kept right on going. . . .'

Because Daddy made such a big deal about him and Travis being Southerners, they went to the Oglethorpe Boys' Academy in Savannah, and not to Choate like Mom had wanted. She pointed out to Daddy that all her friends sent their boys to preparatory schools in the North.

'That's fine for those who want their sons turning into little Yankees. I want mine to know where they come from.'

Staying in Savannah suited the Macken boys fine. Travis liked it because it meant Daddy could take him around the warehouses and factories, teaching him how the business worked. Michael liked it because he could spend his time roaming the woods around their big white mansion, swimming in Turner's Creek or taking out his boat and catching crayfish over the side with a piece of string and some salt bacon. And when they went into the city he could go to River Street and watch the boats. That was what he liked best of all.

He chose just that for his birthday treat. It was his eighth birthday, and that meant that Daddy would leave his work for a few hours and take him anywhere he wanted to go. Travis would come too, of course. And it wasn't actually his birthday today, because on the real date of his birthday Daddy had been in Baltimore. But it was the nearest day to it that he could manage, and Michael didn't mind waiting.

'So, Mikey, how do y'all want to spend your day?' Daddy asked over breakfast.

'I want to go down to River Street.'

'Aw, that's boring!' Travis made a face. 'You always want to go down to River Street.'

'It's Michael's day, Travis,' said Mom quietly. She liked to stand up for Michael on occasion, and took his side against Travis when she felt he needed it.

'Tell you what, why don't we call in at East Bay and I can show you guys some things, then we'll go down to the river and see what we can see.'

Michael smiled and nodded eagerly. He so wanted Daddy to be pleased with him. Daddy was his all-time hero, a great man, just like everybody in Savannah was always telling him. He knew the trip to his father's office was really for Travis's sake, because he liked to see what was going on there, and he knew that Daddy would show them the plaque on the wall again, the Johnny Mercer one, and tell them that this was his empire and it was going to belong to the two of them some day. All that stuff was OK. He didn't mind going along with it because he wanted Daddy to like him. Travis was the golden boy, everyone knew that, and it was hardly Travis's fault that he was born first. Just so long as Daddy was pleased with him too, from time to time.

'See here, you guys.' Daddy called them through to his desk after they had ridden up and down in the new elevator and flicked the buttons on Winona's fancy telephone system. On his desk was a large colour photograph of a ship. Travis immediately climbed up on to the great leather chair so that he could get a better view.

'Neat!'

'Yeah, ain't she just? She's the *Island Star*. Fourteen thousand tons of her. She's been laid up in Baltimore for a while because the guys who owned her couldn't afford to run her any more. But we're going to spend several million dollars refurbishing her and then run her in seven-day cruise trips around Tahiti.'

'Can we go and see her?' begged Travis. 'Please?'

It's not fair, thought Michael, shaking inwardly with the indignation he did not dare show. It's *my* birthday, I should get to decide everything we do. . . .

'Whoa there, Travis. I think that's up to Mikey here, don't you?'

Daddy was smiling at him, but the glow of pride in his voice was for Travis. He loved it that Travis was fascinated by everything to do with the company.

Michael shrugged. 'OK, if we can go to River Street first.'

'It's a deal!' Daddy held out his hand. 'And tell you what, you get to pick where we have lunch, too.'

'McCrory's!' said Michael without hesitation.

So Stanley, Daddy's chauffeur, dropped them on River Street, but it was spoiled somehow, because Daddy kept looking at his watch and Travis was hopping from foot to foot, impatient to get back in the car and drive up to the shipyard. Michael would have been happy to sit there all day and watch the tugs and the river cruisers weaving to and fro. He liked to screw up his eyes and squint at the far horizon, imagining he could see beyond the river mouth to the Atlantic Ocean. He liked the idea of water stretching for miles and miles, all the way to England.

But they only stayed there a few minutes, then went to see the *Island Star* in dry dock, and Travis impressed everyone with the questions he asked. And even though they drove back to McCrory's luncheonette on Drayton Street and Michael was allowed to eat as many home-made Oreos and eat as much pumpkin icecream as he wanted, the day was spoiled somehow.

Cordella Macken was putting the final touches to Michael's birthday dinner. She hoped it would be a nice surprise for him; something that would perhaps make up for the rest of the day. She knew that it was hard for him sometimes, having to be in Travis's shadow all the time. She sat at her dressing table and examined the two framed photographs of her sons. Eleven-year-old Travis was so much like his father, it was uncanny. Thick, golden brown hair, striking blue eyes and a strong, square chin. Michael, with his brown eyes and straight, dark hair, was quite different. Al and Martha both swore he was the double of his late grandaddy, James Macken. She couldn't be sure about that since she had never met her father-in-law, but she did privately think that Michael was even better looking than Travis in his way. He was certainly going to be taller than his older brother. But people didn't notice that, they were so bound up in the idea of Travis being the spit of his father.

Cordella applied a little pale pink lipstick and tidied her hair before going down to the kitchens to talk to Bonnie and Sadie, the cook, about the meal for tonight. She didn't like the staff to see her looking less than her best. She smiled at her reflection, confident in the knowledge that she looked better now than she ever had done. Thirty-six suited her a whole lot better than eighteen had. She had filled out nicely, lost that scrawny look. You couldn't exactly call her curvaceous, but at least she was rounded. Her hair was tinted a pretty shade of ash blonde and set in waves on her shoulders, and she made sure she spent an hour every day by the swimming pool so that she always had a light tan. Al liked her when she was tanned. He appreciated her body more these days, that was for sure. She had proof of it, in fact. Smiling at herself, she patted the round of her stomach.

Martha would be here any minute to help with the preparations. She didn't strictly need the help, not with a full-time staff of five, but she and Martha had become close friends over the years and they liked to do things together, family things.

She went down into the dining room and fussed over the table settings. She had bought a whole load of balloons and streamers in colours to match the green and silver décor; it would look real pretty when they were all in place. She would get Martha to give her a hand fixing them up. When she had checked on the flower arrangements in the drawing room she would see how the meal was coming on. Sadie was preparing Michael's favourite: her spicy fried chicken and creamed squash.

She felt at ease, confident, moving about the house like this. She loved her home, with its cool, spacious interiors and the lawn sloping away down to the tree-lined shore of the creek. Al sometimes talked about moving somewhere even bigger, even grander, but she always resisted. To keep him quiet she would get the interior decorators down from New York to give the place a fresh look. Or they would buy another home. They had an apartment in New York, a ranch-style house with its own golf course in Florida, and a cabin in Colorado's San Juan mountains. They took the boys up there to ski, and already both were showing plenty of talent for the sport, particularly Michael. . . .

Cordella sighed with satisfaction. She loved her life. Who would have thought she could be so lucky?

Martha Neely frowned as she clutched the wheel of her Lincoln convertible. She didn't much like driving at the best of times, and especially not when she had something important on her mind. Wyatt told her she should make more use of the MackenCorp drivers, after all he was the senior vice-president and she was the sister of the chairman and chief executive. But it seemed silly to go to all that trouble just to run out to the airport to drop off her daughter, and then drive on to her sister-in-law's for a girls' afternoon. What would the poor driver do all afternoon while they were fixing party decorations? Martha's mind always ran on these practical lines.

Now she wished she hadn't been to the airport and seen what she had seen. Her eldest daughter, Melissa, was flying up to visit Wyatt's relatives in Minnesota, and Martha had volunteered to put her on the plane. As she was standing at the barrier waving Melissa goodbye, she had seen *her* coming in the opposite direction, through the arrivals gate.

There was no doubt that it had been her. Once you knew Beulah Peabody, you did not forget her. Her hair was still that brilliant, ostentatious shade of red, her figure still as arrestingly voluptuous. She wore a wide-brimmed hat, and Martha remembered how she had liked extravagant hats in the Forties, and how the nonchalant way she wore them made Martha feel plain and homely, like a country mouse. The brim was low over her eyes (which was just as well, because it meant she did not see Martha standing there), so all that was visible of her face was a vivid red gash of a mouth. Against the pastel ginghams and lawns of the Savannah women she looked like a creature from another planet in a simple black Givenchy dress. But then she had been living in Paris for years, which was like another planet if you had never set foot outside Georgia.

She had been half expecting Beulah to come back when Clermont Peabody died nearly a year ago. Everybody had. But there was no sign, no word, and everybody forgot about her again. And now here she was. Her arrival must have had something to do with her daddy's death, even at this late hour, because there was an inheritance involved. There were papers for her to sign before the money could be hers. Perhaps she would do that and then go away again.

Martha spoke to Cordella on the phone nearly every day, so she knew Cordella was unaware of her sister's arrival. She should tell her, she really should. But it wasn't going to be easy. Martha had been there in the days when Beulah was Al's girlfriend and no one gave poor Cordella a second thought. They thought Al would marry Beulah, he certainly had eyes for no one else back then, and the things the two of them got up to. . . . But then Beulah had disappeared and Al had announced he was marrying Cordella. She and Wyatt couldn't help but find it odd, but Al refused to talk about it. And then they had ended up being glad, anyhow, since Cordella was a lot easier to get along with than

Beulah. Beulah was always a mite patronizing, and not at all interested in home and children and the like.

As she turned off Wilmington Island Road and swung her car through the gates of what was known simply, in good old Savannah tradition, as the Macken place, Martha told herself to stop being silly and letting her imagination run away with itself. Beulah had been away from Savannah for most of the last fourteen years, she had a life elsewhere. She would be just passing through. Anyway, when she looked at this beautiful place she knew that of the two Peabody girls, Cordella was the one with everything going for her.

Nevertheless, she decided as she walked up to the elegant front porch, she would just mention that Beulah was in town.

The two women were soon lost in a pleasant world of family news and gossip, comparing and contrasting their offspring and their husbands' endearing and infuriating habits.

'Honey . . .' said Martha carefully as she tied two green balloons together. 'There's something I wanted to tell you. You'll never guess – '

'And I've got something to tell you, too!' Cordella gripped Martha's hands and her eyes were sparkling. 'I swear I am just going to *burst* if I don't tell somebody – I'm pregnant!'

'Why, honey, that's marvellous – '

'I'n't it just? And I just *know* that this time it's going to be a girl!'

Martha hugged her sister-in-law. 'Fingers crossed!' She knew how much Cordella wanted a daughter.

'So. . .' Cordella released herself from the embrace. 'What was it you were going to tell me?'

'Oh . . . oh, nothing.'

'Anyhow, I haven't told Al about the baby yet, because I thought it would be kind of a nice idea to announce it at Michael's party tonight. You know, with everyone gathered here and all.'

'Well. . .'

Cordella's face fell. 'You think it's a bad idea? Why, you think Al would be mad if I didn't tell him first?'

Martha shook her head. 'No, I think it's a fine idea. Why don't y'all go right ahead and do that.'

★ ★ ★

It was exactly the sort of party Cordella loved. Not some fancy corporate affair with a lot of skinny mannequin wives poured into black cocktail dresses straight from the Paris couture houses. There was no one showing off their jewels or their face-lifts or talking about how rich they were. Instead it was just family and a few close friends. Wyatt and Martha were there with their two youngest children, Al's secretary Winona, and some of the couples she and Al met regularly at the country club, with their children. She was pleased to see Michael enjoying himself. His spirits had revived since the boys returned from their day out, when he had seemed a little quiet. Al looked pleased too; that was good.

Warmed by a glow of pride and well-being, Cordella waited until Michael's eight candles had been blown out and the last chorus of *Happy Birthday* had died away before rising to her feet. The silver spoon in her hand made a ladylike tinkling sound as she tapped it against the side of a punch cup. She smiled and blushed in acknowledgement of the surprised looks on the faces of her guests. Cordella was not in the habit of making speeches.

'Since we are here to celebrate a family occasion. . . .' She paused for a moment to ruffle the thick curl on the back of Michael's neck. '. . . It seemed a good moment to announce that the Macken family has another reason to celebrate.'

Al's eyes flashed a question at her. She reached for his hand and held it as she went on. 'Al and I are going to be celebrating another eighth birthday some time in the future . . . we're going to be parents again!'

During Cordella's announcement, no one had paid any attention to Bonnie showing another guest into the dining room. Now, as the clapping and cries of congratulation died down, the guests noticed that Cordella was standing still and rather pale in Al's embrace. One by one they started to turn and look in the direction of the open doors.

'Hello, everybody,' said Beulah.

Michael was to retain a vivid memory of that day. The blur and noise of the party, the green and silver balloons and gaudy coloured streamers, the pink glow of the pomegranate punch in its crystal cups, reflecting the sparkling light of the chandeliers. And then suddenly the room seemed quiet and still, and instead of all the colour he was aware only of the woman who stood smiling at them from the doorway. The colour faded away and there was only the intense creamy whiteness of her skin and the stark black of the hat that completely covered her hair.

He had heard about Aunt Beulah, of course, but only as a name. Nothing in his eight years so far could have prepared him for her . . . he realised later that the word was sexuality. The way she stood there with one hand artfully placed on her hip. The provocative jut of her bosom, which seemed somehow to bear a direct challenge to his mother, pretty in her pastel afternoon frock.

People talked about her for days afterwards, weeks even. They said Aunt Beulah had suddenly grown bored of Europe and was planning to settle in her home town of Savannah. He didn't quite understand why this was so surprising, but evidently it was.

But Aunt Beulah's return was totally eclipsed by the arrival of Honoree. His sister was born six months later and from that moment he forgot about his aunt. He was completely lost in wonder at the beauty and frailty of this tiny little creature. All new babies were tiny, he knew that, but Honoree was extra tiny because she arrived a few weeks early. But she was still beautiful with tiny wisps of blonde hair covering her eggshell skull, long, dark lashes, a tiny rosebud mouth.

Daddy was delighted to have a daughter; Travis thought it was cool to have a kid sister; they thought she was great. But it was different for Mom and him. They *worshipped* Honoree. The two of them spent hours together beside her crib just gazing at her. They marvelled at every detail, took note of every movement. Mom seemed worried that he would be upset not to be the baby of the family, but for Michael being an older brother was blissful. He loved the idea that there was this little, vulnerable creature he could care for. It made him feel strong and proud. And when she was older he would be able to teach her so many things she didn't know about.

They had a nursemaid for the baby, of course, an English Norland nanny in a crisp brown uniform, but Mom was so besotted with her she insisted on doing the feeding and diapering herself when she was at home. And Michael would help her.

'Wanna come help me, Michael?' she would call, and he would bound upstairs to the nursery in her wake. He didn't like to go up there himself too often in case he disturbed Honoree, or the nanny gave him frosty looks.

'You know what to do,' Mom said over her shoulder, and Michael trotted over to the dresser to fetch talcum and cotton wool and baby lotion.

'That's it, hold the pail a second. . . . Hey baby, hey sweet pea. . . .' Mom's voice softened into a contented crooning noise as she touched the tiny waving hands. 'Lotion please, Michael. . . . Look, your big brother's helping me, isn't he? Gonna give him a smile, huh. . . .' She turned to her fellow slave with a conspiratorial grin. 'Guess Travis would think we were pretty slushy, wouldn't he? But I reckon we make a great team, you and me.'

Michael basked in his mother's approbation. You see? he felt like saying to the world, somebody does need me after all.

'I don't know, somehow things just felt different this time around. . . .' Cordella took a sip of her wine, unable to prevent herself pursing her lips a little. She didn't normally drink wine. 'The whole of the pregnancy was different from the beginning. I just felt great from start to finish. With Travis I felt real queasy, and I was so nervous with it being my first and all, and then when I was expecting Michael. . . .' She shivered slightly. 'Well, it wasn't a good time for Al and me. But with Honoree . . . it was just special somehow and I kind of knew all along that she was going to be a girl. And then when she *was* a girl, I just kind of went crazy with the joy of it. I sound silly I know, and I guess all this women's talk must be kind of boring for you, but . . . well, it's nice we can talk like this. After all this time.'

Beulah flicked an imaginary crumb from her cream Courrèges pants suit and took a mouthful of wine, savouring the taste. She didn't find it nice at all, not hearing Cordella's endless homilies on pregnancy and childbirth and the joys of family life. In fact it was one of the most boring lunches she had ever sat through. Some sort of ghoulish curiosity had drawn her to her sister, wanting to make a show of friendship so that she could be witness to these confidences.

But it couldn't be true, could it? After all these years, her sister was still married to her former lover, and happily so, if her accounts were to be believed. And she looked good, you couldn't take that away from her. The descriptions of scenes from the happy home were meant to be proof. Were they offered as a warning, too, she wondered, or was Cordella's faith in her husband as total as it appeared? She set down her glass and pushed back her chair. 'You'll have to excuse me.'

Cordella started and turned pink; for a moment she looked like the mousy, nondescript girl she used to be. 'Oh, Beulah, I'm sorry, I didn't mean to spend the whole time talking about myself. You must think – '

'It's not that. I have something to do, that's all. A meeting. We must do this again some time.' She kissed the air next to Cordella's cheek.

'Just drive around the block a few times, please,' she told the driver when she had hailed a cab. She needed to enjoy a few moments' peace. She took out her compact, powdered her nose and added more lipstick in a subtle red-brown shade. Pink lipsticks argued with her hair. Not bad, she told her reflection, not bad at all. From looking at her skin you would never know she was not twenty-one. The age, the experience were all in the expression of her slanting green eyes. But then her eyes had always looked like that. They had been speaking the language of sex to men since she was sixteen years old. Or was it fifteen?

She snapped the compact shut. 'East Bay Street, please. The Macken building.'

Before she walked through the vast plate glass doors, she paused to smile at the name in gold letters above them. '*Macken*'. It gave her pleasure to see evidence of Al's success, but she was not surprised. They had always known he was going to make it big, the two of them. And all the time she had been abroad she had followed his fortunes in the business press. It had been a sort of hobby with her.

She took the elevator to the top floor where Al's secretary was positioned outside the inner sanctum like a guard dog. She was about the same age as Beulah but looked older with her horn-rimmed glasses and heavily lacquered beehive.

'Miss Peabody. How may I help you?'

'I'd like to see Mr Macken, please.'

'I'm afraid Mr Macken is tied up at the moment.' Winona gave the standard response used to deflect people who presented themselves without an appointment. 'May I – '

'Then I'll just have to help untie him, won't I?' Beulah flashed Winona a saccharine smile and opened the door to the office.

Al was standing at the window with his arms folded, looking out at the Savannah River. Beulah took stock. He was still quite a man. In fact she found him even more attractive now that the gaucheness of youth had been rubbed away. There was power in his stance, and the thick set of his shoulders. He still looks like a railway navvy in a Savile Row suit, she thought, and that's one hell of a turn-on.

He smiled politely when he saw her, but she could see he was annoyed.

'Beulah, well! What can I do for you?'

This was the first time they had been alone. In the company of others, Cordella included, he had been a smooth, Southern gentleman, the perfect brother-in-law. Now he was failing to conceal the fact that her presence disturbed him.

'I guess I just wanted to take a real good look at you, Al.'

'Why did you come back?' The words were more an accusation than a question.

'I always intended to. Why surely y'all didn't think that I was going to stay away for ever just to convenience you and Cordella, did you? I just thought I ought to wait until we were a little older. In our prime.'

She stepped a little closer, inviting him to run his eyes over her body. The front of the Courrèges jacket was veiled in a chiffon scarf that almost, but not quite, concealed the cleft between her breasts.

'Beulah, if you have ideas about starting something. . . .'

She raised an eyebrow.

'Well, I'm happily married now. Me and Cordella both. We have our two fine boys and a new baby we're both crazy over. . . . I know it's kind of hard not to think about how different things might have been for you and me if – '

'Different?' Beulah laughed straight into his face, and for an instant Al was just a poor country boy with a paintbrush in his hand being teased and taunted by a rich girl from the big house.

'Do you think for a minute that I want to trade places with Cordella? To go to fork luncheons at the Junior League and charity bake-ins for the school, and talk about nothing but my children and gettin' pregnant? . . . You and I surely would have had something different, wouldn't we?'

'Beulah. . . .'

She reached out and touched the flesh on the inside of his wrist, just below his watch strap. He shivered.

'I'm not going to start anything with you, *Mister* Macken. You're going to do that all by yourself. Right now you might not think so, but you will, that's for sure.'

Michael woke early on the morning of 3 April 1961, the day his sister was four months old. Four months. He said it out loud to himself. It sounded so much older than three months. Already she could do a whole lot more than she could a month ago. She would reach for her rattle and her favourite fluffy duck. She liked to grab hold of his two thumbs and try and pull herself up. And she was crazy about being bounced on his knee, bending and straightening her tiny legs. Soon, Mom said, she would be able to sit up. And then to creep, and then walk. . . .

He decided he would go and see if she was awake. It was great to be the first person in to her in the morning, to be on the receiving end of those wide, toothless smiles. He crept down the corridor to the nursery, taking special care to be quiet as he passed the nanny's room. Honoree was still asleep though, curled up in the corner of her crib with the fluffy duck beside her. Best to let her sleep. Mom was always telling him she got cranky if she hadn't had enough sleep.

He would never really understand what made him turn and look again. Something in the way she was lying, perhaps, something not quite right. The way she was hunched and slightly stiff looking. Or had he been aware of her unnatural stillness. As he approached the crib and reached out his hand, cold snakes of fear travelled down his body, turning quickly to panic as he felt the terrible coldness of her skin.

'Mom! . . . MOM!'

He snatched her up, tangled in her blankets, started running blindly towards the door, though he knew it was useless. The tiny face was a dull greyish purple and mottled on one cheek where she had been pressing against it. The front of her nightdress was wet with drool.

The nanny ran into the room and she cried out, a sort of twisted scream. Mom was standing right behind her and she just looked at him, her face drained of all colour. 'Oh my God, Michael,' she whispered. 'Oh my God! What's happened?'

The nanny had taken Honoree's body from his arms and was giving her mouth to mouth resuscitation, though they all knew it was useless, and from then on everything was a blur of noise and yelling, Daddy trying to calm Mom's hysterical sobs, yelling for someone to call an ambulance, a doctor. . . .

And then when the paramedics came and took the small, stiff corpse away, wrapped in a blanket, everyone turned their attention to Mom, trying to comfort her somehow, telling her to hold on, to be strong, and no one paid any attention to Michael, who stood still in the nursery knowing he had lost the most precious thing in his life.

Beulah Peabody drove to her sister's house.

She was not a woman who ever drove slowly – she broke the speed limit almost every day of her life – but today the way she managed the car reflected her reluctance to actually arrive, as though by crawling along she might never arrive. She really didn't want to do this.

The phone call from Al's secretary was strange, garbled. Then she calmed down enough to say that Cordella's baby was dead. 'I thought you'd want to know,' she kept saying, apologising the way bearers of bad news always do. 'I thought I ought to tell you.'

Beulah thought back to that night before Cordella's wedding. Cordella had been calm then and strong. She was the one who had Al. It felt as though she had everything. And Beulah had wanted to hurt her, to transfer some of the hurt she was feeling, buried deep down inside where no one could find it. Christ, she had wanted her sister to burn in hell.

And now this.

She pressed her face against the steering wheel, eyes tight shut, trying to summon strength. Then slowly, very slowly, she climbed out of the car, walked to the front door and rang the bell.

The maid who answered was red-eyed from crying, wringing her hands, quite literally. Beulah had thought people only did that in books.

'Oh, Miz Beulah.'

'I came . . . I just . . . can I please see my sister?'

'I don't know, Miz Beulah, she's just so. . . .' The woman broke spontaneously into sobs. 'It's just so terrible to see. . . .'

'I just wanted to say I was sorry.'

'I'll tell her you called.'

Beulah realised the maid was waiting for her to leave. 'Right, well, I guess I'd better go.'

She turned and walked back to the car. As she turned the key in the ignition the front door opened and a figure appeared. It was Cordella.

Beulah got out of the car and walked quickly towards her. She had never seen anything as terrible as the sight of that face, so swollen from crying it looked bruised. Instinctively, she held out her arms.

'I came as soon as Winona told me. You must feel so terrible.'

But Cordella shrank from her embrace. 'You have no idea how I feel.' She spoke in a cold, dead voice. 'How could you? You're not a mother.'

'Cordella – '

'Please, I don't want you here right now. Just go, please, leave me alone.'

They called it 'crib death'. That's what Michael heard the experts say to Mom and Daddy afterwards, the endless stream of doctors summoned to try and explain.

No one knew why it happened, but it had an aftermath more terrible than death itself. It involved Michael talking endlessly to doctors, even to the police, answering questions about exactly what he had found in the room that morning, what he had seen, what he had touched. They explained to him that nothing was his fault, yet everything they asked made him feel it was, that he had *done* something. And he was just the brother, just a kid. Everyone acted like he wasn't supposed to be particularly upset or anything.

And then there was Mom. What happened to her was the most terrible thing of all. For days she ate nothing. For weeks she howled like a dog all night. She wouldn't let anyone pack up Honoree's things or rearrange the room in any way. She would go in there by herself and pace up and down, calling out her dead child's name in a strange high-pitched voice. 'Where are you?' she would call. 'Please come back, oh *please* . . . I just want to see you. I just want to touch you. . . .'

On the day that would have been Honoree's first birthday, the priest came to visit. He and Mom sat up in the nursery, talking in low voices. The door was open a crack and Michael stood listening outside. He couldn't help it. Even in death Honoree exerted fascination for him.

'Sometimes I can't believe it happened, it's as if she never existed. And then I touch her things and I smell her smell and the pain is so bad . . . I just want to hold her. . . .'

The priest murmured comforting words.

'It hurts so much, it feels so bitter. I know it's wrong to be bitter.'

'You still have much to be thankful for, Mrs Macken. You have two fine sons. You are still their mother – '

'But I'm Honoree's mother too. And now she's gone it feels as though she's all I want, as if she's all I ever wanted. . . .'

The priest must have done some good, Michael reflected, because after he left, Mom started packing Honoree's things up into boxes. Daddy and Aunt Martha had been trying to persuade her to do that for months. He plucked up courage and tapped on the door.

'Mom?'

'What?' She answered dully. She wouldn't look him in the face any more, hardly ever kissed or embraced him. It was as if she was angry with him. Why? Because he had got there first, perhaps? Or because he hadn't been able to do anything? He remembered her voice when she saw him, asking him what had happened. Could she really think he was responsible in some way, that he could have harmed her? He remembered the police asking if he and Travis had been jealous when Honoree was born.

He picked up a pink blanket and started to fold it.

'Don't touch that!' his mother snapped. She snatched the blanket and thrust it into one of the boxes.

'I thought I could help you, Mom. Like I always used to help you . . . you know, before.'

'I don't want any help, thank you. No one can help me with this.' And she stood up abruptly and walked out of the room.

Michael took the blanket from the box and put it to his face, inhaling the sweet baby smell. And then he wept, not just for the loss of his sister, but for his mother too. Even she didn't need him now.

Al Macken climbed down the steps of his Lear jet and walked across the tarmac to the limousine. Winona was waiting for him. He hated to waste a minute of the working day, so whenever he was away she would meet him at the airstrip with her clipboard under her arm and ride with him into the city, using the journey to discuss any developments there might have been in his absence.

'Jack Kominsky called from Paris. He says he's still checking out the possibility of co-operation with Niarchos. He says he'll fix a meeting with you in New York. . . . Wyatt says he needs to go through the quarterly report with you. You can call him at home tonight. . . . Oh, and I appointed myself an assistant, as you suggested. She started today.'

'What? Sorry, did I tell you to do that?' Al turned away from staring out of the window, rubbing his eyes.

Winona peered over the rims of her spectacles, her way of expressing disapproval. 'Don't you remember? Before you went to Chicago last week you said the workload was far too much for me to manage by myself, and I should hire someone to help.'

'Yeah, I did too.' He turned back to the window.

'Are you sure you're all right, Mr Macken?'

'Yeah . . . yeah. . . .' He rubbed his eyes again. 'Just a little tired, I guess.'

'I'll fix you some coffee when we get into the office,' said Winona. He did look tired, she thought, had done for months now. Grief for his infant daughter had taken its toll, but most of the strain came from having to be strong for the others, for Cordella and the boys. He didn't like to talk about it too much though. She had tentatively suggested that they ought to try and have another child and he had almost jumped down her throat.

'Good afternoon, Mr Macken.' They were met at the elevator by a smiling young girl who held out her hand for his jacket and briefcase. 'May I get you anything? Coffee? Tea?'

She was perhaps twenty-three or twenty-four, pleasant looking rather than pretty, with a trim figure and waving red hair.

Al ignored her. 'Winona – come through here!'

She followed Al into his office, closing the door behind her.

'Who the hell was that out there?'

'Why, Mr Macken, that was Patricia, my assistant. I was telling you about her just – '

'Get rid of her!'

'Lands' sakes – why? She's awful pleasant and bright too.'

'She doesn't fit in, that's all. Give her a month's pay and hire someone else tomorrow. And don't go gettin' any redheads either. They're too distracting. Something about the way they smell, they have different body odour or something. I read that some place. . . .'

He was mumbling now. With a great effort he straightened himself. 'And forget the coffee please, Winona. Just get together all the stuff I need to look at tonight and get Stanley round. I need to get out of here. . . .'

Tonight was the first time in ages he actually asked Stanley to get a move on and drive faster than the stately pace he usually employed. He couldn't wait to get home.

'Cordella!' he called as soon as he got into the house. He had an overwhelming need to be with her. 'Honey, where are you?'

'In here.'

She had just come into the garden room dressed in a short white tennis dress, her fair hair smoothed back under a broad white Alice band.

'You been out on the court, honey? Well, that's great, that's just terrific.' He was pathetically grateful these days for any sign that Cordella was leading a normal life again. 'Y'all have a good game?'

'I asked the coach from the club to come over for an hour and give me a lesson. I need to work up my serve a bit if I'm going to start playing again.'

'Well, that's good . . . it's good that you want to do that, I mean. . . .'

Al laid his briefcase down and put his arms around his wife, touching her tentatively as if she was made of glass and might implode at the slightest pressure. 'You look real pretty in that dress. You ought to wear skimpy little things like this more often, show off your legs.'

He bent to place his lips over hers, but she deflected him roughly. 'Don't, Al!'

'Honey, why not?'

'I just don't feel like it, that's all.' Her voice was dull, dry. She bent down and started to unlace her sneakers.

'Well, just when the hell are you going to feel like it, that's what I'd like to know? We haven't made love in months not since . . . not since – '

'Go on – you might as well say it.'

'Not since we lost Honoree.' His shoulders sank and he dropped his hands by his sides.

Cordella looked up at him and her expression was cold. It reminded Al of the early days of their marriage, when she had been angry with him all the time. 'And I suppose you're about to tell me we ought to fuck so we can make another little baby. Just like Honoree! Well let me get something straight here, I don't want another baby! Even if it turned out to be a girl, she could never be like Honoree. It would just be an insult to her memory!'

'Honey, for Christ's sakes – '

Cordella ran from the garden room and slammed the door.

'Jesus Christ!' Al went out into the hall. He stood there for a moment with his hands on his hips, his chest heaving with anger. 'Jesus fucking Christ . . .!'

He stormed to the front door and wrenched it open. 'Stanley, where are you? Get your black ass in here!'

'Just puttin' the car away, sir.'

'Well, don't bother. Just give me the goddamn keys!'

Al ran down the steps and climbed behind the wheel of the Cadillac. He drove so rarely he had trouble remembering where the controls were. He threw the car into gear and screeched out onto the Wilmington Island Road, heading for the expressway back to the city. It took him only seconds to realise where he was headed, but rather longer to remember the address, since he had never been before. The red T-bird gave her away. Beulah always did have a weakness for fast cars. It was parked outside a tiny but exquisitely elegant townhouse on Anderson Row. The old Peabody House, the place she detested for being ugly, had been sold.

She was in the shower. When she emerged her red hair was dark and dripping with water, little rivulets that ran down her shoulders and the slope of her breasts into the edge of the towel she wore like a sarong.

'I might have been in bed with someone,' she said.

'I would have thrown him out. Or just climbed right over him.'

There had been a pleasant heat in his groin as he drove around looking for her house, but as soon as he set eyes on her it intensified uncomfortably and he realised he had an erection straining obviously against his thin summer pants. Jesus, he thought, and I haven't even touched her yet.

'Well, what *is* going on here . . .?' Her slanting eyes were laughing as she reached out and touched him with a teasing finger. Before she could finish unbuttoning his fly he pushed her hand away, propelling her to the bed and easing himself into her with the same movement. And as he did so the heat flared up and died away. He ejaculated against her thigh and rolled away with a groan.

'Sorry. . . .'

Beulah wiped herself down with the towel. 'It's been that long, has it?' she asked grimly.

'God, Beulah, don't start, please! This year has been hell. I can't take any more from you, or anyone. Just let me hold you.'

When he reached out to take her in his arms he noticed there were tears in her eyes. 'Beulah, what is it? You want me to go?'

'No!' she said fiercely. 'Not again . . . I guess I just hoped that you would come to me because you wanted me, not because you needed me.'

He kissed her lingeringly on the mouth, then laughed, placing her hand between his legs. 'See? Want, need . . . what's the difference?'

Travis Macken walked slowly along Bay Street, concentrating on placing one foot in front of another. Jesus, he felt strange. He must have drunk more than he intended to. It had seemed no more than a couple of beers, but maybe he just lost count. Oh, and he had a bourbon too, some time toward the end of the evening.

He and his friends had called in for dinner at Euphemia Bailey's boarding house. She still ran the dining room exactly as she had before the war and the queues of diners waiting in line still stretched along West Jones Street. Daddy regularly called in for breakfast and she was always pleased to see the Macken boys and hear their news. After dinner they had gone down to one of the new jazz clubs on River Street, and Travis had lost track of time. He had parked his brand new Corvette down here somewhere, but he couldn't just figure out where. . . . He decided he would walk about a little to clear his head.

The outline of the MackenCorp building loomed up ahead of him. Wherever you went in this town, you could hardly get away from it; it dominated the skyline completely. There were lights in the windows of the top floor, and the Cadillac was still parked out the front, with Stanley sitting there examining his fingernails and reading the sporting pages of the *Savannah Morning News*.

Travis grinned. So Daddy was up there, still working. He'd go up and surprise him and the two of them could ride home together. The old man would be pleased. He liked it when they did that kind of thing, man to man. He'd never had that kind of closeness with his own father, never shared things with him.

He stepped out of the elevator into silent, thickly carpeted gloom. Winona and the other secretaries had long since gone home, and the only light in the place was the thin gleam from the crack around Daddy's closed office door.

He was reaching for the door handle when he realised his father wasn't alone. This surprised him; momentarily he hesitated. The other voice belonged to a woman. Of course! Daddy was fooling around with someone, one of the secretaries probably. He would hardly welcome an interruption from his son. But his hand depressed the handle anyway, and pushed the door very gently until it was a few inches ajar. He could see frustratingly little, but he didn't dare push the door open further. The narrow opening revealed a section of his father's body, from waist to mid-thigh. His strong, muscular buttocks were naked, his pants bunched around his thighs. All he could see of the woman was a shapely knee and calf, and they sure as hell didn't belong to Winona! Her skin was creamy pale against Daddy's dark tan. The disembodied buttocks started to thrust against her rhythmically. There was a gasp, and the leg inched upwards, pressing hard against his back.

Jesus Christ, thought Travis, this is incredible! His skin was tingling and he could feel himself getting hard. It took all his willpower to stop him from reaching down and unbuttoning his chinos. The guy was, what . . . forty-six, forty-seven years old, and he was fucking away like some young stud. What a guy! Sure, he was married, but when you were the chief executive of a multi-million dollar corporation, you could do what the hell you liked. You probably got opportunities like that every day, coming at you from all sides. And it would be like that for *him* too, as soon as he joined Daddy at MackenCorp. He could hardly wait.

Less than twenty-four hours later, Michael Macken stood at the edge of the indoor swimming pool, watching his father complete length after length at a steady crawl.

'Health is wealth' was one of the homilies he was always trotting out at Michael and Travis. 'You can't cry off a merger meeting because you don't feel well. A day lying in bed could cost you millions of dollars.' He was living proof of his own theorem; he worked out fanatically and swam fifty lengths a day, and Michael could not remember him being ill once in the last fifteen years.

'Hey, Dad!'

Al hauled himself out of the pool and stood there with water dripping down his heavy shoulders onto the magnificent triangular torso and trim stomach, flat as a twenty-year-old's. The bastard, Michael thought admiringly, how does he do it? With his year-round tan you couldn't even see the scars on his back any more, where James Macken, had whipped him. Not unless you looked very carefully.

'What can I do for you, son?'

'Dad, can I borrow ten dollars? I'm going to the movies tonight.'

'Take some from my wallet. It's over on the side there . . . take twenty.'

Al dived in neatly and began to plough up and down again.

Michael found the wallet next to his father's Cardin bathrobe, and fumbled through the wad of notes, looking for a twenty-dollar bill, or two tens. They all seemed to be hundreds. Wait a minute, what was this . . .?

He reached into the back of the billfold and pulled out a photograph. It was dog-eared and lined from much handling, but a recent photograph nonetheless, in colour. It was his Aunt Beulah. She was sitting on the edge of a bed (where, in some motel room?), dressed only in a black slip, and the mocking, laughing expression on her face said 'Nothing in life is worth taking seriously'.

Not even adultery. Michael knew all about that. They talked about it in Bible class at school, and his friends liked to speculate about whether or not their parents 'fooled around'. But even now, he found his mind running to all sorts of explanations, making excuses for his father. She was his wife's sister, after all. So it was probably one of Mom's photographs. Daddy probably just found it on the floor some place and kept it for her and forgot to give it back.

He felt better for having reasoned like this, even though in his heart of hearts he knew his mother would never have a photograph of Beulah dressed that way. Laughing like that, in some sort of sexy come-on.

'OK, son? You get the money?'

Michael waved the ten-dollar bills in reply, pushing the photograph guiltily into the recesses of the wallet.

'Y'all have a good time then, you hear?'

With a dismissive wave Al dived into the pool and swam away like some sun-tanned, muscular fish.

'Travis?'

'Yeah?'

'Can I ask you something?'

Michael went looking for his brother and found him, predictably, on the baseball pitch their father had had built at the back of the house. It was supposed to be for both of them, so that they could ask their friends around for a game, but really it was for Travis, so that he could practise his pitching.

'Watch this.' Travis put on his glove and lifted the ball up high, to shoulder level. Then he swung back his shoulder, pivoted on his right foot and hurled the ball with as much force as he could at some imaginary opponent. He was not especially tall for eighteen, but he had his father's powerfully broad shoulders and the pitch was impressive.

'Travis – '

Without even turning round to look at him, Travis picked up the ball again. 'I've got to get in plenty of practice if I'm going to make it onto the college team.'

He was about to leave for his first semester at Harvard Law School. His grades hadn't been all that good, but Daddy had just promised a new wing for the university library, so Travis was in there with all the 'A' grade students, studying the subject that Daddy had picked out for him. After he had completed his law degree, he would take up his position in the Macken Corporation. He seemed quite happy to have the whole thing mapped out for him. Travis was basically lazy, Michael decided. He was just concerned with making himself look good, and leaving the decision-making to somebody else.

He took off the glove and handed it to Michael.

'Here – you take a turn. Tell you what, why don't we have a little wager? I'll wager you ten dollars that you can't pitch it as far as . . . that tree stump over there. Tell you what, the twenty bucks goes to the one who gets it nearest.'

'OK.'

Michael knew he had little chance of winning, but to refuse would give Travis the moral victory, and besides, he found it difficult to resist an opportunity to compete with his brother. He grabbed the ball and swung back, knowing instantly that he hadn't paced himself properly, had not given himself enough time. He threw while the weight of his body was unbalanced, and the ball dropped like a stone several yards in front of the tree.

'Hey, that's not so bad,' said Travis, who could afford to be generous. He swung back and effortlessly pitched to within inches of the tree trunk. 'Ten bucks, please.'

Michael handed over the money. 'Hey, Travis, can I talk to you about something?'

'Sure.' They sat down on the grassy bank on the edge of the field.

'I found a snapshot in Daddy's wallet. Of Aunt Beulah.'

Travis's eyes narrowed. 'What kind of snapshot? You mean. . . .' His hands traced the imaginary hourglass curves of a woman's body.

'Yeah, that kind.'

Travis grinned and shook his head. 'Aunt Beulah, huh? Jeez. . . .'

'You think they're having . . . you know – '

'An affair? I guess so.' Travis was grinning. He seemed to find the idea amusing.

'But, Trav, don't you think that's kind of . . . well, wrong? I mean, what about Mom?'

'Well, I guess she and Dad don't do it any more.'

'No, I meant, well what about love and stuff? I mean, Dad married Mom, so they must love each other. So why would he want to go and do a thing like that with her sister? I mean, why do married people do all that stuff? When you marry someone you make a vow to stay faithful, don't you?'

'Listen, Mikey. . . .' Travis patted his arm. 'Let's just say you've still got a heap of growing up to do if you think marriage has got anything to do with love. Or sex. . . .' He whistled. 'Aunt Beulah! That's something, ain't it though? Have you seen the jugs on the woman . . . hey, and talking of jugs, did you check out that new girl at the tennis club, what's her name . . .?'

'Melody.'

'Melody, that's the one. She has got these breasts that are just begging, and I mean *begging*, to be squeezed! She wears these little tight sweaters, and . . . well, you should take a look some time.'

Michael was not surprised at the turn the conversation had

taken. Apart from his looks and his sporting prowess, all Travis thought about these days was sex. Once he had called Michael into his room and shown him the collection of porn magazines he kept underneath his bed. Not just sweater girls or pin-ups but the real thing. Girls who lay around naked with their legs wide open, looking like they didn't care who saw them. Travis had offered to lend them to Michael, but Michael had refused, even though he was overwhelmed by a hot, squirmy fascination for the little bits he had glimpsed. With Travis, even jerking off would be turned into a contest, and you could bet he'd find some way of being better at it.

Michael went into the house. He found his mother in the kitchen, discussing the evening meal with Sadie. He helped himself to one of the lemon crack cookies cooling on the table.

'Mom, I won't be here for dinner tonight. Me and some of the guys are going to the drive-in.'

'Oh. OK.'

He followed her out of the kitchen. 'Mom?'

'Hmmm?'

'Can I ask you something?'

'What is it?' She sounded distracted, as ever.

'It's about you and Dad.'

'What?' She turned to face him, but her eyes wouldn't meet his. That was how she was these days. She went on as normal, but she just wasn't interested in the people around her. The two of them weren't pals any more. He felt a surge of anger towards her, more than he had felt towards Daddy when he found the photograph. Why was she doing this to him, just disappearing some place where he had no hope of reaching her?

'Forget it,' he said. 'It doesn't matter.'

Michael stayed angry with his parents for the next two years. His mother remained withdrawn and his father travelled more and more without her. Michael speculated to himself about whether Aunt Beulah accompanied him on these trips. He had given up trying to talk to Travis about it. When his brother returned from college for the vacation all he could talk about was sport and his conquests with girls.

Then, slowly, the big empty space at the centre of Michael's life started to fill up. The thing that filled it, quite naturally, was sex. Not doing it, but being interested in doing it. During the summer of 1968, his interest was narrowed down from the general to the specific. From girls to one girl. Melody.

Melody Beck. He wrote it three hundred times inside the cover of the notepad he was using for his history assignment. It was kind of scary, this facet of his character that he had just discovered. A capacity for total obsession. 'Melody Beck' sang through his head from dawn to dusk. He spent his waking hours trying to remember every detail about her, creating elaborate fantasies in which he always came to her rescue like Superman. At night, he dreamed about her.

He had first noticed her because of her breasts. He remembered Travis commenting on them when she first joined the Country Club, and that started him off looking at them whenever he saw her at the club. Then he started to look at the rest of her, and pretty soon he forgot her breasts in favour of her long, slender legs, her thick ash-blonde hair and her grey eyes that crinkled at the corners when she smiled. At the time Travis first pointed her out she wore braces on her teeth, but this summer she had them removed to reveal a dazzling, white smile. Darting about the court in her tennis dress she looked the perfect all-American girl.

Michael was amazed by the thoroughness with which his growing obsession took hold, and the lengths to which it took him. He hung around in the office until the club secretary left her desk, then looked up her name in the register of members. Melody Karen Beck. Date of birth: 15 January 1952. The fact that she had turned sixteen several months ahead of him made her seem even more glamorous and unattainable. He pieced together more and more fragments of information with the zeal of a criminal investigator on his first case. She was in the twelfth grade at a select girls' academy in town, she had an older brother at Georgia State University and a younger sister called Lori. Her father was an eminent gynaecologist, practising at the Georgia Infirmary, and the family lived at a smart address in the centre of the city, in what was now known as the Historic District.

He feasted on these crumbs of information like a starving man, but he tried to restrict the amount of time he spent hanging around the court when she was playing. He didn't want her noticing and thinking he was weird, or goofy. Sometimes he nodded hello when he passed her, and she would smile shyly and hang her head.

The problem with obsession, Michael discovered, was that mere information didn't satisfy the appetite for long. He started to try and get closer.

One afternoon he went into the ladies' locker room when there was nobody about. His mother had left something behind, that was what he planned to tell people if he was caught. He found Melody's peg, recognising it by the blue sports' bag she always carried. She was out on court in her tennis whites, and her clothes were tossed carelessly over the bench. A gingham skirt and a white blouse with a Peter Pan collar. He lifted the blouse and pressed it tentatively to his face. It smelled sweetly of sweat and soap. His pulse quickened so dramatically that he could feel a throbbing in his temples. Underneath the blouse was a pink, lace-edged bra and matching panties. He touched them gently; they felt warm. Then with his heart thumping, he turned and ran from the room.

When he got home that evening he found that he was restless, unable to concentrate. This Melody thing was getting just crazy, he couldn't leave it alone. He told his parents he was going to visit Euphemia Bailey, and drove himself into town in the MG roadster that had been his sixteenth birthday gift.

He identified the Becks' house, a smart colonial villa on Huntingdon Street, shaded by trees that dripped with Spanish moss. He drove around the block, parked and started to saunter past as if he was really headed somewhere else. His heart leapt into his mouth when he realised that Melody was there, sitting on the porch. She wore jeans and her feet were bare. At the Country Club she tied her hair up in a braid or ponytail, but now it fell loose over her shoulders, making her appear older. That was why he hadn't recognised her right away.

She had seen him.

'Well, hi!'

'Hi.' He stopped in his tracks, and his arms flapped awkwardly by his sides. Where the hell was he going, if she asked?

'You're Michael, aren't you? Michael Macken?'

He started. 'How d'you know my name?'

She laughed, a deliciously unselfconscious giggle. 'You're kidding, aren't you? Everyone in Savannah knows who *you* are. I mean, with who your father is, and all.'

He realised suddenly that she was embarrassed, as though *she* was the one who had been caught checking up on *him*.

'Would y'all like some lemonade?'

'Sure. Thanks.' He went and sat next to her on the porch. He was trembling.

'Just wait until I tell the other girls at the club about this, they'll never believe it! And Michael, I just have to ask you something. . . .'

Michael had never really considered before that his name made him something of a celebrity in Savannah, even within the elite confines of the Savannah Country Club. But as Melody plied him with questions about his family's various homes, their cars, their servants, he discovered that she had already found out a lot more about him than he had about her.

'Would you like to come out and see the house some time?' he asked casually.

'You bet I would!'

'We could have a game of tennis, or maybe go and catch a movie or something.'

She grinned. 'Your own tennis court! That would be neat!'

Five hours after sniffing her blouse, he had a date with Melody Beck. He almost died of shock.

Once he had dated Melody several times, Michael allowed himself to relax a little. This was no longer a secret obsession. He was in love. He still thought about her all the time, but now it was the way she had looked at him, the things she had said to him that preoccupied his mind. He could even talk about her with his friends. He hadn't managed to get beyond a chaste kiss on the lips yet, but Melody certainly seemed to like him a lot. Being Michael Macken was turning out to be worthwhile after all.

This knowledge filled him with an intense feeling of inner warmth, something he hadn't experienced since Honoree died. Someone was out there for him. It didn't matter any more that

Mom had no love left for him and Daddy viewed him as second best. He had Melody.

Travis came home from Boston at the end of June, sporting fashionably long hair.

'Say, little brother, what's this I hear about you dating? Who's the lucky girl?'

'Melody Beck.'

'Melody . . . not *the* Melody? The one with the. . . .'

He cupped two imaginary protruberances at the front of his sweater. 'Well, what a guy!'

For once, even Travis was showing an interest in him. He plied Michael with questions about the progress of their relationship, including how 'far' they were going.

'Not even made it to first base yet, huh? Keep trying!'

Michael certainly planned to. He was going to escort Melody to her prom dance the following week, and had made up his mind that they were going to have a proper kiss. And he might even pluck up courage to tell her that he loved her.

'Hey, you look gorgeous!' Michael swivelled round in the front seat of his car to admire Melody when she climbed in beside him. She wore a pure white dress with a boned silk bodice and a flimsy organza skirt. Her hair had been curled into ringlets and caught up with white gardenias. She wore a corsage of gardenias on her wrist, and carried a white lace stole.

She smiled at him. 'You look kind of swell yourself. I like the tux.'

Michael took one hand off the wheel and closed it around Melody's. When they stopped at the next intersection, he leaned across to kiss her cheek, but she stiffened slightly at his touch. She seemed nervous. Maybe she was worried that he would muss up her dress, or her hair.

When they got to the dance, Melody disappeared into the crowd of her friends, swallowed up into a rainbow of frothing skirts, as they all admired one another's gowns. It was a long while before she came back. Michael stood and waited by the punchbowl, fingering the white lace stole she had given him to hold, and pulling at his unfamiliar wing collar. Melody reappeared and they danced together to Patsy Cline singing *Sweet Dreams*, then she spotted the brother of one of her oldest friends.

'I just *have* to go and dance with Marlon, you don't mind, do you?'

She kept this up for most of the evening, darting here and there, treating Michael as though he were little more than a convenient coatstand. Every now and then he thought he saw one of the other boys flash a look of sympathy in his direction.

Finally, he cornered Melody and led her out onto the terrace. If he was ever going to carry out his plan he would just have to get on and do it. Holding both her shoulders to keep her still, he brought his mouth down over hers, and gently, tentatively, covered her lips. Immediately he felt a swimming sensation in his legs, fireworks going off in his brain.

When they died down he realised she wasn't kissing him back. In fact she was keeping her lips firmly closed in an attempt to discourage him.

'Michael, don't, please.'

He let go of her shoulders. 'Melody, what the hell is going on with you? You've been avoiding me all night – '

'I'd like to go home.'

'What, are you ill or something?'

'Something like that. Please, just let's go.'

Maybe it was women's troubles, Michael thought. He had heard guys say that it made girls act funny at certain times of the month. Melody was very quiet all the way home. He didn't try to kiss her again.

'When shall I see you?' he asked, as he climbed out to open the door for her. 'Shall we go out tomorrow? We could go to McCrory's for an icecream soda or something.'

She shrugged her shoulders. 'I don't know, Michael. . . .'

'I wish you'd tell me what's wrong.'

She stood on tip-toe to plant a kiss on his cheek. 'I'll call you tomorrow, OK?'

It didn't feel OK. He had a sick, cold feeling inside his stomach that kept him awake all night like the ringing of an alarm bell. He didn't know if Melody was going to call or not; he didn't intend to sit around and wait. The following evening he called her.

'Oh, hullo, Mrs Beck, I'd like to speak with Melody, please. It's Michael Macken.'

'Michael?' She sounded confused. 'Oh . . . well, I'm afraid Melody's not here just now. She went out. Shall I give her a message?'

'No, thank you.'

The alarm bells were getting louder. If Melody wasn't in when Michael called, her mother usually told him exactly what she was doing: 'Oh, she just popped over to Sue Ann's' or 'She and Lori just went out for a soda, they won't be gone long'. 'She went out' had a sinister ring to it.

He drove down to Huntingdon Street and parked his car a few yards from the house. He would wait. Whatever was going on, he wanted to confront her face to face. Or maybe she was ill. Maybe she just went to the doctor or something. A hundred innocent explanations went through his mind in the two hours he sat and waited.

And then he saw her. Of course! The most obvious explanation and he hadn't even considered it. She was in a car, a car which until seven o'clock that evening had been parked alongside his MG in the garage. Travis's Corvette. When Travis said he was going out on a date, he had barely even listened, let alone bothered to ask with whom. Travis was always going on a date.

Michael's car was parked in the shadow of one of the giant oaks, so they didn't even see him. With the headlights on and the engine still running, Travis leaned over and in one smooth movement pulled on the parking brake and started kissing Melody. Michael couldn't quite suppress a feeling of admiration. You had to hand it to Travis, he knew what he was doing.

And Melody could obviously tell she was in the hands of an expert; she went all limp and soft in his arms, only moving her head slightly to slide her lips to and fro. She was kissing him back. The way her cheeks looked all hollowed, she was using her tongue as well. Travis's fingers roamed over her cashmere sweater like two large brown spiders, squeezing her breasts with the subtlest of movements. Well he would, wouldn't he? That was all he was interested in. Melody Beck's breasts. Michael didn't even feel greatly comforted when Melody pushed his hands away from the edge of her brassiere. She was probably saving the next base for the next date.

All that good, warm feeling that Melody had given him, that feeling of being somebody significant, had evaporated in the time it took Travis to steal a kiss from the girl he thought was his. Why the hell shouldn't she be interested in Travis? He had the Macken name, and more besides. He was a handsome, suave college jock. Why wouldn't she prefer him?

Michael closed his eyes and thumped his steering wheel so hard that his hand was still throbbing when he got home.

'Look, it was no big deal,' said Travis the next day. 'I saw her a couple of times down at the club, and she was coming on kind of . . . you know, friendly. So I asked her for a date. She made out there was nothing going on between you guys. . . . I know what you're thinking, but I didn't get her cherry. It's all yours, buddy. I'm not out to get involved with some school kid and have her cramping my style the whole summer. Just look on my dating her as getting her warmed up for you. She's hot to trot now, just dying for it. So get in there, little brother, get in and give her a fucking that'll make her remember the name Macken for ever. Jesus, she'll probably get it tattooed on her fanny by the time you and I have finished with her. . . .'

Melody phoned Michael that evening. She sounded tearful. Travis had probably just given her the brush-off.

'Michael, I'm so sorry, I don't know what happened to me back there. . . . I met your brother and I guess he just kind of bowled me over. You know, he just paid me all these compliments, and then when he asked me out I kind of thought, why not? it's only one date. . . . Michael, are you still there?'

'Yeah.'

'Well, nothing happened. I mean nothing's going to happen. Travis is going back to Harvard in the fall, so there's no question of getting heavy. . . . I know I acted kind of off at the prom, but I was just feeling a little confused. I didn't know whether I should tell you about seeing Travis or not. In the end I figured what the hell? It probably won't come to anything. . . . Are you still there, Michael?'

'Yeah.'

'So what I'm saying is, all this doesn't mean we can't see each other. We can still go on dating.'

'No,' said Michael. 'I'm sorry, Melody, but I've changed my mind. It's over.'

Michael was relieved when the summer of 1968 came to an end, and he could get on with his final year at high school. But once he was there, he found it hard to concentrate. His grades started to slip from straight As to Bs and even Cs. Rather than being worried, he found he didn't care very much.

Al Macken came up to his room one evening when he had gone upstairs to do his homework. He had his feet on the desk, and the Beach Boys turned up to full volume.

'Jeez, Mikey. . . .' Al surveyed the carpet, strewn with dirty undershorts, socks, sneakers and record sleeves. The bed was like a balled-up pile of laundry with an overflowing ash tray perched on top. 'Your mom said your room was kind of messy but . . . what happened in here? You always used to be a tidy kind of guy.'

Michael shrugged, but made no comment.

'Anyhow. . . .' Al continued to look around the room as though its contents were making him uncomfortable. 'It's your seventeenth birthday next week. I guess you're a little old to be taken down to River Street now?'

'I guess.'

'I have to go to New York on that day, but maybe we could go for a soda some other day, or catch a baseball game. They sent me free season tickets. . . .'

'It's Travis who likes baseball, Dad, not me.'

Michael swung his legs off the desk and waited. He knew his father hadn't come to talk about his birthday.

'Well, let's talk school. You'll be going up to Harvard next fall, but your principal tells me that your grades are not up to the mark. . . .'

Al found a corner of the bed free of clutter and sat down heavily. 'What concerned me about my conversation was not so much the poor grades but some nonsense about you wanting to major in Liberal Studies.'

'Yeah, that's right.'

'But we always said you were going to read Law, then do your MBA.'

'*You* said that, Dad. That was your decision, and Travis went along with it, just like he always does.' Michael turned his dark eyes full on his father's face, and watched him wince. Michael knew his eyes spooked his father, and sometimes it was fun to take advantage of that. 'My decision is to do something different. I think a Law major would bore the shit out of me.'

'Oh?' Al pretended to examine his fingernails. 'Travis seems to be finding it interesting. A challenge. . . . I think you'll be pleasantly surprised when you try it. So I'll tell your principal – '

'You won't tell him shit!' Michael sprang to his feet, his dark eyes flashing. He was taller than his father now, something else which freaked the old man out. 'I'm sorry, Dad, but I made a decision a few months back. I decided I wasn't going to fall into the trap of competing with Travis for the rest of my life. It might give you a kick to see us scoring points in order to please you, but I think there's something sick about it.'

'But, Michael, where's the competition? I built MackenCorp to be big enough for both of you, and still have plenty left over. I want *both* of you guys up there in the boardroom with me. As soon as you graduate you become senior vice-presidents, both of you. That's automatic – '

'Forget it, Dad! This may surprise you but I don't want a seat on the board. I'll leave all that stuff for Travis, the whole goddamn lot of it! He's going his way, and I intend to go mine. If he wants something, then I don't. *That's* automatic!'

FIVE

Cambridge, Massachusetts, 1973

Peg Anderson sat on the edge of Audree Simon's room in their dorm house at Radcliffe, watching her friend make herself up in preparation for a date. Her other great friend, Sara, was on the bed too, which meant there was not much space for Peg. Sara was as broad as she was tall, with bushy dark hair that grew from her head at right angles. She wore round, gold-rimmed glasses – not because she was myopic but as a sort of insignia, the badge of the intellectual. She had a relentlessly cheerful nature and liked nothing better than to sit around and gossip about who was sleeping with whom on campus.

Sara's short, squat body was dominated by an enormous bust which projected from her like a shelf, and which she tried to disguise by wearing loose-fitting smocks. Audree, on the other hand, had no bust at all. Her body was as thin and straight as a boy's and clad unvaryingly in black. Audree (with the emphasis on 'odd', as some of the Radcliffe students joked) came from Mendocino in Northern California, where her mother, a latter-day hippy, ran a herbal drugstore. 'She's, like, basically a witch,' drawled Audree. Audree had long, straight hair which was fiercely peroxided to a shade of lemon yellow.

She had lined up rows of pots containing a variety of fascinating potions, some of them from her mother's pharmacy. She scooped up a handful of green lotion from one, and spread it lavishly over her face until the surface of her skin shone. Then she dabbed little specks of orangey foundation on top and blended it in.

'Hey, Audree, isn't that going to be a little dark?' asked Sara.

'It depends on the lighting,' said Audree confidently. 'Where we're going the lighting's going to be kind of weird. You'll see.'

She slicked iridescent purple shadow onto her eyelids and then carefully outlined their rims with kohl.

Peg placed her chin on her hand with a happy sigh as she watched Audree searching about for the right lipstick. Protected from the world by the comfortable buffer of girlish friendship, she could almost be back in Liverpool with Sandra.

Oh, but this place was so different. Had she ever seen the architectural glories of England's Oxford and Cambridge, she might have been disappointed by Cambridge, Massachusetts, with its more utilitarian scale, the solid red-brick buildings huddled alongside the river, the randomness of Harvard Square, a place that seethed rather than dreamed. But until she came here she had never set foot outside Liverpool, so to her it was a magical place, a seat of learning that was lively and cosmopolitan. The neoclassical red brick and white pillars of Radcliffe Square were elegant and gracious after the Liverpool docks, and the lofty proportions of the college's dorm houses seemed positively palatial.

She had wanted so desperately to belong here, but when she arrived in 1970 Harvard and Radcliffe were going through the most turbulent year of their history. Students who opposed the Vietnam War had been protesting so forcibly against the university's links with the Reserve Army Training Corp that state troopers had been called in to disperse them and there had even been talk of the university having to close to maintain civil order. Peg was dismayed when she found not groups of blonde, suntanned cheerleaders going cheerfully to their classes, but angry young women who blocked off Massachusetts Avenue chanting anti-war slogans and throwing Molotov cocktails. Stores had their fronts shattered and their contents looted, the window of the president's office in Harvard Square was covered in protective plastic.

Peg did not join in any of these activities. She did not dare. To the other students, protesting against the establishment took precedence over getting an education, but for Peg that education meant everything. She had far too much to lose. Even now that they were in their senior year and Cambridge was much quieter, Peg still refused when Audree tried to drag her along to an anti-racist demonstration, or a rally to have pot legalised, or a love-in on Cambridge Common. There were still tensions over curricular reforms, and plans to merge Radcliffe and Harvard, and tensions could erupt into violence at any moment. The Administrative Board could demand that protesters withdraw from the College and, as Peg tried hard to impress on Audree, she could not take the risk because she had too much to lose.

The past three years had been an exercise in merging into the background. She shopped at the Harvard Co-op for jeans and sweat shirts and sneakers that would make her look like all the other students. She wore her long brown hair tied back in a pony tail, and no make-up. Still, she saw men staring at her sometimes when she walked through Harvard Yard. She would smile at them, and laugh when they winked or cat-called. If they tried to take things further, they discovered she was not interested.

Keeping a low profile meant she had a lot of time to devote to her studies, and for the past two years she had achieved the best grades in her year. Thanks to her friendship with Audree and Sara, she had not lived the life of a saint. She had been to parties, drunk a lot of cheap wine and smoked a little pot. She had even been on a few dates, but the men who were interested in her backed off, puzzled when she refused to go past kissing and kidding around. She was aware she was condemned as being a loner or a tease but this did not trouble her. She knew what she wanted, and anyway, just being here made her happy. She liked to walk down to the Harvard Bridge and watch the sailboats on the Charles River. Sometimes she crossed the river and went to explore Boston. Many of the students never ventured further than Cambridge, but Peg enjoyed escaping from the hot-house atmosphere of the campus. She liked to go down to Boston Harbor and look out for ships.

And because old habits are hard to shake off, she would spend time gazing out to the Atlantic, trying to see beyond the horizon. Being in America and facing towards England made her feel like Alice through the Looking Glass, looking at the world from the outside in. Liverpool had been turned into a tiny, make-believe world, and the things that happened there happened in a dream.

She had told her family she would visit them often, but it hadn't been easy. The Morrison Trust provided her with one free air ticket each year, and that was used up by the Christmas vacation. In the spring and summer she had not managed to find the money for the fare. The trust provided what was needed for tuition, board and lodging and some books. A waitressing job provided money for clothes and other essentials. But there was nothing left over for air tickets, and her parents didn't have that sort of money. So she had spent her vacations studying and exploring New England on her own. Last summer she had stayed with Sara's family in Wisconsin.

She still wrote to Jimmy and her parents regularly, knowing how much they relished the descriptions of her new life. It must have sounded like an entirely different world to them. Her father was retiring from the dockyard soon, her mother still worked at the library. Jimmy had a job on the buses now, as a conductor. The Neanderthals played in working men's clubs in the evenings but it was little more than a hobby now they knew they were never going to make it big. He had a steady girlfriend called Angie, and Peg knew it would not be long before they married and started a family. They were already saving up the deposit on their first home.

She wrote to Sandra too. In a way, she missed Sandra most of all. To begin with she wrote back and told Peg what Billy Walsh was up to. After a while she stopped.

'Well, I guess that just about does it.' Audree put down her lipstick and turned round to face Peg and Sara. 'D'you think I look OK?'

'Personally, I think you're wearing too much make-up,' said Sara cheerfully. 'I wouldn't have thought Jerry Blum was the kind of guy who was into it. But still . . . I guess you know him well enough by now.'

'I don't know, we never talked about it.' Audree grabbed a tissue and wiped off some of the foundation. 'And last but not least . . . I'd better not forget to take this!'

She produced a small blue plastic box and opened it with a flourish. Inside was a diaphragm.

'*Audree!*' said Sara.

'I know – they're, like, gross-looking, aren't they?' She sighed. 'When you've been going with a guy for so long that you know to take your diaphragm along it takes away the fun somehow. You know . . . you know how it feels at the beginning?'

Sara giggled. 'You mean when you think you might need to take some protection along but you're still not totally sure?'

'Yeah. And d'you remember what it's like the first time you go all the way with someone, and you just *know* that it's about to happen and you're wondering what he'll be like, you know, how you'll feel when he *actually* penetrates you, like are you going to – ?'

Peg stood up. 'I think I'll go back to my room and do some study.'

'PEG!' Audree gave an exasperated screech. 'Just when the conversation gets real interesting you always run out on us!'

Peg was about to mumble some excuse and slip out when there was a knock and the girl on 'bells' stuck her head round the door.

'Audree, your date called, he says he's just on the way over but to say he's bringing a friend so can you fix up someone to double with.'

'That'll be Hamilton,' said Audree. 'Jerry said he might bring him over. He wants to meet some nice Cliffies, apparently.'

'Tell him to go to Wellesley,' said Sara crossly. They all disliked the patronising name given to Radcliffe girls by Harvard men.

'I tell you, those girls at Wellesley would *love* to get their hands on Hamilton Winslow VI.'

'The sixth!' exclaimed Sara.

'I know, a total WASP. His family have been in Massachusetts for ever, they practically came over with the Pilgrims . . . so, how about a double date? Peg?'

'No, thank you,' said Peg firmly, but she stayed, out of curiosity, until the two men arrived. Jerry Blum had been dating Audree for several months and she had met him before. She liked him, enjoying the combination of his overt radicalism and intense sexuality. It was fun to flirt with Jerry. He was small and dark and wiry, with piercing blue eyes that would look her up and down before fixing on her breasts. She put this down to a kind of starvation on his part; Audree's chest was as flat as a board.

The two men made an odd couple, since Hamilton Winslow was very tall and very blond. He had large, meaty hands that flapped awkwardly at his sides and he blushed when he looked at Peg.

'You have him,' Peg whispered to Sara with a giggle. 'Definitely not my type!' She fled to the sanctuary of her room before there could be any discussion of what constituted her 'type'. She knew Audree and Sarah found it odd that she never dated men more than once or twice, and wasn't interested in sleeping with them. Everyone had sex these days without being married or even going steady, it was not considered a big deal.

The truth was that Peg found the necking pleasant, exciting even, but was afraid to go further in case she liked it too much and had to suffer the inconvenience of falling for the man in question. That might mean a real relationship, which would take more of her time and energy than she was prepared to give. She had become adept at putting off men by talking about how important her work and her future career were to her.

Guaranteed to put them off, she reflected as she sat down at her desk. Men didn't really like women who wanted to go all the way to the top; it threatened them. Study was the only place she could hide. Smiling grimly to herself, she picked up her pen.

'I guess we'd better get round to some studying.'

Michael Macken looked at the girl whose name he could not quite remember. Sherry? Shelley? She was pretty. Well, kind of. She didn't look her best right now, sprawled across the bed with her legs wide apart. Her faded Indian print skirt was twisted around her hips and her skimpy yellow T-shirt was rucked up above her breasts. Both her chest and her pubic area were daubed with dark, sticky streaks; they had been taking it in turns to squirt Hershey's sundae sauce over one another and then lick it off.

He let his gaze wander around the room. Michael had a suite of rooms in Eliot House, and their entire surface area was littered with soiled, expensive clothes, empty cola bottles, beer cans, rumpled editions of the *Boston Globe* and *National Lampoon*, reeking ashtrays.

'Study? What's that?' he asked. A smile spread across his face and he half closed his eyes. Leaning forward, he licked at a chocolate-flavoured nipple.

'Hmmm . . . I think I missed a bit.'

Holding the grubby yellow T-shirt out of the way, he let his mouth travel down towards the girl's navel while his fingers probed the stickiness between her legs. She sighed and squirmed, but after a few seconds pushed his hand away.

'I feel like doing a joint,' she said. 'Do you have any stuff?'

'Well, sure.' Michael looked around the room doubtfully. There probably was some hash here somewhere, but he had no idea where to start looking. 'How about coffee? Jack Daniels?'

'Joint first, please.'

She smoothed her skirt down and settled back on the pillows like a cat preparing for sleep.

There was a knock on the door, and before Michael had a chance to ask the caller to wait a minute, it opened. Al Macken stood there contemplating his son, who was completely naked except for a thin covering of chocolate sauce.

'Looks like I'd better come back later.'

'Was that your girlfriend?' Al asked Michael when he stood in the centre of the same room two hours later. He noted that Michael had made no attempt at tidying up but he had showered and put on T-shirt and jeans. The girl had vanished.

'Girlfriend?' Michael frowned. 'No, she's just, you know, a girl.'

'Well, the two of you surely had plenty to entertain you.' Al checked his disapproving tone, forced a smile. 'Say, the limo's waiting downstairs, and I've got a couple of tickets for the Red Sox. We could drive out to Fenway Park and catch a game.'

'I think you've got the wrong son,' said Michael coldly. 'Travis is the one who's stuck on baseball, remember?'

'Mikey, you're going to have to drop this jealousy thing – '

The telephone rang in the study, and Michael went to answer it. Al overheard him saying, '. . . a sorority party up at Wellesley . . . yeah, that would be cool. I can bring alcohol, sure, why not?'

He felt a surge of irritation at his good-looking, charming, easy-going son. When Michael was off the phone he said: 'Anyways, I didn't come up here to take you out to a baseball game. I need to talk to you.'

Michael wandered round the room looking for socks and shoes. 'Shoot.'

'Your tutor has been in contact with me. He said your grades stink. And the reason they stink is not because you're stupid but because you haven't attended any lectures or handed in a single written assignment for this semester. At this rate, he says, you're not going to commence at all. In fact, if it weren't for the endowments the Macken Corporation has made to this university, you would have been slung out on your ass long ago.'

Michael shrugged. 'Well, that's cool then, isn't it? Because right now Harvard really needs the money. Financially, the place is going down the toilet.'

'Michael!'

'Well what do you want me to say here, Dad?'

'I want to know just what is going on with you. You gave law school a miss in favour of liberal arts; OK, I went along with that. I figured it might even be a good thing to have my two sons major in different specialties. It's kind of a diversification. But right now you seem to be majoring in . . . girls.'

'Dad, don't give me a hard time about – '

The telephone rang again.

'. . . Sure, I'd like that. Why don't you come on over to Eliot later and we can go the party together.'

'It's a pity you can't put the same effort you devote to your social life into your studies,' said Al angrily when Michael had hung up. The two of them faced one another and Al found himself staring once again into James Macken's eyes. Michael's defiance reminded him of himself at eighteen, but he had been defying his father by wanting to do something with his life. Michael's defiance lay in doing nothing.

'Listen son, we're getting nowhere like this. Let's go out.'

Michael refused to ride in the limousine, so they crossed the bridge and walked to Boston Gardens. Families were strolling about, feeding the squirrels, listening to a blues band busking next to the Arlington Street entrance.

'Travis is doing real well in New York,' said Al. 'He's found premises on Park Avenue for the new MackenCorp offices, and he's identified a whole portfolio of interested investors. He seems to like Manhattan too. . . .' He shuddered slightly. 'I don't think

I'd like to trade places. The north-east makes me feel uncomfortable. Places like this – ' he gestured to a crowd of students gathered around a speaker on his soap box – 'make me feel uncomfortable. Part of being an uneducated Southerner, I guess.'

Michael curled his lip. 'You're not about to give me all that hokey about the good old South, are you? To you it's all Rhett Butler and magnolias and pretty women who revere their masterful men. It's all sentimental bullshit.'

'Hey listen, I have no reason to be sentimental about the old South. The town where I was born was just this nothing place in the middle of nowhere. It was hot, and swampy and mean. Everyone was dirt poor and ignorant with it, mistrustful of new ideas. And I could have run off and started up my business in New York, or California, but I didn't. I stayed in Georgia because I wanted to change the way things were, to show that life can be different. And it's because I stayed that I can feel pride now in being a Southerner.'

'Well, I'm not proud!' retorted Michael. 'I try and change the way I talk when I'm here just so people won't realise that I come from the South. Because to people here, the South is where blacks get oppressed and students get killed for their beliefs. It's backward and it's ugly. People down there want to live in the past.'

'Yes, but I'm talking about the *new* South! Things are changing so fast, and the new South is all about the future. It's about investing money so that there's prosperity and decent education, and people have a chance to change their ways. That's where you belong!'

'I don't think I know where I belong,' said Michael quietly. He sat down on a bench beside the pond and asked, 'How's Mom?'

Al shrugged. 'Oh, you know. . . .'

'And how's my aunt?'

Al was taken aback.

'You don't imagine that Travis and I don't know about you and Beulah, do you? We've known for years.'

'Now, Michael, listen – '

'Does Mom know?'

Al looked down at his hands. 'Yes . . . well, I guess so.'

'You mean you haven't talked about it?'

'No.'

'Does she care?'

'I don't know, Michael. I love your mother – God knows, there was a time when I thought I'd never feel that, but I do – but sometimes I'm not sure if she still loves me. You know how she changed when . . . well, you know.'

'When Honoree died.'

Michael meant the words to provoke, but his father merely looked pained.

'Do you love Beulah too?'

Al stood up and they started walking again. 'We go back a long way, to before I married Cordella. We were in love then, but giving her up was the price I had to pay for the Macken Corporation. It was what your grandaddy Peabody wanted, and I badly needed his help, otherwise . . . anyhow, I don't regret it. If I hadn't have married your mother I never would have had you and Travis.'

'And Honoree.'

A shadow passed across Al's face. 'Let her rest in peace, Michael.'

Michael's voice grew hard with anger. 'It would be convenient if we could forget things, wouldn't it? Like the fact that you didn't really have to make a sacrifice at all. You didn't "pay the price", as you put it, unless you believe that losing your daughter was the price God made you pay. You took it all: Mother, Travis and I, the corporation *and* Beulah, the perfect mistress! I bet she's great in the sack – '

'*Shut up!*' Al blocked the path, stopping Michael in his tracks. 'Now just you listen up, boy! I haven't come here to talk about what I've done wrong and how I've been punished! I'm not going to play games here, I'm just going to tell you the bottom line. Finish your studies and graduate, or no more allowance and no more trust fund. You won't have a dime!'

'So, how was Hamilton Winslow VI?' Peg asked Sara. 'I never did find out how your date went.'

'He was a nerd,' said Sara. She scooped powder creamer into

a mug of coffee and lit a cigarette. 'But quite a sweet nerd really, if you like that kind of thing – emotionally retarded WASPs.'

'Which you don't.'

'Which I don't. However, one day my prince will come.' Sara sighed contentedly and dragged on her cigarette. 'Actually, I think he was more interested in you.'

'Really?' Peg walked to the window of her room in Briggs House and looked out at the Radcliffe Quadrangle. It was a warm fall afternoon and the sun glinted on the blue and gold clock tower of North House. The leaves on the tree were just starting to change. Peg loved the seemingly endless palette of colours. At home in Liverpool the leaves just turned brown and dropped to the ground in wet heaps. Here in New England their shading ran through every imaginable hue from lemon to mustard and ginger.

'You ought to go out more, Peg. Audree thinks so too. You're by far the best looking of the three of us – by rights you should be dating every night.'

Peg smiled indulgently at her friend. 'Sarah, it's nice of you to think of me, but this is our senior year, remember? It's only seven months until commencement. I just want to – '

There was a muffled groan, then the door was flung open and Audree stood on the threshold with a towel wrapped round her shoulders to catch the muddy droplets that streamed from her hair.

'It's gone green! Look – my goddam hair has turned green!'

Peg lifted a damp strand and examined it. 'I wouldn't say it was green exactly. Green*ish*.'

'Honest to God, I mixed up the henna exactly like it said on the packet. It had a little chart on the back, and if you're in the "Fair" section you're supposed to turn into "Strawberry blónde".'

'Maybe you're not supposed to use it on peroxide,' Sara suggested. 'It's probably had a weird reaction to the chemicals. A girl back home got green hair when she swam in a pool with too much chlorine in it.'

Audree sighed. 'I just thought being a strawberry blonde would be cool. Mom sent me the stuff from Mendocino, but she said it worked best on brunettes. . . .' A gleam came into her eye. 'Peg! Your hair would be just perfect!'

'No really, Audree, I – '

'Come on! It would be kind of an interesting experiment, don't you think? It's terribly good for the condition and it washes out after a couple of shampoos. . . . '

'*Magnificent!*' said Audree several hours later. 'You look just sensational – doesn't she, Sara?'

Peg had submitted to having her hair smeared in thick green mud and then wrapped in foil for what seemed an eternity. It dried and caked and itched. Then it had to be rinsed out; a lengthy, messy process during which all of them were splattered with rust-coloured stains.

Once her hair was thoroughly clean, Audree had dried it around a circular brush, twisting and flicking it in the hot air until it fell in rippling waves. She held up a mirror to display the finished result.

Peg was forced to agree that the transformation was quite startling. Her nut-brown locks were a glowing shade of Titian that looked almost natural. Being a redhead suited her. It warmed the slightly sallow tone of her skin and accentuated her grey eyes, making them look almost blue.

'We shouldn't let this beauty go to waste,' declared Audree. 'We'll get dressed up, all of us, and go out and hit Cambridge tonight like three sirens from hell!'

'I don't have anyth-'

Audree placed her fingers over Peg's lips. '*Don't* tell me that you don't have anything to wear! I've seen the very thing right here in your wardrobe.'

She rummaged around and found a black velour mini-dress that Peg had bought in a Liverpool boutique on one of her shopping trips with Sandra three years earlier. It had hardly been worn.

'This is perfect. You're gonna knock their eyes out. Wait. Where are you going. . .? We haven't finished with you yet. I'm going to do you a full make-up. You won't know yourself.'

She didn't. Audree stroked smoky shadow around her eyes and blacked her lashes so that her eyes appeared huge and lustrous. Her mouth was painted with a claret-coloured lipstick that accentuated the deep curve of her upper lip. The finishing touches were silver hoops at her ears and bangles on her wrists.

'I don't feel like me,' Peg complained, as the three of them walked down John F. Kennedy Street to the Boat House Bar. 'It must be to do with being a redhead; I feel as if I've borrowed someone else's identity.'

'You have,' said Sara. 'Just for tonight you're a femme fatale.'

Claiming that there wasn't time, neither of the others had made any effort to get dressed up. Sara was dressed in baggy work overalls, and Audree in skintight jeans. Next to them, Peg felt like some over-exotic bloom, a mannequin on her way to a photographic shoot. Once they had ordered a bottle of wine and she had drunk a few glasses, she started to relax. The bar was warm and crowded and smoky. Heads had turned to stare at her as she went to sit down, but she did not mind it in the way she did when she was just plain ordinary old Peg.

'That guy over there keeps staring at you,' whispered Audree. 'Don't look now, but he's on that table in the corner, to your right.'

'Don't worry, I've no intention of looking!' hissed Peg. She poured more wine into her glass.

'Well you should!' giggled Audree. 'Back in high school he would have been described as a "dreamboat".'

Peg raised her head slightly and peered over the rim of her glass. There was no denying he was handsome. Even sitting at a table you could tell he was very tall, and even in this gloom he looked tanned. He had dark brown hair swept back from his forehead, and every so often he ran his hand through it in a way that was distracted rather than vain. He had large hands, Peg noticed, with long, broad fingers.

This is silly, she told herself, now you're getting hung up on the hands of a complete stranger.

'I expect he's waiting for someone.'

'Uh-uh.' Sara shook her head sagely. 'Only one glass. And look at the way he's drinking it. If he was expecting company he wouldn't go so fast.'

The young man had dispensed with the services of the bar staff and had a bottle of bourbon on the table in front of him. He had already drunk about a third of it, draining his tumbler at regular intervals. As he lowered it on the table, his eye caught Peg's. She put her wine glass down, flustered. The way he had looked at her made her feel strange inside.

'I think I'll just go to the ladies' room. . . .'

She stood up and hurried away. Inside the cubicle she locked the door and leaned against it for a while. Then she shook herself. This was crazy! He was just a guy!

She splashed a little water on her face and scrubbed at the dark red lipstick with a tissue, trying to remove some of it. No wonder the man had been staring at her; she looked as if she was out to be picked up. She would go back into the bar and tell Sara and Audree that they should move on, go over the river to one of the jazz clubs in Back Bay, maybe.

When she returned to the bar, Sara and Audree were gone. She glanced out into the street in panic, then saw that only one wine glass remained on the table, with the bottle beside it. They had deliberately left her behind. She had been set up. They had probably been planning this from the moment they dyed her hair and dressed her up, only she had been so preoccupied with the way she looked she hadn't even noticed.

She went back to the table and sat down. Something compelled her to do this, even though her first impulse was to pay the bill and go straight back to Radcliffe. She sipped slowly at her wine, trying to look as if she drank on her own every day. She waited.

Inevitably, he came over to her table. She quelled her panic by remembering her appearance. It's all right, she told herself. I'm in disguise. This isn't really me.

'May I sit down?'

His voice was deep and quiet, with a gentle lilt, an accent she did not recognise save knowing that he was not a Bostonian. He did not sit opposite her but pulled up a chair so that they were side by side. At close quarters he was much younger than she had at first imagined, probably around twenty-one or twenty-two.

He smiled at her as though he was genuinely delighted not to have been sent away. He's rich, she thought suddenly. Those immaculate white teeth were the result of years of expensive dentistry. The Swiss watch he wore was solid gold and the loafers were the kind that cost $200 a pair in Saks. He was sitting up straight, but you could tell that he had drunk a lot.

'It was your hair that made me come over, ma'am – '

Peg laughed. 'Please don't call me "ma'am", it makes me feel a hundred. My name's Peg.'

'Peg?' He frowned a little, and she knew he was thinking the name did not match her appearance. 'It's the colour, I guess. Red hair always did kind of stand out.' He added, almost to himself, 'My aunt has red hair. You sure could say she stands out.'

'Really,' said Peg, in a tone that implied she didn't have the slightest interest in his aunt. He obviously wasn't going to be put off easily, so she asked, 'What's your name?'

'Michael. Michael Macken.'

'Ah. As in the Macken Corporation.'

'You've heard of it?'

'Of course. One of the fifty biggest companies in the USA.'

'You're majoring in business, then?'

'No, economics. But I hope to go on to the Business School, if I can get a place.'

'No kidding?' He laughed, but it was not a sympathetic laugh.

'What's wrong with that?' Peg asked sharply. Her defences shot up, instantly. 'Don't tell me you're one of these men who don't believe in women in business?'

'Honey, I don't believe in *anyone* in business. All those fat cats chasing the same prizes, falling over each other and stabbing each other in the back just to grab a slice of the pie. All trying to prove they're cleverer than the next man. You don't want to be doing all that shit. Go and find yourself something real to do. Something worth your talents.'

Peg bristled. 'Tell me,' she said coldly. 'Have you any idea how patronising that sounds?'

He shrugged. 'That's just the way I see it. And I know plenty about it, believe me.'

'Oh you do, do you? Well allow me to be the judge of what's best for me.'

'Sure. You're just one of those little girls who wants to join in the boys' games.'

Peg stood up to go. 'I don't have to listen to this.'

He put a hand on her wrist. 'Sit down – please.'

She relented.

'Sit down and have a drink with me. Or better still, come with me for a walk. . . . Want to go down to the river?' he asked as they left the bar together. 'I like to go down there sometimes and just look at the water. It reminds me of home.'

Me too, thought Peg, me too. They relapsed into silence as they walked down to Anderson Bridge, close but not touching. It was much colder now that the sun had set, and a damp white mist was settling over the river. Michael took off his jacket and hung it over her shoulders. It smelled musty, of aftershave and marijuana.

He leaned on the bridge. 'You didn't like what I told you before.'

'You said what you thought. I don't happen to agree, that's all.'

'Well I do know a little about the world of business. And if I have to play by the same rules as the rest of my family, I don't want in.'

He looked thoughtful, and for a while didn't seem to want to speak. Peg took the opportunity to look at him more closely. She had always thought the adjective 'piercing' was confined to blue eyes. Michael's eyes were dark brown and still they managed to pierce; sad and sexy at the same time. She tried looking down at his hands instead; large sun-tanned hands with clean white nails.

Michael sighed.

'I was supposed to go to a party tonight, but I had to make a decision,' he said abruptly. 'Peg, which do *you* think is better: to have a whole lot of money, or not to have any?'

'I don't know; I've never really had any. I like to *make* money though. I think it's fun. Power is fun.'

He ran an eye over her vampish dress. 'You don't really look like the kind of girl who would be interested in business.'

'Appearances deceive. This isn't really me.'

He waited for her to explain, but she was silent.

'The kind of money I'm talking about isn't the kind you earn. It's the kind of money you're given when someone else has earned it.'

'I wouldn't like that kind of money,' said Peg emphatically, 'it creates obligations.'

'Yeah. . . .' Michael sighed. 'Money's OK, it's the obligations I don't want.'

'Then you'd be better off without the money.'

'I guess you're right. . . .'

He leaned out over the edge of the bridge, screwing his eyes up to look out as far as he could towards the horizon. Beneath the mist the dark water reflected the neon street lights with quivering pools of amber.

'I used to do this when I was a kid,' he said. 'Hanging out by the river was my favourite thing.'

'Mine too.'

'In England, huh?'

'You don't exactly have to be Einstein to work that out.' Peg was always conscious that she hadn't lost her accent.

'. . . And with no money. What does your daddy do?'

'He builds ships.'

Michael laughed. 'Isn't that strange! So does mine. Only my daddy has a whole heap of money.'

He shivered slightly. Instinctively, moved closer.

There was an awkward pause.

'So, I guess we go back to my place now.'

Peg was taken aback at his arrogance. She stepped away from him, frowning.

'You know you want to.'

Not true, she wanted to say. But it was true. He was looking down at her, long and hard, with those burning dark eyes. Then he kissed her. Long and hard.

Peg experienced the nearest thing to ecstasy she had ever known. The whole of her body shuddered and she had to lean against Michael's chest because her legs would no longer support her. I wanted him to do this, and now he is. And I want more. Not just his lips and tongue, but. . . . The thought disturbed her and she pulled away.

'What's wrong?'

'Nothing's wrong, I – '

'Good.' He kissed her again. 'Come with me.'

She followed him dumbly over the bridge, along Memorial Drive and into Eliot House.

★ ★ ★

Once they were inside, in the warm, slightly stuffy room, Peg was aware she had drunk more than she usually did. That must have been what was making her act like a slut, she told herself, rationalising her behaviour even then. She pushed Michael down onto the bed and began to stroke him all over. She started with her fingers on his wrists, touching the fine dark hair that showed beneath his cuffs. The warmth of his flesh was like a magnet. Tentatively she touched the nape of his neck. The skin was soft there, as soft as a child's. Her fingers seemed to melt into it, and the warm melting feeling ran down her fingers and up her arms, spreading over her body, darting between her legs.

Suddenly hungry for him, she ripped open the buttons of his shirt splaying and pressing her fingers across his naked chest, sucking and biting him. She cried out for sheer pleasure, reaching to his chinos and fumbling angrily at the belt buckle.

At some point during this exercise – and she never understood quite how – Michael had removed her pantyhose and underwear and lifted her onto his lap. There was a jolt of pain as he entered her, melting into a blissful warmth. If someone had told her then that she could do this for always, for ever, she could not have been happier.

She woke two hours later, with a dry mouth and a thumping head. For a moment she forgot where she was, then froze in panic.

Michael was still asleep, breathing quietly. She wriggled her limbs free from under him and dressed in the dark before creeping shamefully away.

'Peg. . .? Are you in there?'
Audree thundered along the corridor and stuck her head around Peg's door.
'Peg, you'll never guess what!' she hissed.
'Audree, I'm working. . . .'
'But, Peg, it's that guy! The one who picked you up in the bar last week!'
Peg felt her insides contract and her skin go cold. She laid down her pencil. 'Are you sure?'
'Of course. There can't be two like that around, he's far too gorgeous. And he's asking for you – '

'He can't be, he doesn't know my surname!'

'Shut up and listen, will you? Jeez! He's asking downstairs in the office for a red-haired girl called Peg. He's trying all the female colleges in Boston, apparently.'

Peg went out onto the landing and peered down the staircase. Michael was standing there in a cashmere overcoat slung over jeans and baseball boots. He had his back to her. She went back into her room quickly and shut the door.

'Audree, I want you to go down and tell him he's got the wrong place. There's only one Peg here but she's got brown hair. A different Peg.'

'But I don't understand, you're the one – '

'Audree, just look at me!' Peg stood in front of the mirror. She was dressed in a plaid skirt and a sweater, with her hair scraped back behind her ears. 'Look, do I have red hair? No! The colour has washed out and I'm myself again, getting on with my life. I'm not the person he went out with that night! That person doesn't exist any more!'

'But Peg – '

'Please, Audree, just do as I ask!'

She closed the door and listened for Audree's footsteps on the staircase. Then she crossed to the window and waited. A few seconds later, Michael came out of Briggs House and crossed the quadrangle with his hands in his pockets and his shoulders hunched. Peg stepped back quickly from the window so he wouldn't see her.

Audree came back into her room.

'Why don't you want to see him again?'

'Because he was rude and arrogant.'

Audree looked at her quizically. 'And?'

'He was rude and arrogant and I slept with him.' Audree had opened her mouth to speak, but Peg cut in: 'Look, it was a mistake, all right? I'd had too much to drink, it didn't mean anything. Best forgotten.'

'He came back looking for you, though. It obviously meant something to him. He could have just slept with you and dropped you. Thousands of guys do it all the time. So what's your problem?'

'Nothing, OK?' Peg glared at her friend. 'He's just a spoilt little rich kid, a Southerner. We have absolutely nothing in common.'

Audree shrugged. 'You're crazy, Peg, you know that?'

After she had gone, Peg stared at the title of her assignment for a full forty minutes, thinking so many negative thoughts about Michael Macken that she finally convinced herself she didn't even like him.

Michael pulled his collar up around his ears as he trudged across Radcliffe Quadrangle and out onto Linnaean Street. He was puzzled. He had only found two Peggies and one Peg in the whole of Cambridge, and he was so sure this was going to be the one. That girl he asked downstairs seemed to think so too, then seemed just as sure that he was wrong.

He went on looking for her for months, wherever he went, wherever there was a crowd of students. He became adept at singling out the girls with red hair, but they were never Peg. He had been so drunk that night he began to wonder if he could picture her at all, and eventually he stopped looking. The memory of her, the overwhelming combination of her bright, sparky intelligence and her sensuality, remained with him.

And Peg Anderson, who had no time for love, or men or commitment, remained hidden.

PART TWO

SIX

1976–1977

It was eight o'clock on a late November morning, and Michael Macken was looking out of the window of his ski cabin in Aspen, Colorado. It was going to be another fine day, he noted with satisfaction. The sun shone through a veil of white mist like a gold coin with its edges blurred. He also noted that the temperature was minus ten; a thick frost but too cold for snow. Already the machines were up there on the ski slopes above the town, blowing out clouds of artificial snow that covered the sides of the mountain like frosting on a cake. If you had enough money, Michael reflected, you didn't even have to let the weather stand in your way.

He showered and dressed and made his way up to the Snowmass village, and the headquarters of Happy Valley Dog-Sledding Inc. As soon as the 200 huskies heard his footfalls on the snow they started to whine and howl; an overwhelming cacophony that rang through the forest.

'Hey, you noisy brutes!' Michael called an affectionate greeting. He could not claim to know each individual dog like a musher could, but he was fond of the animals; they were eager and loyal and hard-working. For part of the year they trained and competed in races, but during the pre-Christmas ski season they took visitors on sleigh rides around the mountains. Michael's job was to spend a couple of hours a day harnessing up, cleaning kennels and maintaining equipment. One of these days he'd be experienced enough to take a sled out by himself, but he wasn't sure if he was going to hang around that long.

There were clients due for an eight o'clock ride, so Michael prepared the sled and helped lead out the thirteen dogs who had been selected to pull it. The chosen few writhed and shivered with pleasure, while their fellows left behind in the kennels howled even louder. Michael helped David, the musher, put the excited dogs into their harnesses, then handed the clients into their seats and tucked blankets and fur rugs around them. They were two young and expensively dressed blondes, 'ski-bunnies' of the type who thronged Aspen in the winter to spend their fathers' money and look out for a millionaire.

As he turned to go back into the kennels he overheard their conversation.

'Do you know who that was?' one of them whispered. 'Only Michael Macken! My uncle's best friend has done business with his father, and apparently he flunked out of Harvard and his father has cut him off without a dime. . . .'

'Really? You mean that guy who just . . .? He was gorgeous!'

'I know! And such a nice guy, too. What a shame he lost out on all that money. . . .'

Michael grinned. He was used to that sort of reaction when people found out about him, and it did not trouble him at all. Why should it? He felt more relaxed, more at ease with himself than he ever had before. He was having a good time. In this last couple of years, since he had defied his father by deliberately failing his final exams at Harvard, he had learned something important. He had learned to like himself.

And he had learned the real value of money. There was no trust fund to fall back on, and no vice-president's salary but there were dividends on shares that Clermont Peabody had bought in his name, and that was just about enough to give him a modest allowance for his food, lodging and clothes. The money he earned from his work at the kennels and his evening job as a barman went to pay for luxuries; a ski pass, nights out at Aspen's discos and bars. He was doing OK. He had enough to enjoy life's good things, what more did he need? And he was free. There were none of the obligations that the Macken money brought in its wake. If he wanted to leave this town then he could, any time he liked.

He probably would do that soon, he decided as he trudged back down to his cabin at midday. He would do a couple more months here, then he was going to head for Europe. He'd go to

St Moritz or Gstaad for the end of the skiing season, then he might wander on down to the south of France. Or Italy. Or Greece. He'd heard you could live very cheaply on the Greek islands and have a hell of a good time too. He could earn a bit of money teaching pretty girls to waterski. . . .

Michael had broken a sweat putting the dogs into harness and hauling heavy sleds out from under cover, so the first thing he did when he got back to his cabin was take a shower. After that he thought he might hit the slopes for a couple of hours and then take a nap before it was time to go and start work behind the bar of the Hotel Jerome. He might collapse into bed at two in the morning if he was lucky, then he would be up again at seven to go up to Snowmass. One thing was for sure, he had learned what it meant to work for a living. To really *work*.

Daddy thought that was what Travis was doing by joining MackenCorp. Working. But old college friends of Michael's who drifted in and out of Aspen from time to time said they had seen Travis in New York and he didn't really work at all. He just dressed up in fancy Yves Saint Laurent suits and sat behind a huge desk all day telling himself, and anyone else who would listen, how powerful he was. Michael wasn't surprised.

Travis Macken knew what it felt like to be royal.

He viewed MackenCorp as a kingdom, with Al as its king, and himself as its prince. Or Crown Prince, now that Michael had conveniently dropped out to go and breed dogs in Colorado, or whatever it was he was supposed to be doing.

Michael could have been royal too, could have had a share of the kingdom, but he just hadn't made the grade. It hadn't been easy for Travis, if he was honest. In order to earn the keys to the kingdom he had had to endure all those tedious years of study at Harvard. It had been really boring. Except for the sport. And the girls.

Travis went into the private washroom that adjoined his enormous office suite on Park Avenue. He came in here a lot. Part of that was to do with having little else to occupy him between his protracted lunch hour and cocktails, but he also liked to look in the mirror and confirm that it was really true. He was really here, heading the New York end of one of America's most powerful corporations. He was directly responsible for the jobs of several hundred people. It didn't matter that he was very poorly qualified to control an investment portfolio of close on a billion dollars. The point was that people believed he could do it. They acknowledged that the kingdom was his.

The reason, he knew, was because he looked so like his father that people started to believe they were the same person.

'You're the spit of Al,' his business contacts used to say in amazement. 'His mirror image!'

Travis smiled at the mirror and the mirror image returned his smile. He wore his hair the same way as his father now, short at the back and sides and swept back off his forehead. Daddy's had streaks of silver mingling with the gold, but that was the only difference. The blue eyes were the same, and the strong cleft chin. They even had their suits made at the same tailor. It was lucky they were so alike. It made his life so much easier, since there was very little left for him to prove. Al Macken had a son who was exactly like him and he had put him in a key position running the New York end of his operations. That was all people wanted to know. So far it had been enough to get them opening their wallets.

Travis washed his hands under gold taps in the onyx basin, and dried them on a freshly laundered linen towel which was then tossed onto the floor. Hell, he employed a woman just to clean up his washroom. He splashed on a little lime-scented cologne, imported specially from London, and combed his hair for the tenth time that afternoon. Then he returned to his vast leather-topped desk (an antique, purchased at Sotheby's) and began to flick through a pile of papers, scanning the pages rather than reading them.

The phone rang.

'Mr Macken, I have Mr Al Macken on one.'

'One second, Sherry, while I have you on the line . . . how about hanging on for a while after the others have gone home? Just you and me?'

'I'm sorry, I've made other arrangements. . . . Putting your call through now.'

'Hey, c'mon, Sherry – !'

'Hello?' Al's voice came on the line.

'Dad, how's it going? How are things down there? And Mom?'

The line was rather faint, but he recognised the excitement in his father's voice. 'Travis, I'm flying up to New York tonight, so we can talk properly later, but I just wanted to tell you that we closed the deal with Fraser. . . . We now own a thousand acres of prime real estate in Montana.'

'That's great, Daddy, congratulations.'

'The reason I'm ringing is because I want you to handle the development project. It'll be easier for you to fly over there than it will for me.'

'Not necessarily – '

'It's virgin land, so there are a lot of possibilities open to us.'

'But, Daddy – '

'Now I want y'all to weigh up some of the possibilities and we can start to discuss them when I see you. This is a real exciting opportunity for us, Travis!'

'Sure.'

'OK, so I'll see you tonight. I'm due at a function at the United Nations Plaza at seven. Shall I see you there?'

'Sure.'

Travis hung up, feeling gloomy. Why did Daddy have to keep pushing him like this? Why couldn't he just let him go on doing what he was best at, wining and dining potential investors and raising the company profile at Manhattan's cocktail parties and charity functions. Real estate development wasn't his thing at all.

He pulled out a fresh sheet of paper and picked up his pen with a sigh. He wrote 'MONTANA PROJECT' on the top line. That was all. His mind was as blank as the paper. It kept wandering back to Sherry. What was the matter with that girl? He flung down his pen and went through into her office. She was watering a plant on the filing cabinet when he walked up behind her. She was a pretty fresh-faced girl, trying to get some experience and save up the money to put herself through college.

'You positive I can't change your mind?'

She started slightly. 'Sorry, I didn't hear you.'

'I really would like y'all to come and have a drink with me tonight.'

'I don't really think I can.'

'C'mon . . .' he wheedled. 'We could go somewhere real fancy. The Oak Room.'

He dropped his head slightly and turned his charm up to full strength, fixing his blue gaze on her from under his lashes. 'Or dinner. Somewhere special. How about Le Cirque?'

'Mr Macken, this is really embarrassing. . . .' Sherry turned away from him, flicking her blonde pony tail over her shoulder as she moved. He caught a tantalizing gust of her scent. 'It's very nice of you to ask me out and everything. I'm flattered, believe me. But I have a boyfriend, you see; we're going steady, and he doesn't like the idea of me seeing you outside working hours.' She shrugged. 'Sorry.'

'Hey, I won't tell him if you won't. Where's the big deal?' He smiled, waiting for Sherry to back down.

She didn't. 'Look, Mr Macken,' she said, facing him from behind her desk. 'I've been thinking about this for a while now, I mean the job's great and I've enjoyed working with you, but this situation makes me a little uncomfortable – '

Travis frowned. 'Which situation are we talking about?'

'You asking me out. I'm very flattered, but like I said, my boyfriend doesn't like it and frankly I feel it's causing unnecessary tension. . . .' She glanced at his face and blushed. 'So, anyway, I've been looking around for another position, and if it's all right with you, I'll be leaving at the end of this week.'

Travis shrugged. 'Sure. I was just trying to be friendly, but if that's what you want. . . .'

He walked out of Sherry's office and closed the door. The situation didn't worry him unduly. Girls like Sherry were two a penny in Manhattan. He was just picking up his phone, to dial the number of the secretarial agency he preferred, when it rang.

'Mr Travis, I have Robert Reydell for you.'

'Put him through. . . . Rob, hi! How're ya doing?'

A happy grin spread across Travis's face. Rob Reydell was his best buddy from Harvard, and the saying was that whenever Rob was around, a good time was not far behind.

'Are you ready to party, my friend?'

'Always. What's the occasion?'

'The Powers boys are in town. There's some sort of a thrash going down at their parents' apartment. And I hear a rumour that Sonya Seddon's going to be there. The strawberry blonde with the terrific mammaries you admired so much.'

'How could I forget!' Travis laughed.

'It should be a seriously good party. Why don't we have a few drinks at the club first and then wander over together?'

'I'm supposed to be seeing my daddy tonight. . . . Shit, he can wait until the morning!'

Rob's laughter came down the line in muffled snorts. 'Spoken like a true Macken, boy!'

Travis was smiling as he picked up his pen. He had completely forgotten about Sherry.

'You have the most beautiful lips in the world.'

Lana Starkewska mouthed the words to her reflection as she applied her lipgloss. She had read somewhere that if you said things like that to yourself often enough you would end up believing them. And that in turn would affect the self-confidence you projected to other people. Self-improvement was a subject she knew a lot about, in fact you could say she had dedicated most of her thirty-four years to carrying it out.

Thirty-four years old. Not so young really, but on the other hand her age was one of the many things about herself that Lana had changed. She usually told people she was twenty-eight. There was no reason why she should be doubted either; she was in terrific shape. She attended keep fit classes regularly, she had invested $100 in buying an exercise cycle, which took up one corner of her tiny bedroom. She used a sun bed every week to maintain her tan. She had had her teeth capped at the rate of one a month, which was all she could afford, her dark-blonde hair was tinted a pale platinum and for her thirtieth birthday she had treated herself to a nose job. Just a small one. A slight refining of the bridge to make it less prominent.

So now Lana had every reason to be pleased with the way she looked. She smiled at herself again as she smoothed her thick, straight hair behind her ears and secured it with a black velvet bow. People sometimes said she looked like the French film star, Catherine Deneuve. Or a petite Angie Dickinson.

Lana took off her robe and went to the closet where she hung her work clothes. She selected a Bill Blass suit in a shade of deep claret. The cut was simple and restrained but the garment still managed to look classy. It said money; money with taste. One of the most important things Lana had learned was that it was much better to buy a few really good outfits than a lot of so-so ones.

With a small sponge dampened with a few drops of eau-de-Cologne, Lana wiped down the suit to remove any specks of fluff or lint. She glanced at the pink label pinned onto the hanger. The date written on it told her when she last took this particular suit to the dry cleaners. She used this system for all her clothes to make sure they were cleaned regularly. Silk stockings were taken from a special satin case in the drawer. The high heeled courts were stuffed with tissue paper, as was the matching handbag. It was essential to take care of your things if you wanted to make a good impression. That was something Lana's mother had taught her. One of many things.

Lana was pleased with the finished result. You would never know she was just a marine insurance clerk from Brooklyn Heights. She looked like a senior executive in some fancy company. Before she made a decision about which coat to take she glanced out of the window to see what the weather was doing. She was not going to ruin her good wool overcoat by getting caught in the rain. From the six-storey apartment she could see across the soaring towers of Wall Street and the financial district. There were plenty of people who believed this was the most stunning view in the world, but today Lana hardly gave it a glance. It looked as if it might rain. She would take her fur-lined raincoat.

She could afford to be blasé about the view; after all, she had seen it every day for over thirty years. The tiny walk-up apartment in the old brownstone on Willow Street was the only home she had ever known. Brooklyn was her home. New York City was her home.

But not according to her mother. 'Never forget that you are an Austrian, and an aristocrat,' she would rasp in her cracked, heavily accented English. 'You are better than these people. You were born to better things.'

The most imporant of the many things that the Countess Starkewska had taught her only child was that you never give up. You keep on going. For her the past was both anchor and rudder in the sea of life, something that she clung on to, to steer her into the future. She would sit in the gloomy, rented apartment with its tobacco-stained brown walls and cracked linoleum and talk about her glorious European past as if the impoverished present didn't matter. When Lana was a child her mother would root around in rubbish tips for bits of bric-à-brac, an outcast table lamp or vase, a broken chair, and haul them, puffing, up the six flights to the apartment, and all the while she would be talking on and on about her girlhood in Austria, about her father's *Schloss*, and the grand parties he gave, her governess and her pony trap. And the narrative thread would lead inevitably to her grand marriage just before the war and then Lana's birth in 1942.

Lana had heard the story of her birth so often during her childhood that she sometimes wondered whether it was just a fairytale. Her father, the young count, was missing in action and her mother went alone with her maid to a private clinic in the Tyrol, near the Swiss border. Like many aristocrats, her husband's family were not in favour of Hitler's régime, and she was fearful for her safety. Moreover, she had already decided that whatever the outcome of the war, she did not want her child raised as a Nazi. As soon as her daughter had been safely delivered, she handed the baby to her maid, who smuggled her out of the nursing home in a pillowcase, pretending she was a bundle of laundry.

'You were a good girl even then,' the Countess would recall with satisfaction. 'You did not make a single sound. If you had . . . well, we would not be here now.'

The infant Lana was taken over the border into Switzerland, and the Countess followed her as soon as she could. They stayed on a remote mountain farm until the end of the war, when they joined thousands of other refugees and sailed to New York. All they had with them was a bag of clothes and some of the Countess's jewellery, which had been given to her by her mother when she married. This was enough to ensure that they escaped the crowded tenements of the Lower East side, where most of the refugees were headed. She sold a ruby bracelet to raise the down payment on the apartment in Willow Street, and they had been here ever since. Lana, who had been only two-and-a-half at the end of the war, could not remember Europe, but she sometimes felt when she looked out over the East River that she had the faintest memory of arriving on the ship, the rush to the railings to get the first glimpse of the Statue of Liberty, the gasps of excitement, the tears.

The other pieces of jewellery had been sold off one by one over the years, to pay for furniture, for the fees and uniform at the Catholic girls academy Lana attended and to supplement the Countess's meagre salary. As a refugee with poor English there were few opportunities open to her, but she was too proud to wait on tables or do anything that involved cleaning up after other people. When she realised that a job she was being offered in Macy's department store involved cleaning the toilets, she delivered a tirade of German and stormed out of the manager's office.

She finally found a job in a dress shop on Brooklyn's Filton Street, a place where her old world manners and *hauteur* were put to good use bullying the customers. By this time all of the jewellery had gone. All except the necklace, that is.

All that was left of the Countess Starkewska's past life were her aristocratic airs and graces and the necklace her mother had given to her on her wedding day. It was a thick collar of milky pearls interspersed with diamonds of at least one carat and a flawless cut. At its centre was a pale emerald, tulip cut with diamond leaves. This, she told Lana, as she took it from its velvet box and laid it lovingly against her skin, she would never sell.

For at least twenty years Lana had fantasised about selling the necklace. It must have been worth fifty thousand dollars, a hundred thousand. More. With the proceeds they could have bought a lovely house on Long Island, or an apartment on the Upper East side, they could have left the drab brown-ness of Willow Street behind for ever. They could even, she suggested tentatively, go on a trip to Europe and see the castle where the Countess was born, look for surviving relatives.

But the Countess was adamant. The necklace would never be sold. It had been handed down by five generations of women on the occasion of their eldest daughter's wedding, and that tradition was not to be broken. On the day Lana married, the necklace would become hers.

The Countess did not appear too concerned that this day had not yet arrived, and was no closer as her daughter reached her mid-thirties. She had stressed all along the importance of waiting for the right man. Only the very best would do for her daughter, and justify the surrender of the priceless Starkewska necklace. And in order to attract the right sort of man, her daughter must tirelessly devote her time to perfecting her appearance. She would not hear of Lana moving out and finding an apartment of her own. All that money wasted on rent, when it could be so much more profitably ploughed into improving her wardrobe and her grooming.

So Lana groomed herself and waited, but she was aware that time was running out. The perfect man would undoubtedly want a family, and in a few years' time she would be out of the running. Lately she had taken to searching Situations Vacant in the *New York Times* and applying for new posts. A change of job might mean a change of social life. If only she had been able to go to college and take a degree. . . .

Well, at least her appearance would never let her down. Lana took one last look in the mirror, folded her fur-lined trench coat neatly over her arm and left the apartment, heading for the subway.

Eight hours later, the Countess Starkewska was in a hurry to get home.

Leaving the junior salesgirl to close up the shop, she acknowledged the calls of 'Goodnight, Countess!' with a nod and a smile and walked down Filton Street to the delicatessen.

'Good evening, Countess,' said the owner, Mario, warmly. He always treated her with deference. Why not, if it kept her happy? She had been a regular customer for twenty-five years. 'Got some great pastrami here, look. . . .' He showed her proudly. 'Or how about some Parma ham? My wife just made cannoli – '

The Countess waved him away impatiently. 'Too expensive.' She bought pumpernickel, zucchini and eggplant, and some dried apricots that were on special. She had visited the butcher in her lunch hour and in her handbag she had secreted a little wax-paper parcel of beef fat he had been about to throw away and gave her for nothing. She would use it to make some dumplings.

'Anything else for you, Countess?'

'No, that is all. Good evening to you.'

She gave Mario the most cursory of smiles before hurrying out of the shop. Normally she would stay and exchange a few words with him about the shockingly filthy state of the streets or the shortcomings of City Hall, but tonight there was no time. She wanted to be sure and catch Lana as soon as she returned from work.

She reached the apartment ten minutes before her daughter did. Lana breezed in looking as fresh and immaculately groomed as ever. 'Always retouch your make-up before you leave the office,' her mother had advised her when she first started work. 'You never know who you might meet on the subway.'

Lana kissed her mother's cheek. 'Good evening, Mama.' She peered into the brown paper bag from the delicatessen. 'You sit down, I'll cook.'

'No,' said the Countess firmly. 'I'll cook. You're going out.'

'I am?'

Her mother smiled; she seemed excited, pleased with herself. 'I heard something when I was at work today. I was listening to two customers talking in the fitting room. Businessmen's wives from Queens.' She sniffed slightly, indicating that they were full of inconsequential social standing. 'They were full of envy because some acquaintance of theirs was going to a soirée for America's top industrialists. So – I make an excuse that a hem needs pinning so I can go in and listen some more.' She waved her daughter in the direction of her bedroom. 'It is at the United Nations Plaza, at seven o'clock. If you change now you can make it.'

'Mama, I'm not on the guest list, they won't let me in.'

'Of course they will, a girl with your style and good breeding. The woman who is going . . . wait I made a note of her name. . . .' She rummaged through her handbag. 'Miriam Arthur. And Mr Harold Arthur. Just say you are with them. It will be the perfect place for you to meet a husband, don't you see? All those rich men. . . .'

'With all their rich wives.'

'Not all of them, I am sure. All right, so we might have to settle for someone who has been divorced. Not ideal, I know, but – ' she shrugged – 'that's the way the world is going. We have to do what we can. Now go – do your best.'

Lana changed into a black velvet shift from Calvin Klein, sheer black stockings and black satin stilettos which made her trim, muscular legs look longer. She swept her hair into a chignon and put diamond studs in her ears.

'Clever girl!' said her mother when she emerged from the bedroom with her fur stole over one arm. 'But there is just one more thing. . . .' She went into her own room and came back with the velvet box that contained the diamond and pearl necklace.

'You must wear it tonight.'

'But Mama, you said not until – '

'I know, I know, but it will bring you luck.'

'Thank you.' Lana lifted the necklace into position, savouring its weight, its coolness against her skin. She smiled at herself when she saw how it looked. The emerald reflected the green lights in her eyes in the most flattering way, as if it had been made especially for her. She looked as though she was already a rich woman.

'Your name, ma'am?'

Lana was walking past the doorman with her most confident smile, hoping he wouldn't stop her. He held a clipboard with guest list, and he was ticking them off as people arrived. She could see 'ARTHUR' at the top, with no tick beside it as yet.

'Mrs Harold Arthur,' she said, drawing back her stole slightly so that the emerald and diamonds flashed under the neon lights. 'My husband will be along later.'

'The banqueting suite is on the penthouse floor, ma'am. Elevator is to your right.'

Lana stalked past him, wondering as she did so what the real Mrs Arthur looked like.

Al Macken looked at his watch for the tenth time in the last half-hour, grimacing in irritation. Where the hell was he?

The rhythm of cocktail party chatter rose and fell around him, white-coated waiters wove their way through the crowds with their trays of champagne held aloft. Al knew a hell of a lot of the people here, most of them in fact, but he wasn't in the mood for talking to them. He was supposed to be out of here, half an hour ago.

Now *there* was someone he didn't know. She was trying to be discreet, but Al could still tell she was sizing him up. Probably because he was on his own. Most of the men had their wives with them. She was a petite blonde, very much in the Manhattan socialite mould: teeth capped, nose fixed, hair expensively coiffed, discreet elegance with good jewellery.

Their eyes met. She smiled and walked over to him. 'Been stood up, huh?'

'Only by my son. I flew up to New York to meet with him, but he's obviously been held up by some – ' he was about to say 'some broad' but thought better of it – 'by some last minute business.' He gave a courtly bow and extended his hand. 'The name's Al Macken, ma'am.'

Lana's eyes gleamed. Working in a marine insurance office she could hardly have failed to hear of the Macken Corporation. And here in front of her was the biggest cherry from that particular bowl. She could not believe her luck.

'It's very nice to meet you at last. . . . I work in shipping too, you see. My name's Lana Starkewska.'

'In shipping? That's interesting. . . . What do you do?'

Lana smiled. She was very adept at avoiding questions she didn't want to answer. Naturally it wouldn't do for Al Macken to know she was a clerk who had gatecrashed.

'Actually I'm looking around for something new at the moment. I don't suppose you might have any contacts?'

She sipped calmly on her glass of champagne and waited.

Al, who had been sizing her up all the time they had been talking, was tempted. There was something about this girl. . . . You couldn't tell what age she was, for example, which was something that always intrigued him. She could have been anything between twenty-five and forty. Beulah was like that. The almond-shaped green eyes reminded him of Beulah, too, and the confident elegance. Feminine, without being fluffy. Just one look into those eyes and you could see that this was no china doll, no pretty ball of fluff. This was a strong woman.

Sure, he was tempted. He felt that sting of attraction just as keenly now as he had when he was a young man of twenty. But there was still Cordella, silent and closed though she was. He still cared about her. And there was Beulah too. Their relationship had mellowed and eased so that it was really just a friendship these days, but from time to time the fires of passion could still be ignited between them. After thirty-five years or more. . . .

No, it was too late for him to start over. He would have to pass on Ms Starkewska. On the other hand, she would be perfect for Travis. He would make a gift of her to his son.

'Well now, ma'am, as it happens I just might be able to help y'all. As you know, our corporation is based in Georgia, but we do have a small office here in New York, and it just so happens that my son is looking for a personal assistant. . . .'

Al didn't know this for certain, but there was a good chance it was true. Travis was always needing a new personal assistant, he got through them at an average rate of one per month. If it didn't look as though they would go to bed with him, he would find some excuse and fire them. If they did go to bed with him, he would grow bored and fire them. He kept telling Travis he should leave secretaries to do their job and look elsewhere for a bit of fun. For a guy as rich and good-looking as Travis Macken, the whole of Manhattan was full of eager young women, it was a gold mine. But the problem with Travis was that underneath all his swagger he was lazy. He couldn't be bothered to look further than his outer office whenever he got a hard-on.

As a result, he never had a decent secretary and he needed someone to hold the place together, someone he could rely on, as Al himself relied on the faithful Winona. She had been around almost as long as Cordella and Beulah, and had probably seen a hell of a lot more of him over the years. . . .

He had a feeling about this young woman. She could be exactly what the Park Avenue office suite needed.

'Ma'am, would y'all wait one moment while I just fix to get hold of a phone? I'd like you to meet my son.'

Lana was hired as personal assistant to Travis Macken and started the job three days later.

The Countess was disgruntled. 'It's a husband you need, not another job. A job you had already. This man you have met who is so important; he should be taking you out, wining and dining you, not putting you to work in his office.'

Lana knew otherwise. Of course she could have dated Travis Macken. But then what? She would have been just one more in a never-ending pageant of pretty blondes he had taken out for dinner. She was not a nubile member of the debutante circuit and in her own right was neither rich enough nor young enough to merit special attention. What she needed to hold his attention was power. And power was earned in the boardroom, not the bedroom.

She did not think very much of the suite of offices on Park Avenue. Sure, it was all very expensive, and a lot of money had been spent, unnecessarily in her opinion, on fancy trimmings. Gilt candelabra and oils in ugly frames. But it was all swank and no taste, no doubt because the Mackens hailed from the South. Southerners thought fancy meant classy, and their idea of style hailed from the pages of *Gone with the Wind*.

All this she viewed as yet another challenge. Before long she would see to it that they called in interior decorators and changed everything. She pictured the place as a cool blend of blues and lilacs, with pale carpets and lots of glass and chrome. One of the first things she did when she had settled into her desk and put away her personal belongings was to find a designers' directory and flick through it, making note of some names and numbers.

There was plenty of time for that in the future though. For now, she had more pressing concerns. She glanced through the interconnecting door at Travis Macken. He was the first on her list of objectives. Tall, impeccably handsome and undeniably rich. He was the Right Man that she and her mother had waited for so patiently all these years. And thank God she *had* waited. No matter that she had seen on their first meeting he was not much more than an expensively educated Ivy League jock. It was only because of his lack of perception that she stood a chance. She would get him.

Travis watched his new assistant arranging her desk. She was very tidy; he liked that.

She bent down to put some papers in a drawer. Her buttocks, in a severely tailored grey skirt, were tight and shapely. Her figure would never get her into Miss America, but she took care of her body, that much was obvious. The thought caused a familiar stirring. She was definitely an interesting proposition. Not really his type, but what the hell. . .?

He would give her a week. No, two weeks, because she was a classy act and would take a little more wooing than the dumb college kids who had occupied that office. He found himself watching her for most of that first day. Not just sizing her up physically, but watching how she did things. She was very confident, very sure of herself. It occurred to him that having a super-efficient secretary might not be such a good thing. Relying on someone meant that it was harder to get rid of them if you felt like it.

'How about going for cocktails?' he called at six o'clock as Lana reached for her coat.

OK, so he had decided to leave it a couple of weeks, but he couldn't help but be curious about how she would react.

'I'm sorry, no. I have to get home.'

'To your boyfriend, huh?'

She shook her head.

'Have far to travel?'

'Just to Brooklyn Heights.'

'Brooklyn . . . y'all live alone there?'

She smiled. 'You ask a lot of questions.'

'I'm interested.'

'I'm afraid I'm not all that interesting. . . .' She snapped shut her briefcase and smoothed her immaculate hair. (What did she need the briefcase for, Travis wondered?)

'And the answer is I don't live alone. I live with my mother.' She smiled again; still cool, still in control.

'So you – '

'I'll see you tomorrow. Good night.'

The next morning Lana came into his office with a folder of papers, which she brandished at him.

'Mr Macken, I'd like a word about this proposal you asked me to type.'

Travis glanced at it. It was a resumé of his ideas for the land development in Montana. Al was still waiting for him to come up with something.

'What's the problem?'

'I took these papers home with me last night and read them.'

'What the . . .? Jesus, you had no right to do that! I don't want employees taking confidential papers out of this building!'

Lana coloured slightly, but pressed on. 'I thought of some ways you might improve it.'

'You did, did you? Could I just remind you here that you were hired as my secretary? I don't remember my father saying anything about editing company reports.'

Lana shrugged and turned to go. 'Yeah, you're right.'

'No wait. . . .' Travis felt that despite her backing down he was left at a disadvantage. He gave her his most charming smile. 'Please – you may as well go ahead and say what you were going to say.'

'All right.' Lana opened the report and started flicking through it. 'You propose to turn the site into a mock-up of a Western town, with amusement arcades, icecream parlour, picnic areas, et cetera.'

'And a camp site.'

'And a camp site . . . but the problem is that this is a very remote area. It's not Coney Island, where you're going to get millions of people passing through each summer. You may get a hundred thousand if you're lucky. If they all spend, say, ten dollars a head, you're going to make a million dollars. Take away your running costs and you're not looking at much profit.'

Travis rested his chin on his hands, watching Lana's face closely. 'So?'

'So I thought we – I mean you – might consider turning it into a luxury resort. It's a beautiful area, rugged, but very secluded. You've got a lake and a river for fishing without having to do anything at all. There's snow in the mountains for skiing, you could have horseback riding. . . . I picture individual log cabins, with a central ranch-house for dining. You know the kind of thing; rustic on the outside, chi-chi and luxurious on the inside. Open fires, spa baths . . . and that sort of building doesn't cost much to put up. You could put in a helicopter pad and a landing strip; again they're inexpensive to build but they add to the prestige of the place and attract the right sort of customer. Stressed-out city types are always looking for that sort of place to get away to – exclusive, with superb cuisine and good sporting facilities. You could call it Treetops or Timbertops, something like that.'

There was a short pause. 'Well, I sure like what I'm hearing so far, but exclusivity has to mean fewer clients.'

Lana nodded. 'Sure. You wouldn't want to go to more than fifty cabins. But if you processed a hundred guests per week, each spending a minimum of $3,000, you're talking turnover of fifteen million. Even with steep running costs, you're going to turn more profit than a wild west town selling candy floss and Hershey bars.'

Travis folded his arms and stared at her. Lana scooped up her papers and turned to go. 'Of course this is only an idea. If you don't like it – '

'No, no,' said Travis hastily. 'No, I'd say so far it has potential. Put what you've said down on paper, and I'll run it past the other members of the board. Could you type it up today?'

Lana smiled demurely. 'Of course. I'm your secretary.'

She sashayed out, closing the door behind her. Travis buried his head in his hands. The rules of the game were changing. He was going to have one hell of a time getting her in the sack now.

'Aren't you going to work this morning?'

The Countess came into her daughter's bedroom with a cup of steaming coffee and a plate of bagels. 'It's nearly eight o'clock, you're usually dressed by now.'

'It's all right, Mama, I'm just going in a little later today.'

'Are you sick?' She felt Lana's forehead. 'You look a little flushed. Would you like me to call Dr Winkler?'

'I'm fine, Mama, honest.' Lana was sitting up against the pillows, pulling a brush through her hair. 'In fact you could say I've never felt better.'

She waited until her mother had gone out of the room and pulled out a folder from under the bed. There on MackenCorp's headed notepaper were the words she had typed herself only yesterday afternoon: '*PROPOSAL FOR DEVELOPMENT OF SITE AT FLATWILLOW, MONTANA.*'

She hadn't just typed the words either, she had written them. They were all her own. All of them.

By 9.30, Travis Macken was pacing his office. Goddammit, the meeting started at ten, where the hell had Lana got to? She was supposed to be here at 8.30. He had already searched his desk and hers for the typed proposal and he couldn't find it. She had obviously put it away in a drawer somewhere or filed it away under her new filing system. Deliberately, no doubt, the ansty little bitch. . . .

He called the office manager and asked her to find Lana's home phone number. His fingers were trembling with rage as he dialled.

'Listen, I don't care if you have to take a day off sick, I don't even care if you have to take a day off to go to the beauty parlour, but I *do* care if you're not here and the fucking proposal has gone missing thirty minutes before the goddam board meeting!'

'It hasn't gone missing,' said Lana calmly. 'I know exactly where it is.'

'It *has* gone missing if you've hidden it somewhere I can't find it. Just what kind of stunt are you trying to pull, lady – ?'

'I haven't hidden it. It's right here. I have it in my hand now, as a matter of fact.'

'Well get your fucking fanny over here then, or I'm going to look a complete asshole!'

'Well now, I don't know about that. . . .'

'What the fu-'

'You will agree with me, I think, that the ideas in this document are mine, and mine alone. And it's not usual for someone to give away ideas like that for free. There's usually some kind of payment.'

'Oh I get it, you want a pay off, right? Well, come on then, name your price. A thousand bucks?'

'No, I don't think so.'

'Five thousand then!'

'I don't want money, Mr Macken, I want a job.'

'You already have a job. You're my personal assistant. I'll tell you what, though, I'll raise the salary. A company car – '

'No. I want an executive position.'

'Jesus Christ, you have to be joking!'

Travis hung up. Then he sat and thought. Sure, he might have a hell of a lot to lose by giving in, but he could gain too. If she wanted to do some of his work for him, so much the better.

He called her back. 'All right, you win.'

'Good. So; you can put it down in writing now, and by the time you've finished I'll be there with the report. It's really a very simple deal.'

But Travis knew the deal was going to be far from simple. It wasn't simple at all.

Michael Macken stretched his limbs like a cat, yawned and looked up at the ceiling. The ceiling fan above his head stood motionless. There was no need to have it switched on through the night now; winter was approaching and temperatures dropped quite low during the hours of darkness.

He started to count, idly, the number of nights he had spent in this little room, with its whitewashed stone walls and low trestle bed. At least a hundred. Since the summer anyway. He climbed off the bed and pushed open the blue wooden shutters, resting his elbows on the stone sill. It was going to be another beautiful day. So what was new? Right across the street from the house, only yards away, the island of Kos came abruptly to an end, dropping away sharply to the Aegean, with white-painted houses nestling on its steep sides. The sun was starting to climb in the sky, sparkling in the sapphire water and turning the bell tower on the church so brilliantly white that it hurt the eyes to look at it.

Michael dressed and wandered down to the taverna in the harbour to get some breakfast. The daughter of its proprietor was sweeping the terrace and smiled shyly when she saw Michael. She had come back to his room with him one night when there had been a crowd down at the bar and they had all drunk too much ouzo. Michael remembered how frightened she had been that her father might find out she had slept with an American. He found the idea of the Greek café owner's wrath rather disturbing and had stayed away from her after that, even though she was touchingly pretty, with glossy black hair and even, white teeth.

He gave her a slight nod of acknowledgement and then went to sit at the table furthest away from the taverna, facing out to sea so that they could avoid eye contact. Her father's dog, a mangy German shepherd, growled as though it could read his thoughts.

After he had eaten his bread and feta cheese he drank the black, treacly coffee as slowly as he could, trying to prolong the meal. Once breakfast was over, there were several hours to fill before lunchtime and very little to do in those hours. There were few tourists on the island now, and the waterskiing season was all but over. If he was lucky he might get to give one or two hours of tuition in a week. His social life had disappeared with the tourists, although there were a few young people from Europe and America backpacking their way round the islands, stopping off on their way east to Kathmandu or India or Thailand.

The truth was that Michael was bored. He had had a good couple of years, he had travelled and met plenty of people, but now he was feeling under-stimulated. His body had had a great deal of stimulation, that was for sure, what with an endless stream of nubile girls, days of sun and surf, ready supplies of coke and hash. It was his brain that was under-used. Even studying had some appeal . . . but no, he couldn't go back to that, not now.

He found himself thinking about Travis quite a lot. He would try and picture him in New York and figure out what he was doing. Apart from making out with pretty girls, of course. It occurred to him that maybe – just maybe – working in the New York office of MackenCorp could be fun. After all, the old man wouldn't be around very much. And there would be a big budget to control, new projects to set up, scope for lots of fresh ideas. And Manhattan was teeming with young graduates of his age, including quite a lot of his buddies from Harvard. It would be good to see some of those guys again. . . .

Shit, he was starting to envy Travis again. Wasn't that exactly what he was trying to get away from? And here he was on the other side of the world, still doing it.

Partly to try and lay the ghost, and partly just to kill more time, he walked up to the town of Kos, to the post office. You could make international calls from the phone there, though the lines were unreliable. He asked the operator to connect him with his parents' house in Savannah. It would be very early in the morning there, but he knew his father would already have left.

He really just wanted to speak to Mom. She worried about him, in fact she seemed a lot more interested in him than she had been when he was around. So he called her from time to time just to let her know where he was. For some reason he had the urge to do that today.

'Mom, hi – it's Michael.'

Her voice was very, very faint. 'How are you, honey?'

'I'm fine. . . . Yes, I'm still in Greece. . . . How is everybody?'

'We're all fine. . . . Your father's just about to go up to New York again to see Travis. . . . Travis is doing real well. He's come up with some great new ideas for a resort development in the Rockies.'

'Good, sounds exciting.' To his surprise, he meant this.

'Listen, honey, there's plenty of work you could be doing over here. You know Daddy would be only too happy to have y'all working at his side. I *know* he feels that way, even after everything he said to you. As far as he's concerned what's past is past and it's just you who's being as stubborn as a mule.'

'But I didn't graduate, Mom. I couldn't keep my side of the bargain.'

'Honey, that doesn't matter now! You've got plenty to offer, Daddy's smart enough to know that.'

'I was thinking I might come back. . . .'

'I'm sorry, sweet pea, I can't hear you! There's a crackling noise on the line.'

Michael raised his voice. 'Doesn't matter, Mom. Could you put my allowance into my American Express account, rather than wiring it to me here? I need to use my credit card.'

When he hung up he had decided. There was nowhere here on the island he could buy a plane ticket. He would have to make the trip to Athens.

He walked back to the harbour to find out about the next ferry to Piraeus.

Lana's first two weeks at MackenCorp had long since elapsed, but Travis had not made any move to seduce her.

He had made an exception to his normal policy and decided to treat Lana as if she was out of bounds. It wasn't easy, but he coped by pretending she was his mother or his sister. Or he reminded himself what might happen if he did seduce her. If she got mad and told him to go to hell, then she was exactly the sort of person you didn't want as an enemy. Not in her new position as executive director. And if she allowed him into her bed, you could be sure that she would use it as a means of grabbing even more power.

True, one evening he did stand behind her and put his hands on her waist, just to see how she would react. It was curious; but she somehow managed to neither reject nor accept the advance. She touched his hand lightly, as if in encouragement, then walked away as cool as ever as if nothing had happened. Her reaction suggested she might be interested as long as it was on her own terms. What else? She was damn smart, that broad.

The truth was that as Travis got to know her better, he felt something he had never felt before: respect. She worked very hard and was full of great ideas. And if the price for having her around taking the load off his shoulders was her being off limits, so be it. New York was full of pussy, after all, it wasn't as if a guy like him needed to go without.

Daddy had been a little unsure about the promotion. Travis should be able to run the New York office single-handed, he had said. One chief and the rest Indians. But he couldn't deny that Lana was good for the company image. She dazzled other businessmen at meetings, always exquisitely chic and with a faintly European air. In a couple of months she had made as many contacts as Travis had in a year.

She breezed into the office in the morning, slung her coat over a hanger and immediately got to work, tapping her pencil against her lip as she thought. They had a little competition going between them to be the first one in; Lana usually won.

'You know, Travis,' she called to him one day ('Mr Macken' had been dropped with the promotion), 'now that the decorators are finished, I'd really like to think about getting an assistant.'

'You've got Paula, we only just hired her.'

'For the typing, yes. I was thinking more at junior management level, someone I could delegate stuff to when I'm out of the office.'

Travis frowned. 'I don't know about that. I don't want things getting so diluted that I'm not – ' He was going to say 'Not making the decisions', but Lana was looking at him in that way she had, head on one side, listening intently but looking as if some part of her somewhere inside was laughing at him. '. . . I don't know.'

Lana started to gather papers together and put them into her briefcase.

'I'm going out. I've got a list of potential investors for the Flatwillow project, then I'm gong to look at a marine re-insurance outfit that I happen to know could be up for sale. There's a whole mint of money in re-insurance. . . .' She draped her coat over her shoulders and touched up her frosted pink lipstick. 'What are you going to do?'

'Well, the accountants are due here later. I guess I'll hang around to see them.'

'It's OK, I'll be back in time to meet with them. Why don't you go down to the health club and have a game of racquets? Or take a turn on the sun bed. You've been looking a little peaky lately.'

Travis glanced at the mirror in his washroom. 'I have?' He did look a little less than his best, but that might be the reflection from the walls, which had been repainted in pastel mint green during Lana's redecoration.

Anyhow, that was all the excuse he needed to take Lana's advice. He went down to the Manhattan Plaza Racquets Club and swam thirty lengths, then thrashed a ball around a court with an old friend from Harvard. After that he was ready for a massage, a session on the tanning bed and a Turkish bath. Showered and changed, he went into the bar and hung around for a while, waiting to see what opportunities presented themselves.

The opportunity that came along was a petite brunette called Kathy. She was there to meet some other guy, but Travis flashed his gold American Express card around sufficiently to persuade her to come out to lunch. After enjoying his permanently reserved table at the Four Seasons they returned to his apartment where they indulged in a line of coke and a couple of hours in bed. Lying tangled in the sheets, satiated but totally relaxed, Travis offered up a prayer of thanks for Ms Lana Starkewska. He was able to enjoy New York so much more since she had been around.

He had left his watch in the shower at the club, and so wasn't entirely sure what time it was when he strolled back into the office. It had been dark for a couple of hours, so he guessed it was around six o'clock. Or perhaps later, since Lana had already gone home. She had left a note on his desk: '*Ring me soonest re Amusement and Cigs*'.

Amusement and Cigs? What the hell was the woman talking about? He screwed up the note and tossed it into the bin, but the phone rang immediately and it was Lana. It was almost spooky, as if she could see him and hear him even when she wasn't there.

'Did you see my note?'

'Yes, I was just about to call you,' Travis lied.

'I've been trying to reach you . . . your father called. There's a company called Atlanta Cigarettes and Amusements Incorporated that's up for sale, and he wants MackenCorp to buy it out and merge it with a similar operation he owns in Savannah. Anyhow, the reason he called is that the company president is in New York at the moment. He wants you to go over and see him in the morning and do a pitch.'

'Do a pitch?'

'You know . . . present some figures and then make an offer based on the figures.'

'But Jesus, Lana – '

'He's called Burrigan and he's expecting you for breakfast at the Carlyle at 8.30.'

'Shit! This is a fine time to tell me!'

'Your father did call at midday. I just didn't know where to locate you.'

Had she tried? Her voice sounded innocent enough, but she did know the number of his apartment and his favourite restaurant. She could have tried and missed him. He would never know. . . .

They both knew what he was going to say next, so he went ahead and said it. 'Couldn't you go and see this guy, Lana? It wouldn't matter what you said, you'd still have him eating out of your hand.'

Her voice as calm and measured as ever, she said, 'No, Travis. I've put in a hell of a day, I've run the show single-handed and

I've covered everything. I think it's unreasonable to expect me to do more tonight.'

'But hell, I know nothing about this fucking company – '

'You've got all night to work on your presentation. And I've left a file of notes in the drawer of your desk.'

With the phone under his ear, Travis groped in the drawer and pulled out a blue file of neatly typed figures. It clearly meant something to Lana, but he couldn't figure it out.

'Lana, *please*!' I'll give you anything you want. A brand new Mercedes! A new apartment! A fur coat, *five* fur coats. . . .'

'I'm sorry, Travis, but there are some things I don't think you can reasonably expect from a mere employee. I don't think you can ask that sort of extra dedication from someone . . . unless perhaps you were married to them.'

Travis felt a cold, sharp tug in his stomach. Was she really trying to say . . .? His fingers trembled slightly as he reached for the file. He knew he recognised it. The blue cover . . . he had seen Lana working on it a couple of days ago. Which meant she must have known about the Atlanta deal all this time.

'Jesus Christ . . .' he whispered into the receiver. 'You knew about this but you left it until now so that you . . . so that I. . . .'

'I want marriage, Travis,' she said quietly. 'Then we can really be an unbeatable team.'

Travis shook his head in disbelief. The expectant silence on the other end of the phone was almost audible, but for a while he couldn't speak.

Uppermost on his mind was not wanting to grapple with these figures all night. But another part of him was thinking, yeah, why the hell not? She was good-looking, intelligent and presentable, a real asset. And once she was his wife and he'd given her a handful of children to keep her busy. . . . His thoughts strayed momentarily to the idea of actually fucking her; there was another incentive. . . . Well, she'd never be able to pull another stunt like this.

'Ok, Lana. First: go to the breakfast meeting tomorrow and come back with a contract for Atlanta Amusements and Cigarettes. Then let my daddy think I set it up alone. After that we can get married any time you like.'

SEVEN

New York 1978

Peg Anderson turned up her collar against the icy wind and trudged through the slush on Central Park South. Yesterday, New Year's Day, it had snowed, but the snow had only dusted the ground for minutes before melting underfoot. Now there were gusts of wind that whipped down Manhattan's streets from the antarctic, and Peg knew from the experience of the past months that this would freeze the streets overnight. Getting around would become slow and difficult for those who, like her, did not own a car and could not afford to take cabs everywhere.

And her one-room apartment on the Upper West side would be freezing. The landlord kept saying he would come round and fix the heating but he never did, and since the place only brought him eighty-five dollars a month in rent, Peg wasn't surprised.

She sighed, hunching her shoulders higher to keep her collar in place over her ears and pressing her fingers down hard into the recesses of her pockets. Every so often she would pass a woman wearing pretty fur ear-muffs and stare after them enviously. How she would love a pair of those! But the ten dollars they cost would keep her in food for several days, and for the moment, keeping herself fed took priority over clothing herself. Her job in the café on Columbus Avenue made her a lot in tips but the hours were only part-time, and in a lean week she might have as little as thirty dollars left after she had paid her rent. When the weather warmed up a little, she would think about starting up her sandwich round again, selling heros to office workers. But at the moment, getting about in the cold was too difficult and the sandwiches arrived almost frozen.

She rounded the corner and a fresh gust of wind whipped

under her collar and made her earlobes smart and tingle. Perhaps she would find some ear-muffs on sale somewhere, or a woollen scarf she could wind around her head. She had heard the top Manhattan department stores had great reductions in January. She buried her head again and quickened her pace until she was in step with the other shoppers heading up Fifth Avenue towards the glittering windows of Saks.

Michael Macken was too hot. His room in the Plaza was overheated to the point of oppression. But he knew that as soon as he got out there onto the streets of Manhattan that goddam wind would freeze him right down to the bone. He remembered winters like this in Boston, and as a Southern boy used to a gentle climate he had thought then he would never get used to it. Sure, the temperatures had been lower in Colorado but the sun had always shone and he had worn special protective clothing. At the moment all he had with him were the clothes he had taken to Greece.

In a moment he would get a cab down to Saks Fifth Avenue or Brooks Brothers and buy himself a cashmere overcoat and some gloves. First, he wanted to speak to his father.

He tried the Savannah numbers for the fifth time that morning. Winona's line at East Bay was constantly engaged and there was no reply at home. His irritation rose to the surface and he slammed the receiver down into the cradle. Crazy, but he was beginning to wish he was back in Greece.

His intention had been to go straight to the top and state his case, but if the organ grinder was not available, he would have to speak to the monkey. He would call in and see Travis later that morning.

Travis Macken was enjoying a leisurely sauna after a game of racquet ball. It had taken longer than he anticipated and he would be back in the office later than he had said, but still he did not hurry. He leaned back on the bench and closed his eyes, enjoying the sensation of sweat breaking out over his tingling body. Lana was at the office; he trusted her to take care of things for him. There was no need to watch her every move now that she was his wife.

They had been married five weeks ago, at St Patrick's cathedral in deference to the Countess's Catholicism. Lana had no family other than her mother, so it had been a quiet affair; just Daddy and Mom, Uncle Wyatt and Aunt Martha and their children and a handful of New York friends. Aunt Beulah had had the good taste to stay away. There had been no point in inviting Michael since they couldn't even be sure he would receive the invitation. He was still bumming around on some beach somewhere, doing nothing with his life.

Lana had worn a very plain, elegant sheath of ivory dupion, cut low to show the fabulous Starkewska diamonds to their best advantage. She rejected the idea of a veil and wore her hair piled in a high chignon and decorated with wisps of trailing ivy, complementing the ivy in her bouquet. His friends were surprised; they had been expecting him to marry some girlish homecoming queen fresh out of puppy fat and teeth braces, or else some well-bred WASP with a pedigree she could trace back to the *Mayflower*. But they all said how classy the bride looked, how stylish. That was what Lana was: a classy woman who had been around and gotten a little bit of experience.

Travis was surprised too, by how much he enjoyed being married to her. Of course she was crazy about him, he knew that. He knew a hell of a lot more about her than she would like to admit. In the short time he'd lived with her he'd found out all sorts of things he hadn't known before. Like she'd told him she was thirty-two, and her birth certificate said she was thirty-five. Like she'd had her tits done by a plastic surgeon, which made them hard and unyielding to the touch. And her hair was dyed blonde, not natural, and she wore as much make-up as that all the time, even when she went to bed. She smoked too, something he hadn't realised. He quite liked finding out her little secrets. It was comforting to know she was not quite as invincible as she liked to think.

OK, so she wasn't that hot in the sack, didn't really seem interested. But sex was a commodity a guy like him could find anywhere. It wasn't necessarily what a wife was for. A wife was for having babies and running the home. And they'd be having a baby real soon. Daddy would be just thrilled shitless to have a grandson, and they would call him Alexander, that would be enough to keep him happy for a good long time.

They hadn't yet discussed Lana giving up work when the babies came along. She would probably want to hire a nanny and keep right on working. Mom wouldn't approve, but actually it was OK by him. He kind of liked the secure feeling of having Lana about the office. Now that she was his wife and their interests were the same, it was natural they should split the running of the business fifty-fifty. She was sweet as pie towards him, he had no more problems with her trying to out-manoeuvre him. And it was only fair that in return for her help he should listen to her ideas from time to time. It was all part of keeping the little woman happy.

As soon as Travis came back to the office, Lana left.

He had made her late for an appointment, but she didn't say anything, just kissed him goodbye and told him she would see him later. If she picked away at him for every little thing he did that annoyed her they would never stop arguing and what would be the point of that? That wasn't the reason she had got married.

As the stretch Mercedes limousine wove its way through the crowded streets of Manhattan, she counted the good things about being Mrs Travis Macken. This car, for a start. Then there was the apartment in Sutton Place. That sure had impressed the hell out of her mother, who saw her years of ambitious dreaming come to fruition.

'You see,' she had said when she admired the bathroom with its enormous Italian marble spa pool, 'you were right to wait.'

Travis and Lana had offered to buy her an apartment of her own on the Upper East side, but she had preferred to stay in Brooklyn Heights. Collecting lampshades and discarded saucepans from skips had become a way of life.

Lana, too, found it hard to shake the habits of a lifetime. Sure, she had spent a lot of money since she married Travis. She had fur coats, and jewellery and charge accounts at all the major stores, with a personal shopper to attend to her needs. But her instinct was still to be careful with money, and to hang her clothes neatly in their dust-proof bags rather than leaving them on the floor for the maid to pick up.

The stretch limo purred its way silently round corners, forcing other vehicles out of its wake, and prompting envious glances. Being rich was OK, Lana reflected. Travis was OK, too. His performance in bed was disappointing, but then she'd kind of expected that. That was what selfish men were like. True, she didn't have very much experience, she'd been far too careful in her pursuit of Mr Right, but she knew enough to know Travis wasn't that great. But then she wasn't in love. That probably had something to do with it.

For Lana, this marriage was about the boardroom rather than the bedroom. That was where she got her kicks. It hadn't taken her long to come to the conclusion Travis was lazy. And he had no original ideas of his own. How could he? He'd spent far too much time trying to imitate his father, and had ended up just a pale copy of the original. He had none of Al's spark.

She was carrying that office now; when they called, people asked to speak to her rather than to Travis, and most of the ideas for future directions were hers. But she didn't mind, she was enjoying being a businesswoman far too much. *This* was what she had been born for, not marriage.

The limo cruised to a halt on East 93rd, and Lana took the elevator to the top floor, where her gynaecologist had her consulting rooms.

'Mrs Macken. . . .' The doctor consulted her notes. 'You're here to discuss the possibility of starting a family.'

'And to have my IUD removed,' said Lana firmly.

'OK, fine. . . .' The doctor indicated that she should take a seat. 'So – you're ready to have a baby.'

'Well. . . .' Lana paused. *Was* she ready to have a baby? She didn't really know. As an only child, with no immediate family, she had no experience of babies. They always looked quite cute in commercials though, and the Countess would be pleased. Anyhow, it was what Travis wanted, and she knew her resistance would be a major obstacle in the smooth running of their marriage.

'Well, sure, my husband and I want a family as soon as possible.'

'OK, so perhaps you'd like to go into the examination room and undress and I'll be through to take a look at you.'

Lana dressed in the cotton gown and dropped her knees open obediently to allow the gynaecologist to insert a speculum. This was one time when it didn't matter how rich you were, she mused. An internal was still an internal and to the doctor all women must look the same.

'So, you're . . . how old?'

'Thirty-five.'

'And how long have you had this IUD in place?'

'About twelve years.'

'Never attempted to get pregnant before?'

'No.'

'Well, you know, you're a little older than most women are when they start to have babies. My advice to you would be to go ahead and start trying, but don't expect anything to happen immediately. It may take a little while.'

'But you think I can have a baby?'

'Let's just wait and see, shall we?'

Lana swung her legs off the table and reached for her pantyhose. 'Umm . . . how can I put this? My husband's very anxious that we have a family straight away. Is there anything I can do to make it happen more quickly?'

'I'm afraid you're just going to have to let nature take its course. But if you're not pregnant six months from now, and you're still worried, come and see me and I'll run some tests.'

Lana pondered over the doctor's words as she left the building. She had sounded a little hesitant. Still, she was fit and healthy, she took good care of herself. . . .

'Drop me on Fifth Avenue,' she told the driver of the limousine. 'I think I'll do a little shopping.'

Saks had a sale on, and after years of having thrift drummed into her by the Countess, she never could resist a sale. The ground floor, wood-panelled and rich with expensive scent, was crowded with well-heeled Manhattan matrons in fur coats and Gucci loafers, picking their way idly through the piles of reduced goods. Lana spotted a pair of chinchilla ear-muffs reduced to twenty-five dollars and reached for them.

Peg Anderson's hand closed over the ear-muffs at the same moment. 'Gosh, I'm sorry. . . .' She released her grip abruptly sending Lana backwards a few steps.

'No, it's OK, you go ahead. I think they'd look really darling on your hair.' She appraised Peg's thick, glossy chestnut locks. 'Maybe the mink would look better against blonde. What do you think?'

Peg, who was still not at ease with the American friendliness to strangers, blushed. 'I don't know, I – '

'Now look at this!' Lana grabbed a cream cashmere scarf from the pile. 'This would be absolutely gorgeous on you! Great on the weekend with a jeans jacket, but also dressy enough to wear to your office.'

Lana had grown up listening to the Countess trying to persuade reluctant customers that a garment would suit them, and that it really was a bargain even though it was twice what they intended to pay.

'Actually, I'm only working in a café at the moment so – '

'You're English, right? I just *adore* your accent – but I guess you think it's me who has the accent. Over here on vacation?'

Peg shook her head. 'I was at Radcliffe, then Harvard Business School, and I've stayed on to look for a job.'

'Really? How fascinating.' Lana's eyes glazed over. She really didn't have time to listen to this kid's life story. 'I have to go now, but why don't you have this for a gift?' She tossed the scarf in Peg's direction and said to the assistant: 'Charge that to my account, please. Mrs Travis Macken.'

Before Peg had a chance to thank her, she had swept out of the store.

'Wait a minute!' Peg hurried after her, but she had jumped into a waiting limousine that pulled out from the kerb and was lost in the traffic.

Macken. As in Michael Macken. Hearing the name caused the strangest sensation, like setting eyes on a ghost. The woman did not sound as though she was from the South, but it was such a distinctive name. . . .

Peg hurried to a public phone booth and looked under 'M'. *The Macken Corporation* . . . of course they had a base in New York, that made perfect sense for a company heavily involved in shipping. Winding her scarf around her neck, she set off at a brisk walk to Park Avenue and 50th.

★ ★ ★

'I've been thinking, honey. . . .' Lana swept into Travis's office and kissed him on the forehead. He was reading the gossip page in the *New York Times* and chuckling to himself.

'About what I was saying to you before Christmas about hiring an assistant. I've only been out of the office an hour and the desk is heaped with messages. And on top of that I have the apartment to run, and dinners to give. And it will be even worse if we start a family. I should be thinking about delegating some of my stuff.'

'So give it to Paula.'

'I don't mean a secretary. I mean a graduate, someone who can help with administration. Take a little responsibility.'

'Sure,' said Travis without looking up.

'Good. I'll get an ad together and run it in the *Times* and the *Herald Tribune*.'

'Great.' Travis laid down the newspaper. 'The Atlanta Cigarette and Amusements figures came in this morning. Want to take a look?'

Lana perched on a corner of the desk and picked up the file. She ran her eye down a column of figures, shaking her head, then checked them again. 'Jesus, Travis, did you see this?'

'No, what?'

'I think their accounts department made a mistake. They transferred the funds to the holding account a week before we actually closed the deal, and we've been credited with the interest. Two hundred thousand dollars of it.'

'So what do we do with it?'

'Well, if it was their mistake I don't see why MackenCorp shouldn't keep it. I'll have it transferred to the company account at Chase Manhattan.'

A gleam came into Travis's eye. He patted Lana's thigh. 'Or . . . we could keep it.'

'*We* could?'

'Yeah. Let's put it into our personal account. Why not? No one knows about its existence but us. And we did close the deal. It would be sort of like a fee.'

'What if your father found out? Strictly speaking, we'd be stealing from the company.'

Travis shrugged. 'He won't find out. Why would he? Anyway, it's only a couple of hundred thousand bucks.'

Lana grinned. 'OK. But we better not make a habit of it.'

The intercom buzzed. 'Someone to see you, Mr Macken. Your brother.'

'Your brother! Were you expecting him, honey?'

'The hell I was!' Travis straightened his tie and pushed the newspaper to the corner of a desk. 'Michael! Good to see you! How're you doing? You're looking good. Check the suntan!'

Michael extended a hand but Travis put both arms around him and embraced him. 'You know, people were just about to give y'all up for dead. . . . Now I want you to meet my wife, Lana.'

Michael shook her hand. 'Yeah, I heard about that. Sorry I missed the wedding.'

'Can we offer you tea or coffee?' asked Lana with her sweetest smile. She could sense that Travis was uncomfortable. 'Did you eat lunch?'

'No thanks, I'll get straight to the point. I want a job.'

Travis laughed and slapped his forehead. 'A job! You are kidding, aren't you? I thought you didn't want anything to do with the old man and the business.'

'I changed my mind.'

'Well, hell, Michael, I'm sorry, but with Lana and I working alongside we've just about got everything covered. We're just about to advertise for a graduate assistant, but that wouldn't really be suitable.'

'Surely you have room for me too? Come on, Trav, there must be *something*. I've actually been thinking this over a lot and I've got a whole bunch of great ideas.'

'Why here? Why not in Savannah?'

'Because I want to be here in New York, that's why.'

'Anything you can do, I can do better, huh?'

'I thought that was your line,' Michael retorted, then coloured slightly. 'Hey, I'm sorry – '

'No, it's OK. I understand you wanting to be in New York. Everyone does. . . .'

Travis spread his hands out on the desk. He was still smiling, but his lips were pinched together. 'Look, this is putting me in a tight position, Mikey. It's Daddy who has the final say about things like this; you know that he's still top dog. He owns this place, I just run it. And you're not exactly his favourite person at the moment.'

'Yeah, but I'm still his son, just like you are. And now I'm back and I want to start over.'

'You're back, but you've been gone one hell of a long time. You're going to have to win back Daddy's faith in you. How does he know he can trust you?'

Michael glared.

'I'll tell you what,' said Travis smoothly. 'I'll call Daddy now and talk it out. I'll back you up. If he agrees, then I'm behind you all the way – '

'No!'

Michael stood up, suddenly. 'No, goddammit! I'm not having you do me any favours where he's concerned. He can either treat me fairly, or not, but without you twisting his arm! I'm sorry about this,' he muttered to Lana as he walked out.

She scrutinized Michael's retreating back. 'You don't want him working here, do you?'

'Got it in one.'

'Shame – he would have made me a great assistant.'

'Are you kidding? You've just seen what a hot-head he is! And he always was a smart alec. Too smart for his own good. We don't want to risk little brother watching everything we do and reporting back to the old man.'

Lana frowned. 'I always thought Michael was the black sheep.'

'Only when he realised he couldn't get Daddy and Mom's attention any other way.'

A pity, thought Lana. Michael had seemed rather interesting. Still, she could tell that having him around would upset Travis and at the moment she didn't want that.

'Honey – '

They were interrupted by the intercom again: 'Someone to see you, Mrs Macken. She says her name is Miss Anderson.'

Peg stood in the foyer of the MackenCorp offices trying to calm herself. The doors of the elevator had just slid shut and she had caught a split-second glimpse of a tall, dark man in a cashmere overcoat. A man who looked just like Michael.

It could easily have been him. If it was the same family, then his father owned these offices. Nonsense, she told herself; it wasn't necessarily him. Manhattan was full of tall, handsome men. And anyway, if it was him then she had just had a lucky escape. She had no wish to meet that arrogant, pushy son of a bitch again.

Lana Macken's husband was another of those tall, handsome men, so classically good-looking and athletic that she felt embarrassed when he had stood up and grasped her hand with such enthusiasm. He looked younger than his wife, too. She was expecting someone middle-aged, distinguished looking, perhaps greying at the temples.

'I hope you don't mind, but I wanted a chance to thank you for the scarf. And also,' she went on boldly, 'to give you this.'

She handed Travis a copy of her resumé. 'I'm looking for a job, so always carry a few copies of this around with me.'

'Excellent . . .' he murmured, turning to raise his eyebrows at Lana, who was sitting next to him on the other side of the desk. 'This really is excellent. A Morrison Scholarship to Radcliffe, graduating *summa cum laude,* then on to Harvard Business where you were a Baker Scholar for outstanding results at the end of the first year. . . . It all makes me wonder why you haven't been snapped up already.'

'I think I can explain.' Peg found herself looking at Lana when she spoke. 'I graduated last year and moved down to New York, and I planned on using some of the contacts I made at Harvard to get a job. The trouble is I'm a British citizen, and in order to get a green card any company wanting to employ me has to prove to Immigration that I can do the job better than a US national. And since I don't have any experience, most of them haven't even wanted to try.'

'Uh-huh, I see.'

'Couldn't you have tried in England?' asked Lana sweetly. 'I'm sure you could have walked into any job you wanted there.'

'I wanted to try and make it over here. It was sort of a personal challenge I'd set myself.'

'Uh-huh.' Travis glanced at Lana, putting the resumé back in its folder. 'It just so happens that we are looking for a graduate to help out, a sort of trainee executive position. And I'm sure, if we come to agreement, we can fix a green card for you. Are you interested?'

'Of course!'

'Great. Drop by tomorrow at 9.30 and we'll run through some details.'

Travis's eyes followed Peg as she walked to the door. He's assessing her legs, thought Lana. She noticed with irritation that the kid had long legs, strong and shapely with well-defined muscles.

'Good legs,' she said grudgingly.

'Couldn't really see them.'

'Bullshit!' Lana lit a cigarette. 'I don't think we should give her the job.'

'Of course we should! We could pay her as little as 10,000 bucks a year, and we'd have a bargain! She obviously has a quick mind. And initiative too, you can't deny that.'

'She's too smart.'

'Don't be crazy.'

'Anyhow, I think you should have tried to work something out with Michael.'

'We've discussed that.'

'And we don't need trouble with Immigration.'

'I can deal with them.'

'So you've got your heart set on this British girl.'

'Yup.'

Lana shrugged. 'OK, honey.' Nine times out of ten she could get around Travis but he could be stubborn, and when he set his jaw like that, she knew there was no point trying to change his mind.

Besides, Miss Anderson was not only too smart, but too cute by far. And she didn't want Travis to see how much that had got her rattled.

EIGHT

New York, 1978

'Peg, could I have a word, honey?'

Lana Macken stood beside Peg Anderson's desk, immaculate in a black and pink Yves Saint Laurent suit and stiletto-heeled courts.

Peg did not look up immediately. She carried on looking over the figures she had just compiled, an informal in-house audit. The lack of movement was deliberate. Lana came to her umpteen times a day with petty queries or non-existent problems, and each time she expected Peg to drop what she was doing and leap to attention. It was a petty power game, and she had decided she was not going to play it.

'If I might have a moment, honey . . .' said Lana, letting the steel show beneath the sickly sweetness.

Peg looked up, slowly.

'There are a couple of things I'd like you to do. . . .' As she spoke, she was trying to read the writing obscured by Peg's hands. 'What's that?'

'Just a review of your business practices,' Peg replied cheerfully. 'I thought I'd go through your files and accounts and see how things could be streamlined.'

Lana opened her mouth to object, but Peg went on quickly. 'I notice, for example, that you're paying far too much for insurance. Who's your broker?'

'We use Keane and Pallenburg.'

'Change them.'

'That's out of the question. The Keanes are old family friends of the Mackens and Travis plays racquets with Manny Keane.'

'Well, they're still ripping you off.'

'I think for the moment it would be better if you stick to the assignments I allocate to you.'

Peg sighed and laid down her pen. 'You're the boss. I just thought that since I have an MBA, I could help you by looking at this stuff.'

From the corner of her eye she saw Lana stiffen. She hated to be reminded that Peg had an MBA from Harvard.

'Dry-cleaning,' she said, tossing the tickets on to the desk. 'Would you be a darling and go collect some stuff for me? It won't take you long. It's right around the corner.'

This sort of ritual humiliation was all part of Lana's game. Peg knew full well that the dry-cleaner she used had a delivery service, and that Lana had a full-time maid whose job it was to take care of Lana's clothes.

'And there's one other thing,' Lana went on with honeyed sweetness. 'I don't think we're going to be able to call you Peg.'

Peg folded her arms across her chest. 'And why's that?'

'It doesn't sound right somehow. *Peg.*' She said the one syllable as though she had something stuck in the back of her throat, giving it a hard, ugly sound. 'That first point of contact we have with clients is so important, and we need you to have a name that's a little more sophisticated, more feminine.'

Peg pretended to look concerned. She found the whole issue ridiculous, but was interested to see how far Lana would take it. 'Peg's short for Margaret. I was christened Margaret Ann.'

'Margaret . . . hmmm . . . Margaret Ann, Ann Margaret . . . I know, how about Margot?'

'Margot? Sounds a bit hard to me.'

'Margot . . .' said Lana thoughtfully. 'Hmmm. . . .'

Peg had learned enough about Lana to know that she would dearly love to provoke an angry or outraged reaction. That would give her the excuse she needed to get rid of someone she viewed not as a cheap and useful resource but some sort of rival. She had also learned that Lana was very effective at getting what she wanted from people, and so she trod carefully.

The personal resentment was easier for her to deal with than the sense of frustration she had from being under-used. The job had enormous potential, but so far she had not found a way to exploit it. Lana always stood in her path, like a couture-clad harpy. She suspected that Travis Macken was more sympathetic and willing to give her a chance to prove herself, but he rarely stood up to his wife. He enjoyed the world of business, but he was lazy and only too happy to let someone else take the tough decisions. It was obvious that as far as the New York office of MackenCorp was concerned, Lana was the one who really held the reins.

Lana leaned on her desk and flicked her thumb on her gold lighter. When her cigarette was alight she turned her head aside to puff the smoke away.

'When you've collected the cleaning, I'd like you to go along to the beauty salon on Park and 60th. Marie will take care of you. She does my hair.'

'It's OK, Lana, really, I've just had my hair cut a couple of weeks ago.'

Lana took a drag on her cigarette, narrowing her eyes in amusement. 'Honey, in the business world grooming is all important. You can never afford to look anything less than your best. Think of it as a treat, on me.'

'Thank you, but I'm quite happy as I am.'

Lana shrugged. 'You know best,' she said in the tone people use when they believe *they* know best. 'I just thought you could use a bit of frosting, brighten yourself up a little.'

'I think one bottle blonde round here is quite enough,' Peg murmured as she stood up to put on her jacket.

'I'm sorry, honey, what was that?'

'Nothing.' Peg grabbed the dry-cleaning tickets and thrust them into her jacket pocket. 'Nothing at all.'

When Peg returned to the office later, she found two purple Bergdorf Goodman carriers on her desk.

'I had Bergdorfs send over a couple of things for you,' Lana explained. 'Think of them as a bonus.'

Peg unpacked a red Dior suit and an Anne Klein day dress in soft cashmere.

'You don't like them? I'll have them sent right back and you can choose something else.'

'No, it's not that, they're lovely. . . .' Peg turned to face Lana. 'It's just that if I'm going to get a bonus I'd rather feel that I've had a chance to earn it.'

Lana ignored this. 'I have another gift . . . here.'

She produced a turquoise Tiffany's box. Inside was a gold charm bracelet, the letters M, A, R, G, O and T hanging from the links.

'Lana . . . this is too much!' She looked down at the glittering trinket. 'Money, I mean. It must have cost – '

'Six hundred dollars,' said Lana briskly. 'Go ahead, put it on.'

Peg did so, reluctantly.

'There ya go! From now on, I'm going to call you Margot!'

As soon as she's gone, thought Peg, I'll take the loathsome thing off. . . .

'Now, before you go tonight, Margot, I'd just like you to do these figures for me.'

She handed Peg a bulging folder. Peg flicked through it eagerly, then realised with a sinking heart that the figures simply needed typing.

'Surely Paula could do this?'

'I know, I know. . . .' Lana gave a mock-guilty shrug. 'It is really a job for Paula, only Travis needs that stuff for tomorrow and I already told Paula she could have an afternoon off to go visit with her folks.'

She swept out, leaving a lingering after-shock of Joy.

Peg was a poor typist, which meant that a job which would have taken Paula an hour and a half took her five hours.

By the time she had made the tenth irreversible error, requiring her to rip up a whole sheet and start again, her back was aching relentlessly and there were beads of sweat breaking out on her forehead. Lana's stupid bracelet was rattling against the keys of the typewriter. She wrenched it off and thrust it into one of the drawers of her desk.

'Hi!'

She started guiltily. Travis Macken stood in the doorway, watching her. He gave her one of his easy smiles and strolled over to the desk.

'She gave you the Point Pleasant stuff, huh?'

'Just to type. I've made one or two minor changes though; I hope you don't mind.'

'You find this interesting?'

'Of course,' said Peg, aware that she sounded a little prim.

'I'm going down to Point Pleasant tomorrow.'
'How nice for you.'
'And I think y'all ought to come with me.'

Peg was horrified to find that she was really looking forward to her day out with Travis Macken.

Horrified because deep down inside, some secret part of her found the idea of being on her own with him rather exciting. The truth was that she rather liked him.

And she found him attractive. Very attractive. It wasn't just his golden good looks, which were a little too conventional for her taste, but his manner. He was so relaxed, so easy; nothing ever seemed to trouble him. He made her feel that everything was easy. And she had a sneaking liking for that Southern drawl, the tantalizing way he could draw out words, the polite little phrases that somehow sounded so sexy. Michael Macken had spoken the same way, of course, but had been a little lighter on the charm. . . .

They sat in the back of the stretch Mercedes, which was mercifully wide enough to prevent any bodily contact. Peg accepted a mineral water from the bar and sipped it slowly, looking out of the window. Her back was growing stiff from the effort of sitting stock-still; if she moved around in the seat her skirt rode up her thighs and she had to tug it down sharply, which drew more atention to her legs than if she had done nothing. In reality her skirt was easily long enough for discretion, but in her imagination the lacey tops of her stockings were dangerously close to being exposed to Travis's burning blue gaze.

He sat with a glass of bourbon in his hand and didn't say much until the limousine reached the waterfront at Point Pleasant and they could see the steely waters of the Atlantic rippling invitingly, with the pleasure palaces of Asbury Park and Atlantic City a grey line on the horizon. Peg's nostrils caught a gust of a familiar smell borne on the wind, a pungent, salty dead-fishy smell.

As soon as he caught sight of the ocean he became animated, jumping out onto the jetty and stretching like a cat.

'I'n't this great? I used to love going down to the waterfront with my daddy when I was a kid. . . .'

He turned and grinned at Peg. 'Too bad we didn't bring a ball with us. We could have gone down onto the beach and played a little softball.'

Peg glanced down at her stiletto courts and black stockings.

'Well, maybe not. . . .'

'Where exactly is the site?' she asked, in an attempt to steer the conversation back from pleasure to business.

'Over there, at the end of that wharf.'

'Aren't we going to walk over and take a closer look?'

'Well sure, if you want to.' Travis looked at her in surprise. 'I didn't figure you'd be that interested in looking at a pile of dirty old metal.'

'That's what we're here for, isn't it?' asked Peg tartly. She attempted to smooth her wind-ruffled hair behind her ears, tucked her briefcase under her arm and began to walk.

Travis fell into step beside her. 'This used to be an old fitting shed. They brought a lot of big old boats up here after the war to fit them out into passenger cruisers. There was quite a lot of money in it then. The old man got into doing that in the 60s. . . .' His silk tie fluttered in the wind, tickling Peg's cheek. He smoothed it down again. 'We got the idea to knock the whole shed down and turn it into a marina complex with a jetty and amusement arcades. Amusement arcades are big down here in the summer, very big. I thought we might try and put up a fast-food joint, but not just doing burgers and fries, some healthy food as well. Salads, seafood, that kind of stuff.'

Peg, who knew that the original idea had been Lana's, nodded. She would have liked to go and look closer, and measure up the place for one or two ideas of her own, but Travis put a hand on her shoulder and wheeled her round abruptly so that they were facing the limousine again.

'Say, it's getting kind of windy. Let's go and get some lunch.'

Peg followed him reluctantly. It seemed a pity to spend so little time out here, after driving all the way from New York. She slowed her pace a little as they reached the Mercedes, its door held open in readiness by the driver. She wanted to go on looking at the ocean. The grey water, with its surface furled by little white, lacy ripples, reminded her of New Brighton. She could hardly fail to remember how it had looked and smelt. She had spent so many hours in her girlhood staring out at it.

Her view was suddenly obscured by Travis's face, inches from her own. He placed a hand on either side of her face, immobilising her, while his lips pressed firmly, heavily against hers. His smell assaulted her nostrils; expensive cologne and a faint trace of Lana. Her cigarettes and Joy. He tasted of toothpaste.

With her lips firmly closed, Peg turned her head and sidestepped his embrace.

'Mr Macken – '

'Travis, please.'

'*Mr* Macken,' said Margot firmly. 'Please don't do anything like that again. I took this job because I really wanted it, and I want to do it well.' She managed to look straight into his blue eyes. 'This may not be easy for someone like you to understand, but I want to make something of myself. I want to get on in life, and the only means I have of doing that is by being good at what I do. And there's no chance of that if the job means I have to be . . . available.'

Travis thrust his hands into the pockets of his cashmere overcoat. 'OK. Only please don't be mad at me, Margot.' He put his head on one side, with a boyish expression.

'I won't if you'll forget about Lana's Margot nonsense and call me by my name!'

'Deal. Peg.'

They laughed, sealing this minor conspiracy against Lana.

'And I want you to promise me you won't fire me for refusing to kiss you. I'd rather wait tables in the crummiest downtown bar than use my MBA in heavy petting sessions with my employer.'

Travis burst out laughing. 'Get in the car . . . come on, Peg, get in the goddam car, I won't bite.' He climbed in beside her.

'So – are we friends?'

'Sure we are.' Travis gave her his reassuring, untroubled grin.

'Good.'

Peg leaned back, but she was not totally relaxed. She found herself stealing the occasional sideways glance at Travis once the car had rejoined the freeway. Finally he saw her doing it, and she looked away, embarrassed. He knows I find him attractive, she thought, and he knows that *I* know. The thought sent a little shiver of excitement through her.

And all the way back to New York City she imagined she

could hear a clock somewhere, just ticking away the time until something happened. Ridiculous, she told herself. Nothing will happen, because I won't *allow* it to happen. It's as simple as that.

Lana Macken lay on a white hospital bed, dressed in a white, standard issue hospital gown.

It was so peaceful here that she almost wished she could stay longer. Just lying here doing nothing, resting. That was something she had done very little of in the past six months. She was always busy doing something, even if it was only shopping or getting her nails fixed. It was quite a relief just to stop, to let time stand still.

The view from the window was nice too. It was colder up here than in the city, and spring was only just arriving. The tops of the trees were just veiled with the newest, palest green leaves, and if she half closed her eyes it looked like there was a green mist in the valley below. Pretty. She had never really spent any time in the country.

She was in a private clinic in upstate New York, near the Finger Lakes. She was using this place rather than the hospital favoured by her gynaecologist in Manhattan because that was also where the wives of all Travis's friends and acquaintances went. It only took one of them to see you there in an obstetric ward and rumours burned their way through cocktail parties and dinners like a forest fire. She had borrowed the company jet to fly her up to Syracuse, telling Travis she was seeing a surgeon to get her breast job remodelled. He never looked at her breasts these days, so he wouldn't notice that there were no fresh scars.

There was a small, ugly scar on her stomach, though, just near her navel. She peered down at it, touched it tentatively, and then in her mind re-ran the conversation she had had with the obstetric surgeon afterwards.

'The laparoscopy was very useful, Mrs Macken, which justified using a surgical procedure. I wouldn't normally carry one out on a patient who had only been trying to conceive for four months, but you felt concerned and you had been using an IUD, so I agreed we should take a look.'

'So I was right, Doctor? There was something wrong?'

'I'm afraid I found very extensive scarring, in the uterus and in both *fallopian tubes. The result of a pelvic infection, which can be a side effect of using an IUD over a period of years. I'm sorry.'*

'Sorry? You mean I can't get pregnant at all?'

'If it were just the tubes, we could try clearing them, but even if you did then conceive, and that would be far from certain given your age, you would face a very high risk of miscarriage due to the intrauterine adhesions. You could be facing a long series of miscarriages, which in turn could worsen the scar tissue. . . . I'm afraid I can't recommend further surgery. I see this quite often in women of your age and sometimes I can help them, but in your case. . . .

'Like I said, I'm sorry. . . .'

Lana hadn't asked him if he was sure, or if it was worth a second opinion. This guy was a world expert in his field, he lectured at Cornell Medical School. If he didn't know what he was talking about, no one would.

Lana felt quite relieved really. Very relieved, even. It was good just to know for certain, to be able to take stock, to plan. It would have been terrible to go on and on trying dutifully, still chasing a faint glimmer of hope that something was going to happen. Having to make sure she screwed Travis at exactly the right time each month. Now that she knew babies and diapers and christening robes and strollers were not going to be for her, she could quite easily wipe them from her agenda completely, when only a week ago she had sneaked into the baby department in Bloomingdales and fingered the toe of a velvet-soft sleepsuit. Sure, a cute baby would have been quite nice, but. . . .

The obstetrician had asked her to consider adoption but she had firmly rejected the suggestion. Travis Macken would rather die than have to adopt a child because he couldn't get his wife pregnant. Or to be precise, he'd rather divorce.

Divorce. That was the next thing she was going to have to think about. There was no question of staying married to Travis now that she knew for sure she could never give him children. As soon as he found out, that would be all the justification he needed to get rid of her. ('But, Lana honey, you knew I wanted a family, I said so from the start. . . .') And she would much rather jump than be pushed. She was going to have to tell him, but she would bide her time until the right moment came along. And she was going to make sure she came out of it with money and prestige. And power. Sure as God made little apples, she wasn't going to give *that* up.

She looked out of the window at the green mist again. Tears pricked at the back of her eyes, but she couldn't really cry. She felt too tired. She would worry about the grieving, the abandoning of her dreams later, but for now she just felt so tired. All she really wanted to do was go home to the old apartment in Brooklyn Heights and climb into bed while the Countess fried up some of her special Wiener schnitzels, followed by apple fritters with whipped cream. And she could take off all her make-up and just let her hair hang down all anyhow and watch some *I Love Lucy* re-runs on the TV. Let someone else have the responsibility of being Mrs Travis Macken. Someone ten years younger; pretty, fertile and eager to please.

Margot. Shit, it was so obvious what would happen. If she told Travis about the divorce right now, the chances were he would fall right into the arms of that uppity little English girl. She was smart enough to be very useful to him, and there was no getting around how sexy she was. She had seen the way Travis looked at her when he thought he was unobserved.

Well, she was damned if she was going to hand her husband to the kid just like that. She would have to get rid of Margot. She would find a way, and it would be soon, but until then, she would hold on to her big announcement.

Travis was going crazy.

He was being *driven* crazy by that gorgeous little English girl. She was so damn cool. Not cool in the way that Lana could be cool, all brisk and controlled and in charge. No, this was different. It was like there was something burning away at the very heart of her but she was damned if she was going to let you have it, or even get near it. So on the outside she was all sassy and razor-sharp, even sometimes downright snappy. Her eyes sometimes looked like she might want you to touch her, but everything else about her, her body language, said loudly, 'Touch me not'. And yet she had an energy and a dynamism that made even Lana seem languid.

That time they went out to Point Pleasant had been great. He had really enjoyed being with her, and for a moment it felt like they might get something going and then – wham! – the defences went up again and the temperature dropped. He'd tried to find opportunities to be alone with her since then, but she was very clever at keeping her distance, and most of the time, Lana was around.

Still, as a game it was kind of fun. Sometimes he went and stood close to her, so close that if he just moved a little he would touch her. And that bothered her. After a while she became tense when she was around him so he didn't need to actually get close to her to get a response, he'd just walk into the same room and she'd look embarrassed. And then she'd remember that control of hers and she'd make some smart-alec remark, or turn frosty again.

The joke was on him in the end, though. Peg was subject to brief moments of embarrassment and discomfiture, but he was having to deal with a raging obsession that grew worse as spring gave way to summer and she started hanging around the office in skimpy dresses that left most of her skin bare. He swore he could smell her when he walked into a room, before he even laid eyes on her. She had an intensely sweet, feminine smell mingling soap powder and spearmint and carnations. He started to get mad at Lana for smoking around the place and masking Peg's heavenly scent with her cigarettes.

Part of the trouble was that he and Lana were hardly ever having sex any more, only when she decided it was the right time for her to get pregnant. No wonder that hadn't happened – they didn't make out enough. So his obsession with his ice princess was being fuelled all the time by plain old-fashioned horniness. Sure, he picked up a girl in a bar occasionally or had a call girl sent over to the office when he was working late. But *she* was always there the next day.

No girl had ever done this to him before. They had always made themselves available to him in the end. He just couldn't figure it out. Lana had kept him at arms' length to begin with, but she had always had the air of someone who would give in at a price. Anyhow, Lana had never been able to get him this hot. She had quite a trim little body and was pleasingly stylish but Peg was cute as hell, gorgeous. She was also single, alone in the city, and from what Travis could make out, she didn't know many people in New York, yet a big, handsome guy with plenty of money couldn't even get a date.

He started to wonder whether there was something a little screwy, a little odd about her. And then he decided he was either going to end up getting so crazy he would rape her or he was just going to have to forget it. So he tried to forget it.

One hot day in August, Lana called Peg through into her office, and said quietly: 'Margot I have a person to person call for you from Liverpool, England.'

Peg glanced down at Lana's face, and instantly felt the blood drain from her own. 'Right. Thanks. I'll take it in reception.'

'Honey. . . .' Lana chewed her bottom lip. 'I've been asked to tell you that it's bad news. I thought I ought to have the call switched through here. . . . I'll leave you alone, OK?'

Shakily, Peg walked to Lana's desk and picked up the phone. She was aware of Lana's face on the other side of the plate glass partition, watching her thoughtfully as she blew smoke up at the ceiling.

'Hello?'

'Peg!'

'Jimmy, what's happened?'

'It's Dad, Peg. He . . . he's had a heart attack.'

'Oh, no. . . .' Peg took a long breath. 'What's happened, has he – ?' Jimmy's voice seemed to grow faint. 'He died, Peg. He died before we even got him to hospital.'

'Oh, Jimmy . . . oh, God – '

'I'm sorry, I can't talk . . . you will come back, won't you?'

'Of course, of course I will. When's the – ?'

'Friday. Why don't you ring when you know what time you're arriving?'

'Sure. But listen, Jimmy . . . oh, God . . . how's Mum?'

'Not too good. But trying to put a brave face on. You know Mum.'

'I'll get the first flight back, Jimmy, I promise. I'll let you know when.'

When she had hung up she sank into a chair, trying to conjure up an image of her father but failing. The only thing that floated into her mind was a picture of her dark blue British passport.

Where was it? Where had she put it? She would need to find it amongst all the clutter in her tiny apartment, and she would need to get a seat on a flight. . . .

'Oh God, Dad. . . .' She spoke the words out loud as the situation sunk in.

'Margot honey, what happened?' Lana was at her elbow proffering a glass of mineral water.

'My father died.' Peg was fighting back a deluge of tears and really just wanted Lana to go away and leave her alone.

'Oh, I'm *so* sorry. . . .'

Peg pressed the backs of her hands against her eyes. 'Anyhow . . . if it's all right with you, I'll get Paula to book me on the evening flight out of JFK. I don't know how long I'll be gone, it depends how my mother is, but it shouldn't be too long – '

'Are you sure you're going to be able to do that?'

Peg looked up. 'Do what?'

'Go and come back like that.'

'It's my father's funeral; I hardly have a choice!'

'Of course you don't, honey. . . .' Lana patted her shoulder. 'It's just the Immigration thing.'

'What thing?'

Lana's voice was as sweetly reasonable as ever. 'Well, from what you told me, your temporary resident's visa that allowed you to study at Harvard expired quite a time ago. So if you go back home you'd have to apply to the American Embassy for another visa to get back into the States. And when they see the discrepancy between the date of expiry and the date of your return, they might refuse you a new visa. The Immigration people over here might start asking questions and find you don't have a green card, and then MackenCorp would get dragged in . . . you see the problem?'

'I see it,' said Peg coldly, 'but right now I really don't care. My father, whom I adored, but haven't seen for more than two years, has just died. Now if going home to bury him means I can't come back to New York, then so be it. This may be a good job, but after all it's just a job, isn't it? Now if you'll excuse me, I have arrangements – '

Lana was still trying not to smile. 'So you're saying you resign your position with the Macken Corporation?'

'It looks as though I don't have any choice, doesn't it?'

NINE

Liverpool and New York, 1978

At the funeral, all Peg could think about was how cold it was. It was supposed to be summer, after all, but the sky was bleak and grey and there was a chill wind blowing in from the Atlantic. And it rained. It rained every single day she was in England.

At the graveside, everyone was in raincoats, without exception, so they looked like a gathering at some professional convention, all members of the same grieving caste. There was Jimmy and his wife, in cheap chainstore black and beige trenchcoats, their mother in a shiny blue mac she'd had for ages, herself in her Burberry, her aunt in belted brown gabardine, her uncle in an ancient, cracked Gannex.

She felt uncomfortable at the wake, which was held in their front room in Virginia Road. Tea and ham sandwiches and bottles of brown ale for the men. She'd been away so long, that was part of it. Mostly, it was guilt, though, guilt that she was the only one who hadn't been there. And by the time she arrived, both their house and Jimmy's were full to bursting with relatives of her father's, so she had had to book a room at a four-star hotel near Lime Street station. The drabness of the impersonal room just added to her sense of alienation.

When the last of the mourners had left, Peg went into the kitchen. Her mother was sitting at the table with an uneaten ham sandwich on the plate in front of her. The black cardigan draped around her shoulders swamped her; she seemed smaller, shrunken.

Peg put an arm around her shoulders.

'Mum . . . I'm sorry. For not visiting sooner. If I'd known – '

'He was proud of you. Proud of what you were doing. You mustn't feel sorry.'

'But I do! What kind of a daughter have I been to you these past years – ?'

'Don't, don't!' Kath Anderson buried her face in her hands. 'Look, love, why don't you go and see Sandra? I know she'd really like you to.'

She wants to be alone, thought Peg. I should have realised that.

'Sure, that's a good idea. Do her parents still live in the same place?'

'Oh, didn't you know? I thought she would have told you . . . she took over the lease of the Eat Inn, down the road. She's opened a café.'

Travis Macken was standing in the doorway of his wife's office.

'Did Peg say when she was coming back?'

'You mean Margot,' Lana corrected him.

'Yeah, Margot.'

'Oh, didn't I tell you, honey?' Lana feigned innocence. 'She told me she wasn't coming back. I pointed out that her position with Immigration would be impossible, and she decided her family was more important.'

'But we could have fixed something with Immigration. . . . Christ, Lana, the girl was good. She worked incredibly hard and she had a first-class brain – '

'And she told me where I could stick the job.'

'But – '

'Anyway, we have more important things to talk about. Come and sit down.'

'I was on my way to a racquet game with Rob.'

'This really is important, believe me.' Lana's smile had faded. Under her perfectly applied make-up she looked pale and drawn.

'You know we've been trying for months now to have a baby?'

'Yup. Sure is fun trying!' The joke was a lame one, and they both knew it. The fact was that the fun had long since vanished. Travis shifted uncomfortably on his seat.

'Well . . . there isn't going to be one. I've had some tests and

I'm — ' she balked at using the bleak word — 'infertile. Barren. I'm never going to have a baby.'

'Are you sure? I mean, what about all these new test-tube treatments. There's lots of ways they can help now.'

Lana shook her head firmly. 'That might take years, and what if it didn't work? No, it's been a lot of fun but it's over, Travis.'

She smiled at his shocked expression. 'C'mon, honey, I was the one who started all this in the first place; at least let me be the one to let you off the hook. New York's full of pretty young things who can give you half a dozen heirs to the Macken empire. I'll fly down to Mexico and get the divorce fixed, then you can start on finding one.'

Travis shook his head slowly. 'How long have you known about this?'

'A while.'

'But you've only just decided to tell me?'

'What difference does it make? You know now. Maybe. . .'

'Maybe what?'

'Maybe it took me some time to get used to the idea myself.'

'So what now?'

'Well . . . why don't you give your attorney a call and work out some sort of settlement? Or we could sit down with him and do it together.'

'OK.'

'Only, there is one thing I'd like you to agree to.'

'What's that?'

'That I get to keep the job. I want to go on working for MackenCorp.'

'For now, sure.'

'Thanks.' Lana forced a smile. When Travis had gone she sank down in her chair, bowing her head. The effort this had taken was enormous, completely draining her. But she was damned if she was ever going to let Travis see how much she was hurting.

Peg couldn't suppress her smile of pleasure as she approached what was now called the Seaview Café. This was what Sandra had always wanted, and now she had achieved it. The brightly lit windows, completely obscured with steam, were hung with cheerful curtains, and Peg knew before she even opened the door that the interior would be warm and welcoming.

Sandra was behind the counter. She stared when she saw Peg, then broke into a smile and held out her arms.

'Peg! Oh, Peggy!'

The girls embraced.

'I heard about your dad, I'm so sorry. . . . Oh, but it's great to see you again, Peg. You look great!'

'So do you!' Sandra had slimmed down considerably, and had a sleek, prosperous look. 'And you're doing what you always wanted to do. How's business?'

'Great! We're doing really well.'

'We?'

Sandra grinned and looked coy. 'My partner and I. Hang on a second. . . .' She went behind the counter and stuck her head into the kitchen. 'Come and look who's here, love!'

Billy Walsh came out from the kitchen, wiping his hands on an apron. He seemed to have gained the weight Sandra had lost, but he was still devastatingly attractive.

'Hi, Peggy!'

Sandra wound her arms around his waist, leaning against Billy's shoulder. There was no doubt that they were a couple as well as partners.

'So you two are – '

Sandra blushed like a schoolgirl. 'Didn't anyone tell you? Well, poor old Billy couldn't be expected to go on waiting for you for ever, Peg! Could you, love?' She looked at Billy adoringly. 'At first we were just working together, running this place, but he noticed me in the end!'

Peg suddenly felt uncomfortable, an intruder with smart New York clothes, and a suntan. The café, which had seemed warm and cosy at first, now seemed claustrophobic, airless. The tea-urn hissed incessantly in the corner, clouding the windows so that you couldn't see out.

'Well anyway, I only popped in to say "hi". I don't want to keep you from your work – '

'Don't be daft! I want to hear all your news. Come and sit down, and Billy will bring us some tea over, won't you, Billy love?'

'Sure.'

Billy filled two cups and brought them to the table, then retreated to the counter. He seemed reluctant to look Peg in the eye.

'So, how long are you over for?'

'For good, as far as I know.' Peg explained the problem with her visa.

'D'you mind?'

'I don't know. . . .' Peg toyed with her cup of tea. She had drunk so much after the funeral that she was already awash with the stuff. 'I liked it over there very much, and I'd just found an interesting job so, yes, I suppose I do mind.'

'Well, their loss is our gain. At least I'll be able to see something of you if you stay in Liverpool. You could always come and work here with Billy and me, tell us everything we're doing wrong.'

'I think three would be a crowd. . . .' Peg glanced in Billy's direction. 'You and Billy Walsh, eh? Does he still drive a motor-bike?'

'No, he's just got a Ford Escort. I wasn't happy about him riding around on the bike after. . .'

'After?'

'Well, it's not official yet, but we're engaged!'

'Congratulations! When's the wedding?'

'Not till next year, probably. Give us time to get some money together. Still time for you to beat me to it!'

Peg shook her head. 'No chance of that!'

'Look, if you hang on a moment while we close up here, the three of us could go out for a drink. It would be just like old times.'

Peg suddenly felt very tired. 'Another time maybe. When I've got over the jet lag.'

Back at the hotel Peg changed out of her black suit, showered and dressed in jeans and a sweatshirt. She switched the television on, then off again, paced to and fro, unable to settle. She felt fretful. Seeing Billy and Sandra together like that, so happy, had touched something deep inside her. Something unsettling. She was the one who had been away, yet they had moved on and changed, leaving her behind.

Her passport sat beside the telephone like a reproach. If she was honest with herself, all she wanted to do now was to get out of Liverpool, jump on a plane and get back to New York. She could go through the business of applying for another visa, but it would only allow her temporary residence, and she would be back to the same problem of working without a green card. It didn't seem a very satisfactory solution. She even considered phoning Lana and apologising in order to enlist her help, but dismissed the idea immediately. Lana would love it, but she would still find a way of saying no.

Going out seemed a preferable option to staying in her room, pacing like a caged animal, so she put on her Burberry and walked down through the city to the docks. Seagulls wheeled over her head, screeching, and the wind whipped the rain onto her cheeks. In the distance she could just see the Mersey ferry rolling across the churning tea-coloured water. Beyond that was the mouth of the estuary, the Atlantic Ocean, America. . . .

The sound and sight of the dock, derelict though it was, suddenly brought her father to life in her mind's eye. She remembered the day he had taken her and Jimmy to the shipyard, the feel of his strong arms as he lifted her up, the bright cheerfulness in his voice as he showed them around his world. How tall he had been. What he had smelled like. Tears sprang to her eyes, and mixed with the rain on her cheeks.

When it grew heavier she turned back to the hotel. She ordered a glass of wine and some sandwiches from room service and watched a comedy show on the television. She slipped into a light doze, then finally fell deeply asleep.

A firm knock at the door woke her.

'Come in.'

The hotel corridor was lit by a single light which gleamed on the hair of the man in the doorway, framing him with a blurred edge of light. Peg groped for the switch on her bedside lamp.

'Hi!'

Travis Macken stood before her with his damp raincoat slung casually over one shoulder. He was so athletic, so sun-tanned and so American he looked like a creature from another planet. And she was so pleased to see him that she almost leapt into his arms.

'Hi!'

She took a couple of steps backwards, staring at him. 'What the hell are you doing here?'

'I want you to come back to New York.'

Peg sat on the end of the bed and started to laugh. 'You mean you've just flown all the way across the Atlantic to say this? You're crazy!'

'I've got a proposition for you.' He caught her eye and grinned. 'A business proposition. Look, I know this all looks pretty crazy, but please would y'all just hear me out?' He looked around the small hotel room, littered with clothes, towels, and the remains of Peg's supper tray. 'We can't talk here, let's go out someplace.'

They walked through the rain-sodden streets to a small Italian trattoria.

'The weather always like this here?' asked Travis.

'Pretty much.'

Travis shuddered. She half expected him to put an arm round her or try and hold her hand, but he kept a respectful distance. In the restaurant they ordered steak and green salad and a bottle of Chianti. Peg couldn't help thinking as she sipped her wine how nice it was to be out having dinner with someone like this. She couldn't remember the last time she had been taken on a dinner date. In New York she was always working so hard, or going to the gym to keep in shape. And she hadn't ever met anyone there that she really liked.

'Lana came to me and hit me with some real heavy news that day you left,' said Travis as he refilled his glass. 'That's what got this whole thing started. She told me she's just found out she couldn't ever give me children. She knows that's real important to me, so she said she'd fly to Mexico to get a divorce. She's there now; it should be through in about a week.'

'I'm sorry,' said Peg stiffly.

Travis shrugged his shoulders. 'Don't be. It was never a big love affair or nothin' like that. Just something that suited us both at the time. The thing is, I want *you* to marry me.'

Peg laughed at Travis, who was smiling engagingly, as if what he had suggested was no more significant than a picnic on the beach. 'You're crazy.'

'Now, y'all promised to hear me out.'

'Yes I did. Sorry. Go on.'

She looked up into Travis's bright blue eyes and felt that familiar shiver go through her.

'Now through circumstances which were not of my own making, I have become single again. And I want you back working with me in New York again. And you want to come back, right?'

'Right?'

'OK, so if the authorities find out that you've been living over there for a couple of years without a visa, they're never goin' to give you a green card. So I figure the only way around the problem is for you and I to get married.'

'Just like that,' said Peg drily.

'This is strictly a business proposition, just for as long as it takes to convince the authorities. If we split up and divorce the minute we get back there, they might be a little suspicious. So we'd have to live together for a while. But it would be separate bedrooms and no strings attached.'

'You're sure this isn't just a ploy?'

'What d'you mean?'

'To get me into bed.'

Travis threw back his head and laughed. 'I'n't that precious?'

'It's just . . . it's such a big thing. I mean, you and Lana have been married less than a year. Didn't you . . . well, don't you love her?'

'Lana and I are good buddies, there's really not much more to it than that. At the time we both had our reasons to want to get married, and it suited us OK, but when you find out you're not going to be able to raise a family together, it kind of changes things.'

Peg spread a piece of cucumber with her fork and examined it thoughtfully.

'But isn't that the flaw in this plan? If having a family is so important, then the last thing you should be doing is arranging a marriage of convenience in which you don't even get to sleep with your wife.'

'I've got plenty of years in which to have kids, I'm in no hurry. And if I do meet someone I want to do that with, then you and I will just quietly divorce, if we haven't already. I don't see this as a long-term thing, just something to help you get back and work in the States again.'

Peg shook her head. 'I don't know, I just don't know. This is all so sudden. . . .' She grinned. 'You're absolutely sure it's a business proposition?'

'Scout's honour. You can even get it in writing if you like.'

'It's tempting, but. . .'

Travis lifted his hands in a gesture of defeat. 'OK, I'm not going to pressure you any more. You're tired, you need to get some sleep.'

He paid the bill and they walked back in silence to the hotel. Peg looked around her at the grimy puddles, and the seagulls scavenging for rubbish in dustbins. At the dirty grey waters of the Mersey, lapping at the edge of the esplanade over in New Brighton. One of those lights on over there was in her mother's bedroom. She would be getting ready for bed now, without her husband. One half of the bed empty.

She found herself reaching out instinctively and touching Travis's arm. She wanted his physical presence suddenly, as a soft of comfort, a talisman. He drew her into him, folding his arms around her and burying his face in her windblown hair. At that moment it was exactly what she needed. He let her stay like that for a long moment before gently pushing her away.

'Business only, remember?'

'If I . . . would there be a promotion for me at MackenCorp? I want to be sure it would be worthwhile coming back.'

'Sure! We'll work something out. You can go as high as you like.'

'In that case the answer's "yes". You've got a deal.' She extended her hand.

'Good girl,' he said, shaking it. 'After all, what have you got to lose?'

Peg waited a couple of days before breaking the news to her mother. She had half expected resistance to her departure, but Kath Anderson was too exhausted to argue. If anything, she seemed relieved that she was going to have one less thing to worry about. On the way back to the hotel they stopped at the

Seaview Café to say goodbye. Sandra gushed and giggled, while Billy looked on silently.

'You are a dark horse!' said Sandra. 'Being whisked away by a gorgeous Yank like that. I told you you could end up being married before me!'

'It's only a business arrangement,' Peg reminded her. 'It's just to allow me to get back into the States.'

'Well, I think you must be mad. Look at him! He looks like a film star!'

Three days after the funeral Peg and Travis took a flight down to Heathrow, where a chauffeur-driven Daimler took them straight to the American Embassy. After Peg had applied for residential status, Travis explained that it would probably be 'more comfortable' for all of them if he and Peg stayed in London until the divorce from Lana had been finalised. Peg shyly admitted she had never been to London before, so the two of them spent a pleasant few days staying at Claridges, shopping and sightseeing. They had separate rooms in the hotel and Travis was the perfect gentleman, kissing her good night at the door when they had dined.

'A deal's a deal,' he kept saying. 'And I intend to stick to it.'

Peg didn't find it easy. She still found Travis attractive and there were times, lying in bed alone at night, when. . . . But then she thought about how complicated everything would be. And it would get in the way of work. She had made a deal with herself, as well as with Travis.

When they had been there a week, the call came through from New York to say that the divorce had been finalised and the papers would be arriving by special air courier the next morning. So at ten o'clock the following day they went to Caxton Hall and were married by special licence, with a business acquaintance and his wife as witnesses. Peg wore a cream shantung suit she had bought in Harrods bridal department, and carried a bunch of pale roses. The four of them had lunch in the Savoy Grill, then the Daimler, which had been waiting outside, drove them to Heathrow to catch the afternoon flight back to New York.

'This is fun,' said Peg as the stewardess in the first-class cabin poured her a glass of vintage champagne. 'I think I could get used to being Mrs Macken.'

'What?' Travis glanced up from his copy of *Time* magazine. 'Oh, yes, sure. Listen, honey, it'll be a while before we get round to buying a place of our own, fixin' it up and stuff, so in the meantime we'll rent an apartment. I got Lana to find us somewhere.'

'You asked *Lana*?'

'Sure, why not? She's good at that kind of thing.'

'It's just that in the circumstances. . .'

'Only a temporary deal, remember.'

'I just would have preferred to choose somewhere myself, that's all.'

The limousine dropped Travis at the office and took Peg and the luggage straight to the apartment.

Her new home was a penthouse in a high-rise block on East 78th, expensive, but cold and characterless. The furnishings, all peach and ivory, brass and leather, looked like something out of a catalogue.

She wandered around, touching things uneasily. Opening the wardrobes in the master bedroom, she found to her amazement they were already full of clothes. She only had to glance through the selection to know who had chosen them. Lana. She had left a note stuck to the mirror on the inside of the wardrobe door.

'Your wedding gift. Hope you like them, L.'

Peg thumbed slowly through suits and day dresses, all of which instantly brought Lana to mind. They were the sort of things she liked to wear herself, elegant and very feminine, tight skirts and revealing, low-cut blouses. All in good taste but not really what Peg would have chosen. Her style was more Annie Hall.

There was even a silky negligee spread out on the bed, and a framed photo of Travis beside it. Peg sat on the bed and looked at it, drawing her arms tightly around her because she felt cold. The building had a centralised air-conditioning system and it was turned up too high. The clothes were meant to be a friendly gesture, weren't they? A parting gesture. . . .

Peg picked up the photograph and shivered again. The cold came from inside her this time. Now that she was back in the hard reality of New York she knew she should have thought this through better in England. Only there her mind had been incapacitated by disorientation and the numbness of grief. Well, she had achieved her wish; she was a US citizen now. But she was also married to a virtual stranger.

She jumped to her feet, unable to stand being in the apartment any longer. Grabbing the key and her briefcase, she raced out into the street and hailed a cab.

'Park and 50th, please. . . .'

Just as she reached Travis's office, the door opened and Lana came out. Far from looking strained by the trauma of divorce, she was sleek and sun-tanned from two weeks in the Mexican sun.

'Lana! I didn't expect to see you here.'

Lana frowned. 'Well of course I'm here, I work here.' She smiled sweetly in the face of Peg's discomfiture. 'Oh, didn't Travis tell you? In addition to the Sutton Place condo, my divorce settlement included a seat on the board at MackenCorp.'

'No, he didn't tell me.'

'But I'm sure there'll still be plenty for you to do about the place.'

Travis came out of the office and placed a heavy hand on Peg's shoulder. 'I think you should run along home now, darlin', get some rest after the flight. We can talk about this later.'

'You bet we will!'

'Go and have a good look around your new home, get to know it a little. You ladies like doing that kind of thing.'

'If they've got nothing between their ears but peanut butter,' she muttered as he walked away.

'Beg your pardon, honey?'

'Nothing.'

Peg was in the bath when Travis came back, turning on the hot tap with her toe every now and then to prolong the time she could spend in there.

'Peg, honey, where are you?'

As soon as she heard his hand turning the handle on the bathroom door she panicked, slipping and stubbing her toe as she scrabbled to climb out of the bath and grab a towel at the same time.

'Oh. . . .'

She stood staring at him with the towel clutched over her breasts and water streaming from the ends of her hair.

'What do y'all think of the apartment?'

'It's fine. Very nice. Look, we need to talk.'

'Sure, but how about getting some clothes on first?' He dragged his eyes away.

'Sorry. . . .'

She threw on a robe and followed him into the sitting room, rubbing at her wet hair with a towel. 'Travis, when you said you were divorcing Lana I thought. . . .'

He poured himself a bourbon. 'You thought what?'

'I thought that was it, the end. I didn't think she would still be around.'

'That was what she wanted. It didn't seem right to fire her.'

'But what about what *I* want? Didn't you realise that this was going to be difficult?'

'Why?' His blue eyes were innocent. 'Nothing's changed except in the eyes of the law. It's not as if you and I are. . . . You worked with her before, why not now?'

Peg faced him, eyes blazing. 'Because, dammit, things *are* different!'

'You mean because you're my wife now, not her?' His expression was mocking.

'No! Because you promised me promotion, and with Lana around that's just impossible. I know what she's like, she'll block me at every turn. I need a free hand if I'm going to make decent business decisions!'

'May I remind you that *I'm* the guy running the New York office and you work for me!' snapped Travis. Then softening, he said, 'Peg honey, try to relax, OK? This is only a temporary situation. You'll get your promotion, just be a little patient.'

'I'm sorry.' Peg breathed out hard. 'Are you hungry? I'll cook you something if you like.'

'You don't have to: that wasn't part of the deal.'

'No, but if we're going to be sharing the same kitchen, I may as well.'

'Sounds great.'

Peg dressed in jeans and went down to the deli to buy pasta and wine and ingredients for a sauce. They ate it on their knees in front of the Mets game, then set off for their different rooms.

'This is something different, huh?' asked Travis as he kissed her good night at the bedroom door.

'It's very civilised,' said Peg. 'More married couples ought to try it.' But despite the quip, she felt uneasy.

Travis spent the following evening at his club and was back late.

'I didn't expect you to be up,' he said, when he saw Peg sitting on the sofa. 'You OK?'

'I just wanted a chance to talk to you alone.'

'Again?'

'Yes, again.'

Travis flung down his sports bag and sat down. 'OK, shoot. But make it quick; I'm beat.'

'Lana and I have really been getting in each other's way at work. We keep bumping into one another, both looking for the same file, both needing to use the same directory. After I'd apologised to her for the hundredth time, she said it didn't matter because we weren't going to be working together for much longer.'

'She did, huh?'

'And she gave me that look. The look that says she knows something I don't know.'

'Well now. . . .' Travis switched on the television and started flicking through the channels. 'There was something I was going to tell you. We're going down to Savannah!'

'To visit your parents?'

He shook his head, grinning. 'Uh-uh. I'm going back there for ever. To live.'

'But. . . .' Peg just stared at his face, she couldn't even speak. 'Just like that? But why? I thought – '

'It's Daddy's decision. He asked to see all our books a few weeks ago, go through the figures. Lana and me had to send all the stuff down to him. I don't know why – he would normally fly up here. But he's been acting kind of flakey. . . . Anyways, he called me up and said that since business has been a bit slower up here lately, and all this talk of a recession, he wants to scale things down in New York. And he thought that since I've divorced Lana and remarried and all, I might want a change. . . .'

Peg stood up abruptly, walked over to the tray of drinks and poured herself a club soda. Travis waved his glass at her, indicating he wanted it refilled with bourbon. She took it from him. 'So . . .?'

'So Lana's going to run the Park Avenue office alone, and I'm going to go back to working with Daddy at MackenCorp, Savannah.'

'And what am I going to do?'

'Well, that's up to you. I can't make you come with me. But we are supposed to be making it look good for the authorities. And if it's promotion you want, well, Savannah is the corporate headquarters. It's a much bigger operation down there.'

Peg sat down. 'I don't know, Travis, it's still a big step. I'm just starting to think of New York as my home.'

The idea of spending time in the southern USA unnerved her, too. The image she had of the South was very much shaped by her radical student days at Radcliffe, where being a Southerner was seen as something to be ashamed of. In Peg's mind it was a place of poverty and oppression, of racial hatred and violence. She closed her eyes and the images that came to mind were the white hoods of the Ku Klux Klan grouped around a flaming cross, the gallows tree described in Billie Holliday's haunting voice.

'You'll love it down there. We'll buy up one of those big old mansions with a real fancy flower garden, like you have back in England. The weather's really great and everyone has lots of parties. It'll be neat. You'll feel just like you're Scarlet O'Hara. . . .'

He saw the look on her face and his good humour evaporated. 'Jesus, what is it with you women? You're never satisfied.'

Peg had never heard him speak like that before, and she was taken aback.

'What about your family?'

'They'll love you.'

'No, I meant the deal. Will you explain?'

'Sure.'

'And your father . . . will he let me work for him?'

'Sure, if I ask him to.'

'When would we be going?'

'Soon. Around the end of the year.'

And there'd be no more Lana. At the moment that seemed the most important thing of all.

'OK,' she said slowly. 'I'll come. On condition that if I hate it, you'll let me divorce you and leave.'

Travis broke into a broad grin of delight and raised a clenched fist in a victory salute. 'Wehay! That's my girl! You won't regret it, honey, believe me.'

He forgot their deal for a moment and bent forward to kiss her full on the lips. 'Georgia, here we come!'

TEN

Savannah, Georgia, 1979

She had expected a dilapidated ante-bellum plantation house in the middle of a mangrove swamp.

But Peg fell in love with the Macken house at Turner's Creek straight away. The cool elegance of the rooms with their slowly sweeping ceiling fans, the gracious sweep of lawn that was almost English in its green perfection, the moss-draped trees overhanging the jetty, making dappled patterns of sunlight on the boardwalk.

She had never been inside such a house before. Sure, some of the apartments she had visited in New York had been impressive, chic and expensive. But this place was crammed throughout with exquisite antiques and oil paintings, classical columns framing enormous gilded mirrors. There was even a ballroom with an old-fashioned oil-fuelled chandelier.

She felt more at ease when she was outside. Even though it was winter the sun was still shining; the air felt warm and balmy.

'We wouldn't wan't y'all to think it was always like this in January,' said Travis's mother as she led her new daughter-in-law round the grounds. 'Sometimes it can be real ugly, cold and wet.'

She smiled shyly at Peg, and Peg returned her smile. What does she think of me, she wondered?

'Travis did explain about how we came to be married?' she asked Cordella.

'He told me how you met, honey, yes.'

'I mean, did he tell you that we . . .?'

'That you what, dear?'

'Oh, never mind. . . . Travis will be along later, he'll explain.'

They were at the Macken house for a family picnic, a ritual gathering Peg was dreading. Especially since the subject had been the cause of her first major row with Travis.

They had just arrived in Savannah, and Peg was all agog to see the famous building that housed the Macken headquarters. Travis was going down to the office with his father, and Peg prepared to accompany him.

He frowned when he saw her putting on a suit. 'It's a picnic you're goin' to, not a convention. Y'all should be wearing jeans or something.'

'The picnic's not till midday. I thought I'd go downtown with you, first. I want to see where I'm going to be working.'

'But Mom will be expecting you along to help prepare the food beforehand. All the wives do. It's like a family tradition.'

'But surely this is different! It's not as if I'm your wife . . . well, in the normal fashion.'

'Mom doesn't know that.'

'She should do.'

'We'll tell her later. But run along for now, and be nice to her. Surely that's not too much to ask? You've got all the time in the world to see the borin' old office.'

So Peg had changed into jeans again and hung around ineffectually while Cordella amd Martha and Martha's daughter packed cold fried chicken and cornbread and salads into large baskets. In the end, Cordella had taken pity on her and said: 'Come on, honey, let me show you around the house.'

She appeared to enjoy sharing her past with Peg and took her round the house, recounting the history of every piece of furniture and painting, telling anecdotes about the old days in Savannah, when men like Clermont Peabody and Al Macken were making their fortunes. Peg started to feel she knew a little more about her husband. She had not known, for example, that Al Macken's father had been a preacher and Al had grown up in poverty.

Cordella was clearly under the impression Peg and Travis had married for love, a misconception that made Peg increasingly uncomfortable. She was glad when Al strolled down the bluff to join them. He seemed short of breath for such a fit man, and as he rested his hand on Peg's shoulder, she was sure she could feel it shaking slightly.

When he saw that the view pleased her, he smiled. 'It surely is lovely, isn't it?'

With his free hand he pointed out across the creek to the Wilmington River. 'That's the Moon River from the old Johnny Mercer song. You know that song?' He started to hum the tune. ' "Moon River, wider than a mile. . . ." But I guess Travis already told you that?'

'No. No, he didn't.'

'Well, you kids just need a little more time to get to know one another.'

'Come on, darling,' said Cordella, patting her husband's wrist. 'You and Travis can go and load up the food. Peg and I will go sit on the porch and I'll have some iced tea sent out.'

As she sipped the cool, scented liquid, Peg reflected that she already felt more at home here than in the house Travis had bought for them. It was an imposing white neocolonial house in Gordonstoun, one of the garden suburbs south east of the business district. Travis had been very proud that he had managed to acquire it for a million dollars; it was nearly a hundred years old, one of the best architectural examples in the area. Everyone wanted to buy places like that.

Peg agreed it was a handsome house, set in a shady garden bright with the jewel colours of azalea and hibiscus, but she couldn't quite quash her disappointment that it wasn't nearer the river. She would have liked to be able to look out over the water. And despite the classical proportions and the exemplary job done by the interior decorators – all pretty English chintzes and old American furniture – the house had the same atmosphere as their apartment in New York. It was as if the house could tell that the marriage was a fake.

Peg didn't allow this to dishearten her. After all, she was going to be an executive with MackenCorp and she did not plan on spending much time at home. And so far, she liked what she had seen of Georgia. Savannah had astonished her. It was a gem of a place, almost unreal in its classical perfection. Since living in Boston she had had little opportunity for walking, but Savannah was perfect for exploring on foot. She loved the cool, shady squares with their canopy of trees that provided relief from the hot, Southern sun. Round every corner she expected to find a Hollywood film crew and a director shouting orders, confirming her suspicion that it was really just a movie set.

Cordella shaded her eyes with her hand and scrutinized Travis's tall, sun-tanned figure as he walked towards them. He had exchanged his suit for baseball cap and shorts. 'Well, here comes your lord and master. Looks like he's coming to tell us it's time to leave.'

They walked down to the water's edge, where picnic hampers, rugs and parasols had been loaded into a fleet of rowing boats.

'It's a pity Michael can't be here,' sighed Cordella. 'Of course, you don't know my younger son, do you? He's at INSEAD in Paris, taking an MBA.'

Peg felt her insides contract and prayed she wasn't blushing. Travis never mentioned his brother and when they were in New York she had all but forgotten his existence. 'Actually, I met him once, years ago. We were at Harvard together.'

'*Really*? Now i'n't that a co-incidence?' She swivelled her head abruptly as a sports car swept into the driveway. 'Hell's teeth, what is *she* doing here?'

A tall, elegant woman with pale, reddish-gold hair climbed out of the car. She was dresed in cream linen shorts and a sleeveless blouse, and carried a huge straw hat. Her hips swayed as she walked towards them and extended a hand to Peg.

'When I heard y'all were having a family picnic to welcome Travis's English bride I thought, "Why, how *nice*. . . ." ' She drawled the word.

'Peggy, this is my sister, Beulah Peabody.'

'Delighted to meet you,' drawled Beulah. 'Been picking up plenty of good old down-home household tips from my sister here, I hope?'

'I doubt I'll find time for that,' Peg replied tartly. 'I'm going to be working alongside Travis in East Bay Street.'

'Really?' Beulah's eyes gleamed. 'Well, I must say my nephew's taste is improving. He used to prefer his women with cotton candy for brains. Mind you, I never met the New Yorker he married before you, but I heard she was no dumb bunny either.'

Cordella pinched her lips. 'Come on, Peg, let's find you a seat.'

She bundled Peg into the first of the boats next to Martha, and made sure that Beulah followed in the second with Wyatt and the Neely children. Martha kept turning her head in the direction of Beulah's over-sized sunhat.

'Really, the nerve of the woman!' she muttered.

'Doesn't Mrs Macken get on with her sister?' Peg enquired innocently.

Martha feigned deafness. 'Did I hear you say you were going to work at MackenCorp?'

'That's right.'

'You know, I was the first woman who ever worked in the company?'

'Oh?'

'Yes!' Martha beamed with pride. 'Right back in the old days, during the war. I helped Al set things up. My, we worked so hard! Of course, I gave it all up once I married Wyatt and the babies started coming along. I expect you'll do the same.'

'Well, the thing is. . . .' Peg looked round helplessly for Travis, but he was deep in conversation with his father. When he looked up she mouthed *'Tell them!'* at him, but he pretended not to understand.

Al, Wyatt and Travis remained locked in conversation when they reached their destination; an island in the middle of the river. Peg caught the occasional tempting snippet as they unloaded the hampers.

'. . . there's a mill over Allendale way we ought to go and take a look at. . . .'

'. . . the satellite franchise is going to be up for grabs next year. . . .'

'. . . good time to move while share prices are low. . . .'

As soon as the rugs were spread out, she sat between Travis and Al in the shade of a cottonwood tree. Hugging her knees, she waited for them to carry on, but they fell silent.

'Peg, would you be a darlin' and come and give me a hand serving this punch?' Cordella called.

'You'd better go help Mom,' said Travis dismissively.

'Only boring old man's talk here, honey,' Wyatt said, grinning.

The men watched Peg as she walked back to join the women.

'Bit of a tomboy, that little lady of yours,' observed Wyatt.

'A real little firecracker,' said Al approvingly. 'And cute as a button with it.'

'I'n't she just?' Travis narrowed his eyes and watched his wife. His daddy was right; she was gorgeous. Absolutely gorgeous. His eyes followed the narrow curve of her waist, and the way her jeans were skintight over her buttocks. Christ, she was still driving him absolutely crazy. And he *was* crazy, to let her do this to him. His daddy wouldn't just sit around and let a woman get away with it. Look what he did to Aunt Beulah.

And Peg was trying to talk to Beulah now, but Mom was just as determined not to let her, giving her little tasks to do like folding up a stack of white linen napkins into pretty shapes. He laughed to himself as he watched her. She sure was finding out that Savannah was nothing like New York.

But then she stood up, her face slightly flushed, and held out her hands.

'Er, excuse me. . . .' She coughed. 'Excuse me, could I have your attention, please? I know you've only just met me, but there's something I want to say while you're all together. . . .'

Damn it, the little vixen really was going to make a fool of him!

'Travis and I have something we want to explain to you – '

'Peg, honey!'

Great, Mom to the rescue!

'Peg, I hate to interrupt, but that cloud's just about to open and drench us all with rain. Just give me a hand folding up the rugs and getting them under the tree. . . .'

'You should have told them!' Peg said angrily.

It was evening, and they were back at their own house. The picnic had been interrupted by rain as Cordella had predicted, and several hours later it was still raining heavily from a dark, dramatic sky. The house was filled with an odd yellowish-grey light.

'This situation is crazy! All your family think we're about to go off into the sunset and live happily ever after. Well, you'd jolly well better tell them the truth before I file for divorce!'

215

'Hey, c'mon, lighten up – '

'I mean it, Travis! The game's over. I want a divorce.'

'I agree that this is crazy. Now come on. . . .' He patted the sofa next to him. 'Come on over here and calm down.'

Reluctantly Peg went and sat next to him. Travis took her hand. 'We'll tell them everything when we're good and ready, OK? For now, this is just about you and me.'

He was stroking her wrist, slowly and rhythmically, and Peg barely had time to realise how nice it felt before he was kissing her, running his teeth over her lips and her teeth, her throat, her breasts. . . .

'Travis, I really don't think this is – '

'You are full of shit!' He spoke angrily, pulling back from her abruptly. 'Just how long did you think you could keep this up, huh? Two hot-blooded young adults, living alone under the same roof. . . .'

He attacked her mouth again. That was how it felt to Peg, for whom the sensation was starting to pass from pleasure into something else altogether.

'Travis, you're hurting me. . . .'

He tugged at her arm until she slid from the velvet sofa onto the floor. With deft movements he unzipped her jeans and tugged her panties down to her knees. Then with a stab of shock she realised he had entered her. He bucked his hips at her hard, grinding her spine into the floor.

'Come on, move a little, baby.'

'I am *not* your baby and I am *not* going to move!' she hissed between clenched teeth. 'We had a deal, remember?'

'Forget the deal! This is the South and you're my wife!'

It was a cold evening in Paris, and in the brightly lit bars and cafés, the windows were clouding with steam from the damp overcoats and scarves draped on the backs of chairs.

Michael Macken was sitting in one such café on the banks of the Seine at the Pont de Sully. He occupied a window table, and through the steamy pane of glass he could just glimpse the Ile St Louis. In the fast fading light of dusk it seemed to float on the river, just above the surface of the water. There were people sitting in restaurants and bars over there on the island, just as he was, but they looked as though they were a thousand miles away.

He ordered black coffee and *Croque Monsieur* and skimmed through the pages of the *Wall Street Journal*, which was mailed to him on a regular subscription. After New York he had decided to travel again, only this time it was to do something constructive. In five months' time he would have his Masters degree in Business Administration, which was more than Travis had ever achieved.

Travis. Christ, the fool had gotten himself married again only days after his divorce from his first wife. He had seen a brief mention in the social pages of the *International Herald Tribune*. There had been a photograph too, poorly reproduced, of the new English bride. He felt the strangest sensation when he saw it; she looked so familiar . . . but it was a bad photograph and the caption only described her as 'Mrs Travis Macken'. Whoever she was, she was very pretty.

There had certainly been no shortage of pretty women in Paris. Michael liked Parisian women. They were sexy, proud and confident. He liked the way they dressed, and the way they carried themselves. When he had first moved here he could have happily sat in a café on the Champs Elysées all day long and watched them walk by.

In a way he preferred just looking at them. He had dated a succession of good-looking young Parisiennes, and now, if he was honest, he was starting to tire of them just the tiniest bit. They ranged from students to socialites, but the things they all had in common were capricious, spoilt temperaments, with a tendency to petulance. And they all took themselves very seriously.

As he walked back to his apartment in the 16th *arrondissement*, Michael wondered if anyone had ever said that the man who was tired of Parisian women was tired of life . . . .

The apartment was so quiet and cold. It echoed. He switched on all the lights in the *salon*, flicked the switch on the stereo and put the kettle to boil. Billie Holiday's plaintive voice filled the apartment, but it made him feel lonely. He had lived on his own too long. He was growing weary of his own company. It was a relief when the music was joined by the jangle of the telephone.

It was his father.

Al set the receiver down with mingled pleasure and guilt.

Pleasure because it had been good to hear Michael's voice after all this time. How long had it been? Years . . . .

Guilt because he had had to lie to get him to come home.

OK, so it was true Cordella was going to have to go into hospital. He hadn't lied about that. But it was only to remove a small cyst from her neck and the doctors had already biopsied it and confirmed it was benign. The way he had phrased this information when he spoke to Michael had implied there might be some possibility the growth was malignant. That Cordella needed her son by her side for support.

Michael was coming anyway, as soon as his term had ended, so Al told himself that the end justified the means. In a flash of memory, Al recalled his father James giving a sermon along those lines. He remembered sitting in the front pew of the small clapboard church in Walthourville, watching the play of the sun on the trees outside the high windows, and squirming. He remembered that his father had gotten particularly roused up on that Sunday morning, and had whipped him like a demon when they got home, saying it would strengthen his character. *The end justifies the means . . . .*

Well, old James Macken would be laughing on the other side of his face now. He probably was, in heaven or hell, wherever the Lord had seen fit to send him. Hell most like. He would say that this illness was God's punishment on him for his greed and ambition and pride, just like he was being punished when Honoree was taken.

Al was sitting at the desk in the library, turning a glass paperweight over and over in his right hand. A violent tremor suddenly seized his right arm, jerking his shoulder upwards and shooting the paperweight onto the floor. It bounced into the corner of the room and shattered into fragments.

With a massive feat of concentration, screwing up his eyes and clenching his jaw, he quelled – or at least controlled – the shaking in his limbs. Slowly, very slowly, placing one foot precisely in front of the other, he walked over to the other side of the room. He bent down and with great care picked up each shard of glass, placing them on his upturned left palm. His hand shook only once, cutting the side of his left thumb on a sharp splinter.

He stood there for a few moments staring down at the deep, garnet-red drops of blood that fell onto the carpet. This was going to get worse, he knew that. At the moment the attacks were fairly infrequent, but John Morrow had warned him that their frequency would increase and pretty soon after that his speech would be affected. Then it was going to get difficult to hide this thing. At the moment nobody knew.

Well, he thought Cordella had her suspicions, but Travis hadn't noticed anything. He had managed to rationalise getting him back to Savannah on business grounds, and Travis had swallowed it absolutely. When he went through the New York revenue figures with Wyatt he had realised it was just as well he had his eldest son back in Savannah where he could keep an eye on him. It seemed that Travis and Lana had been siphoning off interest money into their own account. They might have gotten away with it if the meticulous and eagle-eyed Wyatt hadn't instituted a centralised system that required a copy of each transaction to be sent directly from the files of companies doing business with MackenCorp in New York to his office in Savannah.

It had been a great disappointment to Al, because for a while there Travis had appeared to be going great guns and fixing up deals under his own steam. He hadn't revealed what he knew to his son, but he had explained the centralised accounting to Lana, by way of a veiled warning, and he knew she was far too smart to run the New York office any way but straight. So far she was making a great job of it, in fact she seemed to be doing better than ever before without Travis around to distract her.

That new English wife of Travis's was smart too, in a different way. She was college smart and crackling with energy. Ambitious too, but with any luck that would fade when Travis provided her with a family. Use up some of her energy on her children. She seemed a nice kid, and Cordella had hopes of turning her into a really good wife for their eldest son, one who would learn to stand two paces behind.

Travis needed someone to keep him on the straight and narrow. He was knuckling down all right, but still needed watching, and Al no longer felt comfortable with the idea of

Travis running the show alone. That was why he needed to get Michael back, and find some way of finally healing the rift. They were going to need Michael now.

'Lord, but it's good to be back in Georgia!'

Travis Macken leaned back in the hot tub and raised his champagne glass to the sparkling blue spring sky. 'I don't know why I ever went away, do you, darlin'?'

The girl beside him – Barbara? He couldn't remember – giggled and slipped down into the warm foaming water. She had long auburn curls and large pink-tipped breasts which floated just above the surface of the water, like cream-filled balloons.

She was a PR girl for a company MackenCorp was wooing, and he had taken her out to lunch at the exclusive Jekyll Island Club. He just happened to mention casually over the soft shell crab that MackenCorp maintained a suite at the club and she expressed an interest in seeing the décor. By that time they had finished off two bottles of Krug and she was extremely drunk.

She giggled again as she lost her balance and sank down under the bubbles, emptying the contents of her glass into the water.

'Heard y'all got married recently.'

'That's right. Last summer.' Travis extended a hand and pressed down one of the pale breasts thoughtfully, waiting to see if it would float up to the surface again.

'What's she like, your wife?'

Travis smiled with satisfaction as Barbara's breasts bobbed up and down at his bidding. 'Well now, she's a real little spitfire. One of these women's libbers. And she's English, so there's a lot about living down here she doesn't understand.'

'Sounds like you have your hands full.'

'Oh, she'll learn. . . .' He gulped carelessly from his glass, spilling champagne on Barbara's face. 'My mom really likes her.' He nibbled lazily at a visible segment of the pale globe, licking off the water that streamed down it. 'Before long, we're all going to be just one big happy family. . . .'

Peg Macken woke up and looked around in panic.

The curtains were drawn, but there was sun streaming through them. The clock on the bedside table said two o'clock.

Then she remembered. She had felt a little off-colour in the morning, so she had come home from work to put her feet up for a while. She had slept for two hours. Lurching to her feet, she was overwhelmed by dizziness and nausea. She staggered to the bathroom and hung her head over the toilet bowl. Nothing happened. She splashed her face with cold water and tugged a comb through her hair.

There was a tap on the bedroom door. 'You all right in there, Miz Macken?' It was Betty, the maid.

'Fine, Betty.' Peg opened the bedroom door. 'I just need some fresh air.'

She picked up the car keys, then hesitated. Closing the bedroom door, she went to the telephone and dialled.

'Hello, Beulah, it's Peg. . . . I didn't want to call Cordella, and I couldn't think who else to ask. I need the number of your doctor.'

Michael finished his last mouthful of chicken and dumplings and wiped the gravy from the plate with a hunk of cornbread.

He had been hungry when the plane landed at Savannah airport, and instead of waiting for his father's car to show up, he had taken a cab downtown and gone for lunch at Euphemia Bailey's boarding house on West Jones.

The place was exactly the same, contributing to the fast-growing illusion that he had never left Savannah. There was still no sign or hoarding outside, but you could pinpoint the exact location of the basement dining room by the queue of people stretching down the street. They formed a polite, patient line, exchanging pleasantries with one another until the door was opened at noon and they were ushered in by Euphemia to the large communal tables. Each table was spread with a spotless white cloth and covered with steaming bowls of food; beef stew, barbecued pork, fried chicken, lima beans, rice and gravy, macaroni and cheese. Now she had turned eighty, Euphemia no longer took boarders, but the dining room was open for breakfast and lunch every day, finding plenty of trade amongst the office workers who had colonised the newly renovated Historic District.

Euphemia came and stood by Michael's shoulder and ruffled

his hair affectionately. She was still as spry as ever, her neat curls dyed vivid auburn.

'Now, what can I get you for dessert, boy? Coconut pie? Rum chiffon pie? Fried banana?'

'Coconut pie. What else do you think I came back to Savannah for?'

Euphemia laughed and went into the kitchen to fetch a heaped plateful. 'So – what *have* ya'll come back to Savannah for?'

'To visit my mother. She had an operation.'

Euphemia frowned. 'Saw her the other day and she looked pretty good to me. I see that brother of yours from time to time as well. He comes in here for breakfast when he feels so inclined. . . . Seen your daddy yet?'

Michael shook his head.

'Anyways, enjoy your dessert.'

Michael wrapped his arm round her waist and gave her a hug. 'If this coconut pie is as heavenly as it always used to be, by the time I've finished it, I'll be wanting to stay in Savannah for ever.'

'Maybe you should do exactly that.'

'I've been feeling tired, and very nauseated for a couple of weeks now.'

'Uh-huh. . . .' The doctor gently examined Peg's abdomen. 'Nothing sinister here. . . . I'll just do an internal . . . hold still . . . . Is your menstrual cycle regular?'

Peg felt her skin grow cold. 'Pretty well.'

'And your last period?'

'Ummm . . . it's been a while.'

'About eight weeks?'

'Could be.'

'I'll do a blood test to confirm it, but my guess is that you're eight weeks pregnant. Congratulations!'

'Er . . . thanks.'

Peg's knees were shaking as she climbed down off the couch. If the doctor had wanted she could have told him exactly when the baby was conceived. The day of the picnic. There hadn't been any other occasions. Travis had wheedled and cajoled, he had tried sulking then showering her with flowers and gifts, but she had kept him adamantly at bay.

And now what the hell was going to happen? She sat at the wheel of her Pontiac and thought. There was still time to terminate the pregnancy; she could go back into the doctor's office now and make the appointment. Travis need never know. And then she could file for divorce and leave town. Just like that.

She tried to open the door of the car and go and do it, but she couldn't. She just felt paralysed. It was her baby's life and that was something sacred. She would keep the baby and they would manage somehow, with or without Travis.

And there was her career. She'd barely had time to get her teeth into work here, and she certainly didn't want to give it up. She had slogged her way doggedly through all the company reports, bullied Wyatt into giving her a complete financial breakdown of MackenCorp, read profiles of every business and industry in the state of Georgia. She'd already come up with some good ideas. Al had accepted her suggestions gracefully. He knew good business sense when he saw it, but he never went out of his way to push her or encourage her, reining back her enthusiasm so she didn't outshine Travis.

There was no avoiding the situation any longer, she was just going to have to confront them, both of them.

She threw the car into gear and roared down to East Bay, taking the lift to the mezzanine floor where Travis had his suite of offices.

'Mr Macken said he didn't want to be disturbed – '

She brushed past his secretary.

'Travis, we need to talk.'

Travis was on the phone, and from the laughter in his eyes, she could tell he was speaking to a woman. He hung up.

'I'm pregnant.'

He whistled. 'Jeez. . . .'

'Quite. Now, we both know how and when it happened. And I know that if I keep the baby, I'm going to have to keep up the pretence about our marriage in front of your family. Which I'm prepared to do, for the sake of the child. I am happy for you and I to be on friendly terms, but that's all. No sleeping together. And I intend to go on working alongside you here at MackenCorp. If you use the child to try and squeeze me out of a job, the whole deal is blown out of the water.'

Travis put his head on one side. 'Which means?'

'Which means I divorce you and take your child away from here for ever.'

'No judge will let you get away with that, honey! Not in the good old state of Georgia.'

'He will if I tell him you raped me.' She stared at him, eyes blazing.

'I see. . . .' Travis looked down at his desk. 'I guess we have a deal, then. Another one.'

'And you'd better stick to it this time.'

'Daddy's not going to be happy with you going out to work once he knows you're carrying his grandchild.'

'Leave him to me.'

She swept up to the penthouse and demanded that Winona let her in to see Al.

'So, how's my favourite daughter-in-law?' He kissed her on both cheeks. 'Sit down, you look pooped.'

Peg crossed her legs and folded her hands in her lap. 'There's something I need to discuss with you, Al.'

'Fire away.'

'When I married Travis, we weren't in love with one another. In fact, we hardly knew each other. I was stuck in England with no means of getting back to the States, and Travis offered to marry me so that I could come back and work for MackenCorp. It was supposed to be strictly a short-term arrangement, until we could convincingly get a divorce.'

Al slumped back in his seat. His hands were shaking. 'Well, young lady . . . I had no idea. . . .'

'I wanted to tell you all, but Travis didn't. The thing is . . . I'm expecting his baby.'

Al broke into a broad grin. 'But that's fantastic news, honey! So it worked out after all. From the way he looks at you, I would have been surprised if it hadn't!'

Peg shook her head. 'It was a mistake. Definitely a mistake.'

'So . . .?'

'So I'm here to tell you that I'll have the child and raise it here in Georgia, as long as you let me play my part here in MackenCorp. I can do it, and you know I can.'

'And if I don't, you'll leave?' He was frowning. 'That would break Cordella's heart.'

'Mine isn't an easy situation, Al. I have to be tough.'

He sighed. 'What do you want?'

'Executive vice-president.'

He laughed. 'You know what, you're a cool customer! You remind me a little of Cordella's sister when she was young. . . . All right, you got it. Vice-president in charge of new business development, how does that sound?'

'That sounds fine. Now, if you'll excuse me. . . .' She got to her feet as gracefully as she could. 'I think I'm about to throw up.'

Michael arrived at his parents' house to find both of them out. The maid explained his mother was holding a supper party at short notice, and his father was hoping to be home directly.

He showered and changed into a T-shirt and jeans. His luggage had been taken up to the guest suite, summing up his situation. He was a guest here now, after an absence of nearly seven years.

Like any guest he was anxious to familiarise himself with his surroundings. He walked through the quiet house, noting the changes his mother had made to the place. The door to Honoree's room was closed, and he stood looking at it for a few moments. When he finally opened the door he was surprised to see his mother had had it completely redecorated, had turned it into another guest room. After the initial pang of sadness that Honoree's special place was gone, he felt glad. That meant Mom was finally over her grieving, had let go.

Walking over the lawn and down to the creek he felt the sheer thrill of pleasure to be back in his boyhood haunt. There was the boathouse, same as ever, where Travis used to keep his stack of girlie magazines under a rotten floorboard. In the tree next to it, hanging over the jetty, was the knotted rope they used to swing from, pretending to be Johnny Weissmuller. When the weather was hot in the summer he and Travis would take it in turns to swing the rope out as far as possible over the creek and then let go, plunging into the cool, dark water. And the other one would be sitting in the rowboat, jeering and shouting and splashing water at the would-be Tarzan with the end of the paddle.

He and Travis had been quite good buddies in those days, when they were left to their own devices. Until Melody Beck had come along, anyway. Perhaps they could be buddies again. Especially now that Travis was married, and therefore wouldn't be trying to steal his girlfriends from right under his nose.

He smiled at the memory of Melody Beck. Jesus, that girl had a great body! Old Travis had been right to focus his attention on her breasts. She might have had a great body, but her brain hadn't been so hot. That was a detail he had been able to overlook as a love-sick seventeen-year-old, but it mattered to the adult Michael. What was Melody Beck doing now? She was probably married to some rich young professional, with a couple of kids in tow. Funny, he had always imagined that Travis would end up married to someone just like her.

The sun was sinking low over the river and Michael sat on the edge of the jetty, swinging his legs to and fro, just watching the colours change in the sky. He sat there for a long time. By the time the sun had hit the water in a blaze of scarlet, he had decided he would stay in Savannah. He didn't even care if it meant flunking out of his MBA. He just wanted to be home.

There was just enough light for him to see his father as he crossed the lawn to join him.

'I thought you might be down here.' Al extended his arms and wrapped his son in a tight embrace.

Standing back, Michael was shocked. His father looked much older, and he had lost some weight. He had never carried fat, but there was less muscle. Like the removal of Honoree's shrine, it was a change he had never anticipated.

He pinched his father's shoulder. 'What happened, Daddy, you stop working out? Or did you just get too busy to use the pool?'

'Something like that.'

'Hey, you gotta get back in there, pal. Health is wealth, remember!'

Al managed a ghost of a smile.

'So how's Mom?'

'Oh, she's fine, she's just great.'

'But I thought. . .'

'Look, why don't we go up to the house? We need to talk.'

The only thing that had changed in his father's den was an

addition to the collection of family photographs on the desk. Michael picked it up and stood there, just staring at it.

'Travis's wife. Peggy. She's quite something.'

'I know,' said Michael quietly. 'I used to know her.'

'That so? Then you'll have a lot to talk about over dinner. She and Travis are coming over. It's something of a celebration, actually. They're expecting a baby in the autumn. Our first grandbaby.'

'Really?' Michael's heart sank like a stone.

'Good to have you here, son, it really is.' Al's voice shook suddenly, and he embraced Michael again.

'You said something about Mom needing an operation. What happened?'

'Oh, it was something and nothing. She found a small lump in her neck, but when it was removed the surgeons were one hundred per cent sure that it was non-cancerous. She's fine.'

Michael's eyes narrowed. 'Wait a minute, what's going on here? You asked me to come back and see Mom because you were worried about her, and now she's fine and you tell me there was never anything to worry about. . . .' He shook his head. 'Jesus, just what *is* going on around here?'

'At the time I was worried, and I thought it would do her good to see you. Chrissakes, Michael, you don't see your mother in years and when she's going in for surgery you don't think she wants her son by her side?'

Al was starting to tremble. He made a concerted effort to calm down, slowing his breathing until he had himself under control. 'Look, Michael, there's no point going through all that now. The surgery was weeks ago, your mom's fine, but that doesn't mean the two of us aren't delighted to have you with us at last.'

'I might have been here sooner if. . .'

'If what?'

'Nothing. So what do you really want to see me for?'

'I just thought it was high time you came back. I want you here, working for me.'

Michael smiled wryly. 'I was going to ask you for a job about a year ago, but Travis more or less convinced me there was no chance unless he asked on my behalf.'

'He never mentioned it to me.'

Michael gave an exasperated smile. 'I told him not to. I didn't want Travis setting it up for me. That's when I decided to go to Paris.'

'You should have asked me. I would have been more than happy to hear you out.'

'Hear me out! Jesus Christ, is that all? You've favoured him over me all the way down the line. He can do what he wants, and I – ' Michael clenched his eyes shut and opened them again. 'I fail some lousy exams and you cut me off without a penny, don't speak to me for years. But Travis can have what he damn well pleases, isn't that the truth of it?'

'Hey, come on!' Al put a hand on his shoulder. 'Just forget about Travis, will you? This is between you and me. . . .'

'Yeah, I know, I'm sorry.' Michael tried to tear his eyes away from the photograph of Peg.

'You're my son, and I want you and Travis both working alongside me. There's plenty of room for you both. Peg's joined the team too. We can be a young company again, really go places.'

'Peg works at MackenCorp with Travis?'

'Sure. She's an MBA, a bright cookie.'

'No, I don't think so, Dad. Not with Travis and his wife . . . two's company, three's a crowd. Now if you don't mind, I think I'll skip dinner too and head off to a hotel. I'm not feeling very sociable.'

'Michael, this is crazy! Why the hell won't you stay?'

'I'm sorry, Dad, I can't explain.' He embraced his father. 'See you some time soon, huh?'

ELEVEN

Savannah, Georgia 1979–1980

Peg Macken stood on the shady verandah at the back of her house. It was the middle of November, one of those brilliant fall days with a stinging blue cloudless sky and temperatures in the upper sixties.

She folded her arms across her chest and strolled over to the big old-fashioned baby carriage, a Macken family heirloom. And there inside it was the heir, her six-week-old son, John Alexander Macken. He was utterly beautiful, his red lips puckering as he sucked on an imaginary teat in his sleep. And she was glad he was a boy. It seemed to her that in the Macken family you got a much better deal if you were male.

God, but she was bored! After a lot of bullying by a syndicate of Cordella, Al and Travis she had agreed to take a couple of months off after the birth, at the end of which time a trained nanny was going to arrive from England. But John was a peaceful baby, and with a cook, a housekeeper and a maid for the cleaning and Joel, the driver and handyman, there was nothing for Peg to do in the house. She had resisted Cordella's attempts to teach her to arrange flowers or attend courses in interior decorating and antique appreciation. On the first day of her maternity leave, Cordella had even given her a copy of Anne Oliver's guide to etiquette, but when Peg saw it contained exhortations like 'A lady never leans back at table', she had discreetly disposed of it. The Macken family were never going to turn her into a Southern belle.

John Alexander opened his eyes briefly, then returned to his dreams. He could be asleep for another two hours at least, thought Peg. All the things she could do with that time . . . .

She went into the kitchen. Betty was at the large table in the centre of the room rolling out biscuit dough.

'Betty, you couldn't mind John for a few hours for me, could you? I want to go into the office.'

'Sorry, Miz Macken, when I've finished up here at twelve I've got to go to see the doctor 'bout my chest. But Joel's wife works as a babysitter, you could ask her.'

'Great! Where do they live, Betty? It's near here, isn't it?'

'One thousand twenty-one Henry, ma'am. But – '

'Right, I'll go and ask them now. I can push Johnny down there in the baby carriage. Oh, and pack up some of those cookies in a box and I'll take them as a gift.'

'Ma'am, I don't think you should do that, ma'am.'

'Why not? It's not all that far, and I need the exercise.'

'White folks don't ever walk round there, that's all.'

Peg smiled at her. 'Don't be silly, I'll be fine!'

She wheeled the baby carriage round to the front of the house and set off, heading due west. She walked quickly, fired up by her sense of purpose. Just beyond Pierpont Circle, the gracious, tree-lined crescent where their house had been the first ever built, she came to the busy intersection with Skidaway Drive. After that the landscape changed abruptly. The large, porticoed houses gave way to smaller wooden ones, some of them on stilts, all of them with a makeshift porch of some sort and a small patch of garden around them. They were in an assortment of colours, some neat and well cared for and others simply dilapidated.

It was very quiet, peaceful even. After Betty's words she had expected street gangs and motorbikes but there was nobody about apart from a few children playing on the grass in front of the houses, and old people dozing in rocking chairs on their front porches. They stared at her curiously as she went by. She supposed she must look conspicuous, a well-dressed white woman pushing such a grand baby carriage. But she liked to think the stares were curious rather than hostile. Her fears of racial hatred had not been realised when she moved here, although the black and white communities did not really mix. Georgia had a better reputation than the other Southern states for treating blacks with respect, and in the past they had enjoyed more freedom in Savannah than almost anywhere.

Joel's house was right at the other end of Henry Street, next to the Zion's Temple Holiness Church. It was a one-storey pink-washed building with the tiniest garden Peg had ever seen, smaller even than the patch of concrete in front of her parents' house in New Brighton. Every inch of it was crammed with bright geraniums and over the top of them, suspended on poles to make the best of the limited space, hung a trailing vine. The effect was touchingly pretty and homely.

Peg stepped over the cat dozing in front of the flyscreen and rang the bell.

'Why, Miz Macken, what a surprise! I was jus' fixin' to go out to the Piggly Wiggly.'

'Is your wife in, Joel? I wanted her to babysit for a few hours.'

'No, I'm sorry, she's over at her sister's. Won't be back until later this afternoon.' He bent down and touched the baby's cheek. 'I'n't he precious?'

Peg thrust the box of cookies into his hands. 'Here, have these anyway. Must go now, bye!'

She hurried back down the street, leaving the old man staring after her in a puzzled fashion. John was stirring slightly, so she would have to be quick. It wasn't going to be so easy to off-load him if he was awake and screaming for food.

Back at the house, she threw together a bag containing nappies, a couple of bottles of formula and a pacifier. She picked up the phone and started to dial Cordella's number, then hung up. If she left John with his grandmother, the chances were she would be straight on the line to Al or Travis, and between the two of them they would make sure she didn't manage to get any work done. She dialled Beulah's number instead. She was an unlikely child-minder, but she was family, and Peg felt sure she would understand.

'Beulah, hi, it's Peg. Listen, could you mind John Alexander for a couple of hours?'

Beulah laughed her deep throaty laugh. 'Sure, why not? Bring him on over to meet his wicked great-aunt.'

Peg had the receiver crooked under one ear, and was already shrugging on her suit jacket. 'Great! Be with you in five minutes.'

★ ★ ★

'Well, hello there.' Beulah lit a cigarette and puffed the smoke up at the ceiling. 'Y'all don't mind if I smoke, do you?'

The baby squirmed and whimpered. Through the window, Beulah could see Peg positively bounding down the steps into Anderson Row and leaping behind the wheel of her car like a dog let off the leash. If she had a tail, she would be wagging it, thought Beulah.

There was nothing to it, Peg had said. You just had to give him the milk when he was hungry, and change a diaper when he shat in it. A piece of cake.

The restless whimpers gained in volume until they became a cry, and then a shriek. Beulah watched him for a while, then when she was sure he wasn't going to quit, she stubbed out her cigarette and attempted to pick him up. He shrieked harder, tensing his little body against hers.

'Pipe down, damn you!' She fumbled for a bottle. 'They can always tell when they've got a greenhorn, so they say, like horses. . . . Here, have some of this.'

The baby gulped at the bottle, swallowed a mouthful of air and screamed harder.

'It's only a bottle, OK? You're supposed to like this stuff. . . .'

Beulah carried bottle and baby to the sofa, balancing the child awkwardly on her free arm. 'There ya go, let's try and make ourselves more comfortable, huh?'

The baby gulped hungrily for a few mouthfuls, then seemed distressed and started to scream again.

'This is crazy! What the hell's the matter with you?'

She paced the room, jiggling him against her shoulder, but the indignant cries persisted. She had no idea they cried so loudly. She glanced at her watch. It had been half an hour since Peg had left. She said she was going to be a couple of hours, at least. Christ, how was she going to stay the distance? Rummaging in the change bag she found a pacifier and held it up to the light like a beachcomber with buried treasure.

'This should do the trick!'

John Alexander had other ideas. He chomped on the teat a few times, rolling it around his mouth like a cigar before spitting it angrily onto the floor. Beulah held his tiny body up so that his face was on a level with hers.

'My, you are stubborn! Just like your grandaddy! Now you and I are going to have to have a little talk. . . .'

The wailing continued, becoming thinner and more plaintive. Beulah was sweating and her nerves were beginning to jangle. She tried going into another room and just leaving him to cry, but the noise followed her, haunting her. Was it always like this, she wondered? How on earth had Cordella coped?

Cordella . . . .

Once she had made the decision, her relief was overwhelming, palpable. Swallowing the vestiges of her pride, she picked up the receiver and dialled her sister's number.

'She should never have left the poor mite!'

Cordella was round at Beulah's house within minutes, bristling with indignation.

'I guess she thought he wouldn't come to any harm.'

'Look at the state he's in! And to leave him with someone who has absolutely no experience of babies! What can she have been thinking of?'

She cradled the baby against her shoulder and he calmed instantly. 'Has he been crying long?'

'Mainly since I offered him a drink. He seemed hungry, then he decided he didn't want it.'

'He's probably suffering with gas . . . .D'you wind him?' She glanced at Beulah's face, and decided not to wait for an answer. 'What I don't understand is why she didn't just ask me straight off. I *am* the child's grandmother, after all.'

Beulah smirked to herself behind Cordella's back. 'I really can't imagine,' she said innocently.

Cordella turned round, her face stern. 'It's just fortunate I was able to come around and bail you out, isn't it? What if he'd choked or something?' Her voice trembled. 'Do you know what it's like to have something happen to your child, do you know how terrifying . . .?'

Beulah looked down, humbled. 'No. I guess I don't.'

'Well, I want you to promise me something, Beulah Peabody. I want you to promise me never to interfere with my family again. Just stay away, d'you hear me?'

★ ★ ★

'What the hell were you doing at East Bay this afternoon? Daddy said he saw your car in the parking lot.'

Travis had returned from work, throwing down his jacket and briefcase on the verandah swing seat next to Peg. She was sipping slowly on a mint julep, pushing the baby carriage to and fro rhythmically with her bare toes.

'I went in to do some work.'

'I thought we had an agreement. You could go back to work, but you'd be at home for two months first with Junior here.'

Peg thrashed the glass swizzle stick to and fro angrily. 'Don't talk to me about our agreements.'

'So . . . what the hell did you do with John Alexander?'

From the tone of his voice, Peg could tell he already knew the answer to his question.

'I left him with your aunt.'

'Yeah, with my aunt! Good old Aunt Beulah. A crazy lush with the morals of a rattlesnake. What the fuck were you thinking of? Mom said that – '

' "*Mom said. . . .*" Christ, your family make me sick! They're like the bloody Waltons! I've already had your bloody mother on the phone lecturing me about my duties as a mother. I was *this* close – ' she held up finger and thumb – 'to blowing the whistle on this whole crazy arrangement and telling her a thing or two about how her precious grandson was conceived!'

'You wouldn't have done it, would you though, honey? You know when you're on to a good thing. You've really slept your way to the boardroom in style now, haven't you? We'll never be able to get rid of you!'

'You *bastard*!'

Travis picked up his briefcase and turned to go into the house. 'I guess I just don't understand you women. No sooner have you had the goddam child than you go and dump it on the first person you can find.'

'It was only one afternoon, for goodness's sake – '

'You should have aborted him if you couldn't be bothered to look after him!'

Travis turned on his heel and walked into the house.

Peg was left looking down at the sleeping baby, feeling empty and bereft. 'I'm sorry, little fellow,' she whispered to him. 'You do understand, don't you? I wasn't dumping you, I just needed some time to myself.'

He slept peacefully on. The silence was suddenly overwhelming, and all Peg could think about was how much she longed for her own mother. Kath Anderson was afraid to fly, so she hadn't even seen her new grandson.

If I was anyone else but me, thought Peg, I would just take my baby and go home. Only because I'm me, I can never admit defeat. I just don't know how to.

Al parked his car outside Beulah's house on Anderson Row, remembering as he did so the night he had first come here.

He had been so angry with Cordella, mad as hell. And Beulah had soothed and warmed him at the same time. When he got close to her it had been like a flame bursting out of ice. He smiled to himself a little as he remembered the pleasure they had had that night. When Beulah was hot, she was surely hot.

And there had been other nights since then, but not many lately. None, in fact, for a couple of years. Since he started to get sick.

She met him with the same ironic smile, as if she had seen him only last week. It was hard to believe she was almost sixty. Her figure was as voluptuous as ever, without an ounce of fat, her creamy skin had only the faintest of lines round the mouth and eyes, and her hair was still the same bright copper. It needed tinting now, but it had been expertly done so as not to look in the least bit unnatural. She wore wide-legged cream linen pants and a cream satin shirt, and her whole being exuded a glow of sensual enjoyment and well-being.

Al wondered if there was a new man in her life. She had always had boyfriends – 'beaux' as she liked to call them – beside himself, but she didn't like him to question her about them. Beulah had never been made to be a one-man woman. When he suggested she might have missed out on the joys of marriage and children, she just laughed at him.

Thank God, he thought with a sudden, spreading sense of relief. Thank God I didn't marry her. It's been so much better like this.

'You just missed Cordella,' she said, as he removed his jacket.

'Cordella! What in God's name was she doing here? She doesn't know – ?'

Beulah shook her head quickly. 'No, nothing like that.' She told Al about Peg and the baby and he made predictably indignant noises about a woman's place being in the home.

'Just like you're in your home now?' She put her head on one side in that same teasing way as when he met her in 1939.

'You saying I'm a hypocrite?'

'If the cap fits. . . .'

'The child's only a few weeks old!'

'And Peg is still a person with needs of her own.'

He shrugged in a way that said he didn't have the energy to argue it out with her. He did that a lot lately.

'So.' She smiled expectantly, head on one side.

'So, Beulah. . . .'

'So, Mr Macken, you haven't been around here for a while.'

He shook his head.

'There's something wrong, isn't there?'

He nodded. Beulah motioned to a chair beside the fireplace and he sat down. Without a word she pressed a glass of bourbon into his hand and sat down opposite him, her elegant legs crossed.

Very slowly and deliberately, he started to tell her everything from the beginning, how he had started to feel unwell, how he had gotten scared, how John Morrow had run tests in private and confirmed that he was suffering from Parkinson's disease. A long, slow, humiliating process during which he would gradually lose control of his body. How long and slow was unknown. It would almost certainly shorten his natural span.

He hadn't been able to speak of it to a living soul, and yet it was easy to tell Beulah.

'Have you told Cordella yet?'

He shook his head. 'But she knows. She knows something is wrong. She's noticed things.'

'You should tell her.'

'I know . . . but . . . this will destroy her.'

Beulah shook her head slowly. 'Don't flatter yourself, Macken. Cordella's tougher than that. She's gotten over losing a child. Losing you won't be worse than that.'

There, she had said it. She had mentioned the fact that he would die. She had made it just that: a natural, simple fact.

She poured herself a bourbon and took a gulp. Her eyes met his over the rim of her glass.

'You're going to end it, aren't you?'

He was amazed. 'How did you know that?'

'Because I know you. I know what you can take. Death is one thing, decay another. You can handle dying, but not falling apart. You're too proud.'

He hadn't known it before he came here, but now he knew that that was what he was going to do. He felt a great release of tension, as if an iron bar had been lifted from his neck.

'How will you decide when?'

'It'll be like making an appointment.' He smiled. 'Death – the ultimate date. Why wait?'

She forced herself to smile back.

'I had hoped to get Michael back first. That would have made it easier. We fought, and he walked out; went back to New York, then on to Colorado. He won't take my calls.'

'Would you like me to try?'

Al shook his head. 'It's too late. He's going to have to make up his own mind. I'm going to leave him half the company. That should help.'

Beulah nodded. 'Sure. He'll come back. . . .' Seeing the look in Al's eyes, she leaned forward and squeezed his hand. He stroked her hand. Their eyes met.

'Beulah could we . . . one last time . . .?'

'The last time. . . .' She drew in her breath sharply. 'Already? Why, when are you going to . . .?'

'Soon.'

Travis followed Peg upstairs when she went to bed.

She heard his footsteps behind her on the stairs and shut her bedroom door very firmly behind her.

He knocked on it gently. 'I want to talk to you.'

'I'm not in the mood for talking.'

'*Please?*'

She opened the door slowly. 'OK, two minutes. But after that

I need to get some sleep. Johnny's still waking at two o'clock for a feed.'

Travis sat down on the end of the bed. 'I'm sorry about what I said earlier. About not wanting him an' all. He's a great kid, and I love him.'

Peg sighed. 'When we were shouting at each other before, it was just like. . . .'

'Go on.'

'Just like we were married.'

'We are, remember?'

Peg became conscious he was staring at her, trying to discern the curves of her body underneath her thin wrap.

'Hey c'mon, Peggy, lighten up.' He bent to nuzzle her shoulder, but she edged away instinctively. He caught hold of her sleeve as she escaped and pulled her down towards him, his lips reaching for hers.

'Travis, no!' Peg pushed him away and stood up, pulling her wrap tight around her. 'This was not the arrangement, remember? I'm prepared to be friendly, and to work alongside you – '

'But, Peggy, I'm crazy for you, you know that – '

'No, you're not. You've never even taken the trouble to get to know me! You just want to be able to jump on me from time to time. Well, I'm sorry but you know my position.'

Travis jumped up and flung open the door. 'Oh, yeah, I know your position all right, you cold bitch! Any position but on your back!'

Peg was relieved when Travis flew to Chicago at noon the following day, intending to spend three nights away. She needed time alone, to think.

The house was very quiet. Betty had the afternoon off and had gone home leaving the evening meal in the icebox. Rita, the maid, worked only in the mornings. John Alexander was having his afternoon nap, and Peg decided to go and sit in his nursery, enjoying the very special silence of a sleeping infant. Through the bedroom window she could see Joel clearing the flowerbeds to make way for next spring. He moved in the very precise and deliberate way of someone who has lost much of the suppleness in his back and limbs. Peg wondered how old he was. His black curls were edged with grey and his face was etched with deep lines. Didn't Betty tell her once that he had worked for the family for fifty years, for Cordella and her mother before her? She felt a pang of sadness at the idea of not seeing him any more.

So was that it? Did the sadness mean she had decided? She was almost certain, only . . . . The house was so quiet, so damned quiet. And John looked so peaceful lying there in his crib. Her state of mind left her feeling oddly distanced from him, as though he was part of a picture and she was just an observer, looking at it. This was *his* home, these people were *his* family. He would always have a place here.

But for her, this was so crazy. It was clear that Travis was not going to be able to abide by their agreement, or at least only with constant rearguard action on her part. It had seemed on the surface that by marrying him she was getting herself the chance of a brilliant career in business. But she could see now that the Mackens would always hold her back. Her importance now was in the role of John's mother, and they would always be able to use that against her.

No, it wasn't worth it. She could find herself a career somewhere else; she had the ability, it was just a question of confidence. Maybe now was the time to return to England. She would have to leave without telling anyone and present Travis with a *fait accompli*.

She parked John in his stroller in the garden under Joel's supervision and went for a jog to relieve some of her stress. When she returned she took a bath, washed her hair, sorted through her clothes. By then John was awake again, so she fed him and left him lying on a blanket on her bed while she packed some clothes and toys for him.

She called the airport and reserved a first class seat on the flight to John F. Kennedy airport at eight o'clock the following morning. Then she bathed John, gave him a bottle and put him to bed, ate supper alone in the kitchen and went upstairs to bed at nine o'clock.

It was going to be difficult to sleep, she knew that. She tried reading for a while but couldn't concentrate, so she resorted to the TV instead. By the end of the Johnny Carson show she was asleep.

A heavy tread on the stairs woke her. She jerked into consciousness. The TV was still on, a Rowan and Martin re-run.

The door opened and Travis came into the room. He stood at the end of the bed looking down at the open suitcase on the ottoman.

'You're in Chicago,' she said stupidly.

He looked up at her. 'My father's dead.'

Travis sat on the edge of the bed, and Peg stood beside him for what felt like hours while he said over and over, 'I can't believe he's done this to me, I can't believe he's done this to me.'

She tried to offer some sort of comfort, but he didn't seem to be aware of what she was saying. Finally, when she murmured something about not getting upset, he rounded on her.

'I'm not upset, damn it, I'm mad as hell! The guy goes and drops dead of a heart attack just like that, out of the blue, and it turns out he'd got the whole thing planned!'

'He couldn't have planned a heart attack, how could he?'

'I don't mean his death, dummy, I mean what happened to MackenCorp afterwards. He's carved the Georgia end up into two equal pieces, one for me and one for Michael. With the condition that we have to work alongside each other or we lose the whole lot to the federal exchequer. I mean, Michael, for Chrissakes! He hasn't been near the place in years, he just dropped out and bummed around the world like some overgrown beachboy, never did a day's work for MackenCorp, and he gets to walk off with half of a multi-million dollar corporation!'

'Even so, half of – '

'But that's not the best part, oh no!' Travis stood up and roamed around the room, picking things up, putting them down again. 'No, sir! Wait till you hear the best part! Daddy's turned the whole thing into some sort of race against the clock so that unless we show profit after a year, we lose the whole thing anyway. I mean, why did he do that? What the hell is the point? He's never going to know if we made it or not. Michael and I could work together for a year and then not speak for another fifty and he still wouldn't know about it. He just wants to go on manipulating people even after he's dead.'

Travis picked up Peg's hairbrush from the bed and started to slap it rhythmically against his palm.

'What . . . what did Michael say, do you know?' So great was the effort to sound casual that Peg's voice trembled audibly.

'Oh, it's not just me that's mad about it. Winona called him and she said he just swore. Said he didn't want anything to do with it.'

Peg breathed out, heavily. 'Well, there you are then. If he pulls out of the arrangement, you get everything.'

'Uh-uh.' Travis shook his head. 'I checked with my lawyer and he said that if Michael refused, then all the assets would be frozen under probate laws until the whole thing was straightened out in court.'

'Would he do that, d'you think? Pull out?'

'I don't know, do I? How do I know?' Travis's voice rose angrily.

Peg tried to quell her own confused thoughts and concentrate on keeping Travis calm. 'Did you call your mother?'

'Not yet.'

'I think you should. Or I could.'

Travis shrugged. His gaze roamed around the room and lighted on the half-packed suitcase. 'You going somewhere?'

'I was going to make a trip to New York.' There was not much point telling him now. 'To do some shopping.'

'Oh. Well, you'll have to cancel. You can hardly go now, can you?'

'No,' said Peg. 'I can't.'

Beulah Peabody brought her car to a halt on the driveway outside the Macken house, and sat still for a while, collecting her thoughts. She smoothed her hands over her black linen skirt. It seemed right to wear black. Al wouldn't have given a damn, but Cordella would appreciate the gesture.

She looked up at the house. Funny to think she had only visited it a handful of times in all these years. The first time had been on her nephew's birthday. She had realised then that she shouldn't make a habit of visiting. If she needed to see Cordella, she would just have to see her elsewhere.

It was a lovely place, you couldn't deny that. Al and Cordella had turned it into one of the finest properties in the county. She had once thought she would end up living in a place like this.

But it wasn't the kind of place you wanted to be on your own. It needed to be full of people.

Cordella answered the door herself. She, too, was wearing black, Beulah noted, a simple jersey dress. It made her look too thin, but Cordella was not one to abandon propriety for the sake of elegance. When Cordella got thin, she just looked scrawny. Beulah became acutely aware of her own voluptuous bosom. She wished she had brought a scarf or something to cover it up.

Beulah had anticipated, at the very least, a cool reception, but Cordella seemed pleased to see her. She took her sister into her thin arms and embraced her.

'I guess y'all want to see him?'

'Yes, I would, if that's all right.'

Cordella led her through the house, to the ballroom, vast and empty but for a grand piano in one corner and the magnificent whale-oil chandelier. The room had been filled with flowers: white gardenias and lilies.

'I thought we ought to put him in here. It seemed most dignified, somehow.'

The open coffin lay on a catafalque at the end of the room. The two sisters stood beside it and looked down. Cordella crossed herself.

'He looks . . . he looks so well,' said Beulah lamely. Al lay before her, as sun-tanned and handsome as he had been in life. The only thing missing was the spark of life, the energy that radiated from him.

'I know,' said Cordella quietly. 'Kind of funny, i'n't it? I keep on expecting him to sit right up and laugh at me. And I sometimes . . . oh, this sounds so stupid.'

'What?'

'I just wish he could open his eyes, so I could look at them one more time. They were so blue.' She sighed a long, painful sigh that came from the very depths of her being.

Beulah kept on staring down at him, unable to avert her gaze. 'Cordella . . . I have to say you're taking this awful well. Losing him.'

'I guess that's because he was never mine to lose.' Cordella's voice had a hard, tight edge to it. 'He never chose me, after all. He just ended up with me.'

'He loved you, though.'

'I guess, in a way.'

'And you loved him.'

'We shared a lot of good things together. He wasn't an easy man to love.'

'No man worth loving ever is.'

'Anyhow. . . .' Cordella glanced sideways at her sister. 'Why should I be taking his death any better than you? If he belonged to anyone, it was to you.'

Beulah shook her head. 'No, Cordella. Don't you see? He wasn't mine either. He couldn't give all of himself to either of us. There were things he needed from you, and things he needed from me. And because of who he was, he never had to choose. Al always got what he wanted.'

Cordella nodded.

'Tell me something, I can't help but be curious. Did you always know about him and me?'

'Yes.'

'He tell you?'

She shook her head. 'I guessed. I don't know how, but I just knew. It just seemed . . . natural somehow, when you came back, that he'd go back to you.'

'But didn't you ever try to stop him being with me? Didn't you want him to yourself?'

'I never really felt I had the right. Perhaps I felt guilty that he ended up with me, when it was you he had wanted all along.'

'Or perhaps you just realised it was better this way. That we were meant to share him.'

'Is that what *you* thought?' Cordella sounded curious.

'I had to find some way to live with the fact you had all those things.'

'What things?'

'Marriage, children.'

Cordella stared. 'I never thought you wanted any of that. I just thought. . .'

Beulah shrugged. 'Why, because that's what Al thought? I just never let him know what I really wanted. Too proud, I guess.'

'He might have left me for you. After Daddy died.'

Beulah shook her head. 'No. You were better at all that

domestic stuff. I would have been a lousy wife and Al knew it. He was so smart, remember? He just made sure we got different bits. I got the sex. You got the kids. We both know which lasts longer.'

Her face softened as she looked down at her dead lover's face. She reached into the coffin to touch his face, then pulled her hand away, when she saw Cordella watching her.

'It's all right, go ahead.'

Beulah stroked his cheek. 'So cold. . . .' She touched his hand, clasped loosely round a camellia.

'I put that there,' said Cordella. They looked up, simultaneously, at the huge vases of flowers on the piano. 'Why don't you . . .?'

Beulah walked over to the flowers and picked a lily in full bloom; creamy white, showy, its petals opened in invitation. She laid it in Al's hand, entwined with Cordella's fragile, feminine camellia.

Cordella smiled her approval. 'Two flowers,' she said, putting her arm round Beulah's waist. 'He would have liked that, wouldn't he?'

'He should be here,' said Travis angrily. 'He should have come to his own father's funeral.'

They were at the cemetery, making their way from the huddle of limousines to the edge of the Macken plot, with its gaping mouth of earth. There had been at least two hundred friends and business acquaintances at the church service, but at Cordella's request they had all dispersed, leaving the family to witness the burial alone. There were Peg and Travis, Wyatt and Martha and their children, Beulah, Winona, and the servants who had served Al for years. But no Michael.

'He'll come,' said Cordella quietly. 'I know he will.'

As the priest read the burial prayers, Peg could not quell the urge to look over her shoulder, back down the path to the cemetery gates. She glanced back several times, nervously, waiting. So she was the first to see him. He was walking slowly towards them, dressed in a black overcoat. His head was bare, and his dark, silky hair fluttered slightly in the breeze.

Peg could afford to go on staring, since she had the protection of the black veil that obscured her face. Travis was staring too, angrily, as Michael reached down and scooped up a handful of earth and crumbled it onto the top of the coffin. He stepped back and shut his eyes tight, screwing up his face as if he were fighting back tears.

'He's got some nerve,' muttered Travis. 'Staying away until the last minute, upsetting Mom, then showing up and acting like some melodramatic college girl. . . .'

'He looks upset,' whispered Peg. 'He must have really loved your father.'

But this was not what Travis wanted to hear. Peg realised he felt threatened by his brother's last-minute appearance, and she shared her husband's indignation. The nerve of the man, just waltzing back here to play the role of the returning prodigal! After ignoring them all for years . . . .

She also realised she would be able to avoid having to speak to Michael, at least for now. Cordella hovered after it was all over, looking as though she would like to make a formal re-introduction, but Travis took Peg firmly by the elbow and steered her past Michael. Peg was aware of his stony glance as she passed, and she returned it, through her veil. If he had thought she was going to rush over and talk about old times then he was wrong. She had no intention of talking to him at all, if she could help it.

'Mom!' Travis wove his way through the others, pulling Peg along behind him until they had fallen into step with Cordella.

'Mom, are you OK?'

Cordella tried to smile at him. 'Sure.'

'You want us to ride with you? Back to the house?'

'No, it's OK, honey, I'll go on ahead and make sure everything's ready for the guests.'

She wants to be on her own, thought Peg. Why can't he see that she just wants five minutes alone with her own thoughts?

'Only, Mom . . . I wondered if you might like to spend some time with young John Alexander. If you thought it would cheer you up, we could bring him around for a while.'

Cordella smiled. 'Thank you, darling, that *would* be nice. Maybe later.'

'You hear that, honey?' Travis hissed to Peg as he led her to the waiting limousine. 'I hope you're not planning on taking any trips in the near future. You can see what Mom's little grandson means to her now.'

Neither Beulah nor Michael attended the wake at the Macken house in Turner's Creek.

Michael was planning to return to France immediately. Beulah was flying to California for a few days' vacation with friends, so she offered him a ride to the airport.

They sat in silence all the way. Beulah turned and looked at Michael from time to time; he kept expecting her to speak but she didn't. A faintly serene smile hovered around the corners of her mouth. Michael felt angry with her. What was she made of, ice? She had been his father's mistress for years, had had far more of the man than *he* ever had, and here she was acting as though everything was . . . well, OK.

When they reached the airport and he started to unload the cases from the trunk, she said: 'You shouldn't be doing this, you know.'

'Doing what?'

'Running away.'

He dropped her suitcase at her feet. 'If you mean not accepting what my father laid out in his will, that's not running away. I just don't want any part in his games.'

'It's no game. It was just something he wanted. He wanted to give you and Travis an even break. It meant the world to him that you two might one day work alongside one another.'

'Is that so?' Michael shouldered his flight bag. 'Well, excuse me for not seeing it your way. I believe that if he really thought that he would have told me. Anyway, Travis seems to be doing pretty well sharing the show with that pushy little English wife of his. Daddy was probably going to change that will and blow me out completely, he just never got around to it before he had the heart attack.'

Beulah shook her head slowly. 'You're wrong. . . . Listen, Michael, just sit down a minute.' She linked her arm through his and led him to one of the plush benches in the arrivals area. 'Two things you should know. First: Al tried very hard to get hold of you before he died. It was the main thing on his mind. Second:

it wasn't a heart attack, he committed suicide. So he made the arrangement for the company in the full knowledge he was about to die. He wanted to give you a chance to succeed.'

'He killed himself? Are you sure? Why would he do that?'

'He was ill, and he didn't want to just fall apart, so he ended it. That takes courage.'

Michael shook his head slowly. 'And nobody knew.'

'Just me and John Morrow and Winona. And now you.'

Michael buried his head in his hands, rubbing his temples. 'Jesus . . . he really hated to be ill, didn't he? He couldn't stand anything to get the better of him, not even death. He had to push death around too.' He permitted himself a small smile. 'You have to admire the arrogance of the man.'

Beulah also smiled, resting her hand lightly on his back. 'Michael, I know you and I don't know one another very well, but I always thought you were more like him than Travis is. Even though Travis looks the spit of him . . . . Y'all just remind me of him when he was young. He had this sparkle. . . .'

Her eyes misted with tears suddenly. She reached for a handkerchief and dabbed them away. 'So you see, I'm kind of sad you're not going to show the same courage that your father showed. I don't know what it is here in Savannah that you're afraid of, but I think it's one hell of a shame you're just going to keep on running. I thought you might decide it was time you stayed and showed them and yourself what you can do.'

Beulah waited, patiently, and was rewarded with a grin, and a shrug of defeat. 'Any chance you can lend me that car of yours while you're away?'

She handed the keys to him. Michael stood up and tossed them into the air, catching them with a flourish.

Travis returned home from the wake in a maudlin frame of mind. He sat in the den and proceeded to drink his way through a bottle of Wild Turkey.

Peg peeped at him through the door, then decided it was best to leave him alone.

'Betty, would you mind listening out for Johnny, please? I just need to go out for some fresh air.'

She took the car and headed downtown. She went and took a

look at the Savannah River then drove round and round aimlessly for a while, but in the end it was impossible to tear herself away from the MackenCorp building on East Bay.

She stared up at the soaring plate glass tower that would always dominate the Savannah skyline. Then without knowing why, her fingers were on the car door handle. . . .

Another car swerved left and pulled in to the kerb in front of her. Beulah's car. But it wasn't Beulah who climbed out, it was Michael.

Peg's instinctive reaction was to duck down behind the steering wheel but to continue to watch him. He was carrying an attaché case and a bundle of files, and he walked purposefully to the front doors of the building, produced a key for the security lock and let himself in. A few minutes later, lights went on on the fifteenth floor. At least he had not taken his belongings to the sixteenth-floor penthouse, that would for ever seem like Al's domain.

It was obvious Michael was intending to stay in Savannah and accept the terms of Al's will. Peg clutched the steering wheel for a few minutes while she grappled with the feelings of anger and indignation this idea threw up. She felt directly challenged, as though he was trespassing on her domain. She watched silently, eyes narrowed, as Michael left the building empty-handed, climbed into Beulah's car and drove off into the night.

She didn't really know what was propelling her, but her automatic response was to get out of her car, enter the building and go up to the fifteenth floor. The office Michael had commandeered was just across the hall from Travis's and one floor above her own. The room was still under-furnished and impersonal; he had just dumped the stuff on the desk and left.

Peg flicked through the files. They were mostly training manuals and case studies from INSEAD. Michael was pretty new to the business world, after all; it was unlikely there would be anything very exciting. There was no personal stuff, no photos or letters.

Except a small brown envelope at the bottom of a box; wrinkled and scuffed from repeated handling. She unfolded it and looked inside. An earring: nothing fancy, just a plain silver hoop. She had been wearing earrings just like that on the night she met Michael in Harvard. She remembered now, remembered looking in the mirror the next morning and noticing her naked earlobe. And realising she must have lost it during. . . .

Angrily, she thrust the small silver hoop into the envelope and tossed it back into the box. Just what did he think he was doing, keeping it all these years?

He can't get away with swanning back here like this, she thought, as she slammed the door of his office so that it rocked on its hinges. *He just can't.*

TWELVE

Savannah, Georgia 1980

Peg Macken took a deep breath and looked at herself in the mirror. Not bad, she told her reflection, not bad. She smiled.

She had been out shopping in the new mall south of town and bought herself a few new business clothes. The choice here was nothing like that in New York, and she supposed that was something to do with the Southern idea that women had no place going out to work in an office. Most of the clothes she had seen were fluffy and feminine; pretty blouses and dirndl skirts, little-girl dresses in adult sizes.

Still, she had found herself a few decent designer suits. This one was a Calvin Klein, made of soft, beige wool and flowing easily along the lines of her body. She wore dark stockings and court shoes and had her thick golden brown hair dragged back with a velvet bow.

She didn't normally wear much make-up, but today she went over her face with particular care, outlining her mouth three times with a lipstick brush before she got it right. Her hand shook slightly, tickling her lips with the bristles of the brush. She was nervous, really nervous. She had no idea why. It really didn't make sense.

Travis appeared in the bedroom doorway. 'What you doin', honey?'

Peg flung him a scathing glance and returned to rifling through the contents of her make-up bag in search of lip gloss. 'Getting ready, of course.'

'You surely weren't thinking of coming downtown today, were you?'

'Of course, why not?'

'Well, Elaine has only been with us a matter of days. She doesn't know her way around the house, and she certainly hasn't had time to get to know John Alexander!'

'Betty's perfectly capable of showing her all she needs in the house, and as for John Alexander – come with me. . . .'

She grabbed Travis's wrist and yanked him along the landing in her wake. When they reached the nursery she flung the door open. 'See!'

There, on the carpet in the sunny blue and yellow room, sat the new English nanny in her crisp brown uniform, bouncing a delighted John Alexander on her lap. He was so engrossed in the game that he didn't even turn his head to look at his mother.

'Elaine is more than capable of coping single-handed here. She's been professionally trained at the best nursery training college in Britain: that's what you're paying $600 a month for. . . .'

She was already skimming down the curved staircase and hunting around for her briefcase and trenchcoat. 'There's no way in the world that I'm going to miss the first board meeting of the new regime. I am still vice-president of the company, remember?'

'So you're going to forget about your kid, right?'

'He'll be fine. So just stop trying to treat me like a wife. I mean, I know I am your wife, but I'm not ever going to be a . . . *wife*.'

Travis narrowed his eyes suspiciously, watching her every move. 'It's been a year and a half now. I think the attorneys would swallow it if we filed for divorce. And now Daddy's gone . . . I thought you would want to get on with your own life.'

'I do,' said Peg firmly, shrugging her coat over her shoulders. 'Believe me, Travis, I do. But I thought I ought to stick around for the twelve-month period of Al's little trial. You're going to have to stay two steps ahead of that brother of yours, and I thought you could use my help.' She gave him a saucy sidelong look. 'Strictly business, of course. . . .'

'Don't want that kid brother of mine thinking I can't keep my wife in line,' Travis grumbled, but he held the front door open for her, and helped her into the waiting limousine. Peg knew as much as he did about the way the company was run, if not more, and he knew he could use her expertise.

'My wife and I are going straight to East Bay,' he told the driver, and gave her a reluctant grin.

The boardroom was on the penthouse floor, with dizzying views over the Savannah River. The twenty-foot walnut table had been polished until it gleamed like satin; blotter, pens and crystal decanters of iced water had been set out at each of the eight places.

It's a ridiculously large table for eight people, thought Peg. We're going to have to shout to make ourselves heard . . . .

Then she noticed that one of the chairs was already occupied, by Michael.

'What's she doing here?' he asked, frowning at Travis, then before he could answer snarled at Peg: 'I thought you'd just had a baby.'

'I have,' said Peg coolly. 'Your nephew. He's three months old.'

'Only we have a quaint old tradition here in the South. We believe in women taking the trouble to raise their own children, rather than leaving it to strangers while they run around getting in to things they don't really understand.'

Peg ignored him and went to sit beside Travis. She glanced at Michael occasionally while the others trooped in. He's still an arrogant bastard, she thought. And he looks arrogant, too. At Harvard he had dressed casually in jeans and sweatshirts, just like anyone else. Now he wore a suit from a leading Paris couture house, handmade and beautifully fitted, an exquisitely laundered shirt and a floral Hermès tie.

Wyatt Neely, MackenCorp's chief accountant and longest serving member of the board, was chairing the meeting. The other members were Ed Roger, head of the company's team of legal advisers and the most senior board member after Wyatt, Frank Earle, the head of personnel, Grant Stedman, in charge of press and public relations, and Raymond Lorimer, head of the marketing division. All men, Peg noted. Except for Winona, sitting discreetly in the corner to take the minutes.

'Good morning, gentlemen,' said Wyatt. He glanced in Peg's

direction and coloured slightly. 'And Mrs Macken. This is something of a sad occasion, the first board meeting since the death of the founder of this corporation, and one of my closest friends. . . .'

He took out a handkerchief and blew his nose.

'Now, y'all are familiar with the terms of Al's will in regard to this company. He took steps to ensure a period of twelve months in which MackenCorp would have not one, but two chief executives – his two sons, Michael and Travis. Now Travis is familiar with this boardroom, but could I please extend a welcome to Michael, who now has his Masters in Business Administration.'

The others, including Travis, smiled at Michael. Peg stared straight ahead, tapping her pen on her blotter.

'Over the past weeks, I have had some discussion with my colleagues here, and we decided that in order for Michael and Travis to work comfortably alongside one another, they should take over responsibility for two quite separate areas of the corporation. In view of his recent experience in New York, I'd like to suggest that Travis heads up our Investments division, while Michael here could take responsibility for Mergers and Acquisitions. Are you gentlemen in favour?'

'Sure,' said Travis. Michael just nodded.

'OK, we'll consider that carried. Now. . .' Wyatt glanced nervously in Peg's direction. 'Mrs Macken here is not a voting member of this board, but she is an acting vice-president, and I agreed to her request that she attend this meeting. With her considerable experience in new project development, which I believe was her specialist subject at Harvard – ' he waited for Peg's nod of concurrence – 'we thought it might be appropriate for her to act as Michael's assistant in Mergers for the year, just while he gets to know his way around a little more.'

'His *assistant*! You've got to be joking!' Peg looked around wildly for Travis's support, but he avoided her eye.

'So, all those in favour?' said Wyatt.

Ed, Frank, Raymond, Grant and Wyatt raised their hands straight away. Travis hesitated, then put his up.

'Those against?'

Michael and Peg's arms shot up.

'Motion carried.'

Peg stormed after Travis when he went downstairs to his office. 'What the hell did you do that for?'

'Do what, honey?'

'Vote for me becoming Michael's assistant.'

Travis sat down coolly and swung his legs up onto his desk. 'I voted for it because I thought it was kind of a good idea. You can be our spy in the camp, keep an eye on my little brother for me.'

'But his assistant! I already have far more experience than he does! He should have been made *my* assistant.'

'Well, honey, if you don't like the situation you know what you can do.'

Peg glared at him.

'There's a beautiful little baby boy lying in his crib at home, just waiting for his mommy. Some women would just love to have the chance to stay home all day with that cute little guy.'

Peg gritted her teeth, refusing to rise to the bait. 'Anyway, I'm surprised you're so sanguine about me working closely with your brother.'

'What do you mean?'

'Well, personally, I don't like him but he is single and very attractive.'

Travis laughed. 'You're hardly his type, darling. He likes his girls blonde and dumb. Anyhow. . .'

He paused, and Peg knew he had been about to say, 'You're married'.

'Anyhow what?'

'Nothing. How about we go down to the Pirate House and have some surf and turf and a bottle of champagne to celebrate the new order?'

'Shouldn't you go and talk to Michael? Sort out a few ground rules?'

'Nah, Michael can go to hell.'

'Quite,' said Peg.

After they had feasted on lobster and clams at the Pirate House seafood restaurant, Travis and Peg walked in Emmet Park near the riverfront. The oak trees were still thickly furred with grey-green moss, but the magnolias had dropped their leaves and were bare of blossoms.

'It's going to be so nice when the magnolias are in bloom again,' said Peg, realising as she did so that she was looking forward to the spring coming, and being in Georgia to see them.

'Savannah's not such a bad place to live, is it?' asked Travis.

'Not bad at all,' Peg agreed reluctantly.

They strolled around the Harbor Light, which Peg thought like an oversized streetlamp sprouting up in the middle of the park.

'Well, this is nice, isn't it?' said Travis.

'Yes,' said Peg, feeling confused.

For a second he looked as though he was going to take her hand, then thought better of it. 'Well, I guess I should get my ass back to East Bay and have that talk with little brother.'

'I'll come with you. I want to get some ideas down on paper to discuss with him tomorrow. Particularly that reclaimed land deal in Florida. I'm really excited about that – '

'Sorry, honey, but you're going to have to head back to Gordonstoun. Mom phoned me and said she wanted to come by and see John Alexander. I thought you ought to be there to introduce her to Elaine. It'll be a bit awkward for the poor girl otherwise.'

Peg sighed heavily. 'I wish you could have told me before.'

'Sorry, honey, we were having such a good time, I guess it slipped my mind.'

'What time will you be coming home?'

'About six, I guess.'

'Fine. When you get back at six, you can take over with supervising Elaine, and I'll go back to the office. I'll just have to work this evening instead.' She climbed into the car beside him and added mischievously, 'You'll be able to show Elaine how to give the baby a bath.'

The next morning, Peg woke up with a headache and her stomach knotted with tension and she resented both intensely. She had set her alarm for 6.45 because she wanted to get into work before Michael, prove she was on the ball. But when she arrived at ten-to-eight he was already there. Her behind had barely touched her chair before his secretary, Lizzy, was on the phone.

'Mr Macken would like you to come up for a meeting. Is eight o'clock all right?'

He could have phoned and asked me himself, thought Peg grumpily. She dragged her feet reluctantly all the way up to the fifteenth floor.

'Hi!' he said, without looking up. 'Come and sit down and let's go through some things.'

Peg sat down opposite him and folded her hands in her lap.

'No, come and sit next to me. I want you to see what I'm doing.'

He pointed to a chair on his left, indicating that she should sit in it. He still hadn't looked at her. She could smell his aftershave, which she didn't like.

'OK.' He picked up a blank pad of paper and a pen. 'We have a lot of stuff to get through this morning . . . .First, let's write down the names of the key personnel within the division.' He began sketching out a family tree, with arrows going in various directions. 'Now we need to look at the areas of management and expertise they cover, see where they overlap and how they can be streamlined.'

The scribbling speeded up and the diagram became even more complex. Peg, whose eyes were crossing with the effort of concentrating, rested one elbow on the desk and supported her head in her hand.

'I'm sorry this is so boring for you,' Michael said, 'but it has to be done.'

'Did I say I was bored?'

'No, but – '

'Then don't assume you know what's going on in my head,' said Peg archly. 'That would be a big mistake.'

When he had finished writing, Michael tore off the sheets of paper and handed them to Peg. 'Right, take these away with you and have a think about it. See if you come up with any ideas.'

He's treating me like a kid with homework, thought Peg bitterly. She snatched the paper and stalked towards the door.

'And be back in my office at 11.30 sharp, please. We're going on a site visit.'

In the afternoon they drove out to one of MackenCorp's newest acquisitions; a textile mill in Monroe, a small town between Atlanta and Savannah. It had been started up in the days when Georgia's main crop was cotton, and now survived by weaving synthetic broadcloths in addition to heavyweight cotton drill.

'Right now this place is turning over $450,000,000 a year and we're employing 5,000 workers,' said Michael as they climbed out of the car.

'I plan on increasing turnover to a billion dollars a year, and keeping costs down by introducing new technology. Somehow we're going to have to convince the mill workers that the new machinery will increase productivity by making cloth faster, not by replacing men. And that's not going to be easy.'

Peg looked sideways at him. 'You really do intend to try and meet Al's challenge, don't you?' She was reflecting that Travis didn't seem interested in the company's performance at all, only protecting his own place in it.

'Sure I do.'

'It's just that you never seemed very interested in MackenCorp before.'

'I've changed. It does happen sometimes, you know.' For the first time all day he looked at her with his intensely brown eyes, raising one eyebrow slightly.

'Come on, they're waiting for us. . . .'

Bill, the foreman, showed Peg and Michael around the shop floor. He had been apologetic when he saw Peg. 'It's kind of hot in here, ma'am. Not really the place for a lady.'

'That's quite all right,' Peg replied primly, longing to pull off her jacket and her pantyhose. 'I'm fine.'

'I think working conditions would be greatly improved if we updated this building. We could have much better ventilation and it wouldn't be so hot. If it's like this now, what's it going to be like in the summer?'

Michael ran his finger around the edge of his collar as he spoke. It was as hot as hell in here now, in mid-March. How did these guys survive it? And the noise! The constant hum and whirr and grind of the looms was overwhelming. And her ladyship there was looking as cool as a cucumber, as always . . . .

'The new machinery would be a hell of a lot quieter too. You must make sure the men understand that – '

'And over here,' Peg interjected, striding into a corner of the factory floor, 'we could add on a new rest area.'

'Yeah,' said Michael. 'That's a good idea. New johns, drinks machines, table football, a pool table, whatever.'

Bill grinned. 'They sure would like that. I'll tell 'em.'

'We're going to have to close down for a couple of weeks while the work's done.'

'That's going to put us behind with our orders, Mr Macken.'

'I know.' He scratched his head. 'I don't see what else we can do.'

'We could try and work out some productivity bonus scheme,' Peg interjected quickly. 'It could run in the weeks before and after the place is closed, to keep us up to our deadlines. Something to encourage the men to work some extra hours.'

'Let's think about that, and we'll talk again.'

As they left the factory Michael made an attempt to pat Peg on the shoulder, but she dodged it. 'Nice work. I'm impressed.'

Peg nodded. She was exhausted. It wasn't just the heat and noise, but the effort of having to think, think, think all the time, to have an answer for everything and to have an instant pool of ideas in her head so that she could pluck them out when they were needed. She had enjoyed it though, more than she had expected to.

They leaned back in the limo and let the icy gusts from the air-conditioning float over their flushed faces.

'One down, but plenty to go,' observed Michael. 'I want us to do similar raids on Southern Atlantic Cargo and Atlanta Cigarettes and Amusements. And then there's Georgia Satellite Inc. and Machemica. . . .'

Peg groaned. 'I just hope some of them have air-conditioning.'

'We'll get a cold drink in a little while. Our next stop won't take long.'

It turned out to be about an hour. Michael was addressing a syndicate of local businessmen about new strategies in corporate planning. Peg, listening from the audience, had expected his lack of experience to show but he spoke well, clearly and with authority, and the audience loved him.

He has a nice voice, thought Peg grudgingly, during the applause. That tends to make things sound more convincing than they are. As if he could read her thoughts, Michael caught her eye and smiled.

The atmosphere was a little more relaxed on the return journey. They drove back to the city along Highway 204, along a soulless commercial strip past the Krispy Chick Drive Inn, a sporting goods store, Piggly Wiggly meat wholesalers, a pawnbrokers, pre-owned car lot and the Chatham County Mortuary.

'I promised you something to drink, didn't I? Jesse, stop the car just here, will you?'

The chauffeur pulled into the parking lot of the Oasis Diner, a squat brick building as bleak and featureless as the land around it. The décor was an odd mixture of bland and tawdry; beige tiled walls, wood-look formica and orange plastic cushions in the booths. There was a cake stand of Danish pastries on the counter, and above it a sign that read '*Shirts must be worn to be served*'. An ageing truckie munched his way solemnly through a plate of fried eggs in one corner, two giggling teenage girls smoked incessantly in another. The three waitresses stood in the corner silently, watching him. Next to the restroom door was a jukebox with records that hadn't been changed in a long time. Peg glanced at them as she walked past, remembering the makeshift juke box on the beach in New Brighton. There were no Beatles records here, just Conway Twitty and Sam Cooke.

They eased themselves into one of the booths and scanned the menu. Chopped steak melts, steak dinners, grits, Bert's chilli soup . . . the diner was baking hot and airless, awash with the smell of frying, and the thought of chilli soup made Peg shudder. The vinyl seat was already making the back of her thighs stick. She ordered an iced cola.

Michael looked around at the diner and laughed. 'Jesus, I haven't been in one of these places for years. Not since I was at Harvard.'

Peg looked down at the menu quickly, pretending to study the photograph of an icecream sundae.

'Shouldn't we talk about when we were in Harvard?' Michael asked quietly.

Peg shook her head.

'No, I guess maybe you're right. We have to work alongside one another. And you're married to my brother, anyhow – '

'About Travis and I . . .'

'What?'

'Oh, nothing, doesn't matter.'

'I guess that makes you my sister-in-law. I never thought of it that way before.'

Peg permitted a small smile. 'No, neither did I.'

At the end of the day Michael went back to his apartment on the corner of Carlton and Bull.

It was the first place he had ever really been able to call his own, and he was enjoying it. The high-ceilinged rooms were sparsely furnished, with white walls bare except for a collection of abstract oils. The polished wooden floors were covered with old Turkish kelims and there were a lot of books, books everywhere. He flung himself on the sofa and enjoyed the silence for five minutes, eyes closed, before flicking on the stereo and grabbing a cold beer from the fridge. Christ, what a day it had been. And having to work with Peg. . . .

He wondered what she and Travis were doing now, tried to picture them in their fancy white mansion. Perhaps they would be playing with their baby together, leaning over the edge of the crib and congratulating themselves on the beautiful child they had managed to produce. Or sitting on the verandah together enjoying a sundowner and talking about how their day had gone. Sharing.

The flat suddenly seemed too empty, the light from the tall windows harsh and cold. Michael went to take a hot bath and then lay on his bed watching the baseball game on TV until it grew dark. As he turned the light out, all he could think about was how much he was looking forward to going to work in the morning.

'Hey, my little man, what's the matter? Hey, c'mon now.'

Peg held the baby against her shoulder and rocked him to and fro.

'I think he's just got a little bit of a cold,' said Elaine. 'His nose was running a bit this afternoon, and he's a bit snuffly now.'

She was tactfully trying to put the blame for his behaviour somewhere other than at the door of his absentee mother.

'He's not usually this cranky in the evening,' said Peg. 'And I'm sorry for being so late back. I don't want you to think I'm going to get back at nine o'clock every night. It's just that with my mother-in-law coming over and having to take time off this afternoon, and so much to get done....'

This is awful, she thought. The poor nanny's only just started and already I'm apologising and making excuses. And Travis and his mother between them are determined to try and keep me chained to the house, even if the chain is long enough to let me out of the front door occasionally.

Outside in the driveway, she heard Travis's car backing out. He was on his way to play racquet ball, leaving almost as soon as Peg walked in the door. 'Did my husband give you a hand with bathtime?'

'Well . . . he stuck his head around the door.' Elaine gave a wry smile. 'We often find that dads aren't all that interested at this stage. He'll come into his own later, when Johnny here is walking and starting to kick a ball around.'

It took Peg longer than usual to settle her son, and she was relieved when he was finally asleep and she could go and wallow in the bath with a glass of wine. Relieved, too, that Travis wasn't around to distract her. She wanted to replay the events of the day like a video in her mind. Some of it had been quite good.

'What's that you're working on?'

Travis materialised in Peg's office and started reading over her shoulder.

'That Florida thing I told you about. Look, there's the piece of land, see, right next to Coronado Beach.'

'Looks like a piece of old swamp to me.'

'Reclaimed swamp,' said Peg, smiling sweetly.

'What are you going to do with it? Build a trailer park?'

'I see it as a sort of theme park. There's a lot of interesting Indian history in the area, and we could have a sea park, a dolphinarium, but tie it all in with a natural history theme. That sort of thing is very popular at the moment.'

Travis sniffed. 'Sounds kind of trashy to me.'

'Well, it's not down to you, is it?'

Travis laughed. 'Michael wouldn't know a good idea if it jumped up and bit him in the balls.'

'I wouldn't be too sure about that.' Peg swivelled round to look at Travis, who was dressed in sweats and jogging shoes. 'At least he's working hard to get the turnover figures up, and not disappearing to the gym, or the tennis court or wherever else you go. . . .'

The last words were laden with meaning. She was sure Travis saw other women behind her back. Which he had every right to, given the nature of their arrangement; it was just that he was so sneaky about it, and wasted so much time. He hardly ever spent any time with his son.

'There are only nine months left until the anniversary of Al's death,' she reminded him. 'That's not such a long time. We should all be working our socks off to come up with new ideas if you want to keep the company.'

'As long as your divorce settlement depends on it, baby, I don't need to worry. I know I've got you working plenty for both of us. That was what you wanted, wasn't it? The career of the century?'

He flashed her a smile, shouldered his tennis racquet and sauntered out of the room.

Peg gathered up her papers and set off for Michael's office. She didn't mind coming in here quite as much as she used to. At first she had hated it. He made her feel as if she were a nuisance, in the way, pestering him even.

'What is it?' he said as she knocked, then smiled when he saw it was Peg.

'I just wanted you to take a look at this.' She put the papers on his desk and he ran an eye over them.

Standing next to him, Peg noticed how his dark hair curled over the collar of his blue Oxford cloth shirt. He should get a hair cut, she thought. She could smell the tang of his aftershave too. She was getting used to it now.

'This looks interesting,' said Michael, 'but it needs a little more research. If necessary, you should fly down there and take a look. I'll come with you if you like.'

She waited for him to go on, but he just looked back at his work and said, 'If that's all. . . .'

He did that a lot, just switching off and dismissing her. It was like a portcullis slamming down, shutting him in.

'What's your problem?' Peg found herself saying.

He sighed and laid down his pen. 'What?'

'Why do you have to be so rude all the time?'

'I wasn't aware that I was being rude. . . . Look, some other time, OK?' He looked back at his desk, signalling that she should go. She did, slamming the door hard.

Michael came to see her later.

'I'm sorry, I was rude.' He rubbed the bridge of his nose with thumb and forefinger. 'I guess I've been overdoing it with the work, not taking time out to relax. . . . Listen, do you want to go out somewhere?'

'Go out?'

'On one of our raids.'

Peg laughed. 'Yes, sure.'

'Great. I'll have the car brought round to the front in five minutes.'

When Peg had collected her briefcase and emerged from the huge doors at the front of the building, she found Michael waiting for her at the wheel of Beulah's sportscar.

'What happened to the limo?'

Michael shrugged. 'Don't tell anyone this, but I've never much cared for being chauffeur-driven. I much prefer to drive myself.'

'So do I,' confessed Peg.

'But Travis doesn't?' He raised an eyebrow.

'I guess not. In fact, now I think about it, I've never travelled anywhere with Travis except in the first-class seat of a plane or the back of a stretch limousine.'

'Some women would think that was the definition of a good husband,' observed Michael. He slipped a tape of Vivaldi's *Four Seasons* into the stereo and drove with confidence to a new site on Montgomery Cross Road where they owned a part share in the first of a chain of seafood restaurants.

'I'm beginning to feel like an old hand at this,' said Peg as she donned her hard hat and walked out to inspect the construction work. The heels of her courts slipped on the rutted mud and Michael grasped her elbow to steady her.

'If you tell me this is no place for a lady, I'll kill you,' she said with a grin, breaking free from his grasp and disappearing in the direction of what was to be the front entrance of the building.

'Hey, wait a minute, slow down! You go so fast all the time!'

'Up there,' said Peg, pointing to the roof of the building, a shell of gleaming new tiles almost complete. 'Above where the sign saying "Ocean Fresh Restaurant" is going to be. I think we should have some easily identifiable logo, an equivalent of the McDonalds "M" . . . a blue fish leaping on the crest of the wave, perhaps. Something nice and bright, so that the customers can spot it from a distance and take steps to pull over. And I think keep the décor simple, clean and clinical, white tiles and stuff.'

She was suddenly aware she was talking too fast, the words falling over each other in their hurry to get out.

'Good,' said Michael. 'I'll send a memo to the architects and designers to liaise with you before they go any further. We're in discussion at the moment about opening in Macon and Atlanta too, so the identity of the chain is important.'

The sun was low in the sky now, and the men working on the site were starting to lay down their tools and head for home.

'I don't know about you,' said Michael, 'but I'm real hungry. Want to go and grab something to eat on the way home?'

'OK,' said Peg, who wasn't hungry at all.

They went back to the Oasis Diner, and as soon as they had crammed into the vinyl booth and smelt the coffee and french fries, Peg felt very hungry indeed. She ordered a cheeseburger.

The waitress stood with pen poised over her pad, then shouted commands at the short-order cook, a young, nervous, coloured boy. They used the sort of diner shorthand that customers never understood.

'Medium over, smothered, Vern . . . hold the onion and treble the cheese.'

Peg noticed it was the same waitress that had served them last time. A pretty girl of about twenty with a mane of tousled blonde hair and a cupid's bow mouth slicked with bubble-gum pink lip gloss. She wore an orange and brown striped overall, with a badge on her right breast that said 'HI – I'M SUMMER' and an ugly orange polyester kerchief round her hair. Her jaws worked constantly on a piece of chewing gum.

Having bellowed Peg's order, she proceeded to ignore her.

'Hi!' she said to Michael, dragging out the syllable with a pronounced Southern drawl. 'Nice to see y'all again. You live round here?'

As she spoke Peg glimpsed a moist wad of chewing gum in the girl's mouth. She heaved it back between her teeth and started working her jaws on it, then flicked it in Peg's direction on the end of her tongue, a sort of veiled insult.

'I live in the city,' Michael was saying. 'I have an apartment downtown.'

He gave the girl a dazzling smile and she simpered back at him. Feeling irritated, Peg stood up.

'I should call home. I told the nanny I would be back by six.'

She found herself glancing in Michael's direction as she dialled. The waitress was leaning on the edge of the table now, talking animatedly around her gum.

'Hello, Elaine? This is Mrs Macken. I was just calling to say I was going to be home a little bit later than I anticipated.'

'I'm sorry, Mrs Macken, but it's my night off. I've arranged to go out.'

'Of course it is, I'm sorry. How about my husband, is he back yet?'

'No sign of him yet, I'm afraid.'

'OK, never mind. I'll sort something out.' Peg hung up, then dialled Travis's office.

'Travis, is there any chance of you leaving for home right now to relieve Elaine?'

'I'm afraid not, honey. I'm kind of tied up right now.'

Peg was sure she could hear giggling in the background.

'Tell you what, why don't I ask Mom to go on over? I'm sure she'd love to help out.'

'No! I don't want you getting your mother involved.'

'Then I'm sorry, I can't help you.'

Peg hung up and walked slowly back to the table. 'Michael, I'm sorry but I'm going to have to leave now.' She explained about Elaine.

'Why don't you call Mom? I'm sure she'd be happy to go on over to your house and look after the baby.'

Peg sighed. 'That's what Travis suggested, but I don't want to do that.'

'Why the hell not? She's the kid's grandmother.'

'Because . . . oh, it would take too long to explain. It's a difficult situation, but fortunately one that's not going to last many more months.'

She snatched up her briefcase and overcoat. 'Shall we go?'

Michael stood up and followed her, watched with sulky disapproval by Summer the waitress.

'Wait one second, we'd better pay for the food we ordered.'

He doubled back and thrust a twenty-dollar bill into Summer's hand. Then he opened his wallet and took out something else; one of his business cards.

Summer smiled like a contented cat, and stuck the card into the pocket of her overall.

'You seem kind of down, honey,' Travis observed the next morning when he came down to the dining room for breakfast. He poured himself a cup of black coffee and helped himself to a pile of Betty's hot corn muffins with cane syrup. For someone who had been out until the small hours of the morning, he looked remarkably chipper.

'I'm fine.' Peg continued to read her copy of the *Savannah Morning News*. 'Where were you last night?'

'Does it matter?'

Peg folded the paper and stood up to go. 'No, I suppose not.'

'How's the little fella? He OK?'

'Why don't you go and see for yourself?' Peg turned and swept out of the room.

'Peg! Peggy, come back here. . . .'

She turned.

'Listen, why don't you let me take you out for dinner tonight to cheer you up. Just the two of us.' He saw the expression on her face. 'No strings, no passes, I promise. We could go to the Boar's Head. That's kind of fun.'

'Oh . . . OK, why not?'

As the day wore on, Peg started to look forward to going out.

She'd never really had much time for dinner dates, or dating of any kind. But sometimes it was fun to get dressed up and be escorted out somewhere, be paid a little attention. She made an effort over getting ready that evening. After John Alexander was asleep she soaked in a hot bath, washed her hair and set it on rollers so that it bounced around her shoulders in waves, and took time over her make-up. She dressed in a low-cut black silk dress, sheer stockings and black patent courts, clipped diamond earrings onto her ears and sprayed herself generously with Jicky.

'Wow!' said Travis when he saw her. 'You really are a beautiful girl, Peggy.'

'Woman,' Peg corrected him. 'I'm almost thirty, after all, and the mother of a strapping six-month-old son.'

The Boar's Head restaurant was in a converted warehouse on the waterfront, with fresh flowers, candles and trailing greenery making it cosy and intimate. Travis and Peg were shown to a table overlooking the water, and the head waiter immediately brought an ice bucket containing vintage champagne.

'One thing y'all ought to have learned, honey,' said Travis as he poured the champagne into two crystal glasses, 'is that we Southerners know how to treat our women.'

Suddenly he started to laugh. 'Well, ain't that a coincidence! Look over there!'

He pointed to a corner table, where Michael was sitting with a pretty blonde girl dressed in a strapless red dress. She was giggling into a tall cocktail glass brimming with umbrellas and plastic flowers.

'She's a cute little thing, I must say.'

'She's the waitress from the diner we went to,' said Peg indignantly. 'She can't be much more than half his age!'

'Lucky boy!' said Travis. 'Look at the tits on her. Just like little puppy dog's noses!'

Peg scowled. 'Don't descend to his level, for God's sake, Travis! You should have seen the way he picked her up at the diner. She was all over him and he lapped it up! It was so blatant, so . . . casual. It was revolting!'

'Hey, calm down! The guy's young and single. He's just taking the girl out for dinner, there's no law against that, is there?'

'I suppose not. She just looks like a tramp, that's all.'

'Well, why don't we ask them over to join us, then we can find out.'

He raised his hand to wave them over, but Peg quickly grabbed his wrist and tugged it down again. 'Don't you dare! I see enough of Michael during the day without having to spend the evening with him and one of his . . . conquests!'

They ordered lobster and veal and a bottle of Chablis, but Peg pushed her food around the plate and left most of it. She found herself turning around every few minutes to scrutinize Michael and Summer, who was getting very tipsy and laughing a lot, her tousled blonde hair falling forward into her plate. Once Michael looked up and saw Peg. His eyes met hers in a long, cool look, then he ignored her painstakingly for the rest of the evening.

Peg waved away the dessert menu. 'I'd like to go home now, if that's OK with you. I've lost my appetite.'

'I don't really understand why you were so hard on Michael,' said Travis as the limousine purred past the rows of palm trees that lined Victory Drive. 'As long as he puts the interests of MackenCorp first, he's free to do what he likes in his private life. Anyway, I thought you guys were getting on well.'

'He's all right to work with,' said Peg, 'but personally I find him cold, arrogant and abrasive.'

'I see. . . .' Travis looked thoughtful. 'Only for a moment back there in the restaurant I thought I'd misunderstood.'

'No,' said Peg firmly, as the limousine swept into the circular driveway and came to a halt outside the pristine white columns of the porch. 'There's nothing to misunderstand.'

Peg was woken the next morning by the phone ringing. Groaning, she rolled over in bed and switched on the light. It was six o'clock.

Travis had already answered the call in his room, and a few minutes later he tapped on the door of her room.

Peg tugged on her bathrobe. 'What is it? Is there something wrong?' She had a sudden surge of panic, thinking that the call might have been from Liverpool. She remembered Jimmy calling with the news of her father.

'That was Wyatt calling. He's holding an emergency board meeting this morning, and he wanted to make sure we knew about it before the story breaks.'

Peg ran her fingers through her hair. 'What story? You mean something to do with Michael and the girl?'

'No, dummy! Frank Earle's secretary has filed an official complaint against him. For sexual harassment. She wants us to take action and fire him, or she's threatening to take him to court and sue him. The story would be sure to get into the media at national level, and that would be disastrous for MackenCorp at this stage. Totally disastrous!'

'But surely if he's guilty – '

'Don't you see, it could make a difference to us achieving our ten per cent growth target, and then we'd stand to lose everything. Every damn thing!'

THIRTEEN

Savannah, Georgia 1980

'We'll have to buy her off.'

Travis was addressing the other members of the board at the emergency meeting. Peg had been given permission to attend on the same condition as before, that she was not eligible to vote. Frank Earle's chair was ominously empty.

'I agree,' said Wyatt. 'We can't risk this getting into the press. Not at such a critical moment in the corporation's history. It would amount to this girl bad-mouthing the company and its policy makers. Shareholders would lose confidence. It could affect the price of stock.'

'What if she doesn't accept?' asked Peg quietly.

'Don't be foolish, darlin',' drawled Raymond Lorimer. 'Everyone has their price, especially a two-bit secretary earing $10,000 a year. It's just a question of finding out what it is and shutting her big mouth as quickly as possible.'

'And what about Frank Earle?'

'I'm sorry, I don't know what you mean.' Wyatt was tapping his pencil impatiently, and Travis shot Peg a warning look.

'I mean, what sort of disciplinary measures will he be subject to?'

'Well, none, of course! He'll just carry on as normal, that's the whole point of calling this meeting and fixing this thing now.'

Peg could feel her cheeks glowing as her anger reached boiling point. 'But what if she really has a case?'

'Oh come on, honey!' It was Travis who spoke up. 'Where's the harm in patting a girl's fanny? Happens all the time. And that Maura's a sassy little thing. She was probably forgetting her manners.'

Peg jumped to her feet. 'I don't believe you! All of you! You think you're Rhett bloody Butler in *Gone with the Wind*, standing around on some plantation with your horse whips, deciding how to keep the womenfolk in line. This girl is your employee too, she needs your protection far more than Frank Earle. I think one of us should at least take the trouble to talk to her and find out what happened.'

'No sense doin' that, honey,' said Grant Stedman. 'Just give her more to holler about later.'

'Well, I'm sorry,' said Peg coldly. 'But I represent this company too. My career is on the line just as much as any of yours. And if you're not going to deal honestly in this, then I shall speak to the press myself.'

There was a sharp intake of breath, and an exchange of disconcerted glances. Only Michael continued to look straight ahead, the tips of his fingers pressed lightly together in a steeple.

'Honey, you are way out of order!' bellowed Travis. 'Now you know fine well the conditions under which you were allowed to attend this meeting. And as a voting member of this board I am now exercising my right to ask you to leave.'

Peg felt like a humiliated child. 'No!' she said defiantly.

'I'm afraid you have no choice.'

She had never heard Travis's voice so cold and unconcerned. Stricken, she looked around the circle of faces, waiting for someone to defend her. There was silence.

Slowly she turned and with as much dignity as she could muster, walked out of the room.

A few minutes later Peg's secretary buzzed through on the intercom.

'Mr Macken to see you.'

'I'm not seeing him, or anyone else.'

'I'm sorry, but he's insisting.'

There was a brief tap on the office door, and it opened.

'Go to hell, Travis!'

It was Michael.

'What do *you* want?' she asked rudely.

'I just wanted to say that I agree with you one hundred per cent. If I'd said so in the boardroom it would have caused a dog fight, but I think you're right, and you can count on my support if you want it.'

'Thank you,' she said coldly.

'Yes . . . well. . . .' He shrugged. 'I just wanted to say it.'

'I appreciate it. Now, if you don't mind, I'd like you to go.'

She had already turned her back on him, so he would not see her hands trembling.

Peg splashed her hands and face with cold water in the washroom and set off to the personnel department three floors below, choosing to use the back stairs rather than take the elevator.

As she reached out to push open the heavy doors to the reception area, she saw Frank Earle coming through them in the opposite direction. He was a thick-set man with thinning blond hair and a yellowish moustache. He raised his eyebrows raffishly when he saw Peg.

She blocked his path. 'Well, you have some nerve, I must say!'

'I don't know what you're talking about.'

'I wonder if your secretary would know? As a matter of fact, I was just on my way to find her.'

Earle glared at her. 'Don't try to scare me, girlie, because I have nothing to be scared about. In fact your husband has already given me his word that this company will support me one hundred per cent!'

Peg gave him a contemptuous stare and swept past. The outer office next to Earle's was empty; the desk looking unnaturally tidy, as though it had just been cleared. She went back to the receptionist.

'Can I help you, Miz Macken?'

'Yes. I'm looking for Maura Johnson.'

The receptionist exchanged nervous glances with the typist at the next desk.

'I'm afraid she's not here.'

'Can you tell me where she is?'

The girl looked in the direction that Earle had just gone, and lowered her voice. 'The truth is, she didn't want me to tell nobody.'

'Please. I just want to talk to her. I want to help.'

'OK.' The girl handed her a file. 'Her address is in there. But you didn't get it from me. I don't want to get mixed up in this.'

Maura Johnson lived west of West Boundary in one of the poorer neighbourhoods on the edge of the city. There was no way you could pretend that the Johnson house was anything but a mess. Rotting window frames, shutters hanging askew on one hinge, grimy curtains at the windows. A tired-looking dog was tied up under the stoop. In one corner of the yard a middle-aged man in overalls was tinkering around with bits of an engine. He had a transistor radio at his feet, tuned in to the country and western station, and barely looked up when Peg's car came into the yard.

You could see these houses from the airport road, when you drove into the city from the west. Peg had looked down at them from the freeway many times, shuddering at their squalor, wondering who lived in them. Now she knew. And she was shocked, because with crystal clarity she could see what losing her job meant to someone like Maura Johnson.

The fly screen was pulled back and a young girl came onto the step. Peg had seen Maura around the Macken building occasionally, but she didn't recognise her at first. She wore no make-up on her pale freckled face, and her reddish hair hung limply round her face. She wore jeans and a T-shirt and her feet were bare. Peg hadn't realised how young she was. She couldn't be much more than eighteen or nineteen.

She looked Peg up and down, taking in her primrose-yellow Valentino suit and under-stated but expensive costume jewellery.

'I have nothing to say – '

She started to close the fly screen in Peg's face, but Peg resisted and pushed it open again.

'Maura, please. I want to help.'

'Yeah, by giving me money!'

Peg shook her head. 'No! I just want to talk. Can we go inside?'

Maura sat down on the stoop. 'We can talk here.'

Peg sat beside her, smoothing her skirt over her knees. 'There are certain people at MackenCorp who want to give you money to get you to drop your claim. But I think that's wrong.'

Maura gave a bitter laugh. 'Don't think I don't need the money.

Christ, just look at this place! My daddy's unemployed and my mom had to give up her job because of high blood pressure. I reckon if I take that bastard Earle to court I can sue him for a whole lot more money than they'd offer me!'

'What exactly did he do to you?'

Maura buried her face against her arm, shaking her head.

'If you go to court, you're going to have to tell a judge about it.'

'He . . . well, he was always standing a little close to me, you know? Crowding me. And he'd brush against me sometimes, but I figured most guys did that, it di'n't bother me too much. And then I was bending over the desk to reach something off a shelf . . . and I felt him behind me, kind of pressing up against me, and I turned round and he had his fly undone and his. . . .'

She laughed grimly. 'Sounds kind of ridiculous when you tell it like that.'

'Well, that's what you'd have to tell a courtroom full of people,' said Peg. 'It's important that you think about that. And there'd be a hell of a lot else as well.'

'I know.'

'Do you?' Peg deliberately dropped the kind, coaxing tone of voice. 'You'd be asked if you were a virgin. How many men you'd done it with and how often. Earle wouldn't get asked anything like that, but that's not how justice works. It's you who has to prove her moral character. They'd ask what you get up to in bed with your boyfriend, and whether you're sexually satisfied. What you were wearing that day, how much of your thighs were visible and whether you wore an uplift brassiere. In other words, was it all your fault?'

Maura buried her head and began to sob.

'And then there's afterwards. There would be a hell of a lot of bad publicity for Frank Earle and MackenCorp, but what about you? You'd be on every TV network, your photo would be on the front of the *Morning News*. And everywhere you went for ever afterwards people would say, "Isn't that the girl in that court case?" It would affect any job you might have in the future, it might even make it difficult to find work.'

'I'd have the money.' Maura sniffed.

'Would you, though? You might lose.'

Maura lifted her head and stared at Peg, her freckled face damp and blotchy. 'I thought you said you wanted to help!' she said angrily. 'But you're on *their* side, aren't you?'

Peg shook her head. 'I just want to make sure you know how distressing and damaging taking Earle to court would be. Anyway, what is it you really want? What do you think would be just?'

'I want my job back. And I want that bastard to lose his. So he can't do that to someone else.'

'Exactly.' Peg smiled. 'That's what I thought. So I'm here to do a deal with you.'

Maura looked wary.

'You say nothing to the media, and I get you reinstated, have Earle fired, plus he has to pay you compensation from his own pocket.'

'You see, you did come here to buy me off.'

'Accepting money from him is optional. I just thought it would make the package even more tempting.'

Maura laughed. 'You surely are some businesswoman!' She held out her hand. 'OK, you got yourself a deal.'

It wasn't until the following afternoon that Peg asked for a private interview with Michael.

She knew there was no time to waste, but it took until then before she could face seeing him. She kept thinking of the giggling Summer spilling her sticky cocktail all over his fingers, and the thought turned her stomach.

He was standing at the full length window, with his hands thrust into his pockets and his face half in profile. He looked very pensive, and Peg was reminded suddenly of that night on the Harvard Bridge, when they had leaned over the Charles River and talked. And had an argument.

'Peg!' The beaming smile when he swung round to face her was quite spontaneous.

Peg frowned. 'Your offer to help in the Earle business – was it genuine?'

'Of course.' He motioned to her to sit down.

Peg sat on the edge of her seat and twirled her tortoiseshell spectacles, chewing the ends of the arms.

'I didn't know you needed glasses,' said Michael.

'I don't really. They're just a sort of executive toy, to make me look more grown up than I really am.'

'Put them on. Let me see what you look like when you wear them.'

Peg obliged.

'You look like a Cliffie.'

'I am a Cliffie, remember?' She gave him an impudent grin. 'Now, about the harassment case. I do agree with Travis and his pals on one issue, and that is that the adverse publicity of a court case could be very damaging to MackenCorp. Especially as I discovered Travis has given Earle an undertaking that we'll back him all the way. That could involve us in damages and costs as well as bad publicity.'

Michael folded his hands across his laps. 'Go on . . . no, keep the glasses on, please. I think they look cute.'

'I talked to Maura Johnson. She agrees to drop the legal suit on condition that we reinstate her and fire Earle.'

Michael breathed out. 'And you want me to . . .?'

'Much as I'd like to be the one to deal with that slimeball, I think that part should come from you. You'll have to tell the other board members, of course, but if they object you can tell them I, for one, will not hesitate to speak out to the press against Earle.'

Michael laughed. 'They surely are going to regret kicking you out of that board meeting! OK, I'll deal with it. I gave you my word, after all. But what about you and Travis. I mean you guys are married, how are you going to square it with him.'

'I don't know,' said Peg. 'But I think you'll agree that's my problem.'

Michael spent the next day locked in meetings with the other board members and representatives of MackenCorp's legal department, and at five o'clock he called a meeting of the entire payroll, every employee from directors to cleaners. They packed the conference room, spilling out onto the aisles between the seats and standing room at the back. No one knew what the meeting was for, so there was a lot of hushed giggling and whispered speculation that died down when Michael stood up on the podium.

'Thank you for coming, folks. I intend to be very brief, I promise.' He cleared his throat. 'A few days ago, a junior member of staff made an official complaint against her boss, about an alleged incident of sexual harassment. . . .'

The whispering started up again. Michael waited a few seconds until it had stopped.

'After appropriate steps were taken to investigate this complaint, at noon today I received the resignation of the man in question, who also happened to be a member of the board of this corporation.'

There was an exchange of shocked looks among the members of the audience.

'Now, I am going to have to rely on each and every one of you not to speak to the press – or anyone outside this building – about this matter. I think y'all know that anyone who discusses company matters in that way will face serious consequences. But I called this meeting to tell you about this because I feel it is of vital importance that the men amongst you know that that sort of behaviour will not be tolerated, and that women feel that if they have any such grievance, it will be looked into and they will receive the full support of the corporation if their complaint turns out to have basis in fact. I wanted to state very clearly at this point – ' he paused, looking around the attentive faces – 'that the MackenCorp is not amongst the places in the United States where a blind eye is turned to sexual harassment, coercion or assault!'

There was a stunned silence, then the whole audience burst into rapturous applause. Peg, seated in the front row of the auditorium, jumped up spontaneously, followed by Winona and Wyatt, and very soon everyone was on their feet giving Michael a standing ovation that lasted several minutes.

The other board members stayed behind to congratulate Michael when the conference room had emptied, with the exception of Travis, who walked out when the applause began.

Peg hung round awkwardly until the others had gone. She held out her hand to shake Michael's, then suddenly thought better of it and thrust it behind her back, leaving him grabbing at air.

'Um . . . I just wanted to say well done. And to thank you.'

'No need to thank me. Like I said before, it just happened that I thought you were right.'

'Well, thanks anyway.' She turned to go.

'Peg, I . . . I was going to ask if you felt like having dinner with me.'

'No, thank you.'

He followed her out of the conference room. 'Are you angry with me about something?'

'No, it's just – '

'Travis, right? Only, I couldn't help noticing that he goes out a lot at night. Without you.'

His brown eyes were on her face with that same burning gaze she remembered from before. She tried to forget them, along with all the other things that had imprinted themselves on her memory: the way his glossy dark hair curled over the edge of his collar, his large hands with their strong, square fingers.

She looked away.

'Well . . . I have to get back to the baby.'

'Sure. Sure you do.' He shrugged. 'Well, see you around.'

It was Elaine's regular night off, an occasion that Peg had come to view as something of a luxury. It meant she could bath John Alexander alone and have a protracted cuddle with him before settling him down for the night. He was more animated and interesting now, and tonight he rewarded her with one of his best songs and his repertoire of tricks, which included blowing bubbles in her face and biting her chin.

The other thing she enjoyed about Elaine's night off was having the house completely to herself. It meant she could dress in sloppy old sweatshirt and jogging pants and go and sit with her feet up on the kitchen table watching *All in the Family* and eating her way through a packet of Oreos.

She was just finishing the packet when Travis returned. 'I'm surprised you're not out with the all-American hero,' he said bitterly.

Peg could smell the bourbon on his breath. 'I don't know what you're talking about,' she said calmly.

'You're always going on about how we did a deal . . . since when was it part of the deal to make me look like an idiot? Publicly siding with Saint Michael . . . the two of you were trying to make a fool out of me!'

'We were just doing what we thought was right!' retorted Peg, taken aback at how easily the 'we' tripped off her tongue.

Travis noticed the tortoiseshell glasses. 'What the fuck have you got those things on for?'

'To see the TV. And because I rather like them.'

'Take them off, they don't suit you. . . .'

Over the intercom there was a sound of fretting from John Alexander, which gradually built up into an indignant wail.

'Where's the goddam nanny, for Chrissakes?'

'It's her night off.' Peg swung her legs off the table. 'I'll just go see what he wants.'

She came down again a few seconds later with the baby over her shoulder, clipping her personal stereo onto her waist band with her free hand.

'Unfortunately, I'm going out for a run now, so that just leaves you.' She plonked the baby on his lap and he immediately started to cry again.

Peg put the stereo headphones over her ears. 'Don't worry, he just needs a dry diaper.'

As she reached the front door, Travis called out indignantly: 'Goddammit, he shat himself!'

'Did he?' asked Peg sweetly. 'I'm sorry: without my glasses on, I didn't see that.'

FOURTEEN

Savannah, Georgia 1980

Peg was dreaming about sand, lots of lovely wet sand, cool underfoot, oozing between her toes, then getting firmer and drier until it was like warm golden sugar, with the occasional knobbly bit of seaweed sticking into the sole of her foot. There was the occasional rejected popsicle stick or, if you were unlucky, a hot gummy nugget of chewing gum.

When Peg woke up, she thought she was on the beach in New Brighton. She kept her eyes tightly shut, reliving the familiar sensations. The salt and vinegar smell, the bad-tempered shrieking of the seagulls. And her father's firm shoulders beneath her backside and his hair twined through her fingers as he took her for a ride along Marine Promenade on his shoulders.

She eventually had to open her eyes, and when she did so, she felt intensely homesick. She desperately wanted to go back to Liverpool, right there and then, just to make sure all the familiar things were still there.

She pulled back the curtains and looked out at the garden. The colourful display from the frangipani and hibiscus was fading now. The summer was almost over here. In less than three months, the anniversary of Al's death would have rolled around, and the future of MackenCorp would be decided. At least then she and John Alexander might be able to go back to Liverpool for a visit. The thought cheered her as she dressed for work.

When she heard Travis going downstairs into the hall, she grabbed her suit jacket and attaché case and flew down the stairs after him. For the past few months they had barely spoken to one another and had travelled to and from work separately; he in the limousine, she in her Pontiac.

'Travis, wait! I need to talk with you!'

He paused with one hand on the front door. 'Make it quick, I'm leaving right now.'

'Can I ride with you, please? There's something I want to ask you about.'

They climbed into the back seat of the limousine.

'OK, shoot.' Travis looked straight ahead, with a bored expression on his face.

'Well . . . it's been months now since Frank Earle left, and I'm slightly surprised that the board hasn't appointed a new chief of personnel.'

'We've been working on it.'

'I was thinking of putting myself forward for the job.'

'You?' Travis laughed. 'I guess I shouldn't be surprised. You've shown you're prepared to put your career before everything, even your own child. A seat on the board and a voting share of one per cent must be what life is all about for you.'

His bitterness made Peg wince. 'I don't happen to think it's such a crummy idea. In the eighteen months we've been living here, I've got to know the Savannah office and the people in it. My management training from Harvard will stand me in good stead, and besides, I'm already the most senior vice president in the place. It makes sense, surely?'

'It just isn't as simple as that, honey.'

'It's because the other board members don't want to appoint a woman to the board, isn't it?' she hissed.

Travis cocked his head on one side. 'My, my, y'all are getting paranoid, aren't you? Weren't you the one that started all that hokum about MackenCorp not allowing sexual harassment? Well, it follows that it's no place for sexual discrimination, either, doesn't it?'

'Get to the point, Travis.'

'The appointment is due to be decided at a board meeting later today, so I'll let you know.' He smiled suddenly. 'Better still, why don't you come along and hear for yourself?'

Lana Macken took in her new surroundings from the back of the cab.

Savannah looked small and rather mean, she decided, as they

approached it from the west on the airport road. When they hit the centre and the Historic District with its stunning, unspoilt houses she had to concede that yes, it was kind of pretty. But still Hicksville. Like most New Yorkers, she viewed her native city as the centre of the universe.

The cab took her to the Wisteria Inn, a small luxurious hotel in Gaston Street, converted from a Georgian house. The owner led her to her suite, converted from a carriage house and decorated in the frothy and extravagant style of the Old South. Lana, whose taste was more restrained, had never seen so many pieces of antique furniture and bric à brac crammed into such a small space, from the huge carved tester bed, to the claw-footed bath and the tinkling crystal chandeliers.

'I'm sure Scarlett O'Hara would have felt right at home here.'

The owner, taking this as a compliment, smiled. 'Will you be staying long, ma'am?'

'I don't know yet.'

'Unfortunately this suite is only available until the end of the month.'

'That should be fine. I don't plan on staying any longer than that.'

'Well . . . there are cordials and sweets laid out for you there, and if there's anything else you require. . . .'

'I'd like you to chill some champagne, please.'

'Certainly. I'll have some put in the ice-box for you. And perhaps you would like some help with your unpacking?'

'No, thank you. I prefer to do that myself.'

Once she was alone, Lana proceeded to unpack her three large cases with loving care. She could not have handled the clothes more gently if they had been newborn infants; the suits in their zipped covers, individually numbered, the shoes protected by shoe trees and velvet shoe bags, the underwear wrapped in lemon scented tissue paper and tied with ribbons.

Underneath the tissue paper parcels was a black velvet box. Lana opened it and took out the necklace, savouring its weight and coldness. The tulip-cut emerald at the centre caught the light with a burst of pale green fire. She had never worn it since the day of her marriage to Travis. But she still thought of it as a talisman, a lucky charm.

She put the necklace away, dressed in a purple Ungaro suit and ordered a cab to take her to East Bay Street. She was welcomed outside the front entrance by Travis's secretary, who ushered her upstairs to the boardroom.

Travis stood up to greet her. 'Gentlemen. . . .'

Lana noted Peg's sulky look at this omission. 'Gentlemen, I'd like to introduce you to MackenCorp's new director of personnel, recently head of our New York bureau – Mrs Lana Macken.'

Lana beamed and went around the table shaking hands. Peg withheld hers. Her face was pink with indignation. 'You can't do that! You can't just appoint someone without consultation.'

'The hell I can't!' said Travis coolly. 'I own forty per cent of this corporation, and I also have Wyatt's support, which carries another ten per cent of the voting share.'

Michael glanced at him. 'Wyatt?'

He shrugged sheepishly. 'Al always spoke very highly of Mrs Macken's work in New York and she *is* already a member of the board as stipulated in her divorce settlement.'

'So . . . even without Ed's five per cent and Raymond and Grant's two per cent each, the appointment is carried!'

Lana planted herself in Peg's path as she left the boardroom.

'Congratulations,' said Peg sulkily.

'And congratulations to you too, Margot! I hear you had a baby boy. How is he?'

'Fine.'

'Travis has told me all about him. He never stops talking about the little guy.'

'Really?'

'Well, he's a man with a son and heir now. I guess that kind of changes everything, doesn't it?'

She gave Peg one of her sweetest smiles. 'I'll be seeing you around, honey. . . .'

When he left East Bay that evening, Travis stopped at the liquor store on Drayton Street and bought the best bottle of French champagne he could find. Then he drove to the Wisteria Inn and presented himself at Lana's suite.

'They say great minds think alike. . . .' She flashed a smile over her shoulder as she went to the ice-box to take out her chilled bottle. 'We'll start with mine, shall we?'

Lana's platinum hair was still pinned up in a French pleat, but she had replaced the suit with a wrapper of pale rose satin. Her feet were bare, and as she moved to pour the champagne, Travis could see that underneath the wrapper she was naked.

She arranged herself decorously on the bed, sipping from her champagne glass with her little finger crooked. If she was a cat, she'd be purring, thought Travis. He felt ungainly in one of the spindly antique chairs next to the bed, not sure what she expected.

Lana's eyes locked on his, and her lips curved upwards in a provocative smile. He moved over to sit next to her on the edge of the bed.

'Poor baby', she cooed, unfastening his tie. 'You look tired.'

'Still got plenty of energy for celebrating.' Travis gave her one of his boyish grins.

Lana ran a frosted pink fingertip over the cleft in his chin. 'That was some kind of bombshell you dropped on those guys today,' she said thoughtfully.

'It was only Peg who minded.'

'And there was me thinking she'd be glad to have another woman around the place.'

'She wanted the job for herself!'

'Poor little Margot,' said Lana, entirely without sympathy. 'She always did want to walk before she could run. Anyhow. . . .' Her eyes narrowed slightly. 'Didn't her position as your wife – your *current* wife – give her a little bargaining power there?'

Travis poured himself another glass of champagne. 'This is the good old deep South, not New York City. Things aren't quite the same around here.'

'I meant, couldn't she just wrap you around that cute little finger of hers?'

Travis shook his head vigorously. 'Uh-uh, no way. It's not that kind of a marriage. Strictly business only.'

Lana smiled over the rim of her champagne glass, touching it gently with her tongue. 'Just like ours, huh? Funny, I always thought you had the hots for her. And you did manage to produce that cute little baby. He *is* yours, isn't he?'

Travis sighed. 'Yup. And yes, I did have the hots for her, but after that one night when she fell pregnant, she made it clear she wasn't going to put out for me. She may be cute as hell, but she's also the stubbornest, most self-righteous little English bitch I ever had the misfortune to meet.'

While he was speaking, Lana had unbuttoned Travis's cuff and slipped her fingers into his shirt, trailing the tips of her nails over his wrist with a movement that was so exquisite Travis felt an instant reaction in his groin.

'What, turn down a husky guy like you? What is the matter with the girl?' Lana picked up Travis's right hand and started to suck the tip of one finger. 'You know, I couldn't help noticing the way she looked at Michael. Did you notice that? She never took her eyes off him. I just wondered – '

Travis shook his head. 'Nah, the two of them couldn't find a damn word to say to one another when he moved back here. Besides. . . .' He removed his fingers from Lana's mouth and ran them over her chin and down her throat to the opening of her wrapper. 'He's dating some blonde waitress.'

At that moment, Travis was not in the least interested in the subject of his wife and his brother. His hand slipped into the front of the satin wrapper and he cupped her breast, kneading and pressing until he heard her sharp intake of breath. 'Lana, darlin', you have no idea how good it is to see you.' He nuzzled her neck, inhaling her scent. 'I have missed you like crazy!'

His fingers went to work again, teasing her nipple then bending forward to follow suit with his tongue.

Lana gently but firmly pushed him away. 'Honey, you're a married man.'

'That don't mean – '

'And besides, you and I have business matters to discuss.'

She straightened up on the bed and pulled her wrapper shut as if she were closing a window. Travis continued to stare at her, his eyes glazed with lust.

'You and I have not yet discussed the terms of my contract, beyond my seat on the board and my voting share of one per cent.'

'I told you you could name your salary.'

'It's not just the money. . . .' Lana sprang to her feet and crossed the room to the marble-topped Victorian washstand. She picked up a comb and teased the tip of her fringe. 'I don't know how much time I can commit to staying down here. I mean . . . *Savannah*!'

'What's wrong with it? Savannah's a beautiful city!'

'Sure, it's very pretty if you want to spend your life living on a Hollywood set. But in business terms, this is toy town!'

Travis sighed. He remembered these moods of Lana's only too well.

'If I'm going to stick around and our old partnership is going to be revived – ' she turned round and gave him her most suggestive smirk – 'there are going to have to be some big changes around here.'

Peg woke late the next morning. She had slept through the alarm and felt thick-headed. Even after a jog, a shower and three cups of Betty's coffee, she had a heavy, dragging feeling that she could not shake off. It was even harder than usual to tear herself away from John Alexander, who was crowing cheerfully as he pulled himself up to standing and cruised around the nursery holding on to the furniture. Elaine brought him to the door to wave, and his cheerful 'Bye-bye!' wrenched at her heart. Reluctantly, she kissed his blond curls and climbed behind the wheel of the Pontiac.

Once at work, she shut herself in her office and asked her secretary to hold all her calls. She settled her spectacles on her nose, laid a piece of MackenCorp headed stationery in front of her and started to write.

Dear Travis,
 I think you and I both realise that we have reached the point of no return. I have been feeling for a while now that our 'deal' has served its purpose and it's time I moved on. I suppose your giving the Head of Personnel's job to Lana instead of me indicates you feel the same. I will always be grateful to you for giving me my US citizenship and letting me have this chance. The best thing to come out of it all is our beautiful son, and I could never regret that part of it. I want you to realise that whatever happens, I will let you visit with him as much as you like. I hope that where John Alexander is concerned, you and I can –

There was a tap at the door and a tall, rangy figure loomed into her line of vision. Peg pushed the letter hastily under a pile of papers.

'Hello, Wyatt.' Peg smiled. She had always rather liked the gentle, courtly man who had been loyal to MackenCorp for more than forty years.

'I've never seen you in those before.' He pointed to her spectacles. 'Looks kind of intellectual.'

'Good. I'll take that as a compliment . . . . What can I do for you, Wyatt?'

'Travis's wife. . . .' He blushed. 'I mean, his other wife.'

'His ex-wife,' Peg corrected him, trying to hide her smile of amusement.

'She's called a board meeting, and from the look of the agenda I thought you'd want to be present. So, if I might escort you. . . .'

'Thank you, Wyatt, that's very kind.'

Peg knew as soon as she saw Lana that she was up to something. She was as icily immaculate as ever, in a dove-grey wool dress with organdie ruffles at the neck and wrists. Peg wedged her spectacles on the end of her nose and adopted her fiercest frown.

'I'll get straight to the point,' said Lana. 'I've been appointed to make some changes round here, and I'd like to begin by telling you what I think is needed.'

You have to hand it to her, thought Peg, she knows how to get their attention. Travis, Ed, Wyatt and the others were staring transfixed at this exquisitely dressed china doll with the rasping Brooklyn accent who looked at them as though she would take a chainsaw to their genitals if she had to. Only Michael was still doodling on his pad.

'The first thing is this: MackenCorp is in the wrong place.'

'It's the finest building in Savannah!' protested Wyatt.

'I don't mean the wrong street, I mean the wrong city! I'd like to propose that we move the headquarters of the corporation to Atlanta.'

'Seconded!' said Travis, a little too quickly.

There was a general murmur of dismay.

'Now hear me out. Atlanta is going through a considerable expansion. It's the twelfth biggest city in the States, and with the exception of Houston, by far the most important business centre south of Washington, D.C. It opens up massive new opportunities in terms of services, personnel and communications. Visitors come to a charming old town like Savannah for vacations; they don't come here to do business. . . .'

Travis was nodding sagely. You hypocrite, thought Peg, giving him a withering look.

'It was different in the days when this was one of the centres of the shipping industry. But that's all changed. Savannah may still be a port, but everything that comes through here goes straight to Atlanta.' Lana looked round the circle of faces. 'And that's where we should be.'

Wyatt Neely was the first to break the embarrassed silence. 'Well now, I never thought I would see the day when in this boardroom of all places – ' he gestured through the huge windows at the sparkle of the Savannah River – 'I would have to listen to someone say that MackenCorp and Savannah should part company. And I can tell you something else: Al would never have stood for this kind of talk, and I think y'all know it!'

Michael got to his feet. 'I don't intend any disrespect to my father's memory when I say that right now, it doesn't matter what he would have thought. Daddy was never one to stand in the way of progress, and that's what has kept this corporation growing and expanding since 1939, when it was just a shack with a telephone and one tugboat for hire. The point is that the Macken Corporation has always continued that growth and development, despite what . . . Mrs Macken – ' he smiled politely at Lana – 'sees as the handicap of being in Savannah. We may not be in a city like Atlanta, but we've always been well placed to take advantage of any new business opportunity in the state of Georgia.'

Peg held up her pen. 'I'd also like to point out that we still have premises in New York, and if we wish to expand nationally, or even internationally, an office in the north-east puts us in a good position to do so. Moving from this building to the business district in Atlanta would really only be window dressing. . . .' She fixed her gaze on Travis's face. 'Or playing house.'

'We should at least carry out some feasibility studies,' said Travis. 'Look at some figures.'

Wyatt held up a hand. 'I am acting chairman of this board for a few more weeks, and I say we should put this to the vote. Those in favour of developing this Atlanta proposal?'

Travis, Lana, Ed, Grant and Raymond all put up their hands. Lana's probably bribed them with promises of fancy new office suites and more staff, thought Peg.

'OK, so that's Travis's forty per cent, plus Miz Macken's one, Ed's five, Grant and Raymond's two each . . . that's a round fifty per cent. And against?'

This latter question was a formality. Michael and Wyatt showed their hands. It was an even split; fifty-fifty.

'Now what?' demanded Travis. 'I mean, we didn't lose and you guys didn't win.'

'In cases like this we need a deciding vote,' Wyatt explained. 'Al used to ask a senior member of personnel to vote. In this case I'd like to invite Mrs Peg Macken to do so, since she is a vice-president of this company and aware of all the issues.'

They all looked at Peg. 'I've already expressed my views,' she said quietly. 'I vote we abandon this farcical proposal of a move to Atlanta.'

'Motion over-ruled!'

'What the hell did you do that for?'

Travis burst through the front door of their house in Gordonstoun that evening and immediately rounded on Peg.

'I don't want to discuss it, Travis.'

She tried to retreat to her bedroom but he followed her upstairs, forcing the door open and pushing past her into the room. 'Well, I damn well *do* want to discuss it! Just what exactly is going on around here? Since when did you become Michael's fucking poodle?'

'I just happened to agree with him, that's all.'

'It just happened, huh? There have been rather a lot of coincidences like that lately. . . .'

He slumped down on the edge of the bed, looking suddenly exhausted. 'This is an impossible situation, and I think we all know it. I called my attorney in New York today and filed for divorce.'

Peg breathed out heavily. 'Lana's revenge, huh?'

'Lana doesn't even know about it. Anyhow, I'm going to tell you what the terms will be – '

'But – '

'No, this time *I* get to tell *you* what the deal is. You get a generous settlement and custody of John Alexander. In return, you have to consult me regarding his education, and you have to relinquish your employment with the Macken Corporation.'

He went on, more gently. 'You can keep the house for now, if you like, I can move out.'

'Thanks, but that won't be necessary.' She opened the bedroom door. 'Now, if you don't mind, I have a lot to do.'

Travis drove to the florists on Habersham Street and bought every single pink rose in stock, several hundred dollars' worth. It was such a large bouquet that it took up the whole back seat of his Mercedes sports, and when Lana opened the front door of her suite, all she could see was roses.

'How pretty!' she exclaimed. 'Champagne?'

She was wearing a different wrapper this evening, a short one made of Swiss lace. Travis noted with approval that her trim muscular legs were tanned a warm golden brown. He put his hands on her waist. 'The flowers are kind of an apology. For what happened in the boardroom.'

'I adore them, they are to *die* for,' Lana purred, pressing the petals against her lips. 'But there's really no need for an apology. Business is business.'

She seemed remarkably light-hearted about her defeat, and Travis said so.

'I didn't really expect to win,' she said candidly. 'I was just testing the water.'

'Oh.' Travis felt oddly disappointed. 'Well, so long as you're not mad at me.'

'Not at all. You were there for me today, and that's what counts.'

She had taken him by the hand and was walking backwards to the bed. 'In fact, I was kind of hoping you would come around tonight.'

'You were, huh?' Travis slipped a hand between Lana's thighs and wiggled a finger expertly under the elastic of her silk panties.

He was amazed by how much he wanted her. He had never been this hot for her when they lived in New York. Maybe it had taken two years with the ice maiden Peg for him to appreciate what he had lost.

He was on top of her now, his knee parting her thighs while his fingers fumbled with the belt of her wrapper.

'Let's get this thing off. . . . Christ!'

As he slipped if off her shoulders he realised that underneath she was wearing the Starkewska necklace. The stones glistened against Lana's milky skin, dazzling in their perfection.

'This is the piece you wore on our wedding day!'

Lana smiled as she slipped her arms around his neck. 'I'm so glad you remember, darling!'

FIFTEEN

Savannah, Georgia 1980

The phone rang at nine the following morning, shattering Peg's concentration. There were three suitcases open on the floor, and she was in the process of emptying the contents of the closets into them.

'Peg?'

'Yes?'

'Peg . . . it's Michael.'

'Oh.'

'You've forgotten.'

'Forgotten what?'

'Today's the day we arranged to go on that site visit to Coronado Beach.'

'It is? Oh . . . I had forgotten, actually, but – '

'I'll come by and pick you up.'

Peg replaced the receiver slowly. She ought not to go, she reasoned. She would just have to tell Michael that she wasn't going to be working with him any more. She tugged a brush through her hair and applied some lipstick, but kept on her Levis, sweatshirt and jogging shoes.

As soon as she opened the door and saw Michael standing there, smiling at her, she knew she couldn't do it. It was a beautiful early fall day, warm and balmy, and John Alexander was out in the stroller with Elaine. There didn't seem to be any good reason for not going along. Michael looked a little surprised at her informal dress, but made no comment.

'I thought we'd take Highway Seventeen down the coast,' he said as Peg climbed into the front seat of his Mustang. 'Have you been down that road before?'

Peg shook her head.

'You'll love it; it's really beautiful.'

His cheerfulness should have been infectious, but Peg felt more and more gloomy, falling silent as they left Savannah behind. When he pointed out landmarks or places of interest, she just nodded.

'There used to be coastal plantations along here. That's where Sea Island cotton was grown: supposed to be one of the best varieties of cotton . . . but it's so swampy here that the plantation owners all used to move out in the summer to escape the mosquitoes. . . . Are you OK?'

'Yes. I'm fine.' Peg continued to stare straight ahead through the windscreen.

'You sure?'

'Of course I'm sure,' she snapped.

'You seem a little tense, that's all. I couldn't help wondering – '

'How's Summer?' Peg asked abruptly.

'Summer?'

'You know, the girl you picked up at the diner. I thought you were dating her.'

Michael shook his head. 'No. I only took her out to dinner once. She wasn't exactly my type. Besides, I spent the whole evening staring at you.'

He took his eyes off the road to look at her and she felt compelled to meet his gaze. She could see the lighter, tawny rings around the rim of his pupils that made his dark brown eyes seem to glow. 'And when I saw you look at me I wondered if you were thinking about that night at Harvard.'

'No, of course not, I – '

'I think about it all the time.'

'Don't, Michael!'

'Well, we never did get around to talking about that time. Couldn't we do that now?'

Peg bit her lip and gave a brief, stubborn shake of her head.

Michael shrugged. 'OK. If that's the way you want it. . . .'

They had left Chatham County and were heading towards Midway. 'Over there, due west, is Walthourville, where Daddy came from,' Michael told her. 'And to the east is the Midway

River. I thought we could take a little detour down there; it's real pretty.'

From the road they could see glimpses of flat marshland edged with forest. The luxuriant foliage was every imaginable shade of green. 'That's a magnolia bay . . . that's myrtle . . . that spiky stuff is wire grass . . . there's a dogwood.'

Michael pointed out the different plants to Peg.

'Magical, isn't it? Indians used to live right here in these forests for thousands of years. They had game to hunt, fish and oysters on the seashore . . . so much that they didn't mind sharing it with the white man when he moved in. And then the white man started clearing the forests to export lumber and grow cotton. . . . Look!' He slowed the car and pointed to a large pale bird circling on the edge of the swamp. 'That's a white ibis!'

'You really love Georgia, don't you?' Peg said suddenly, unable to ignore the fact that Michael had taught her more about the state in two hours than Travis had in two years.

'Yes. I was crazy to leave.'

'But you stayed away so long. Lived in Europe. Don't you want to do that again?'

Michael shook his head. 'I thought at first that if I failed in this contest to be chief executive of MackenCorp I would just head on out again. But now I don't want to. I want to stay in Savannah, because for the first time in my life I feel as if I'm really achieving something. So even if I lose, I'll try and work something out with Travis. I'm sure we can figure something out.'

'Oh. . . .' Peg felt almost physically overwhelmed by her reaction to this news. It was a heaviness in her chest; the sinking of her heart. 'Oh, I see.'

They had reached the mouth of the river now, and Michael pulled the car over onto the bluff. They were surrounded by a broad expanse of marsh, trimmed with shingle, stretching out to the broad Atlantic.

'If you don't mind getting your shoes wet, we can go down to the water's edge.'

Peg shook her head. 'You go. I don't feel like it.'

'What's wrong with you? You're usually so energetic everyone else is running to keep up . . . come on!'

He took her hand and pulled her out of the car. Apart from the birds bobbing about in the grasses, the place was completely deserted.

'It *is* beautiful. . . .' Peg sighed, looking out to the horizon. 'Over there somewhere is England. If Ireland wasn't in the way, we could probably see Liverpool.'

The words caught in her throat as she spoke. She was overwhelmed with longing for her childhood, her home, her father . . . .

Michael was close behind her and she felt his fingers on her back, very gentle. Her breathing quickened.

'Peggy. . . .'

He put his hands on her shoulders and turned her around. She already knew he was going to kiss her and her mouth sought his; blindly, instinctively. Everything flooded back into her consciousness in that instant; the smell of him, the feel of him, how much she had wanted him and how deeply she had buried that desire.

She pushed him roughly away. 'No, Michael, don't! There's no point in this!'

She turned and started wading back through the damp grass to the car.

'Peg, Chrissakes, wait!'

'I'm going back to England,' she flung over her shoulder. 'Travis and I are splitting up, and our marriage was a sham in the first place.'

He ran to catch up with her. 'But if you're leaving Travis . . . well, that's great, isn't it? You can stay here with me.'

'No, I can't! I'm being hounded out of MackenCorp and I couldn't stay with Travis and Lana around . . . it would just be impossible. Forget it!'

She wrenched open the door of the car and flung herself inside. When Michael sat in the driving seat she kept her eyes fixed straight ahead.

'Letting you kiss me like that was a mistake, OK? Now, if you don't mind, I think I'd better not come down to Florida. Could you please just drive me back to Savannah.'

'Now?'

'Right now.'

★ ★ ★

Peg wouldn't let Michael drive her to the house, insisting that he set her down as soon as they reached the city limits. She took a cab back to the house, left a note for Travis, collected John Alexander and drove him to his grandmother's house at Turner's Creek.

The place had an air of tranquillity Peg found instantly soothing. Cordella was in the garden room, arranging flowers.

'Well, hello!' Her face lit up when she saw John Alexander. 'Hello there, young man. You and Mommy are just in time for some of Sadie's peanut cookies.'

'I'm not staying,' said Peg quickly. She saw Cordella looking down at her jeans and sand-crusted sneakers. 'I just came to tell you that I'm going to England.'

Cordella twirled one of John's golden curls around her finger. 'Going to visit with your other grandma, huh, cute stuff?'

'Actually, we're going over to stay. . . .' Peg took a deep breath. 'Travis and I are splitting up. And we weren't really married anyway.'

Cordella looked at her quizzically.

'I mean we *are* married, but we weren't ever in love. It's sort of complicated. . . . I ended up married to the wrong brother.'

She expected Cordella to look shocked, but she carried on snipping the stalks of her lilies, quite tranquil. 'We have a way of doing that in this family. Al married the wrong sister. However. . . .' She smiled at Peg. 'It all worked out for the best, and I'm sure it will for you.'

The phone rang. Cordella removed her gardening glove to answer it.

'It's for you,' she told Peg, taking the baby from her arms. 'Travis.'

'I just got your note,' Travis said. 'Are you still planning on leaving tonight?'

'Yes.'

'I have a message for you from Lana. She says she must see you before you go. She wants you to meet her in Forsyth Park in half an hour.'

'No way!'

'OK, please yourself. But she did say it was important.'

★ ★ ★

Michael drove around endlessly, making four circuits of the city before he had calmed down sufficiently to drive up to the white-columned porch of the house in Pierpoint Circle.

Travis answered the door.

'Where's Peg?' Michael snarled. 'I want to see her.'

'She's not here.'

'I don't believe you!'

'Don't be so damned ridiculous, Michael, look!'

He beckoned his brother up the stairs. 'Come see for yourself!'

He showed Michael into Peg's bedroom, where the half-filled suitcases still covered every available space.

'So she really is going,' said Michael softly. 'What did you do to drive her away, huh?'

The two brothers were the same height and stood facing one another head to head, one blond and blue-eyed, the other with eyes even darker than his dark chestnut hair.

'You always did have to shit on my chances, didn't you, Travis? You just can't help taking everything that's mine!'

Michael's eyes were so brilliant with rage Travis instinctively took a pace backwards. 'I don't know what the fuck you're talking about – most of the time I never did.'

'I met Peg back in Harvard. I fell in love with her – for the first time in my life I was really, really in love with someone . . . and then the next thing I know, good old Travis has gone and married her!'

'Chrissakes, Mikey . . . take it easy. Firstly, I never knew all that . . . and I'm not standing in your way now, you can see that! It's up to Peg to decide what she wants, and as you can see, what she wants is to leave both of us behind and go back to England.'

'Yeah, you're right, I'm sorry. . . .'

Michael turned on his heel and walked out of the room.

'Mikey, wait . . . if you still want to see that flaky, stubborn bitch, I can tell you where she might be in about half an hour from now. . . .'

Peg's curiosity got the better of her, and she left the baby with Cordella and went to Forsyth Park.

She sat on a bench in the centre, watching the water tumble

down the white column of an ornamental fountain. Office girls taking a walk in their lunch hour strolled past her, chattering and laughing. Occasionally a chipmunk darted across the grass to snatch a discarded potato chip. Peg felt numb, detached. She was hot too, as the October sun reached its zenith and pierced the morning haze. She stripped off her sweatshirt and hung it around her shoulders.

After half an hour there was no sign of Lana. Peg looked down impatiently at her watch, then stood up to leave.

'Peg!'

She spun round.

'It's all right, I'm not going to hassle you; I just came to say goodbye.'

Michael bent down and kissed her swiftly on the lips. 'I love you, Peg, you stupid girl!'

'I love you, too,' she called, but he was already out of earshot.

Peg watched him disappear, then turned and walked slowly to her car.

By the time she reached the Wisteria Inn Peg's sadness had turned to rage, and she was spoiling for a fight. 'What's the big idea?' she stormed at Lana. 'Dragging me out there and not showing up!'

Lana was reclining languidly on a watered silk chaise longue, dressed in a pale lilac suit, every single blonde hair in place. Peg's hair, by contrast, had been whipped by the salt wind, and her jeans and sneakers looked even more grimy in this exquisite, frilled boudoir.

'Oh dear, didn't Michael show up?' asked Lana with a pussycat smile.

'Yes, he . . . how did you know?'

'Oh good!' Lana swung her legs off the chaise longue and sat up poker-straight. 'It's time you and I had a little talk, Margot. Sit down. . . . How about a glass of champagne?'

Peg eyed her warily. 'Why do I feel like I'm being set up?'

'I guess in a way you are. . . . You and I have never been friends, have we? Which is a shame, if you think how alike we are.'

Peg looked at Lana, then down at her clothes, and laughed.

'Think about it. We both became wives of one of the Mackens

as a means of getting what we wanted. And it taught us both the same lesson. That putting ambition first, making it the prime motivator, doesn't necessarily get you what you want.'

'Or at least, it doesn't let you keep it,' said Peg thoughtfully.

'Precisely. Until now, what we did has backfired on both of us.'

'Are you saying – ?'

'We're both businesswomen, so I'm suggesting you and I go into partnership. Just answer a question first. Are you in love with Michael Macken?'

'Yes.'

'I knew it. And you want to marry him?'

'But I can't! He wants to stay on here in Savannah, and I can't, not now, it wouldn't work – '

Lana held up a French-manicured hand. 'Hold on one second, just answer the question. Do you want to stay in Savannah with Michael, yes or no?'

'Yes – after a long trip to England to see my family.'

Lana beamed. 'You have no idea how solemn you looked when you said that: I wish I had a camera. OK, so here's the thing: I want Travis back, you want Michael. It looks as though you and I have the workings of a deal. Now I have no intention of staying down here in Hicksville a moment longer than I have to.'

'But I thought – '

Lana raised her hand again. 'Hear me out, please. What if I take Travis back to New York with me and leave you and Michael to play at being the twentieth-century Rhett and Scarlett?'

Peg felt her heart thumping with excitement. 'Will Travis go?'

'Sure he will. He has lots of friends there, and a son and heir down here, so he doesn't have to worry about missing out on that dynastic thing. I think he'll cope with being a father at a distance.'

Peg nodded ruefully. 'I think you're right.'

'Besides, he's always much happier when he's being told what to do. And right now, he'll do anything I tell him to.'

Peg laughed.

'It's no laughing matter, honey. As soon as I arrived in Savannah I saw that the Southern men have had their own way round here for too long. When you voted against me in that meeting, do you realise it was probably the first time a woman had ever made a difference in that building?'

Peg smiled ruefully. 'I kidded myself that happened when I started working there.'

'Whatever. There's supposed to be a new age dawning for the South, and if that's the truth then I think it's high time the Macken wives called the shots, don't you?'

Peg grinned broadly. 'Sounds wonderful.'

'So . . . the corporation split evenly; half the assets controlled from New York, half from Georgia. Travis and I in charge up there, you and Michael down here. That way neither of the brothers wins and neither loses and everyone is happy.'

'Al would have approved.'

'So Margot, do we have a deal?'

Peg held out her hand. 'We do . . . but only if you call me Peg!'

'You'd better go tell Michael that you're planning on coming back from England. . . . No, wait!'

Lana stood up and linked her arm through Peg's. 'I happen to know Travis and Michael have gone down to East Bay to discuss the future of the Macken corporation. And since we've decided what the new order is going to be. . . .'

Peg grinned. 'Let's go and break it to them together.'